Captain Abou stared at Goldsmith as if he had gone crazy. "It's going to be damn tough for my entire platoon to fight our way out of here let alone your five-man recon team! It's suicidal!"

Goldsmith sensed the fear in his men, A stay-behind-mission was exciting to talk about. But it was a different ball game when you were surrounded by NVA soldiers looking to blow you away.

"I know the risk, sir,"—Goldsmith moved closer to Tyriver so his One-One could see his face clearly in the moonlight—"but this mission means a lot to us."

That's all Tyriver needed to hear to fire up his courage. "Let's move it, sir!" he hissed.

Getting out when the getting was good made sense. But not when American POWs needed help so bad . . .

FIELDS OF HONOR #5

✪✪✪✪✪✪✪✪✪✪✪✪✪✪✪✪✪✪✪✪✪✪✪✪

THE BRONZE STAR

Donald E. Zlotnik
Major (Ret.), U.S. Army Special Forces

A SIGNET BOOK

SIGNET
Published by the Penguin Group
Penguin Books USA Inc., 375 Hudson Street,
New York, New York 10014, U.S.A.
Penguin Books Ltd, 27 Wrights Lane,
London W8 5TZ, England
Penguin Books Australia Ltd, Ringwood,
Victoria, Australia
Penguin Books Canada Ltd, 10 Alcorn Avenue,
Toronto, Ontario, Canada M4V 3B2
Penguin Books (N.Z.) Ltd, 182–190 Wairau Road,
Auckland 10, New Zealand

Penguin Books Ltd, Registered Offices:
Harmondsworth, Middlesex, England

First published by Signet, an imprint of New American Library,
a division of Penguin Books USA Inc.

First Printing, January, 1992
10 9 8 7 6 5 4 3 2 1

ARMY REGULATION (AR) 672-5-1

2-15 Bronze Star Medal

The Bronze Star Medal is awarded to any person who, while serving in any capacity in or with the Army of the United States after 6 December 1941, distinguishes himself by heroic or meritorious achievement or service, not involving participation in aerial flight, in connection with military operations against an armed enemy; while engaged in military operations involving conflict with an opposing armed force in which the United States is not a belligerent party.

a. *Heroism*. Awards may be made for acts of heroism, performed under circumstances described above, which are of lesser degree than required for the award of the Silver Star.

b. Meritorious achievement or meritorious service.

(1) Awards may be made to recognize single acts of merit or meritorious service. The required achievement or service while of a lesser degree than is required for the award of the Legion of Merit must nevertheless have been meritorious and accomplished with distinction.

—Extracted from the regulation

CHAPTER 1

✪✪✪✪✪✪✪✪✪✪✪

CHRISTMAS, 1941

She squeezed her eyelids together, forcing the remaining tears to spread out over her cheeks. The tiny bundle she was holding in the crook of her right arm moved, and she looked down at her newborn son.

The large snowflakes that had been blowing up against the window had melted almost instantly, reflecting the outside light in an array of interesting shapes. The weather had changed outside of her hospital room during the early afternoon, and now the snowflakes had changed to small chunks of ice that were sharply cracking against the maternity ward window. The sound drew the young mother's attention away from her baby. She thought of the chatter of machine-gun fire in the war movies she had seen with her husband.

The woman's upper lip trembled as she struggled to stop the flow of tears and contain her sobs. The baby's upper lip quivered as if in answer to his mother's silent call, but he was only testing his instinctive ability to suckle.

She smiled down at her son through her tears and used her left index finger to tickle the baby's upper lip. He responded to the touch by placing his mouth into high gear. He was hungry.

She had told the nurses and her doctor that she would breast-feed the child, even though she had been encouraged to use bottle feeding to reduce the possibility of infection. She had breast-fed her first son and had enjoyed the bonding. She had nothing else to give her children but her love.

She reached over to a nearby nightstand and removed

a sterile cotton pad from a small box. She massaged her left breast until a clear liquid began to flow and then used the pad to ensure that her nipple was sanitary for her newborn son's first feeding. It would be another day before she started producing actual milk. The clear liquid was nature's way of making sure the infant's system was working properly before it began consuming the rich mother's milk.

The feeding process eased her grief a little. It was less than three weeks since the Japanese fleet had attacked Pearl Harbor, and the nation was bracing for a Japanese invasion on the West Coast. Not only that, but Hitler was winning all over Europe.

The only good news was that her husband had been called back to work at the General Motors foundry after having been laid off for over six months. The nation's industry was already beginning to gear up for war production.

She looked down at her newborn and tried smiling. "Oh, my little war boy, what kind of a world have I brought you into?"

The maternity room door swung open and the duty nurse entered carrying a small tray of pills in tiny paper cups. "Well! He's starting to feed. That's a good sign." She looked down at the young mother's chart and added, "Has he cried yet?"

The mother shook her head and smiled down at her son.

"Hmmm." The nurse looked up from the foot of the hospital bed and stared at the suckling infant. "It is very unusual—very unusual. Did you know that he didn't cry when the doctor slapped his bottom?"

"No, I didn't know that."

"He just inhaled a lungful of air and sounded like he sighed—but he didn't cry." The nurse frowned. She had never heard of an infant who didn't cry. "He didn't cry to be fed?"

The mother shook her head slowly from side to side. "I just knew he was hungry."

"I'm concerned that we might have a small problem."

"What kind of a problem?" The mother looked up

at the nurse, who instantly busied herself with the pill tray.

"Nothing serious, but he might have a problem with his vocal cords or . . ."

"Or what?"

"Don't worry, dear, he'll be just fine. Saint Luke's is a fine hospital and your doctor is one of the best."

"Or what, Nurse." The mother kept her voice even but firm.

"Sometimes there are mental problems when infants don't cry." The nurse hurried to finish filling out the mother's chart.

The mother smiled down at her son. She could see the bright blue, unfocused eyes staring at her breast as he fed, and she wondered if the color would change when he got older. For a second it seemed to her that a light was coming from *inside* the boy's eyes. "You don't have to worry about his vocal cords or his brain. He's just fine. He comes from tough stock."

The nurse used the comment to change the delicate subject. "Is his father coming to see him this morning?"

There was a long pause before the mother answered. She knew that her husband had spent most of Christmas Eve with his drinking buddies at Trump's Saloon. He had called her twice from the neighborhood bar, located only three blocks away up Janes Street. She knew that it would be late that afternoon before he even woke up. "Probably much later. He's with our two-year-old son and it's Christmas morning—you know how that goes," she lied. She had left her other son at her mother's house, knowing that her husband would end up drunk and incapable of caring for little Tommy.

The nurse accepted the mother's answer. "It is quite a special event—being born on Christmas morning!"

"Yes, he is my little angel. My war boy."

"War boy?" The nurse paused in the doorway. Associating angels with war wasn't a very Christian thing to say.

The mother smiled again but didn't answer the nurse.

"Make sure you let us know at the station as soon as he cries." She turned halfway around and added, "I could maybe just give him a *light* slap to, uh, make sure that there isn't any problem."

The mother shook her head slowly and looked down at her infant. "No, there will be plenty of time for him to learn how to cry. We don't have to inflict pain on him to see if he can do it."

Feeling guilty, the nurse tried to distance herself from her own recommendation. "I didn't mean to imply that I wanted to hurt him. But it's not normal for an infant not to cry."

"We aren't living in normal times, Nurse, and my son isn't a normal baby. He's special. Anyone who's born on Christmas morning is special—right?"

"Yes." The nurse hurried out of the ward. She was beginning to feel very uneasy, and she only huffed a curt greeting to the hospital administrator as she passed him in the hall.

The mother waited until the door had closed before speaking to her nursing son. "You're not even a day old yet and this nasty old world wants to inflict pain on you, little one. Well, don't you worry none! Mommy is here to protect you."

The infant's eyes tried turning toward the sound of the voice without moving his mouth from the nipple. The blue irises sparkled in the reflection of the bed lamp light.

The door to the maternity ward opened again and a male administrative clerk entered. He saw the woman nursing and turned his head toward the window. "Sorry."

She covered her breast with a portion of her sheet.

The clerk coughed to clear the embarrassment from his voice. "Have you decided on a name for him yet, Mrs. Goldsmith?"

"His father hasn't made it here yet. How long can you wait before you have to finish filling out his birth certificate?"

"The doctor would like to sign it before going home. It is Christmas, you know, and he wants to get back to his family." He smiled, but inside he felt like going over to the telephone and calling the woman's husband. What kind of a father would miss his child's birth? He had checked the woman's visitors chart and had seen that she hadn't received a visitor since she had arrived at the hospital alone in a taxi cab.

The woman read the anger in the man's kind eyes. She knew that the whole hospital staff would keep checking on her and the baby until all of the routine affairs had been taken care of. "So you want a name for my little war boy."

"What did you call him?" The man grinned.

"War boy."

"Hmmm, that's a decent name for him. After all, we are at war." The man was kidding to raise the mother's spirits a little.

"No, I think we'll call him Alex-Paul."

"Alexander Paul Goldsmith?"

"No, Alex-Paul. Just Alex with a dash and then Paul. That way he'll be named after his uncle and his father."

The administrator twisted his mouth and nodded his head. "It's different. I like the sound of it. Alex-Paul."

The mother smiled.

CHAPTER TWO

✪✪✪✪✪✪✪✪✪✪✪✪✪✪✪

BLACK MOON

She released an explosive snort and held her head up high to face the danger.

The creature that was threatening her newborn calf had climbed into the large tree in the thicket of bamboo she had chosen as a birthing place, a short distance from the rest of the herd. Her danger snort brought a series of answering snorts from the herd bull and a number of the calfless females. Even tigers were cautious of a herd of alerted gaurs, but the creature that took refuge in the jungle tree wasn't responding to her threatening snorts.

She moved closer to her newborn calf as it struggled to gain its feet for the first time. She alternated between licking the calf and tossing her horns in the direction of the tree creature, ignoring the growing number of army ants that had found her afterbirth. One of the large warrior ants crawled up on the calf's nose and sunk its pincers in the tender flesh. The calf bawled and lunged up on his wobbly legs.

The mother gaur mistook the calf's bawl of pain as having been caused by the creature hiding in the tree and she charged through the thick bamboo and vines, using her fifteen hundred pounds as a battering ram. She stopped just short of the base of the tree and tossed her respectable rack of horns up at the tree creature.

"Go! Get away from here!" The strange noise made the female gaur even more nervous, and she responded with a deep snort. "Go! I don't mean your baby any harm!"

The mother gaur gave a distress call and the whole herd came to her rescue. The newborn ran over to his mother's side for protection while the herd bull circled the tree, challenging the intruder to fight him.

The sound of dogs barking brought the herd around to face a new danger, and the man in the tree was temporarily forgotten. A number of high-pitched voices called to each other when the NVA scouts realized that they had stumbled on a whole herd of jungle cattle. One of their dogs yelped and tried backing away in the restrictive bamboo undergrowth from the charging bull gaur. The body of the dying tracker dog flew through the air and landed with a crash on the tops of the bamboo.

The man in the tall tree removed his .22-caliber Hi-Standard pistol fitted with a factory silencer and waited. The NVA tracking team had been chasing him all afternoon, and even if he hadn't accidentally run into the female gaur, he would have only been a few hundred meters farther down the mountainside. The tree was as good a place as any to make a last-ditch stand.

The NVA dogs whined and circled around the area. The reek of the wild cattle overrode the smell of the man they had been tracking. One of the dogs found the afterbirth, and the colony of army ants attacked the dog instantly. It yelped in surprise and then screamed.

A sharp command was given in Vietnamese and the handlers called their dogs back and started moving down the mountainside away from the herd of wild cattle.

Alex-Paul sighed softly and replaced his pistol in its holster. The gaur herd had given him a short reprieve, but he knew that the tracking team would swing around when they reached the valley floor and try to pick up his old trail again. He had a couple of hours to rest before it would be necessary to leave the tree.

He slipped off his very light, almost empty rucksack and tucked it in the crook of a large branch sticking out almost parallel to the jungle floor. He had decided to climb up above the secondary growth of the jungle and get a reading on where he was. The small ten-square-click map he had been given for his recon team's patrol had long ago become ineffective, but he was hoping that he could identify some kind of landmark for a compass heading. He knew that he had been heading in a generally southerly direction for the past three weeks, and soon he would be able to head east again and back into South Vietnam without running into any large NVA patrols. It had been just a case of rotten luck to have run into a NVA tracking team that had dogs with them.

He climbed quickly and with confidence up the trunk of the large jungle giant, using the thick vines that surrounded the tree for hand and footholds. The fingertips on the thin kidskin gloves he was wearing were starting to wear through, but they still gave him some protection against insect bites. The piece of camouflage cloth he wore on his head had come from a parachute. The cloth hung down well past his elbows, and he wore it in the fashion of an Arabian sheik. The headpiece was designed to protect his neck and face at night from insect bites and also to act as lightweight camouflage in the jungle. He wore a dark blue navy SEAL wool brimless watch cap under the nylon cloth to act as a sponge for his sweat and as a barrier against the tenacious mosquitoes. During the day or when he was moving through the jungle, he tucked the excess part of his camouflage headress in behind his load-bearing harness, but at night he could release the cloth and pull his legs up to his chest and form a tent.

The American reconnaissance man wore a well-worn camouflage tiger suit, and the only part of him that could possibly be detected in the jungle by sight were his eyes.

His electric blue eyes were a recon man's curse. Even when he squinted in order to hide the whites of his eyes, the electric blue irises shone as if the color had a light all its own. The blue was a blessing when it came to women, but it had always been a curse when it came to dealing with men. For some reason it brought the worst out of another male when he looked at them, and if he stared, it almost always ended up in a fight.

The sun's rays warmed his dirty face when he broke through the secondary layer of trees surrounding the jungle giant he was climbing. He saw a scorpion on a vine a few inches away from his gloved hand. He wondered why the creature was so high up on the tree before curling his index finger against his thumb and flicking the threatening creature out over the treetops. Alex-Paul felt a shiver ripple down his back. He knew that even something as minor as a scorpion's sting would hasten his death at the hands of the North Vietnamese soldiers who controlled the Laotian jungle.

Lieutenant Goldsmith looked out over the wide valley through which the Ho Chi Minh trail coursed. It presently harbored a large force of NVA soldiers. He had been trying to get through the valley for three days, but had run into NVA patrols twice before stumbling on a gasoline pipeline and a large depot, which explained the unusually high NVA activity in the area. The gasoline pipeline started back in North Vietnam and bordered the trail all the way down to where Cambodia jutted out toward Saigon. He leaned against the tree trunk and pulled the piece of loose cloth tape off the face of his army issue watch and looked at the time and then back down at the valley. He would know soon if the NVA had found and disarmed the special shape charges he had attached to the main underground storage tank and pumping station.

He moved around the tree and removed his Lensatic compass from the carrying pouch attached to the left side of his harness. The compass needle spun around and then jerked back and forth until it settled down pointing north. Alex-Paul looked over to the east and felt a strong emotional pull as he saw a thin column of smoke. He replaced his compass in its canvas case and climbed higher up the tree so that he could get a better look at the source of the smoke. He could see a dark red spot that had been carved out of the jungle and a pair of tiny dots circling the clearing. A new American base was being cut out of the jungle on the side of the faraway mountain. The column of black smoke went straight up in the windless blue sky. Alex-Paul assumed that the soldiers occupying the new site were burning their human waste using diesel fuel. It was very difficult to judge the distance to the base looking over the tops of the jungle, but the tiny helicopters gave him something to gauge by and he estimated that he was at least twenty miles as the crow flies from the safety of the forward base camp.

It might as well have been a thousand miles through shark-infested ocean.

Goldsmith's thoughts returned to the NVA pipeline

that had been the target for his recon team. Finding the
pipeline had been very difficult. SOG headquarters had
known about the NVA project to build a gasoline pipeline from North Vietnam to the south for over three
years, but every attempt at locating the pipe had resulted
in failure.

The thoughts about the pipeline made Alex-Paul
remember the accidental encounter with an NVA company that had taken the lives of his teammates. His hands
gripped the vines growing on the tree and he closed his
eyes. The rays of the sun warming his face was the only
comfort nature gave him as his mind slipped back to
when he still had companions in the hostile jungle.

Sergeant Archer paused and turned his head slowly in
an arc that started with his chin pressed against his left
shoulder and ended when his chin touched the harness
of his right shoulder. He was the only member of the
team who was wearing the new night goggles, which
made him look like a creature from a science fiction
movie. The goggles turned the black shadows of the night
jungle into shades of bright green.

Archer felt the slight pressure against his rucksack
from Goldsmith's hand. The five-man recon team had
been moving along the Ho Chi Minh trail, holding onto
each other's rucksacks in the extreme darkness, with
Archer guiding them. It was dangerous walking on the
trail, but moving through the thick jungle that bordered
the NVA highway was near to impossible. All the same,
because they were well within NVA-held territory, their
chances of surviving an accidental run-in with an NVA
patrol were actually very good. The enemy would be very
hesitant in firing on anyone moving on the trail at night,
assuming that the travelers were their own couriers.

Archer could see where the vehicle tracks left the trail
and veered toward a motor park hidden beneath the jungle canopy. He searched the area surrounding the
entrance for guards before reaching back and touching
his lieutenant's chest to signal that he was moving forward again.

The night was so dark that the only thing Goldsmith
and the rest of his team could see as they walked behind

Sergeant Archer were the small pieces of reflector tape attached to the rucksack of the man in front of them, and even that small source of comfort couldn't be seen most of the time because of the clouds that often hide the moon.

Suddenly the whole team heard the loud sound of the tank engine starting up and they froze. The Russian-built PT-76 amphibious light tank was less than fifty feet off the trail.

Archer knew that the nearness of the tank had scared the rest of his teammates, who couldn't see anything in the dark, and he reached back and patted his lieutenant's chest. Goldsmith reached back and reassured the man behind him that he was still there, and touches of reassurance were passed along to the last man in line.

Goldsmith used the noise from the diesel engine to risk speaking in Sergeant Archer's ear: "Let's use the noise to get past this night laager site before dawn breaks."

Archer squeezed Goldsmith's shoulder instead of speaking and started inching past the opening in the jungle where the tanks had pulled off the main path.

The five-man team had moved well past the tank laager site and the sounds of the jungle were taking over again when a thirty-six-inch Chinese Claymore antipersonnel mine detonated. Lieutenant Goldsmith was the only team member who heard the detonation. He felt something hit his rucksack with enough force to spin him around and knock him down. The rest of his team had died instantly. Sergeant Archer's body and full rucksack had absorbed most of the steel ball bearings from the explosion. The angle that the Claymore mine had been set at had placed Archer directly in the path of the pellets and the man behind Goldsmith had lost half of his right side.

Alex-Paul fought to maintain consciousness, but in the darkness he was having trouble figuring out if he was awake or his eyes were closed. He finally reached up and felt his eyes: he was stunned but awake. His hand reached out for Archer and came to rest on the goggles still attached to the sergeant's head. Alex-Paul felt warm blood on his hand and removed the goggles. He slipped them on and saw instantly that his whole team had been killed. The man who had been traveling in the middle of the compact formation had received the full force of the detonation and had been cut in half. Archer's body was torn apart and lay on the trail in an unnatural position. Alex-Paul struggled to his feet and took a partial step toward the radioman and stopped. The radio was riddled with the ball bearings the Claymore had dispersed.

He paused for only a few seconds to look down at his teammates to ensure that they were all dead and then slipped across the road into the jungle. He moved quickly through the thick bamboo until he found a small clearing and then he dropped down to listen. He could hear the sound of NVA soldiers' voices as they called to each other.

He listened.

Alex-Paul had attended the Presidio of Monterey's Language School and he had a working knowledge of Vietnamese. The NVA soldiers were calling to each other in excited voices, thinking that the Claymore had killed a deer. The excitement in their voices increased when the first soldier's flashlight revealed the dead Americans. He called back to someone still in the laager site, and a sharp command echoed along the trail.

Alex-Paul listened to the NVA company waking up and knew that he had to use the night goggles to put as much distance between the NVA unit and himself before daylight. He moved at a steady pace the remainder of the night through the jungle in a large arc to the west. He had crossed back over the Ho Chi Minh trail just as the first rays of the morning sun broke through the secondary growth of the jungle.

The NVA knew that American SOG reconnaissance teams always traveled in teams of five or in Hatchet platoons of thirty commandos and five Americans. They would find his track off the main trail as soon as it became light. Alex-Paul figured that he had only a couple of hours' head start on the enemy. He stumbled onto a narrow jungle stream soon after crossing the main trail and decided to use the ankle-deep waterway to throw the NVA off his trail. He used every trick that he had learned while training with the Apache Indians in New

Mexico during his escape-and-evasion training. He left the trail twice and doubled back into the stream and before he left the stream for good, he had gone almost a half mile downstream and created a false exit before doubling back into the water. He then returned to the site where he had created a false exit. Climbing a tree, he used the branches as a means of crossing over to the other side of a bamboo patch before dropping down again in the jungle. His first attempt of leaving the stream on the ground was the trail that the NVA had accepted, and when they saw that he had doubled back to the water again, they didn't think of coming back to the site again to check for a *second* entry after they found his last false exit from the stream a mile farther south.

The trick had given Goldsmith a chance to make it back to South Vietnam. He would have made the escape sooner except that the NVA had decided to launch a major invasion through that area at the same time and the jungle was filled with small NVA units. Each time Alex-Paul tried turning east, he ran into NVA patrols. He hadn't been detected, though, until he had run into the most recent patrol—and the tracker dogs.

Goldsmith felt the warmth of the sun leave his face and he opened his eyes. A wall of black monsoon clouds had blocked out the sun and were filling the northern end of the valley. The huge cloud bank spread all the way to the west into Laos. He adjusted his grip on the vines and quickly glanced around the tree. The monsoon storm would reach his location in a matter of minutes, and he wanted to make it down to the fork where he had left his rucksack before the vines became too slippery.

Alex-Paul climbed backward down to the fork and quickly checked his rucksack, thinking to make a place for himself in the crook of the tree. He removed a version of a Roman short sword that he had had Randall, the famous knife maker, design for him when he was still in school back at Fort Bragg. Randall had a shop in Orlando, Florida, where he made custom hunting knives for wealthy hunters. He had accepted Alex-Paul's request only because the idea of making a copy of a Roman short sword had caught his imagination. Alex-Paul had sent the knife maker the researched material he had needed to make the sword, and the only change from the original design was the hollow handle with the screw-on cap. Randall had placed a lead weight in the handle to balance the sword, but the weight could easily be removed and the hollow handle could be used to turn the sword into a very effective spear.

Alex-Paul carried the sword between his shoulder blades in a custom-made sheath that Randall had also made. The sheath was a part of his combat webgear and fit snugly between his rucksack frame and his shoulder harness. He had been intrigued with Roman short swords ever since he had studied the Roman empire in college. The sword was the main reason the Roman army had conquered most of the known world.

A cool breeze reached Alex-Paul and he didn't need to look up to know that the rain was rapidly approaching. He chopped off a couple more branches of leaves and stacked them in the crook of the tree to make a nest to sit in during the storm.

Suddenly the head of a tree python stuck out of the leaves only inches in front of Alex-Paul's sword. He jerked his wrist and slashed off the snake's head. The creature's body was coiled around a secondary branch, and Alex-Paul reached out and snatched the coils before they could follow the lifeless head down to the jungle floor. The snake responded by trying to coil around his arm.

Alex-Paul moved backward along the branch, balancing himself using the wiggling snake he held in one hand and his steel sword in the other. He felt the leaf nest he had made with his boot and squatted down. The headless snake was still twitching as he threw it on the nest. It wouldn't go anywhere and as soon as it was totally lifeless, he would skin it and eat the protein-rich flesh raw.

He sat down on the nest with his back resting against the tree's trunk and adjusted the five-foot tree python between his boot heels as he removed his nylon headpiece from behind his neck and pulled it out over his shoulders. He glanced up at the dark clouds just as he felt a first huge raindrop hit his forehead, and then he removed a package of cigarettes that he had stuffed into a side pocket of his rucksack. The cigarettes were in a plastic bag to protect them from the rain, but he could feel that the one he removed from the half-empty pack was damp. The matches had been designed to light even if they were wet, but he could only hope that the cigarette would still burn. He got a flame with the first strike of the match, but the Kool sputtered and hissed before it caught on fire.

Alex-Paul pulled his nylon shoulder cape tight against his buttocks and tucked the lightweight cloth in and pushed his legs out a little so that the cloth formed a tiny tent in front of him. He left a small crack for the smoke to escape and inhaled his first lungful in over a week. The monsoon rains would give him a chance to smoke without the smell from the cigarette being detected.

The raindrops started splashing the outside of the parachute cloth in a pitter-patter, and then it seemed as if someone had turned on a fire hose. The nylon cloth stopped most of the water from coming inside of Alex-Paul's little tent, but his pants and boots were still saturated in seconds. He didn't care about getting wet as long as he could finish his cigarette first. He always carried a pack of Kools with him when he was on a mission, even though he never smoked out in the field. The cigarettes were for the helicopter ride home after extraction or if they linked up with an American unit in the field.

Alex-Paul cupped his cigarette in his hand to give it a little more protection from the rain and then checked his nylon hootch, making small adjustments to channel the penetrating water away from the front of his body. The cigarette was finished way too soon, and he thought about lighting up another one but gave up the idea. He didn't want to risk losing a single cigarette to the monsoon rain and decided to skin the snake while it was still raining. He flipped back the flaps of his headpiece and felt the cold rain hitting his face. It was dark out under the rain clouds, but he could still see enough in the partial light to skin the snake. Alex-Paul laid the snake meat out on the limb and let the rain wash the blood off it and the blade of his twenty-two-inch sword before replacing the sword in its sheath and biting into the moist meat. The first bite told him just how hungry he was, and he didn't stop eating until he had torn a couple pounds of meat off the snake's skeleton.

The rain continued in a solid sheet the whole time he ate. Alex-Paul first rubbed his hands under a small waterfall created by a nearby branch, then decided to remove his clothes and shower in the storm.

He folded his jacket carefully in the crook of the tree and removed his boots and trousers. He rubbed his socks in the rain before removing them and wringing them out a couple of times to remove the dirt. It was a poor way to do his laundry, but the best he could do without any soap. Alex-Paul cleaned his uniform the same way. He squatted naked on the tree limb and felt the refreshing clean water cleanse his skin. When he had finished, he stood up and stretched, looking up at the dark sky through the layers of tree limbs. It felt good not to be weighed down with clothes and combat gear. He felt as if he was going to float off the limb and disappear in the rain-filled sky.

The feeling of cleanliness was replaced by a cold chill and then a desperate feeling of loneliness that reached his very soul.

Alex-Paul dropped down again on the branch in a squat and looked out over the jungle. He shivered and blinked the water out of his eyes.

He knew that he would survive. It was the thought of what he was turning into that bothered him the most.

CHAPTER THREE

✪✪✪✪✪✪✪✪✪✪✪✪✪✪✪✪✪

EARLY SURVIVAL TRAINING

The sun fell behind the monsoon clouds and the gray light that had filtered down through the leaves disappeared. The jungle became black, with zero visibility. Lieutenant Goldsmith was forced to rely solely on his sense of touch. He could only hear the tons of water hitting the leaves of the tree and the sound of the water running over the ground below him. He was like the rest of the creatures in the jungle—hiding to wait out the storm.

The monsoon rain had lowered the temperature in the jungle thirty degrees in less than an hour, but it felt like much more to Alex-Paul. He started shivering and rubbed his arms and legs to generate a little body heat. He slipped on his washed uniform and boots before wrapping up in his nylon poncho liner to wait out the storm that he knew would stop as fast as it had started.

Shivering again, he tried thinking about something that would take his mind off his present condition. He was good at escaping through his mind. It was a condition he had developed early on as a child being raised by his grandmother after his mother died when he had just turned seven. The first few years had been all right because his brother was still living with them, but when he turned seventeen, he joined the paratroopers.

Goldsmith smiled to himself in the dark as his thoughts went back to his early teenage years. He had just turned fourteen the Christmas before the hottest summer ever recorded in the General Motors town of Saginaw, Michigan. His grandmother had asked him to remove the storm windows from two of the side windows on the house so that they could get a breeze flowing through the house. She had kept the storm windows on the house through most of the summer as an added protection against break-ins while they slept. Just removing the windows caused him to work up a sweat, and his white cotton T-shirt became molded to his wiry young body.

She watched her grandson work through the lace curtains that covered all of the windows in her house and smiled. He was growing into a handsome young man. Her smile changed to a frown when she thought of the boy's father, but she had to give the man credit: the boys had gotten their good looks from him. Her daughter had been from solid German stock, but she had not been beautiful, though the boys had inherited their mother's blond hair and blue eyes. The father had been a handsome devil regardless—and a damn drunk. Sadly, the boys knew about their father's drinking, but they did not know of their greater heritage. Their paternal grandfather, a prosperous Jewish merchant in Poland, had been murdered by an anti-Semitic mob. His wife had Anglicized her name to Goldsmith when she had passed through Ellis Island, fleeing to safety in America.

The old woman tapped the window with her knuckles. "Alex-Paul, put the storm window in the shed and come inside!"

"Okay, Grams."

She pressed her head against the glass and watched him carry the heavy storm window around to the back of the small house. She heard the back screen door open and close and used her fingers to comb the lace curtain straight again before turning around to face her grandson. "It's so hot out today and you've worked so hard that I thought we could have a special treat." She reached into her apron pocket and removed a brand-new five-dollar bill. "Would you run to Princing's Drugstore and get us a half gallon of their vanilla ice cream?"

"Sure, Gram—but why not get it from the grocery store, it's closer."

"I like Princing's vanilla better, and besides, you can

get yourself a nickel phosphate as a reward for the hard work you've been doing."

"It's nothing, Grams."

"It is hard work, Alex-Paul! Your grandfather used to complain every year when it was time to remove the storm windows." She looked away from her sweating grandson and slipped into a reverie for a couple of seconds. "And besides, you're going to have to put them back up before it gets dark."

"Sure, Grams." Alex-Paul took the five-dollar bill and slipped it into the front pocket of his Levis.

The old woman's gaze followed the money. "Make sure that you don't lose it. That money has to do us until my Social Security check arrives next week."

Alex-Paul nodded and left the house through the back door. He paused in the shed long enough to remove the money and fold the new bill as small as he could before slipping it into his mouth next to his lower left jaw. He twisted his lips a couple of times and adjusted the bill before testing in a low voice to see if the money interfered with his talking. When he was satisfied, he left the house through the shed door and casually strolled back through their garden toward some blackberry and raspberry bushes. The ripe berries were covered with bees and hornets, but he knew from having to pick them that the bees would leave him alone if he moved slowly through the berry patch.

Alex-Paul slipped up over his fence in a fluid movement that he had rehearsed at least a thousand times. He knew every single inch of ground between his house and the grocery store, located on the corner of Janes and 15th Street, and Princing & Brennan's Drugstore, up a block on 14th Street. The critical part of his trip was crossing over 15th Street and making it to the alley beyond.

He followed the fence line west until he reached Grandpa Refie's gate and paused. Grandpa Refie had died during the spring. He had been eighty-nine and had lived in his house alone for the past fifteen years after his wife had died from cancer. Grandpa Refie's backyard had been a preteen's dream because it was filled with fruit trees and berry bushes. Alex-Paul had spent many enjoyable evenings sneaking over the fence and raiding the old man's fruit trees along with his friends.

The sound of voices coming from the street drew Alex-Paul's attention away from his daydreaming. He slipped around the back corner of the old garage and pressed his cheek against the dry wood. A tall stand of hollyhocks reached up halfway to the garage roof, and Alex-Paul eased himself between the tall stalks of the flowering plants. He could hear the golden northern bumblebees landing on the dark red flowers surrounding his head, but he paid them little attention. He had all of his senses directed on the gang of teenagers who were passing in front of Grandpa Refie's house. One of the teenagers kicked out at the "FOR SALE" sign in the front yard, and Alex-Paul heard the dull thud from his hiding place. He reached over and wrapped his hand around a couple of the hollyhock stalks and pulled the flowering rods over so that they stuck out around the edge of the garage. He moved his head so that his left eye could see the street. One of the deep red hollyhock flowers rested next to the side of his head, and Alex-Paul could feel the bumble-bees pass his ear as they entered the flower for pollen. He wasn't afraid of the working bees, knowing they would leave him alone. It was the teenagers who threatened his mission to the store.

Alex-Paul recognized the last of the teenagers in the group. The kid had been in his ninth-grade math class and had seemed like a nice guy who had been forced to join the gang during the summer. Whenever he saw the kid when he was by himself, the youth always spoke to him, but when he was with the older guys, he ignored him. Alex-Paul was used to being treated like that.

The sound of the gang faded, but Alex-Paul waited a couple more minutes before releasing the hollyhocks and pulling his head back from the edge of the garage. A bumblebee buzzed his head angrily and then landed on a light pink hollyhock flower farther down the way.

Alex-Paul reached up and brushed the pollen off his cheek from where the flowers had rested and slipped through Grandpa Refie's backyard. He moved swiftly through the tall weeds of the next yard and dropped to a low crouch next to the wire fence that stopped at the

wired-shut gate that used to enter his friend John's backyard. John's family had moved away from the neighborhood three years earlier, but Alex-Paul still referred to
the dark brown garage as John's.

He listened.

A dog barked at something down the block and a car
passed out on the road. Everything was quiet. Alex-Paul
was a little nervous because the gang had been moving
in the same direction he was. The row of backyards ran
parallel to the streets. Alex-Paul listened hard to tell if
the gang was still moving toward the grocery store or if
they had stopped at one of the houses on the street. He
had to make sure that the gang was not going toward the
drugstore and decided on climbing up on the flat roof of
John's garage to see. He used the sections of the wire
fence as footholds and quickly climbed until he could
reach the top edge of the brown garage. The back window had been boarded up with thin wood slats from an
orange crate, but Alex-Paul had been there when John
had done the nailing and they had left a space just wide
enough for a toehold so that they could climb up on the
roof and use the raised vantage point during their preteen
green apple fights with the 14th Street gang.

Alex-Paul crouched on the open rooftop and quickly
scanned the nearby backyards before risking standing up
and looking over at the sidewalks between the houses on
both 16th and 15th Streets. He couldn't see the gang
anywhere and decided that they had stopped at one of
their houses.

He dropped behind the garage next to a huge rhubarb
plant and made a mental note to pick some of the sour-
tasting stalks for his grandmother, who loved making
rhubarb pie. Alex-Paul slipped around the corner and
stopped behind the partially open side door of the garage
to make a final check before trying to slip across the
wide-open backyard to 15th Street. Once he had reached
the alley behind, he could move quickly to the sanctuary
of the drugstore. Alex-Paul moved around the jammed,
partially opened door and stepped back into the shadow
of the garage for one final check before dashing toward
the street.

"Hello, motherfucker."

Alex-Paul felt a sinking feeling in his stomach before he turned around to look back at the shadows of the garage. He had found the missing gang.

"Wha'cha doing comin' in our garage?" The voice came from a dark corner where some coal was piled. Alex-Paul remembered the day when the coal truck had dropped off the load over five years earlier. John's father had converted the house to a gas heater the following year, and the coal had remained in the garage gathering dust.

"Just passin' by."

"I's seen you at school." It was the voice of the kid who had been in his freshman math class. "He ain't no trouble, Reggie. Le 'im go."

Alex-Paul made a move to leave and felt a hand grab his shoulder. "Hold it, motherfucker! I say when you can go!"

Alex-Paul stopped.

"Where you goin'?"

"A friend's house."

"Where?"

"Over on Cherry Street."

"You lie!"

Alex-Paul remained silent.

"Are you goin' to the store?"

Alex-Paul continued standing silently, trying to figure out how many of the gang were in the garage.

"Search the motherfucker!"

Forms materialized from the shadows and grabbed his arms while another pair of hands reached in his pockets.

"Nothin'."

The hands still held him.

"Take off your shoes!"

Alex-Paul was shoved down onto the wooden floor of the garage. He removed his tennis shoes and handed them to the older teenager who had appeared from the coal bin.

"Socks!"

Alex-Paul obeyed.

"He's hiding the money in his underwear!" It was a new voice coming from the main part of the garage, divided by the wooden three-quarter wall that held back the pile of coal.

Alex-Paul felt a sinking feeling. The whole gang was inside of the garage.

"Take off yer clothes!"

"I've gotta go." Alex-Paul tried breaking free, but the open doorway was blocked by the bodies of three teens.

"Go in there and take off yer clothes, or I'll personally kick your ass and *tear* off your clothes!"

Alex-Paul felt the teens pushing him into the main section of the unused garage. He resigned himself to a strip search, knowing that he was going to have to use his wits to escape the gang or get his ass severely kicked for their afternoon entertainment. He pulled his T-shirt up over his head and dropped it on the handlebars of an old bike. He flipped the buttons open on his Levis and slipped them off in a fluid movement. "Okay?"

"Take off yer underwear."

"You queer or something?" The words slipped out before Alex-Paul could stop them, and he braced himself for the blow that he knew would be coming.

The fist impacted against his jaw where the five dollar bill was hidden. Alex-Paul felt the blood seeping out of his gums.

"Take 'em off!"

Alex-Paul shoved his Fruit of the Looms down off his hips and used his foot to flip the briefs back up to his hand.

"He's got a big cock for a white boy." The voice was a girl's.

Alex-Paul had thought only the gang members were in the dark garage and hadn't been embarrassed undressing in front of guys—he had done that in gym classes since the seventh grade—but the girl's voice brought a blush to his cheeks. He tried putting his underwear back on but was stopped.

"Where's the money, motherfucker!"

"I told you, I don't have any money!" Alex-Paul let his voice reflect his hate.

"Hmmm, a cocky little motherfucker!"

He was thrown roughly down on the wide wooden

planks that lined the floor of the old garage, and he felt hands holding down his arms and legs.

"Let's see if this little honky likes losing his little cock."

Alex-Paul felt the cold knife blade resting against his lower abdomen right above the base of his penis. He felt a flash of fear for the first time since his capture. Up until then he had thought the gang was just shaking him down for some money.

He felt a hand touch his crotch and instinctively tried squeezing his legs to protect his reproductive organs.

"I can feel hair down there." It was the girl's voice again.

"Don't get that motherfucker hard now! Your pussy is for us, bitch."

"Bitch?" The girl's voice rose as she turned around. "You calling me a bitch? This boy's dick is three times as big as yours and he ain't even hard yet!"

The garage filled with laughter.

The leader threw Alex-Paul's underwear at him and screamed, "Get your ass out of here before I cut your dick off!"

Alex-Paul paused only long enough to gather his clothes and ran out of the garage back into dazzling sunshine. He ran over to the back of the house and faced the garage door as he dressed. Three gang members stepped out of the doorway and laughed at him as he slipped his T-shirt on over his head.

Alex-Paul memorized the faces of the teenagers. He would someday get his revenge. Living in the ghetto had taught him that it was much wiser to wait to repay a wrong than to act when he was outnumbered.

That was the first lesson he learned in guerilla warfare.

The cold chill from the monsoon rain drew Goldsmith's attention back to the present. The storm had passed and the tons of water still falling was from the coated tree leaves. It would be another hour before he could move through the jungle wearing the night goggles. He adjusted his position on the limb and felt for his package of cigarettes. He could risk one more smoke before it became too dangerous. He held the smoke deeply in his lungs and returned to thoughts of his childhood. He had gotten his revenge on the gang, but he had waited three months to do it.

It was his first week at Saginaw High School, and the gangs had already put out the word to the other students that if they tried taking home their books, they would get their asses kicked. It was a way for the gang members to hold down the grading curves in the classes.

Alex-Paul had already decided on sneaking his books home by using a nerdy backpack. He waited until all of the buses had left before trying to sneak out of the side door of the high school and running the three miles to his house. He liked running and the backpack made him feel like he was a mountain man, which was one of his running daydreams that he used to pass the time as he ran. He knew that daydreaming like that was childish, but as long as no one else knew about them, they couldn't do any harm.

The gang that operated around his neighborhood always rode the bus that picked up the high school students on the corner of Janes and 14th streets. He hadn't even *tried* riding the bus and had resigned himself to either running or walking to school.

He removed his backpack from his locker and pulled his navy watch cap down to his ears. The dark blue wool cap hid his curly blond hair, which waved like a flag in the breeze when he ran. It was still very warm out during the first few weeks of school, but he would rather sweat a little wearing the watch cap than draw attention and have to fight his way home.

Alex-Paul stepped out of the side door of the school and met three of his neighborhood gang members, who were leaning up against a well-worn railing.

"Well, it's naked boy again."

Alex-Paul started running past the group and felt his shoulder yanked backward as his pack was torn loose.

"Books! This fucker is breaking the rules and takin' books home with him!"

"Leave him alone, Reggie, he ain't botherin' us." It was the math student again.

"I'm gettin' the impression that you *like* this boy."

Reggie tore the first five pages out of Alex-Paul's biology book and let the wind blow them out across the school yard.

"Stop that!" Alex-Paul reached for his books. "I can't afford to pay for new books!"

"Really, motherfucker?" Reggie continued tearing the pages out of all of the smaller youth's books. "Well, you are goin' to have to either buy new books or not take your homework home—like the rest of us. We're gettin' by just fine!"

Alex-Paul felt tears coming. "You motherfucking idiot!" He swung and hit Reggie against the side of his neck.

He felt the first blow, but after that the punches all blended in together. He dropped onto the dirt intersection where the main sidewalk met the one from the side door and didn't get up until the sun had set. He lay in the dirt for over an hour, and no teacher or any other students saw him lying there.

The weekend gave Alex-Paul enough time to heal so that he could make it to school on Monday. The three-mile walk had at first seemed impossible to make until his muscles loosened up and the throbbing pain left his body. The weekend had been horrible, and he had spent both days in bed taking huge doses of aspirin to ease the pain. He had told his grandmother that he had been injured playing a rough game of football, and she had been kind enough not to press the issue.

The kids in his classes felt sorry for him, but didn't say anything to draw the gang's attention. It had spread quickly around the school that Alex-Paul had tried smuggling books out of school and had received a severe ass-kicking, along with his books having been torn up.

Reggie was in his history class, which was the last hour, and he started laughing the instant Alex-Paul walked into the classroom. The rest of the gang in the class joined in and were joined by the other kids, who knew better than to get Reggie mad at them.

Alex-Paul took his seat, keeping his eyes averted from any of the black kids, and opened his book to where it started at chapter five.

As the teacher lectured in a bored drone, Alex-Paul plotted his next move. He already had the locker combinations to four of the gang's hall lockers. He needed only to gain the combination to Reggie's locker before he could make his move.

On Thursday, the kid who had a locker next to Reggie's slipped Alex-Paul a note with the combination numbers written on it. The kid's hand shook as he passed the slip of paper.

There was a light rain falling on Monday morning when Alex-Paul slipped out of bed a half hour early. He wanted to arrive at school before the buses arrived. He dressed quickly and made himself two pieces of toast before slipping out the back door. He paused in the shed and removed three items: his baseball glove, bat, and a baseball. He tucked the baseball in the right rear pocket of his Levis and hopped down the steps to the narrow sidewalk before breaking into a long-distance jog. He had left his book bag at school since the incident. It took him a half mile to adjust his body movement to the weight of the wooden bat, but he settled into his normal pace by the time he had reached the edge of the Polish neighborhoods near Weber Street.

The school janitors had just opened the school doors when Alex-Paul arrived at the gym entrance. He ran down the hallway to his locker and stashed his baseball equipment before removing his bookbag. The first locker he stopped at was Reggie's. He opened it on his first try and went through the stack of books at the bottom until he found the history book. He switched his torn book for Reggie's new one and slammed the locker shut. He visited each one of the gang member's lockers, switching books until he had replaced all of them. The last locker he visited was the one that belonged to the girl who had made fun of him in John's garage. He unbuttoned his Levis and looked both ways down the hall before urinating on the books and paper that were cluttering up the bottom. When urine started leaking out onto the marble floor in front of the locker, Alex-Paul cut off the flow. He had made his point.

During third hour in biology class, he heard that there had been an incident during homeroom. A girl had slapped Reggie's face and had accused him of peeing on her books because she had refused to suck his dick.

Alex-Paul kept a straight face and played as if he was just hearing the news. He shrugged and looked up at the notes the teacher had left on the blackboard for the class to copy before she arrived.

Not one of the gang members had noticed that their books had been switched when the last bell rang. Alex-Paul hurried to reach his locker before the rows of buses parked out in back of the school left. He removed the bat, slipping the worn glove over the handle, and shoved the baseball in the side pocket of his book bag before throwing a strap of the bag over his left shoulder. The baseball bat he rested on his right shoulder.

The buses were almost full when Alex-Paul stepped out the back door and hurried past the wall where the swimming pool extension stuck out. He took his time walking past the bus, but no one paid any attention to him. He stopped when he reached the back end of the bus and walked back down along the opposite side. He was just thinking he had failed when Reggie came charging out of the open door, followed by eight of his cronies. Even though Alex-Paul had been baiting the gang, he had allowed himself to be caught off guard because he had expected Reggie to react instantly to seeing him carrying his bookbag. It was a good lesson for Alex-Paul and one that he would never forget.

"You are a dumb, and I mean dumb, mutherfucker. Didn't you learn your lesson about those books the first time!" Reggie was balling up his fist to take his first punch at the smaller boy when he felt his whole arm go numb.

Alex-Paul had dropped his bookbag onto the asphalt and slipped the glove off the end of his bat. With a fluid movement he swung the bat as if taking a homerun swing. The bat connected just below Reggie's shoulder.

There was no pain—yet. Reggie looked startled and took another step toward the kid whose ass he had kicked easily the week before. This time he felt extreme pain as the bat came down next to his head and broke his collarbone.

Reggie screamed like a girl and dropped to his knees.

By this time Alex-Paul had already taken a couple of steps to Reggie's left to give himself room to swing the bat. With a level swing he whacked Reggie's lieutenant in the thigh. He groaned and dropped to the asphalt, holding his leg in both hands.

The third gang member was too close for Alex-Paul to swing his bat so he turned sideways and poked backward with the fat end of the bat, catching his attacker right in his solar plexus. He gasped and fell sideways.

The remaining gang members stopped attacking and spread out to look for an opening in Alex-Paul's defense, but the back of the swimming pool wall protected the smaller boy from being circled.

A squad of teachers followed the assistant principal over to where the fight was. The parking lot squad was well versed in breaking up fights by the buses, which was a popular place for students to settle their differences.

"Put down the bat, young man—now!"

Obeying the assistant principal, Alex-Paul was instantly charged by three of the gang members, but he was ready for them. He threw the baseball and hit the closest one right between the eyes. The sound of the baseball striking flesh echoed among the rows of parked buses.

Two of the shop teachers, carrying Fiberglas and wooden paddles they had made for their classrooms, restrained the two remaining gang members.

Alex-Paul noticed that it didn't take very much for the teachers to stop the two bigger kids. He knew that he had won the fight, and for the first time he looked up at the hundreds of faces staring open-mouthed out of the bus windows down at him.

The rest of the school year, there were threats made on his life by the gangs and he was expelled for two weeks, but it was worth it. The remaining three years of his high school life were incident free. The incident with the baseball bat in front of half the school had sealed his reputation as being crazy to the extreme.

Lieutenant Goldsmith shoved his poncho liner off his shoulders and stretched. It was time for him to start off again. He paused just long enough to smile and think about the second lesson he had learned about dealing with an enemy that was larger and stronger than your own force: plan and rehearse your plan until you know what you are going to do as well as a ballet dancer knows his program, and then execute the plan with vigor and determination.

Most people who grow up the victim spend their whole lives hating those who oppressed them. Lieutenant Goldsmith was just the opposite. He thanked the gangs for turning him into one of the best reconnaissance men in the United States Special Forces. Growing up under such hostile conditions had taught him how to survive.

Goldsmith reached for his rucksack and felt in the large inside pocket for the night goggles. The moon had broken through the tails of the monsoon clouds and gave off enough light for the goggles to function.

He turned on the switch and the tree branch turned a bright green. He could make out what was left of the snake stretched out over the limb and decided to leave it there. The dead meat might attract some unwanted guests as he moved through the night jungle.

Goldsmith adjusted his side holster with its .22-caliber pistol and he reached back to make sure the handle of his short sword was where it should be for easy withdrawal before stuffing his wet poncho liner in his rucksack and climbing backward down to the jungle floor. He let the sides of his headress hang down over his shoulders. The mosquitoes would be coming out from their hiding places by the millions.

He paused only long enough to confirm his heading, using his Lensatic compass, and started weaving his way through the jungle in a due easterly direction.

CHAPTER FOUR

✪✪✪✪✪✪✪✪✪✪✪✪✪✪✪

ROUND EYES

Lieutenant Goldsmith took his time for the first thousand meters. The terrain was mostly rolling hills covered with thick jungle in the valleys and tall elephant grass on the hilltops. He knew that his team's operations area had been in the foothills of the mountains. The idea had been that the gasoline pipeline coming down from the north had to follow the lie of the land. Otherwise, the NVA would have been forced to operate pumping stations and there were ways of detecting the heat and sound from the station engines. The staff planners at Command and Control North had been right about the pipeline, but they had failed to come up with an accurate estimate on how well it was guarded.

Goldsmith stopped moving through the jungle. Thoughts about the pipeline made him check his watch again. It had been almost twelve hours since he had installed the last of the shape charges on the pipeline. The charges had been set to go off a hour apart. He had followed the pipeline for almost five hundred meters, placing one of the small high-tech charges every two hundred meters or so, before he stumbled on a main storage and pumping station.

An NVA team had just finished refueling a large convoy and were taking a late-morning siesta; even the small guard detachment were sleeping underneath their bamboo hootch. It had been easy locating the underground tank and digging through the loose top covering to place the small shape charge directly against the steel side of the storage tank. The NVA, paranoid about the critical pumping stations being detected through spy satellites,

moved them often. They had used slave laborers from
the Laotian Hmong mountain tribesmen to dig over a
hundred large holes, and then they camouflaged them
for future use. That was why the soil on top of the large
storage tank was so loose that it could be moved easily.

Goldsmith stopped and dropped to a squat. The failure
of the new CIA-provided shape charges was bothering
him. Sergeant Archer had been the team engineer and
explosives expert, but all of the team members had been
trained to use explosives. He was sure that he had set
the charges right. The only possible answer was that the
NVA had found the small charges and neutralized them.

The idea of the charges failing still bothered him, and
before he started again through the jungle, Goldsmith
removed the last of the devices from his rucksack. The
small, quarter-pound device was mostly composed of a
plastic explosive, a high-tech detonating device, and a
sabot about the size of a fat thumbtack. The idea was
for the sabot to penetrate the side of a steel pipe or even
an inch of steel. There was a small tracer producing a
high-energy fire that had been designed to create instant
fumes from the gasoline or diesel fuel as it passed
through the liquid so that the following detonation would
be enhanced. He stared at the palm-sized device through
the night goggles, and in the green light he tried figuring
out if he had done something wrong when he set the
timer. The charge had a safety and he was sure that he
had armed the charge properly. Shaking his head, he
squeezed the shape charge in his hand and felt the tiny
switch next to the electronic timer.

Goldsmith frowned as he realized that the switch was
a selector for an additional twelve hours on the timer so
that the device could go up to a twenty-four-hour delay
setting. He had not checked the switch when he had set
the times. The selectors could have all been set for an
additional twelve hours. Sergeant Archer had checked all
five of the devices personally for each one of the team
members and had placed them in each man's rucksack
himself.

Suddenly Goldsmith heard a deep cough. He removed
his pistol and scanned the surrounding jungle through the
night goggles. The cough had come from something other

than a human—it had been too deep. He listened intently for another cough to locate the exact direction of the sound. "Tiger" popped into Goldsmith's mind, and he tapped the small-caliber pistol in his hand. It would be useless against a big cat. He hefted the quarter-pound shape charge in his left hand and decided that if a tiger came for him, the worst he could do would be to blow both of them up. He used his thumb to place the timer on five seconds and rested his thumb against the start switch.

Fifteen minutes later, he heard a growl followed shortly by a wild pig's squeal. It had been a hunting tiger. Goldsmith turned off the shape charge and slipped it back in his pack before removing his short sword from its sheath. He started moving again through the night jungle, carrying his silenced pistol in his gloved hand, thumb resting on its safety switch, and his short sword in his right hand.

A muffled thud reached him through the dense layers of ground-level jungle growth, and he paused to turn toward the direction of the sound: down in the valley. Goldsmith shrugged and checked his compass to make sure that he was still headed east. He was following the contour of the land to conserve his energy, so his course had been snakelike.

An hour later, he heard a second muffled explosion from the valley below, and he frowned. Even using delayed fuses, B-52 bombers would have dropped more than two bombs.

Then a new thought occurred to him. He smiled and checked his watch. If the explosions were his shape charges blowing up the pipeline, there should be a granddaddy of them all in about an hour.

Time slipped by quickly as he concentrated on the jungle surrounding him. He knew that the farther east he moved, the more danger he would face. Not only would the number of NVA on the alert increase, but he would have to negotiate through American long-range patrols and then through regular line units. The LRRPs would be tough to pass through because they would be using the jungle just as he was and they wouldn't hesitate to shoot first if he surprised a team. The larger American

units would be easier to locate because regardless how
hard a company commander tried, he could not move
a whole American company through the jungle without
sounding like an express train. Base areas would be
tough to approach also, because they had small stationary outposts in the jungle that would be listening for any
sounds approaching their positions. As good as he was
at stalking through the jungle, he knew that he made
some sounds that a listening post would detect.

Goldsmith shrugged his shoulders under his almost
empty pack and moved forward. He would tackle the
problems one at a time. Right now he had to get through
the NVA outposts that lined the Laos–South Vietnam
border.

The jungle thinned as he started climbing uphill and
the eight-foot elephant grass replaced the bamboo. Using
his short sword to keep the sharp blades of grass away
from his exposed face, he pushed his way through the
sea of waving grass until he reached the top of the hill.
Then he started walking in a tight circle, slowly
expanding his spiral until he could see in the distance.
Goldsmith moved back to the center of his circle of
knocked-down elephant grass and looked back down in
the valley and then over to the east. He could see a
bright silver-green thumb-wide strip below him and knew
that he had found the Dak Poyo River. It was a major
landmark that told him he was at least thirty thousand
meters below his assigned ten-square kilometer area of
operations! He had covered a lot of distance alone on
the ground after his team had been killed. Then again,
however, if the dull thuds he had heard earlier had been
his shape charges going off, he had accomplished their
mission.

He turned around toward the high mountains that
dominated the interior of Laos. Using the river behind
him, he oriented himself with the landscape. He had
brought only the ten-square-kilometer map with him into
the AO, but he had spent hours back at the CCN command bunker studying the maps of their entire operations
area. The cleared area he had seen from his perch in the
giant tree had to be the old Special Forces A-camp at
A Ro that had been closed down back in 1965, but was

still used on occasion by the Marines as a forward operational base during their border surveillance missions.

Goldsmith stared at the clearly defined mountains to his west and then again down at the wide valley. The moon had broken through the clouds and was providing enough light for his night goggles to turn everything into shades of detailed green.

Seeing a billowing green cloud erupt through the treetops down in the valley, he stared, puzzled at the strange phenomenon. If he had been watching the growing cloud without the night goggles, he would have recognized the yellow-orange ball of fire immediately.

The sound of an explosion reached him and he knew that his shape charges had worked. By accidentally setting the charges for an extra twelve hours delay, he had given himself time to get well clear of the pipeline.

Goldsmith took only a few minutes to enjoy the fireball, which began to expand in two long strips from its center. He oriented himself to the river to his east and then hurried down. He knew the explosion would stir up the NVA like a rock hitting a hornet's nest. He planned on using their anger to make it across the river before daylight. The NVA would center their attention on the area surrounding the destroyed pumping station. He was sure he had already passed their line of defense for the Ho Chi Minh trail, and he had to avoid only the large NVA units along the border now to make it back into South Vietnam.

The river looked shallow from where he lay watching the strong current flowing south from the mountains. He wished that another monsoon storm would come to cover his crossing, but the night sky was already starting to show signs of daybreak, which meant that he would have to spend another day inside of Laos before attempting a river crossing. The Dak Poyo River was still a good ten kilometers inside Laos, but he figured that he could cover that distance before nightfall if he had an early start.

His trip from the high ground had brought him to a Montagnard trail that had been used for centuries by the Hmong tribesmen of Laos and the Montagnards of South Vietnam. Goldsmith thanked himself a hundred times during his walk down from the hills for the time he had

spent memorizing the maps of the area. He had missed
the Montagnard trail only by a few hundred meters, and
that was excellent, considering he didn't have a map of
the area.

The Montagnard trail was the fastest way to cover
ground, and at the same time it gave him an advantage
if he had an accidental encounter with NVA soldiers.
The NVA would not be expecting a lone American soldier walking a trail in their backyard, and as long as he
kept his senses honed, he should be able to hear the
NVA first and slip into the jungle until they had passed
him. The only real danger was running into an NVA unit
resting alongside of the trail, but that was a chance he
was going to have to take. Trying to make it back to
South Vietnam through virgin jungle would take more
strength than he had left.

At the sound of truck engines, he ducked down against
the matted-down bamboo. The first truck pulled to a
halt at the river's edge, and a North Vietnamese soldier
appeared from the riverbank only a hundred meters from
where he was hiding. The driver and guide exchanged
words, and the NVA soldier started walking out into the
river. Goldsmith was shocked when he saw that the
muddy-colored water only came halfway up the man's
calf. A large dead tree swept down the river and struck
something submerged in the water. Goldsmith inched
forward from his hiding place to get a better view of
what was going on upstream. He would have sworn the
river was at least over his head, but the NVA soldier was
almost in the middle of the river and the water was still
the same distance on his calves.

The NVA guide yelled something back, and another
NVA soldier stopped the second truck from going into
the river. A crew of five NVA soldiers waded out in the
water and worked the tree free by lifting it up. A loud
scraping sound reached Goldsmith, and slowly it dawned
on him what he was watching. The NVA had built a
bridge that was submerged a foot beneath the muddy
water!

Lieutenant Goldsmith started counting the vehicles as
they crossed over the bridge, but stopped when he
reached twenty. By that time he had decided that he had

to cross the river while the convoy was occupying the attention of the crew assigned to maintain the bridge.

He hurried to make a small raft out of pieces of wood and bamboo that lined the riverbank, and as he worked he cursed himself for wasting so much time watching the convoy. He hoped that there were still a few more trucks to cross as he placed his rucksack on the small raft—which looked like a clump of dirt and underbrush that had broken away from the riverbank—and eased himself into the cold, mountain-fed water. The current sucked his legs down instantly, and Goldsmith was forced to grab onto the raft. The speed with which the raft was pulled downriver was faster than he had judged, and his dangling legs were acting like a rudder for the strong current to push against. He had wanted to keep an eye on the NVA soldiers working on the bridge, but the situation required that all of his attention be focused on getting across the river. If the NVA saw him in the pale morning light, he would know about it shortly.

The current carried him a half mile downstream before his boots touched the bottom of the river again. He had been frog-kicking to help move the raft laterally, and when he stood up, the water was below his waist. He had just enough time to grab his rucksack before the current pulled the raft back out into the main stream.

Goldsmith glanced upriver only once before slipping into the jungle. It was now a matter of slipping across the border and linking up with an American unit. He moved through the jungle for a few hundred meters before removing the night goggles. It had turned daylight since he had left the river. He replaced the goggles in his rucksack and took a break for his eyes to adjust to normal light. It felt good seeing things as they really were again.

He then removed his boots and socks so that he could wring out the excess water from his socks, which were making too much noise as he walked. He continued removing articles of clothing, one at a time, until he had twisted as much water out of the material as he could. While he was doing this, he planned his route through the jungle. NVA trucks were using the old Montagnard trail, which meant that there would be trail watchers and infantry nearby from either local Vietcong units or NVA reserves. But if he tried traveling parallel to the trail in the jungle, he knew that he not only would have a difficult time maintaining a true course, but that it would be nearly impossible to break through the jungle without making noise. He was better off to move cautiously along the trail and slip into the jungle at the first hint of any other travelers.

Alex-Paul stepped out onto the trail and paused to listen for any sign of a human presence. He started walking east in a low crouch, and slowly he straightened up and increased his pace. Danger could come from either direction, and it was increased if he moved too slowly on the trail. He had to move at a pace faster than an NVA column so that any troops coming from the west wouldn't catch up to him. At the same time, though, he couldn't race ahead or he might blunder into NVA moving east back into Laos.

In the first hour, three false alarms caused him to duck into the thick bamboo and underbrush that grew right at the edge of the truck tire tracks. Once the jungle was so thick that he couldn't shove in far enough to hide, and he was forced to drop down and scurry underneath the bamboo.

Goldsmith moved along the shadowed side of the trail as it wound through the rolling hills, slipping across the trail when necessary to remain in the shadows. The walking was easy because the trail was going downhill all the way.

Then he heard a thud and a cry of pain.

Goldsmith slipped into the jungle at an angle so that anyone coming from the east would have to look back over their shoulder to see where he had left the trail. He dropped to the ground less than three feet from the worn trail but was completely camouflaged by the undergrowth and his uniform. He could see patches of the trail if he raised his head slightly. The sound of people walking reached him, and he lowered his chest against the thick layer of wet leaves.

"Fuck! Let them shoot me, I can't go much farther."

Alex-Paul heard the words clearly, and he was raising

himself off the ground before he realized that an American voice was out of place on the trail.

A thick ghetto accent answered the first voice: "Keep quiet, or they'll fucking zap your ass!"

A chatter of voices was followed by a heavy thud. This language he didn't recognize. He had taken Vietnamese at the language school, and he had worked with the Montagnards and knew a few of their words, but the high-pitched, nasal chattering wasn't anything he had heard before.

He risked raising himself enough to catch glimpses of the men as they passed within a couple of meters of his position. He saw a black soldier trying to help a smaller white soldier stay on his feet with a pole tied to his arms. A small man wearing a red-and-white-checkered cloth around his head entered the picture. He screamed something at the black soldier and hit him with the flat side of the stock of his AK-47. Standing next to the black soldier, the man was so small that Goldsmith thought he was a boy until he turned slightly and Goldsmith saw his face. The small man was over forty years old. Another American entered the limited open space on the trail, and in the second he passed, Goldsmith saw a camouflaged 101st Airborne Division patch on his shoulder. Then a pair of little men appeared in his small window onto the trail, and two more Americans stumbled past, wearing bamboo yokes behind their heads with their arms tied to them at their wrists and again behind their elbows.

Lieutenant Goldsmith felt a chill and then a tremendous desire to urinate as he realized the five American soldiers had been captured by the Pathet Lao! The North Vietnamese made attempts at abiding by the Geneva Convention rules of warfare—the Pathet Lao did not. The Laotian communists tortured their prisoners for nighttime entertainment, and under the best of conditions they used South Vietnamese and American prisoners as personal slaves to their officers—buying and selling the captives as they saw fit.

He was leaving his hiding place to attack the Pathet Lao guards when voices reached him from the main force of Pathet Lao coming up the trail from the east. Goldsmith lowered himself to the ground and checked his watch. If he could survive, knowing the exact time the prisoners passed his position would help locate them in Laos. A man could walk only so far in a given amount of time.

Over a hundred Pathet Lao passed his hiding place before he risked taking another look. Goldsmith knew that there would be a rear guard, but he didn't know how far back they were. He waited.

He heard them before they appeared on the trail, carrying their weapons over their shoulders. Two Pathet Lao were talking to each other and smoking American cigarettes. Goldsmith didn't have any trouble figuring out where the Marlboros had come from as he squeezed the trigger. The pop of the silenced pistol was so soft you had to listen for it. The second Pathet Lao soldier had only enough time to look surprised at his comrade when another bullet ripped through his left temple. He dropped onto the trail dead alongside his fellow rear guardsman.

Lieutenant Goldsmith pulled their bodies off the trail and spent a couple of minutes fixing the brush so that it would be very difficult to find them. In a few days their smell would draw the attention of passersby, but by then, with a little luck, he would be drinking a cold beer on some American base camp.

Goldsmith glanced back over his shoulder, feeling tremendous pity for the American soldiers who had been captured. They were living Goldsmith's worst fear. Death was absolutely nothing to him, but being captured was something he knew he could not handle.

Goldsmith stared back down the trail, and he spoke for the first time since he had tried scaring off the mother gaur. "I'll be back, motherfuckers!"

He crossed over the Laos–Vietnam border a little past high noon without realizing it. There weren't any of the stone signs marking the border on the Montagnard trails that were common along the major Vietnamese highways. Goldsmith continued on the trail, carrying his pistol at the ready in his left hand and his black-bladed short sword in his right. He couldn't get the thought of the POWs out of his mind, and he knew that unless he could concentrate on his own situation, he would end up making a fatal error of judgment. The terrain was opening up again, and huge stands of elephant grass began narrowing the trail.

Without giving it much thought, he angled off the trail and stopped to pull the elephant grass closed behind him. He could negotiate through the grass without making much noise, and his compass would keep him on an easterly course. He figured that he could keep going for another few hours and then laager for the night in the tall grass. Early the next morning he would make the dash for the old Special Forces camp at A Ro.

The sun was directly overhead, and the heat felt good against his face. Steam was coming off his wet uniform and from his rucksack as the sun's rays began drying out the material. Goldsmith decided to take a much needed break and dry out a little before trying to link up with an American unit. He knew he could negotiate the grass better if he dried out a little, and the abrasions from the wet cloth that had been rubbing against his bare skin would dry out.

Lieutenant Goldsmith thought that the soft voices were coming from his dream and blinked his eyes rapidly to wake up. He had dozed off in the bright sunshine.

"Left." The single word came from only a few meters away in the tall grass and was barely a whisper. "A trail."

Another voice answered in a deeper whisper. "Check it out—but be careful."

Goldsmith listened for a foreign voice. The POW incident had made him very gun-shy.

Hearing a lone soldier moving through the elephant grass, he decided on risking a contact.

"Round eyes." Goldsmith didn't know why those particular words came out of his mouth, but it brought an instant reaction. He heard the clicks of a dozen safeties coming off weapons and a lot more noise as the soldiers shifted their positions in the tall grass to focus on where the voice had come from. A lot of people had snuck up on his position when he had been sleeping.

"Who are you?" Ten feet away, the voice was louder than a whisper but lower than normal conversation.

"Lieutenant Goldsmith. I'm E&Eing from Laos."

There was a long pause before the same voice answered him again. "Show yourself—very slowly."

Goldsmith stood up and took a deep breath before pushing the grass away in front of him. He had holstered his pistol and resheathed his sword so that he would not present a hostile appearance to the American patrol.

The tackle from his right side was unexpected, and he landed flat on his back with all of the air knocked out of him.

"Don't fucking move!" A paratrooper laid a K-Bar fighting knife against Goldsmith's throat.

A young-looking officer appeared from the grass and stood over the two of them. "Goldsmith?"

He smiled. "Yep."

The paratrooper let the lieutenant get to his feet.

"You say that you are coming out of Laos—alone?"

"Yes, my recon team was hit by a Chinese Claymore. I'm the only survivor."

The paratrooper who had tackled Goldsmith looked at him with growing respect.

"I'm Lieutenant Kolinski with the 101st." The platoon leader held out his hand and Goldsmith shook it.

"I saw some of your buddies back there a ways . . ." He used his thumb to point out the direction over his shoulder.

"You did? How long ago?" The lieutenant's voice was beginning to rise and he caught himself. "How many?"

"Five—four white guys and a black guy."

"That's them!" At that moment the lieutenant was joined by a trio of sergeants who had been watching in the grass.

One of them addressed Goldsmith: "How many NVA were with them?"

"They weren't NVA—Pathet Lao."

"Fuck!" The lieutenant's voice dropped in despair.

"How many of them?" The sergeant's eyes narrowed.

"A company—maybe a hundred of them. I took out their rear guard—two men."

"How long ago?"

"Three or four hours."

"We can still catch them, Lieutenant." The sergeant hefted his M-16.

"They're already in Laos. We can't cross the border."

"He did." The sergeant pointed at Goldsmith with his M-16. "I'm going, sir. There's no way that I'm going to leave a fellow paratrooper alive in those butchers' hands!"

"Okay, but what about him?" The lieutenant nodded at Goldsmith.

"He can come with us or wait here."

"Better yet," Goldsmith said, knowing he didn't have the strength to go back into Laos with a combat patrol, "give me one of your radios and I'll take care of myself—and a couple of smoke grenades. I'll move east a couple of clicks and call in for an extraction. My unit has airborne forward air controllers up all the time a team is inserted. I'll be out of your hair in no time at all."

The lieutenant nodded and one of his radio operators dropped his PRC-25 at Goldsmith's feet. "Try to get it back to us—I've signed for it."

"The FAC can give you some really good support if you want it. Gunships and fast-movers are on call."

The airborne lieutenant nodded in agreement. "Our people might have some trouble getting clearance to fire in Laos."

Goldsmith looked over at the platoon radio operator. "He's on frequency 88.7 with a call sign of Bucking Dog 65. What's your unit, Lieutenant, so I can get your radio back to you?"

"Bravo Company, 1st Battalion of the 101st—Lieutenant Kolinski."

"Be seeing you soon." Goldsmith slipped the PRC-25 into his rucksack and pulled the drawstrings tight around it.

"You were really out there alone?" The paratrooper lieutenant still couldn't believe that the Green Beret officer had been alone in the jungle and acting so damn calm about the whole affair.

"Not by choice." Goldsmith lifted the now heavy rucksack over his shoulder. "You'd better get moving if you want to rescue your men."

"You sure you'll be all right out here alone?"

"Yes. You're going to need all of the firepower you can muster when you catch up to those Pathet Lao."

"Let's move it, sir!" The sergeant had already started moving the platoon west through the tall grass.

"You can travel faster if you use the trail. Now that I'm off it, anything you see on it is fair game."

Then Goldsmith disappeared in the sea of tall grass. He followed the trail the platoon had made in the grass for a half hour before stopping and setting the frequency on the radio to 88.7 and squeezing the handset. "Bucking Dog 65, this is Viper 6 . . . over."

The response was instantaneous. "Viper Six, Bucking Dog! I missed you! Where are you, over."

"Viper 6, near A Ro. I'm off my map, over."

"A Ro?" The forward air controller's voice reflected his shock. Goldsmith was over twenty-five miles south of his insertion point.

"Roger that, Bucking Dog, and I'm really ready to come home . . . over."

"Bucking Dog, do you have any special requests? Over," the FAC said, referring to wounded and KIAs.

"Negative, just one person coming out, over."

There was a long silence and then the FAC answered in a hushed voice. "Roger, Viper. Extraction team is on their way. Be prepared to pop smoke, out."

CHAPTER FIVE

⊛⊛⊛⊛⊛⊛⊛⊛⊛⊛⊛⊛⊛⊛⊛

TALL TOWER

"It's all very hard to believe." The officer wearing a silver eagle on the collar of his camouflage uniform walked over to the Plexiglas window and looked out over the raked sand at the cement wall of the tactical operations center. "He lost his team, but he doesn't have a single combat wound. He openly stated that he used NVA trails and he actually had his team walking down the Ho Chi Minh trail when the Chinese Claymore killed his teammates." The colonel shook his head before continuing, "It's too much."

"What do you think happened, Colonel Shunball?" The officer sitting behind a large Philippine mahogany desk turned slightly in his swivel chair to face his boss.

"I think the NVA ambushed the team and Lieutenant Goldsmith panicked and ran." The SOG chief twisted the end of his handlebar mustache.

"How do we then explain the hole in Lieutenant Goldsmith's rucksack and the Claymore ball bearing that was found on the bottom of his pack after it had bent his carrying frame?" Major Ricks had waited for an opening in the conversation before submitting that critical piece of evidence. He knew that his boss had intentionally left that fact out of the report.

Lieutenant Colonel MacCall flashed an angry look at his executive officer and tried brushing the comment off. "He could have staged that to support his story. Goldsmith is a very smart man."

"Why would he lie?" The major knew that he would have to press the issue now, or the lieutenant would end up in serious trouble. Even a rumor getting out to the

51

rest of the recon teams that Goldsmith had left his team and ran would get the lieutenant killed. Cowardice was tolerated among the elite combat soldiers, on a one-time basis. Anyone who had ever served in combat knew that anyone could freeze under fire, but forgiveness came from telling the truth and then making sure that it never happened again.

"He might want to look like a hero to the rest of the recon company." The lieutenant colonel glanced over at his boss and then quickly added, "A lot of people would do anything for a couple of decorations without having to really earn them."

The colonel pointed over at the gray-headed major, who was the only officer in the room wearing short-sleeved khakis and unauthorized penny loafers. "What do you think, Speedy?"

He had been waiting for the colonel to ask him that question. "I think that we should trust Lieutenant Goldsmith."

The lieutenant colonel stood behind his desk and leaned forward. "Do you actually believe that a second lieutenant, with nine months in-country, could pull something like that off?"

"What was RT Viper's mission, sir?" The respectful pronoun didn't sound right coming from the older major's mouth.

"Locate the NVA gasoline pipeline and if possible destroy a portion of it." The lieutenant colonel's words were clipped, and his voice carried the tone of a schoolboy being forced to recite his lesson before the class.

"He not only accomplished his team's mission, *alone*, but he did it in such a manner that the Air Force could make out the direction the pipeline was laid out in and could saturate-bomb over ten miles of the pipeline. Add to that his sighting of five American POWs from the 101st and his successful link-up with elements of that division, and you do have a very successful mission."

"Damn it!" The Command and Control North commander smashed his fist onto his desk. "The platoon he sent after those POWs was damn near wiped out!"

"Goldsmith warned the lieutenant from the 101st that there were over a hundred Pathet Lao with the POWs, and Goldsmith had even supplied the radio frequency and air support of his FAC cover when he realized the airborne lieutenant was going after his men."

"The Pathet Lao cut the throats of those five POWs!"

The major remained calm. He could see that he was winning the colonel over, even though the senior commander was an old friend and classmate of his boss. "We can't blame Goldsmith for that!"

"He could have guided the platoon." The lieutenant colonel thought he had played a verbal ace.

"Goldsmith mentioned in his statement that he would have, except he didn't think he had the strength left after living off the jungle for over a week—and the airborne lieutenant, Kolinski, mentioned in his statement that he didn't think Goldsmith would have been much good to him and would have slowed his platoon down. Kolinski accepts full responsibility for his actions."

The lieutenant colonel shook his head. "I don't care what the statements *implied*. There are just too many holes in Goldsmith's story, and besides, he has a history of getting into trouble."

"What kind of trouble?" the colonel said, interested by the CCN commander's comment.

"Lieutenant Goldsmith was thrown out of a line unit for stirring up trouble with black soldiers."

"Sir?" A captain who had been listening to the conversation from across the room spoke up.

"Yes?" Colonel Shunball squinted as he sized up the young officer.

"I've read the complete report from the 5th Division, and what it said was that the black soldiers in that unit did not accept Lieutenant Goldsmith's style of leadership—that leaves a *lot* of unanswered questions. I think we should stick to the issue at hand and his performance with us on his first mission."

The colonel smiled. "And"—he leaned forward to read the captain's nametag— "Captain Barr, what do you think about Lieutenant Goldsmith's performance?"

"Well, sir, if we don't believe what our recon leaders tell us during their debriefings, we had better start getting used to using spy satellites for our information."

"How's that?" The colonel glanced over at his commander and saw the white jawline.

Captain Barr continued, "If the other recon leaders hear that we are calling Lieutenant Goldsmith a liar, we might as well shut down the program. They aren't going to risk their lives to be called liars."

"Is that what the other recon leaders are saying?" The colonel, an old-time reconnaissance man himself, knew that rumors had already started in the CCN compound, and he didn't want them spreading to his other units at CCS and CCC.

"That's the word I've got, sir."

"What do *you* think we should do?"

"I'd give him a fucking decoration, sir—sorry." The young captain started blushing over the escaped cuss word.

The colonel ignored the mistake and nodded his head. "I agree. Until we have something more positive, we've got to take Lieutenant Goldsmith's word. Decorate him, Jack."

"Sir!"

"Decorate him!" The colonel's voice lowered as a sign that the conversation was closed.

"Yes, sir."

The major looked over at the captain and winked. What they had rehearsed in Barr's office had worked. It had looked as though Major Ricks had been responding to his boss's request to gather evidence to hang the new lieutenant, but Ricks had done just the opposite. Lieutenant Colonel MacCall was *officially* the commander of Command and Control North, but everybody, including the Vietnamese commandos, knew that Major Ricks was the real power in the long-range reconnaissance operation. You could cross the command-appointed commanders at CNN, but only a fool would cross Speedy Ricks.

"I've got to tap a kidney and fly back to Saigon." The colonel started leaving the office and paused. "Do you have that paperwork we talked about on the secure telephone for me?"

"Yes, sir, I'll get it for you." MacCall waited until his boss left his office to go to the latrine before speaking to the captain, who served as his administration officer. "Write Goldsmith up for a Bronze Star for Valor."

"A Bronze Star, sir?" The young captain was shocked.

"Yes! What in the hell do you think he deserves? A fucking Medal of Honor?"

Captain Barr wanted to say yes, but he caught the look Major Ricks was giving him out of the corner of his eye and said, "Whatever you say, sir."

"Good!" Lieutenant Colonel MacCall left his office through a small side door leading directly into his private administrative office, where he had two clerks working on special projects for him. He took a large manila envelope off the clerk's desk that had Colonel Shunball's name written across the front in bold Magic Marker letters. The envelope contained a smaller box and a cardboard-protected packet of papers.

MacCall left the clerk's office through the exit without going back into his office, where he had left his executive officer. Catching his boss leaving the private latrine in the hall, he handed him the sealed packet. "I really was hoping for your support in there, sir."

"You should have done your homework. Ricks and that kid had done theirs." Shunball hefted the package in his right hand. "Thanks, I appreciate this. General Elms over with the support command would like a Silver Star—if you could arrange it for us."

"Sure, sir. Just remember that I would like to make the five percent list coming out at the end of the year."

"Consider it done."

"And you know that I've promised both of my special clerks appointments to Officer's Candidate School for their help."

"Just send me their paperwork. You're doing a great job here for us, Jack. Don't let this thing with Goldsmith get you down. If he's the kind of officer I think he is, you'll have plenty of chances to nail his ass for your classmate."

A look of shock came over the lieutenant colonel's face. "How in the hell did you know?"

"I run the top spook organization in Vietnam. Do you think I would waste all of that talent just to fight the NVA? I've known for a long time that you and the commander from the 1st Brigade of the 5th Division were asshole buddies from the Point."

"*Friends*, sir—not asshole buddies. We watch out for each other."

"Well, I've got a very good idea what happened back there with our blond-haired lieutenant, and it has nothing to do with *his* racial prejudices."

"Just because my friend is a black officer, sir, doesn't mean that he is—"

The colonel held up his hand. "I'm not calling any officer prejudiced—not yet." He patted MacCall's shoulder with the sealed envelope. "Thanks again. You don't need to walk me out. I can find my helicopter out there on the pad."

Lieutenant Colonel MacCall watched his boss stride across the sand to the helipad, and then turned on his heels to go back and take a hunk out of his executive officer's ass.

Lieutenant Goldsmith watched the helicopter warming up from his seat on the top platform of a fifty-foot rappeling tower. Sitting with his legs crossed, he was wearing a pair of cut-offs made from what Special Forces troops called a leopard camouflage suit. The rappeling tower was where he went to be alone. He could see the activity of the whole camp from the elevated position, and he didn't think anyone knew that he used the rarely used platform as a secret hiding place.

Colonel Shunball hurried to buckle himself into the nylon seat and started tearing the large manila envelope open before the chopper had left the ground. He removed a small cardboard box from inside the envelope and then removed a small blue leather box from the larger one. He hesitated and smiled before he opened the presentation box and stared in at the beautiful Distinguished Service Cross displayed on a tan velvet backing. His smile widened. He was looking down at the top of the CCN headquarters building when his eyes caught sight of a figure sitting cross-legged on the top of the rappeling platform as his chopper pilot circled the structure to get a heading for Saigon. A blond-haired man sitting on the platform stared back. Then the man turned his head to look back out over the South China Sea, which bordered the backside of the large compound.

Colonel Shunball's helicopter gained altitude in order to pass over Marble Mountain to the south and follow the coastline. The colonel tried leaning out of the chopper so that he could get another look at the man. Feeling guilty over having Lieutenant Colonel Ricks write up a phony award for him, he snapped the presentation box shut before putting it away in the manila envelope.

In the next moment he was angry at himself for feeling guilty. Sure, he hadn't done what the award citation said, but he had been screwed out of a Distinguished Service Cross back in Korea when he had been a young second lieutenant and this award was making up for that mistake!

Colonel Shunball turned on the intercom headset and barked at the pilot: "Let's set a record getting back to Saigon! I have an important meeting!" He turned off the headset before the pilot could answer and threw it onto the seat next to him.

A sea breeze blew in off the water and dampened the heat from the nearby beach. Lieutenant Goldsmith scanned the base camp below him like a hunting hawk. His eyes missed nothing. He watched a team practicing for a patrol on the mock live-fire rifle range that occupied a portion of an unused rice paddy. Goldsmith frowned, wondering how the Vietnamese could grow rice in sand, and then he saw a stream that meandered down from the low foothills. Top soil had washed down over the centuries to make the narrow strip of land very fertile.

The sun reflected off a piece of bare metal on the top of the mountain that seemed like a mistake of nature to break up the miles of bare beach. Goldsmith stared at the spot and could barely make out a couple of moving figures. He remembered having been briefed on his arrival that a Marine outpost and radio-relay site occupied the unusual mountain, which was composed almost entirely of a gray marble. He wondered who occupied the *side* of the jagged cliffs. From his perch on the tower, he could see a solid row of American units for miles back up the beach toward Da Nang. When American units started building up in the area, the Vietnamese govern-

ment had given them the unoccupied beaches to the
south of the ancient city. The Vietnamese had little use
for white sand beaches and sun tanning was strictly a
Caucasian pastime. In Vietnam, a dark face was the sign
of a peasant who had spent his whole life working in the
rice paddies. The wealthy and middle-class Vietnamese
made a point out of staying out of the sun.

Alex-Paul had learned about the Vietnamese social
structure during his tour of duty at the Presidio of Monterey Language School. His instructor had been a young
woman from a wealthy Vietnamese family, who had
bought property in California and were applying for
American citizenship. She would mix Vietnamese customs and social lore in with the lessons. Goldsmith
smiled to himself, feeling the wind blowing past his ears
as he sat facing the sea. The Vietnamese instructor had
become very upset when he had asked her: "If having
light-colored skin is a sign of social status in your country, what do the Vietnamese people think of black American soldiers?" She blushed and tried avoiding the
question, but the two black officers in the class pushed
her for an answer. She commented that at first black
soldiers had shocked the Vietnamese people, but they
had become used to them as the American troop strength
had built up.

The smile left Goldsmith's face. He wondered why
blacks were automatically looked down upon in just
about every country—including countries that had never
seen blacks before, like Vietnam and the Indochina area.

The sound of someone climbing up the ladder drew
Goldsmith out of his reverie. He really did not want visitors. He waited until a head appeared above the platform
before turning to see who his visitor was.

"I hope I'm not disturbing you."

Goldsmith recognized the site's administrative officer
and shrugged. "I was just about ready to leave." He
started to get up and reached down for the poncho liner
he had been sitting on.

"Please, I came up here to talk to you."

"I spent five and a half hours debriefing the staff over
at the TOC, sir—"

"You don't have to address me as 'sir' when we're alone. I'm Rob Barr—you can call me Rob."

Goldsmith took the offered hand and then dropped down again, crossing his legs. "I'm Alex-Paul Goldsmith. OCS-commissioned." He glanced quickly over at the captain for a response.

Barr openly laughed before commenting. "Hey, I received my commission from ROTC at Iowa State! You don't have to worry about my membership in any self-interest groups." He was referring to the infamous West Point Protective Association, which West Point graduates claimed did not exist, but every officer without a West Point commission who had ever served in combat knew that was a lie. "I read your personnel file—that's my job—and I noticed that you had an unusual first name."

"I'm named after my father and his brother."

Captain Barr saw that small talk wasn't getting him anywhere and changed the subject. "I see that you've found my special getaway place."

"I'm sorry, I thought that no one ever used this tower."

"Every once in a while we run our commandos through a tower exercise, but for the most part you're right. It isn't used." Barr looked over Goldsmith's shoulder and added. "Colonel Shunball just left. He was in a meeting with Colonel MacCall and Major Ricks. The conversation was about you." Barr could see the walls going up in the young lieutenant's eyes.

"About what?"

Captain Barr's eyes locked for a second with Goldsmith's, and he was forced to look away. "The mission you were on."

"I figured something was wrong by the way they debriefed me. What does the colonel think—I ran off and left Sergeant Archer and the rest of my team to die?"

Barr felt his face getting warm. Goldsmith had guessed correctly. "Something like that, but Ricks supported you and so did I—"

"Thanks," Goldsmith replied icily.

"I think it's because it was your first mission. No one

really knows you very well, and ever since you arrived here, you've pretty much kept to yourself."

"I'm not very sociable." Goldsmith locked eyes with the captain again, but this time Barr held his gaze. "I didn't think a unit like CCN cared about popularity contests."

"We don't. It's just that you arrived here from another unit in-country, and everybody is wondering what happened—"

"You mean if I was a coward and they booted me out?"

Barr spoke what he was thinking: "Are you some kind of a fucking mind reader?"

Goldsmith chuckled. "Not really. It's just that I've been down this road before."

"What happened between you and your battalion commander? I've read the report, but it really doesn't make sense."

"There was a riot and I was the duty officer. I stopped the riot—that's about it."

"Your ex-battalion commander states that you opened fire on American troops."

"The soldiers were rioting in a combat zone because they claimed that blacks were forced to work harder than whites. It was bullshit and everyone knew it."

Captain Barr nodded his head. He had heard about the racial problems in the line units, but Special Forces had been spared that kind of hatred. Blacks in the elite unit were from among the best soldiers in the army, and they had been required to meet the same standards for entry as white soldiers. "The colonel told me to put you in for a Bronze Star for Valor."

"Thanks."

"I'm a little embarrassed."

"Why?" Goldsmith said looking out over the camp.

"What you did deserves a lot higher award."

"A Bronze Star is just fine."

"I've worked it out so that we can give you *three* Bronze Stars."

"Why?"

"I've been ordered to give you a Bronze Star for Valor and that's what I'll do. But the colonel didn't say that I had to give you only one." Barr changed his position on the platform and stretched out his legs. "Maybe you don't know what you've done, Alex-Paul, but walking out of Laos is a big deal. You are only the second recon man at CCN who had the guts to stay alone in the jungle. Lieutenant Bourne pulled a stay-behind mission a couple of years ago, but he ended up getting killed. What you did was heroic. You've earned a Bronze Star for blowing up the pipeline, another one for having the guts to E&E, and a third one for taking out the two Pathet Lao. Actually, you should get a DSC for what you've done."

"That's a very high award, Cap—Rob."

Goldsmith didn't see what flashed over the captain's face, but he caught the strain in his voice. "If you only knew what was going on . . . you'd understand."

"I'd like to finish out my tour in peace here. What do I need to do to get the colonel off my ass?"

"Let me take care of MacCall. I haven't figured out why he's on your ass so hard. He should be happy with your mission." Barr's forehead wrinkled. "Do you know if your ex-battalion commander is a friend of MacCall's?"

Goldsmith shrugged.

"Let me check that out." Barr stood up and turned toward the ladder. "Are you coming down for chow?"

"No, I brought some C-rations in my rucksack."

Captain Barr started backing down the ladder and then paused at neck level. "I almost forgot. The colonel has assigned Sergeant Tyriver to you as your One-One, along with three of our best Meo tribesmen." Barr's head disappeared below the level of the deck and popped back up again. "Tyriver's been in-country for two straight years. He's one of the best recon men in Vietnam."

"It sounds like the colonel doesn't trust me." Goldsmith turned around slowly and looked Barr in the eye. "You'd better get down that ladder. There's a hornet's nest behind the first rafter beam."

Noticing the hornets circling his head, Barr nearly let go of the ladder. He stopped halfway down the tower and called back up to Goldsmith. "I should be seeing Tyriver in the mess hall. Do you mind if I send him over here after supper?"

"Sure." Goldsmith watched the captain cross the compound to the mess hall, located near the ocean in the back of the compound. He liked the captain, but he hesitated to make friends. He didn't want to owe anybody anything, and he didn't want people owing him. He just wanted to pull as many recon missions as possible. He planned on staying in Vietnam until he had saved enough money to buy a small piece of land back in the States and maybe hunt or trap for a living. He knew one thing for sure: he was sick and tired of the human race and the constant games people played with each other.

His first nine months in Vietnam had been one long power struggle with his battalion commander. Whatever he did, it was wrong as far as the officer was concerned. He had either been too aggressive or too soft on the troops. Nothing was ever right and once the other officers in the battalion saw that the commander had marked him, every one of them shunned him.

The recruiter for SOG had only been passing through the brigade headquarters when he had run into Goldsmith. Only a week later Alex-Paul received verbal orders to report to Command and Control North.

After the first question Lieutenant Colonel MacCall had asked him, he knew that his ex-battalion commander had talked to his new commander. McCall had asked him if he minded serving on a recon team with a black sergeant for a second-in-command.

Goldsmith felt the sun on the back of his neck as it started slipping below the mountains. He remained sitting, facing the sea, and reached into his rucksack to remove a full bottle of Jack Daniel's. It was past six o'clock, and the small CCN NCO club had opened its doors, signaling that it was okay to start drinking on the compound.

He opened the bottle and took a long draw of the smooth whiskey before setting the bottle down. The sun's warmth left his neck and touched the back of his head. Goldsmith felt a chill and released the air he was holding in his lungs. His throat burned and he coughed.

"That shit will burn a hole in your windpipe, sir."

Goldsmith turned his head toward the voice. The soldier had caught him daydreaming and had actually made it past three creaky rungs on the ladder. Two of the rungs were right next to each other, which meant that the climber would have to skip both of them. "Sergeant Tyriver?"

"Yes, sir. Captain Barr told me that you were over here, but everybody in camp knows that you've been sitting up here all afternoon."

"I thought I was getting away by coming up here."

"Actually, sir, this is a pretty popular spot inside the compound. It's used a lot, but everyone respects the privacy of the person using it and pretty much leaves him alone. The southern corner of the beach is another spot, and so is the roof of the storage shed in the S-4's compound."

"Thanks for the information."

"If you want me to leave . . ." Tyriver remained waiting on the top of the ladder even though there were a half-dozen hornets buzzing around his head.

"Naw, come on up. I can't drink this whole bottle by myself anyway."

"Thanks." Tyriver selected a spot off to one side, so that he wouldn't obstruct the lieutenant's view of the sea, and reached over for the open bottle.

Goldsmith removed a can of C-ration franks and beans from his pack and used the P-38 can opener he wore around his neck. "That booze is going right to my head. I'd better get something in my stomach before I decide to fly off this tower."

Tyriver grinned in the fading light. "That has been tried a couple of times before. All five members from RT Copperhead jumped off the top together one night."

"Really?" Goldsmith buried the white plastic spoon in the cold rations and looked over at Tyriver. "How many died?"

"No one. The sand broke their fall, but there were a couple of broken bones and the CO was incredibly pissed because it took the recon team out of action for a month."

"God takes care of fools and drunks—or so they say."

"That was a really good mission you pulled. We're all sorry that Sergeant Archer got zapped along with the rest of your team, but he knew the risk. CCN has lost over twenty-five complete teams since we were formed as a reconnaissance unit." Tyriver dropped that information to let the lieutenant know that what had happened to his team was not unusual. "In fact, Captain Barr pulled our personnel files, and it seems that last year alone, CNN had over four hundred casualties and we only have two hundred and five Americans assigned. I'm not including our commandos either."

"High rate of wounded and dead."

"I don't think there's a single man down in the recon company or with the Hatchet platoons who hasn't been wounded at least once."

"I hated to lose my first team." Goldsmith reached for the bottle and Tyriver handed it to him.

The sergeant watched as the lieutenant kept the bottle up to his lips for a long time. "You accomplished your mission, sir."

Goldsmith nodded his head and thought before answering. "That I did. Yep, I sure did that."

"That's all that counts here at CCN, sir."

Goldsmith turned and stared at the sergeant. Tyriver matched his stare for some time. "I *asked* to be your One-One, sir. I like your style."

Goldsmith nodded his head and grunted.

"We can pick up a mission tomorrow, if you feel you're ready, sir." Tyriver took the pause as a negative and added, "We'd have to accept the mission tomorrow, but we'll have two weeks of special training, and we really don't have to take a mission for another couple of months. I just got out of the field and so did you. We can coast until you feel up to it."

Goldsmith's electric blue eyes sparkled in the fading light as if they had a power source all of their own. "What kind of mission?"

"Project Cherry." Tyriver scooted closer to Goldsmith so that he could whisper the top-secret information. The act was more of a response based on his training than a need for secrecy sitting on top of the isolated tower. "Your POW sighting has generated a lot of interest in the high command. The whiz kids in Saigon think that there might be a Pathet Lao POW camp in the area."

"I was told that the Pathet Lao cut the throats of the five men I saw on the trail."

"They did. That's commie S.O.P. if they know they can't keep the POWs from being rescued."

"Those are shitty standard-operational-procedures for any army." Goldsmith took another long swig to erase the faces on the trail. "But I guess being dead is better than being a captive of the Pathet Lao."

"I agree." Tyriver's brief statement carried a lot of hidden meaning. He was telling Goldsmith that if he ever was wounded in Laos that he would rather be killed than left behind.

"I agree too . . ." Goldsmith passed the same message back to his One-One.

"So what do you think, sir?"

"Let's do it. At least I know all of the local roads in the area."

Goldsmith's comment brought a chuckle from Tyriver. The lieutenant smiled back at the sergeant. He liked the man's style, and he instinctively knew he could trust him.

"Let's get drunk, sir."

"That might cause a problem climbing down from here."

"The captain knows we're up here. We can sleep it off and climb down for breakfast."

"Done!" Goldsmith handed the bottle over to Tyriver. Getting drunk sounded like a very good idea.

CHAPTER SIX

✪✪✪✪✪✪✪✪✪✪✪✪✪✪

UNDERWATER BRIDGE

The night on the tower was not wasted getting drunk. The hours were spent getting to know each other, as the two men talked about their days growing up back in the States and many of their disappointments and successes.

The Jack Daniel's acted more as a conversational lubricant than as an intoxicant for the two men as they felt out each other's strong and weak points. A CCN recon team was composed of two Americans and three commandos indigenous to the area they were assigned to reconnoiter. Survival meant that the two Americans had to know each other very well, and both Goldsmith and Tyriver knew they had no time to waste if they were going to accept the POW snatch mission.

'What's this about you carrying only silenced pistols on patrol?' Tyriver was using one of the four corner supports of the tower as a backrest. He sat with his legs stretched out and crossed in front of him.

"I believe that recon teams have a better chance for survival during an accidental encounter with an enemy force if they use small-caliber, silenced weapons."

"Makes sense, but .22-caliber pistols don't give very much firepower."

Goldsmith sat with his legs hanging over the side of the tower used for helicopter rappeling instruction. As he talked, he felt the strong sea breeze move his feet back and forth. "We don't need a lot of firepower in the jungle—just something to take out anyone who gets too close to where we're hiding. Think about it for a couple of seconds. If you're in the jungle hiding and the NVA discover you, what happens when you fire your CAR-15?"

"The rest of the NVA are drawn to your hiding place."

"Right! But with a silenced weapon, you can take out the NVA who are getting too close to you and no one knows about it. One man can do a hell of a lot of damage to an NVA platoon before they wise up."

"I like the concept, but I would feel much more comfortable if we had a little more firepower. Would you agree to silenced Swedish-Ks?"

"How will you cover the sound of the blow-back bolt when you fire it?"

"That can only be heard close-up in the jungle. It's worth the trade-off."

"Okay, you carry the Swedish-K and I'll stick to my silenced pistol."

Tyriver liked Goldsmith's willingness to be flexible. "What about the little people?"

"What do you recommend?"

"They like automatic weapons."

"Can you get your hands on four silenced Swedish-Ks?"

"Sir, you're in SOG now. We can get our hands on anything." Tyriver lifted his head and stared at the morning sun, which was beginning to break along the fine line at the edge of the sea. "We should clean up and get some breakfast before telling the area-studies officers that we want the snatch mission."

Goldsmith stood and stretched. "The night passed by fast. I didn't get much more than a buzz off that bottle." He reached down, shoved his poncho liner into his rucksack, and pulled the drawstring shut before putting the pack over his shoulders. "Race you down to the ground."

"You're on!" Tyriver was sitting closer to the ladder and he didn't have a pack to carry. He dived and reached the ladder first.

At the same moment Goldsmith disappeared off the edge of the platform. He grabbed a helicopter strut that had been mounted at the edge of the tower to simulate footing for a helicopter rappel, and let his right foot swing up under the tower so that he could kick the rafter where the hornets had built their nest.

The defenders reacted instantly, swarming out to attack the creature on the ladder.

"Motherfuck!" Seeing the swarm of hornets emerge from behind the rafter, Sergeant Tyriver locked his boots on the outside edges of the wooden ladder and started sliding down to the ground.

Goldsmith had already dropped to one of the large cross-beams and swung from strut to strut until he was low enough to drop to the sand.

The hornets followed Tyriver down to the ground a couple of seconds behind Goldsmith, and they were starting their attack to defend their nest when Tyriver reached down and started throwing handfuls of sand up in the air. The tactic worked. The hornets broke off their assault and hovered up out of range of the sand cloud.

Goldsmith was halfway across the training area when Tyriver caught up to him. "That was a fucking cheap trick, Lieutenant!"

"Did they get you?"

"Fuck, no!" Tyriver brushed the back of his head with his hand to remove the sand. "I can't believe you jumped down from that tower!"

"I didn't jump. Let's call it a controlled fall."

"Has anyone told you that you're fucking crazy, Lieutenant?"

"A couple of times." Goldsmith grinned and patted Tyriver's shoulder. "That was quick thinking back there, using the sand to distract the hornets."

"I'm a fucking survivor, Lieutenant. Remember that!"

"I will, you can be sure of that."

There were a dozen men already in the communal shower building when Goldsmith arrived carrying his shaving kit and towel. He had been assigned a room in the staff officers' hootch until the Recon Company commander could find space for him in one of their team hootches. RT Viper's two NCOs had been sharing a hootch with RT Coral, and all of the men were noncommissioned officers. Lieutenant Colonel MacCall frowned on a single officer sharing living space with a bunch of NCOs.

"You're up early, Goldsmith."

"I didn't think administrative officers got up before nine."

"Old habits are hard to break." Captain Barr pulled his towel back and forth across his back as he talked. "Did you spend the night up on the tower with Tyriver?"

"Yes." Goldsmith hung his towel on a nearby hook and placed his shaving kit on a bench below it.

"So what do you think? Can the two of you work together?" At that moment Captain Barr noticed an unusual scar on Goldsmith's left shoulder blade. It looked like a very large polio vaccination, except it was over two inches across. "That's a strange scar."

"I got that during a cinder fight when I was ten. It was my first war wound doing battle with the Cherry Street gang."

Barr smiled and shook his head. He appreciated Goldsmith's honesty. There were a lot of people claiming old scars as new battle wounds to justify Purple Hearts. "So, what about Sergeant Tyriver—what do you think of him?"

Goldsmith glanced around the shower room at the other officers and NCOs, who acted as if they hadn't been listening to the conversation, and then answered the S-1. "He's a top-of-the-shelf recon man."

"Good! Then I'll tell your company commander that you accept the assignment."

"Tyriver mentioned that he was a Special Forces-trained medic. Isn't he a little valuable for a recon team member?"

Barr chuckled and wrapped his towel around his waist. "He caused all kinds of hell before they released him from the aid station. He's done very well for himself, with over twenty SOG missions under his belt."

"How many successful?"

Barr glanced around the room of listening men and caught a lot of embarrassed looks before they turned away. Goldsmith had asked a very sensitive question. "I don't really know, except he has made a very good name for himself." Barr pointed over at a man entering the showers. "Hey, Bruce! How many successful missions does Tyriver have?"

The tall, skinny man paused in the shower entrance and spoke without looking back over his shoulder, giving his voice an echo. "Eight out of twenty-one."

"Thanks!" Barr nodded toward the shower room. "He's our senior area-studies man for the northern area. Eight out of twenty-one is exceptional. Most of our missions don't last a full day before the NVA make contact with them."

"Why?"

Barr shrugged. "I'm just the administrative guy. I don't do recon."

Goldsmith nodded and picked up his soap box. "I've got to meet Tyriver for breakfast. We want to get over to the TOC and volunteer for the prisoner-snatch mission."

Everyone in the room and those lined up at the sinks stopped and looked over at Goldsmith.

"You don't need to hurry."

"Why?"

"POW snatches come under Project Cherry, and that particular program has the highest death rate of all the SOG projects. Not many people are volunteering for stuff like that."

"Does Tyriver know that?"

"Sure, why shouldn't he?" Barr picked his things off the bench and started to leave. "I'll see you for breakfast and we can finish this conversation."

Goldsmith didn't notice everyone staring at him in the showers. Rumors had already started spreading about him, especially his mission. Sergeant Archer's friends were deeply concerned about the rumor that the lieutenant had panicked and left his team to die. Now the lieutenant was volunteering for one of the most dangerous missions in Southeast Asia. Cowards did not volunteer for suicide missions.

One of the men followed Goldsmith into the shower room. He spoke for only a few moments before moving across the room, but Goldsmith heard his words clearly through the shower spray: "We don't talk about missions outside the tactical-operations center."

Goldsmith recognized the voice of Major Ricks.

* * *

Sergeant Tyriver was late joining Goldsmith at his table. The lieutenant was finishing his coffee and was about ready to leave.

"Sorry, sir."

"No problem, David."

Tyriver smiled. He had not told the lieutenant his first name, which meant Goldsmith had known about him all along. "They have good food here—they say it's the best in Vietnam. Our mess sergeant has been here since the camp opened. He's getting to be a very rich man."

"How's that?"

"He runs the black market from Marble Mountain down to the C-team."

"And he's not in jail?"

Tyriver looked over the bite of the omelet he had on his fork. "Not lately, Lieutenant. About a year ago one of our COs tried cleaning up his operation and the food got so bad that even the commandos threatened to riot, so the old man backed off. You see, he's making a lot of money on the side, but at the same time he makes sure we have the best food and lots of it."

Goldsmith shrugged, deciding to keep his opinion to himself. He didn't mind shady deals as long as it benefited the troops and no single individual made a profit.

Tyriver saw the look on his lieutenant's face and added a word of caution: "If you don't agree with that, you'd better be very careful, Lieutenant. There are some powerful people in SOG who are doing much worse, and they'll have your ass killed before they back off."

"Killed?"

"Suicide missions. They're just as good as a hit man."

"We should get over to the TOC and state our *desires*. I've heard that POW snatches *are* suicide missions."

"Yeah, but voluntary ones." At that moment Tyriver started choking on the food he had just shoved in his mouth, because he was hurrying to finish eating. "Fuck it!" He stacked a layer of sausages on a piece of toast and covered it with scrambled eggs mixed with cheese and then another piece of toast. "Let's go."

Major Ricks and four area-studies officers were standing in front of the master map, which covered the com-

pleted Command and Control area of operations and all
of their permanent launch sites. The scale of the map was
1:50,000, which covered one entire wall of the reinforced
cement bunker. The operations sergeant who had designed
the map had used his imagination: he had placed the
map between two sheets of half-inch Plexiglas and then
installed bright fluorescent lights behind and around the
map board. The effect was unique. In the dimly lit bunker the map stood out in exaggerated detail. The noncommissioned officer had also colored in the valley
floors, creating a spiderweb of logical routes for the
NVA to use, and he had even worked out a detailed
scheme by following the contour lines from North Vietnam through their AO that showed the best possible
route for the NVA pipeline. This was the map that had
given Goldsmith the information he needed for his first
mission. The NVA had relied on gravity whenever possible to move the gasoline through the pipe.

"Here and here . . ." Major Ricks tapped the map
with a grease pencil, "maybe even back along the base
of these mountains—here."

"That whole area has been recently photographed by
satellite, and nothing has shown up, sir." The senior
area-studies officer marked out a large rectangle on the
map, using a white grease pencil that became almost iridescent in the lighting.

Major Ricks glanced away from the map and saw Lieutenant Goldsmith and Sergeant Tyriver watching them.
He nodded and beckoned for the two recon men to join
them. "Where did you say that underwater bridge was?"

"Here sir." Goldsmith pointed at a small symbol on
the map. The CCN staff had already updated the map
based on his debriefing. They had even put on a symbol
for a POW sighting where Goldsmith had seen the five
Americans with the Pathet Lao.

"What do you think we should do with the bridge?"
Ricks said, returning his attention back to his staff
advisers.

"We can try bombing it, but the odds are against any
positive results and we would still have to send in a team
to confirm the damage. Or we could send in a team to
blow it." The senior area-studies officer knew his job

very well. "I go with a Hatchet Platoon—engineer heavy." The captain turned toward Goldsmith. "What was the bridge made out of? Wood or steel?"

"Steel, sir."

One of the junior area-studies officers spoke up. "I thought you said in your debriefing that the bridge was underwater and the river was very muddy. How could you see the bridge?" It was a valid question.

"An uprooted tree hit the bridge when I was observing the activity, and the NVA were forced to pry it up so that it could float over the surface of the submerged bridge. I noticed that the water level on the NVA soldiers' legs did not increase, which meant that the bridge was very solid, and I could hear the sound that the log made crossing the bridge. It was wood rubbing against steel."

Everyone was impressed with Goldsmith's professional demeanor and self-control.

It was Sergeant Tyriver who broke the silence by winking at the staff officer.

"Logical answer." The junior staff officer had gained a new respect for the recon lieutenant.

"So we'll have to plan on blowing a sunken reinforced steel bridge." Ricks looked over at one of the staff planners who had been standing in the rear of the growing group. "Can we handle something like that, George?"

"No problem, sir. The water will help act as a tamping material, and we have some very good plastic explosives that will not only destroy the bridge, but make a large enough crater on the river bottom to render the site unusable."

"Good. Let's go that way, then." Ricks reached up and patted Goldsmith's shoulder. "I know what you want to talk about, but that mission has already been assigned to RT Diamondback."

"The area is large enough for two recon teams, sir." Tyriver's voice was very low as he tried maneuvering the executive officer's position to one of more flexibility.

Ricks smiled and shook his head slowly. "No, Tyriver. Goldsmith has just come out of the field, and even though he looks healthy, our medics tell us that he is going to need a couple of weeks to heal."

Goldsmith had been staring at the map, only partially

listening to the conversation. "Sir, how about letting us go in with the Hatchet Platoon to destroy the bridge? It would be an excellent chance for my new team to work out some of our kinks without having the full responsibility of a mission."

Major Ricks' mouth was forming the word no, but what Goldsmith was proposing made good sense. It was a perfect opportunity for a new team to shake out its operating procedures, and besides, Goldsmith had been at the bridge site before and could help locate it. "You're very convincing."

"It's logical, sir." Goldsmith said, mimicking the area-studies officer's voice.

"Work it out with George Martin—he's our resident demolitions expert." Ricks started stepping down from the raised platform in front of the map and hesitated. "The name RT Viper is being retired. Do you have any suggestions for a new name? It has to be a reptile. All of the northern AO teams are named after reptiles and the southern teams after states."

Goldsmith looked at Tyriver, who shrugged as he answered, "All the good names have already been taken or retired."

"How about RT Massasauga?" Goldsmith looked from Ricks to Tyriver for confirmation.

"Massasauga? What kind of fucking snake is that?" Tyriver shook his head. "It sounds like a river or something."

"The massasauga is a shy rattlesnake that lives near the mouths of rivers. It avoids confrontation but will strike if molested."

"That's us! We're small but tough motherfuckers!" Tyriver thumped his chest and pointed out something that none of them had realized before. Both Tyriver and Goldsmith were very short, only a few inches taller than their commandos. "And a good recon team avoids confrontations with the enemy."

"Then RT Massasauga it is!" Major Ricks shook the packet of papers in his hand. "Get your team together and get ready to enter isolation for your area briefing with the Hatchet Platoon. By the way, where are you planning on living, Lieutenant?"

Goldsmith shrugged. "Where I'm at will be fine, sir."

"He can move into my hootch down by the beach, sir. The other RT moved out to live with their men down in the commando barracks. They wanted to learn Meo."

"It's up to Goldsmith and your company commander. Colonel MacCall has given all of the commanders guidance about NCOs and officers living together."

Tyriver knew about the new rule. "He said that as long as they were serving on the same recon team that it was all right."

"Fine, then, work it out and start thinking about a list of special equipment that you'll be needing for this mission. We want to give our supply people as much notice as possible."

"Yes, sir." Goldsmith nodded for Tyriver to follow the area-studies officer responsible for planning their mission back into his office.

Captain Martin sat with his feet crossed over a corner of his desk, talking to another captain when RT Massasauga entered the large office. The area-studies officer's desk occupied a corner near the door, and the rest of the space was filled with maps spread out on tables and stacks of reference books. Three sergeants stood next to a table, analyzing a long strip of aerial photographs.

"Lieutenant Goldsmith!" Martin beckoned for him to join them at his desk. "This is Captain Abou, he's going to be commanding the Hatchet Platoon—and the mission."

Goldsmith held out his hand to shake Abou's hand. As they did, he saw the hatred in the senior officer's eyes. All the same, the captain's voice remained calm. "You've made quite a reputation for yourself on your first time out."

"Thank you, sir."

"Getting your whole fucking team killed!"

The NCOs stopped and looked up from their photographs. The room became so quiet that they could hear the air conditioner.

Sergeant Tyriver flashed a look over at Captain Martin to see if he was going to do anything, but the area-studies officer remained an observer.

Goldsmith pushed Captain Abou's hand away when he

released it and turned his attention to Martin. "We came here to talk about the underwater bridge, sir."

Captain Martin nodded and pointed toward a trio of NCOs. "We've photographed that section of the Dak Poyo and discovered something very interesting. Come and I'll show both of you."

Captain Abou flashed a hate-filled look over at Goldsmith, who responded by looking over at Tyriver and sighing.

"Here's where you claim you saw the bridge—and look at this interesting little item." Captain Martin used the tip of an X-acto knife as a pointer on the photograph.

"Interesting." Goldsmith knew that the underwater bridge was there, but the area-studies team had needed proof. The ripple running straight across the river showed that something man-made was under the surface of the water. Nature rarely did her work in perfectly straight lines.

"What's interesting is that that picture was taken during the dry season. This series of photographs was taken early this morning." Captain Martin paused to let the efficiency of his staff operation sink in. "You can't see the straight line ripple in the deeper water."

"So we now know that *Goldsmith* told the truth," Captain Abou said, pronouncing the lieutenant's name as if his tongue had suddenly been covered with shit. "Let's go in there and blow that fucking thing up."

Sergeant Tyriver was about to speak, but Goldsmith grabbed his arm and shook his head to stop him. Obviously, something was bothering the captain, and Goldsmith wanted him to play his hand out before they went into the field.

"We're assigning two of CCN's best demolition men to your Hatchet Platoon, Abou, for that purpose. Your platoon's mission will be to secure the eastern side of the river. Each one of your commandos will be issued one LAW rocket. Goldsmith reported that the bridge had heavy vehicular traffic, and we might get lucky and surprise a convoy."

"Sir?"

"Yes, Goldsmith?"

"Why get lucky? Why don't we enter the area like

recon men and wait to blow the bridge when there *is* a convoy crossing it? We can have prearranged air strikes on call in both directions on the road so that we can napalm the hell out of the jungle. The convoy I saw was carrying troops and ammunition."

"Because we are a damn Hatchet Platoon, Lieutenant! We kick ass! Not hide in the fucking grass!" Captain Abou's voice rose to a scream before he had finished.

Captain Martin's jaw muscles flexed before he answered his peer: "I think you'd better give whatever is bothering you a rest, Abou. You're making an ass out of yourself."

"You plan the damn mission, then! Call me when you're ready to brief me!" Abou turned on his heel and stormed toward the exit.

Sergeant Tyriver's soft voice reached him and brought the captain to a halt. "We will."

"What did you say, Sergeant?"

"I said that *we will* plan the mission and get back to you—*sir*."

Captain Abou stormed out of the room.

"What's bothering him?" Tyriver shook his head and looked at Captain Martin for an answer.

"I don't know. Normally he's so damn professional that he's boring during mission planning."

"I think we'll find out soon enough." Goldsmith returned his attention to the NCOs and the aerial map. "He seemed pissed over my first mission for some reason. Was he a friend of Sergeant Archer's?"

"Not particularly. He isn't very fond of blacks."

"Fuck 'im." Tyriver growled, bending over the photographs showing where the bridge was located.

"Careful, Sergeant, you're talking about an officer," Martin gently reprimanded. He liked Tyriver, and Captain Abou had been way out of line.

"Here's where I think the trail goes through the jungle, sir." Goldsmith picked up a blue grease pencil and started marking out the trail as he remembered it.

The next few hours in the area-studies room were ones of intense planning. They worked through lunch and the only thing that stopped them was a TOC alert. The recon team that had been sent in to search for the POW camp had made contact within an hour after their insertion and were requesting extraction. All of the area-studies chiefs were required to monitor the crisis and give advice to the senior officer directing the assets from the TOC control center. SOG recon teams had everything available in Southeast Asia at their call.

Goldsmith and Tyriver stayed in the back of the control center and watched as the staff worked the extraction of the team through the launch-site commander. It was like watching a ballet with everyone wearing camouflage uniforms in front of the illuminated backdrop of maps.

Captain Martin had not been involved in the mission planning for the team being extracted, so he joined Goldsmith against the back wall of the center.

Goldsmith leaned over and whispered in the captain's ear, "I'd like to ask a favor, sir."

Martin looked over and then beckoned with his head for them to step back into the TOC storage room. Goldsmith pulled Tyriver in behind him.

"Shoot—what can I do for you?"

"Sir, I'd like for you to talk to Major Ricks and convince him that it would be good business to let RT Massasauga stay behind at the underwater bridge site after we blow it." A long pause followed. Goldsmith had thought that the senior officer would quickly discard the idea and had been ready to submit a torrent of solid reasons why a stay-behind team made sense.

Captain Martin nodded and opened the door again. He had said nothing.

"Sorry about that, David. I just couldn't stand there listening to that mission failing and not do *something*. There is a POW camp over there in Laos somewhere."

"Hey, L.T., it's a good idea. The Hatchet Platoon will be an excellent cover for a stay-behind team, especially after they blow the bridge. It will look like the bridge was the whole mission." Tyriver nodded in the direction of the exit. "Come on, let's move your things over to my hootch before it gets dark. We've been in here half the day already!"

Goldsmith followed his One-One out of the CNN tactical operations center, which was one huge, open, top-secret vault. They passed through the three gates and showed their badges to the guards to get *out* of the area.

The two members of RT Massasauga kept to the cement and wooden sidewalks until they reached the perimeter road. The sand between the buildings was raked everyday and was kept free of footprints, a system that was part of overall camp security. A few years earlier, a large NVA sapper team had actually entered the compound and caused a great deal of damage. It wasn't the damage or even the lives that were lost that had caused so much concern, though, but the fact that a SOG camp had been infiltrated by the enemy. Since that attack, security inside the compound was absolute, and a security violation could earn a member of the program his walking papers to a line unit.

"I think you'll like the hootch. It's right on the beach perimeter. You can hear the waves." Tyriver started walking faster. "How much stuff do you have, sir? We can borrow a jeep to haul it."

"Not very much, Tyriver. I carried it in here, so we should be able to carry it over to the beach side of camp."

"I didn't want to say anything in front of Major Ricks, but the men over in Recon Company don't think very much of the staffers, and it wouldn't be very wise for you to be staying in their hootch."

"You know, David, I'm developing a lot of respect for those area-studies people. They sure acted a hell of a lot more professional than Captain Abou."

"What do you think his problem is, Lieutenant?"

Goldsmith shook his head in bewilderment. "I don't know, but I'm really getting fucking tired of it."

"Sounds like that kind of shit has been going on for a long time for you, sir."

"If you only knew the half of it!" Goldsmith entered the long staff hootch and led the way down a dark hallway to his room. A blast of air-conditioned air hit his face when he opened the door.

"It's like a fucking freezer in here!" Tyriver said, rubbing his bare arms.

"My roommate likes to sleep cold at night. And he leaves the air conditioner running all day long. Actually, I'm glad to be moving out of here. It's nice to sleep cool at night—and it did help heal all of the jungle crap I picked up—but air conditioning fucks up your system for working in the jungle."

"You don't have to worry about being too cold in our hootch at night, L.T., but it isn't too bad with the sea breezes, and because we are so close to the water, we get very little sand blowing through the cracks."

"Are you talking about that little hootch built way in the back of the Recon Company area?"

"Yep! It used to belong to the once living legends of CNN: Lieutenant Bourne and Sergeant Cooper."

"I've heard Bourne's name mentioned before."

"He made quite a name for himself—even won the Medal of Honor. Sergeant Cooper survived, but the lieutenant died."

"We've got some big shoes to fill, Sergeant David Tyriver." Goldsmith grinned and adjusted his rucksack. "Let's get out of this engineered atmosphere and back to the real world."

The sergeant's hootch had been built sideways to the sea, with the exits facing north and south to keep the sand from blowing in. Tyriver walked around to the southern entrance and opened the door. "Home sweet home—for at least part of our lives."

Goldsmith entered a small room just big enough for two cots and a pair of homemade dresser drawers that were no more than four wooden mortar-round boxes stacked on their sides and nailed together. The doors all hung down so that they could be lifted up and items stored inside. A small doorway filled the space between the two dressers, and a long piece of camouflage parachute silk was drawn across it. "What's back there?"

Tyriver pulled the curtain back and led Goldsmith into the other half of the hootch. "This is where our commandos live. They're probably down on the beach catching snails. Damn, they love to eat those slimy fucking creatures by the pound!" Tyriver shook his shoulders in disgust.

Goldsmith checked out the items in the small room. Two sets of homemade bunk beds were built against the walls, and the commandos' equipment and weapons were neatly stacked against the walls. The room had a different human smell that Goldsmith noticed immediately. He had heard that Americans had a different smell, which stemmed from a different diet.

Tyriver stuck his head out of the Montagnard entrance to the hootch to see if the three commandos were sitting outside. The area surrounding the hootch was vacant. "They should be back soon. All three of them speak a little English. And Y-Brei understands almost everything concerning patroling, if you use simple words and speak slowly."

"I assume this is my bunk?" Goldsmith dropped his rucksack onto the bunk farthest from a sliding Plexiglas window that looked out over the sea.

"Seniority has its privileges, Lieutenant."

"Whatever. I don't plan on spending much time back here anyway."

"We've got a couple of hours before supper. Let's change and go down to the beach for a while." Tyriver was already pulling his sweat-stained tiger jacket over his head.

"Sounds good."

Goldsmith followed Tyriver's example and wore cutoff shorts and unlaced jungle boots down to the beach. The sand in the compound was too hot to wear shower slippers on.

"You know, my first couple of days here were spent mostly in isolation. I really didn't have a chance to enjoy the benefits of the camp." Goldsmith pulled his boots off and left them next to the gate guards' wooden hut. The row of boots let the guards know how many men were out on the beach when it came time to lock the gate for the evening. The beachfront was open all the way north to the last American compound, almost five miles away, but the beach was closed at the base of Marble Mountain, the last American outpost to the south.

"There they are! I told you they would be catching those damn snails!" Tyriver waved at the three Montagnards wading waist deep in the surf.

"This beach would sell for a lot of money back in the States." Goldsmith picked up a handful of the fine sand and let it drain out between his fingers.

"Yeah, like back in Malibu—wall-to-wall condos!" Tyriver waved for the Montagnards to come back to

shore and walked across the beach toward where they
had stacked their gear around a five-gallon bucket. He
leaned over the bucket and wrinkled his nose. "Montagnard escargot—ugh!"

"Yes! Escargot!"

Tyriver turned around and grinned. "Lieutenant Goldsmith, meet Y-Brei. He's the one that I told you speaks
very good English."

Y-Brei grinned at the compliment and held out his
hand to shake. "We cook escargot tonight, maybe Lieutenant wish to eat with Montagnards?"

"Yes." Goldsmith smiled and looked down in the
bucket at a mass of moving half-inch snails.

"And this is Y-Bluc and Y-Clack," Tyriver said, finishing the introductions.

"We will make a fine team!" Lieutenant Goldsmith
shook hands with each of the men. At the same time he
noticed the naked trio were compact and well built. None
of them had suffered from any of the childhood jungle
diseases that claimed so many young Montagnard lives,
or if they had, they had survived and become stronger.
The tallest of the trio came barely up to Goldsmith's
chest, and he was a short man for an American.

Tyriver read his thoughts. "Don't worry about them.
They can carry a hundred-pound pack all day through
the jungle."

"Have you ever seen a fat Montagnard, David?"

"Come to think of it, no, I haven't. Even the little
ones are built like their fathers, except they might have
protruding bellies."

The Yards started getting dressed in their tiger uniforms. They had caught enough of the small snails for a
good feast, which would be supplemented with a home
brew called *numpai*.

"You're in for a treat tonight. Those snails end up
tasting and *looking* like boiled snot!" Tyriver waved back
at the Yards as they moved down the beach.

"I can't insult our teammates. If they can eat it, so can
we."

"We?"

"We."

"Aw, shit!"

Goldsmith started walking faster once they had left the wet sand that bordered the surf. "Let's go see the supply officer for our special gear."

"Don't you want to take a break down here for a little while?" Tyriver loved the sea and spent as much time as he could down on the beach.

"Maybe later, once we've got everything in order for this mission and the area-studies team finishes their planning for us."

Tyriver grinned and hurried to catch up to his One-Zero. He liked the lieutenant's intensity.

CHAPTER SEVEN

✪✪✪✪✪✪✪✪✪✪✪✪✪✪✪✪✪✪✪✪✪

SAGINAW COUNTY JAIL

Lieutenant Goldsmith was pleased with the response they got from the supply section. The officers and NCOs had responded to his requests just as the area-studies people had. Everyone was totally professional and they supported all of the recon teams with the same zealousness—there weren't any of the buddy-buddy cliques found in the regular line units.

The supply officer remembered Goldsmith from his first mission, but all he could remember was a blurred figure passing through the building. Sergeant Archer had been assigned as the team leader for the mission and had done all of the planning. Assigning an NCO as a team leader over an officer was common practice in SOG units for the first few missions, until the officer had gotten his feet on the ground.

"So, do you feel better, Lieutenant?" Tyriver asked, anxious to return to the beach.

"Much."

"Well, I'm beach bound. Are you coming?"

"Maybe later. I've got some thinking to do. I'll meet you back there."

Sergeant Tyriver caught the strange tone in his lieutenant's voice and hesitated before turning to take the perimeter road through the Hatchet Platoon area around to the Recon hootches. He accepted the fact that Lieutenant Goldsmith was a little different from the rest of the recon men, but being a little different was the reason all of them had ended up with the super-secret reconnaissance unit. Pausing, Tyriver looked back, wondering if he had said something wrong. Then he disregarded the idea as being paranoid. The lieutenant was a loner even when he was among loners.

As Goldsmith cut through the buildings next to the generator shack, he felt the hundred-kilowatt generators beating their constant rhythm in his bones. The seven large units had been intentionally located near the main TOC so that they could be protected in the event of a ground attack. Goldsmith walked quickly down the sidewalk and turned into the main entrance of the top-secret open vault that was also the operations center. He hurried so that he would not be seen.

The guard at the steel vault door checked his identification against the photo identification of every member of the organization, which was kept in a binder. Goldsmith was signaled into the vault with a bored nod.

All of the area-studies rooms were very busy, but the main map area was empty except for the staff NCO, who was posting information on the main map using stick-on symbols.

Goldsmith placed a chair in front of the area where his team was going to be inserted and crossed his arms over the back of the reversed chair. He stared at the map, memorizing all of the terrain features inside the ten-click square surrounding the bridge symbol. He remained sitting cowboy-style on the chair for over a half hour before standing up.

"If you don't mind my asking, Lieutenant, what are you doing?" the staff NCO asked, approaching from the rear. "You did the same thing last time you were assigned a mission."

Goldsmith turned around on the chair and smiled. "I'm memorizing the map for a thirty-click area surrounding the objective."

"*Thirty* thousand meters?"

"Yes, it saved my ass on my last mission when I worked my way off my insertion map, so I think that I'll make a habit out of memorizing the terrain. Actually, it really does help if you can visualize the hills and main terrain features before insertion. That way you aren't so confused when you jump off the helicopter."

The NCO shrugged. Each one of the recon team leaders had his own set of peculiarities.

"What do these skull and crossbones represent?" Goldsmith tapped the map with his outstretched finger in a dozen different places.

"We use those to depict POW camps or POW sightings. The skull and crossbones seem appropriate, considering the high KIA rate in rescue attempts and the low survival rate of Americans taken prisoner by the Pathet Lao."

Goldsmith nodded and the staff sergeant moved down the wall of maps. The skull and crossbones seemed to glare back at Goldsmith as he stared at them dotting the Laotian countryside. He felt fear bubbling inside him again. It was an old fear dating back to teenage days. He was terrified of being taken prisoner and being confined. Goldsmith rested his chin on his right fist as he leaned on the chair. As he stared at the illuminated map, slowly his eyes lost their focus and he slipped into a reverie.

He saw them standing in the recessed entrance of Tubman's Grill, which occupied the corner of Janes Avenue and 12th streets. There were five of them and they all were wearing the blue engineer handkerchiefs around their heads that signified they were full members of the Pachucos. Junior gang members carried the handkerchiefs in their back pockets, with a large portion hanging out, or they tucked half of the handkerchiefs in their waistbands so that they could be seen.

Alex-Paul didn't have any outstanding problems with any of the Pachucos, and normally they would go their own way. The all-Mexican gang kept to themselves and only caused problems if an outsider tried messing with one of their members or a Mexican girl.

It was too late for him to cross over to the other side of the busy street, and he knew that if he tried walking past them on the sidewalk, it would be too much of a direct challenge to go uncontested. Alex-Paul decided that the best discretionary move would be to turn off Janes Avenue onto 12th Street, go behind Tubman's Grill, and use the alley until the Pachucos had passed.

The alley, though, was normally even more dangerous than walking down the main thoroughfare.

Alex-Paul glanced sideways just as he reached the restaurant wall to see if the Pachucos were going to come after him. All he saw was an empty sidewalk. He hurried down the alley to get as much distance as he could between him and the threat.

"Where ya goin?" Someone asked in a thick Tex-Mex accent. "You don't like speaking to Mexican people?"

Alex-Paul moved away from the back of Tubman's Grill into the alley, and the five Pachucos spread out around him.

"We're short about five dollars for lunch. You might want to help us out a little?"

"I'm broke." Alex-Paul removed his hands from the pockets of the cotton jacket his brother had sent him from Fort Campbell, Kentucky. The back of the black jacket had a two-foot rendition of the airborne division's shoulder patch: the head of a bald eagle with its beak open. The division motto was inscribed over his left breast in bold white letters: "SCREAMING EAGLES."

"How much ya got?"

"I said, nothing," Alex-Paul lied. He had a ten-dollar bill in his pocket that he needed for his probation officer. He was required to give the man ten dollars a week to pay off his court costs. Failure to pay the money would be a breach in probation, and his suspended sentence of thirty days in jail would be activated.

"You don't mind if we empty your pockets, then?"

"Yeah, I mind."

"Say, ain't you that kid who used a baseball bat on some blacks back in high school?"

"I'm still in high school—a senior. I start my last semester when Christmas break is over with," Alex-Paul said, trying to change the subject.

"Yeah, you're the guy. I was in your class, but I quit." The Tex-Mex accent thickened. "You know, us Mexicans aren't very good with the white man's schools."

"You used to hang around with Mike Verdusco, right?" One of the Pachucos who had blocked his escape back out to 12th Street spoke from the edge of Alex-Paul's peripheral vision.

Alex-Paul answered without taking his eyes off the leader. "Yeah, Mike and I are still good friends. He left for the Marines last week."

"Too bad he isn't here now to save your lily-white ass." The Tex-Mex took a step forward. "Money or an ass-kicking. You choose."

Alex-Paul opened his mouth to speak and started reaching into his Levis watch pocket. Then he twisted around and grabbed the edge of the small shed behind the restaurant, used for garbage cans. He had pulled himself up onto the roof before the Pachucos realized that he was trying to escape.

A thin coat of ice covered the asphalt shingles, and Alex-Paul felt his tennis shoes slip. He hit the roof flat on his back, sending out a dozen large cracks in the thin ice from the point of his impact. He felt the fingers slip through his hair and then the impact when a Pachuco grabbed his hair and slammed the side of his head against the roof of the shed. The Pachuco was joined by two more of his gang, and they pulled Alex-Paul off the roof.

"So, motherfucker! You want an ass-kicking!"

Alex-Paul used his free hand and thigh to block a kick that had been meant for his groin.

The Pachuco leader, still holding his hair from behind, yanked his head backward. Alex-Paul responded by burying his right elbow in the gang leader's stomach. He heard the air leaving the man's lungs. The Pachuco let go and Alex-Paul took up a defensive position with his back against the wooden alley fence. He glanced over at the back door of Tubman's Grill, hoping desperately that someone would come out.

"Ain't nobody going to save your Anglo ass, mother-fucker!"

Alex-Paul caught the glimmer of a switchblade in the sun-light, and picked up a piece of cardboard to use as a shield. It wasn't much, but he figured if he could get the Pachuco to bury the blade in the cardboard, he could disarm him. Alex-Paul knew that the Pachucos weren't afraid to use their knives. The summer before his brother had gone into the paratroopers, four Pachucos had jumped him two blocks away from Saint Luke's Hospital and shoved a four-inch blade all the way in next to his belly button. Tom had walked the two blocks to the hospital's emergency room, holding the knife between his fingers. According to the rules of the gangs, he had deserved what he got because the all-white gang he belonged to was at war with the Pachucos and he had made the foolish mistake of trying to go somewhere alone. Part of the reason a person joined a gang was for the protection it gave its members. Even if you were going over to your girlfriend's house, you stopped by and picked up a couple of your gang to walk you over there.

"No, I don't want this little motherfucker cut. He's going to get the boot."

All of the Pachucos came at him at the same time, and Alex-Paul had only enough time to get in a couple of punches before he felt himself falling. He locked his forearms in front of his face and pulled his legs up to protect his crotch. He had seen what happened when a lone victim was down on the ground, and he prepared himself for the kicks to start coming.

"Look at the little punk!" The Pachuco leader stood over Alex-Paul with his right foot drawn back. "Pull him up on his feet."

Two Pachucos held his arms while their leader ran his hands through Alex-Paul's pockets. "Well, you don't have any money."

Alex-Paul shrugged.

The Pachuco leader smiled and stuck his forefinger down in the watch pocket. "What's dis?" He removed the folded ten-dollar bill and held it up so that his comrades could see. "Hey, lunch!"

"I need the money to pay my parole officer," Alex-Paul said, hoping that the mention of the court official would give him a break.

"You in trouble with the law, *hombre*?" The gang leader started strutting toward the back door of the restaurant holding the bill high over his head. "Come on, hombres! It's chow time!" The two Pachucos holding Alex-Paul started releasing him when their leader turned around. "But before we eat, maybe we should teach this Anglo that we are not like blacks. If he decides to put some baseball bat action on us, we'll kill his skinny little ass!" He nodded and one of the bigger Pachucos took up position in front of Alex-Paul. Throwing rapid fire punches, he hit him three times in the stomach and once alongside the head in a space of a couple of seconds.

Alex-Paul felt himself falling almost before he felt the punches. The Pachucos released their hold on him and ran to join their leader.

It took a full minute for him to catch his breath. He was starting to get scared that he might never be able to breathe again when the first breath came. He struggled to his hands and knees, and waited until his dizziness left him before getting to his feet.

"Fuck!" Rubbing his jaw, Alex-Paul winced at the pain. He took one small step and then another. He knew he had to get out of the alley and away from the restaurant before the Pachucos decided to come back and really kick his ass while they waited for the food they had ordered with his money to be prepared.

He stumbled a half block and then started feeling a little better, with the exception of his jaw. By the end of the block, he felt much better and started thinking about what he should do. If he didn't show up at the probation officer's office, a warrant for his arrest would be issued, and if he showed up without the money, he would be in trouble. Alex-Paul decided that the worst of the two choices would be not to show up. He removed his white wool scarf and tied it around his forehead. He let the long loose ends hang down behind his back before zipping up the light jacket. He not only wore a flannel shirt and an old gym sweatshirt under his jacket, but had a worn pair of lined leather gloves. He would be warm enough if he ran over to city hall, but he knew that once he started running in the cold air, he would have to continue running the whole eight miles or he would end up very sick. The run was nothing when he was in good shape. It was the punches in his stomach that bothered him—a stitch in his side would force him to walk.

Alex-Paul shrugged and started running south along 12th Street. He *didn't* have a stitch in his side, and worrying about something that didn't exist was foolish. He had to get to the meeting with his probation officer on time.

*   *   *

The warm air hit him the instant he stepped into the main hallway of city hall. He felt as if he was going to puke. Sweat ran down both sides of his face, and he felt a slightly burning sensation when the salty sweat touched the spot where the Pachuco had hit him. He glanced up at the large clock at the end of the hall and smiled to himself. He had made good time. He still had twenty-three minutes left before the appointment.

Alex-Paul hurried down the marble hallway and turned into the men's room. It was slightly cooler inside the large room, and he was starting to remove his jacket when he heard a commode flushing. He removed his headband scarf and hung it around his neck before leaning over a sink and turning on the cold water to wash his face. The man left the restroom without washing his hands. Alex-Paul squatted down to see if there were any other occupants in the stalls before removing his jacket and his sweatshirt. His flannel shirt was stuck against his body and he decided to remove it too. An inch of his Levis waistband was saturated with sweat. Alex-Paul took a deep breath of warm air and shuddered. It had been a very good run.

The door to the restroom opened and a very well-dressed man entered. As he walked over to the urinals, he at first ignored Alex-Paul. Then he did a double-take. Alex-Paul was standing in front of a washbasin, using paper towels to blot the sweat off his upper body.

"Do you always run around city hall half naked, young man?" the man said over his shoulder.

Alex-Paul smiled at the stranger's reflection in the mirror above the sink. "I ran over here."

"How far?"

"About eight or nine miles."

"In this weather?" The man continued looking at Alex-Paul over his shoulder.

"I don't have much choice. I can't afford a bus and I have to be here."

"For what?"

"I'm on probation."

The man's gaze roved down Alex-Paul's body. The teenager didn't realize the effect he was having on his observer. His upper torso was well developed from years

of hard exercise, and the old Levis he wore had become
a little too small and outlined his buttocks and legs. With
his matted-down curly blond hair, Alex-Paul could have
been posing for a teen magazine picture.

The man turned away from the urinal, and Alex-Paul
saw his penis sticking straight out of his open fly.

The man noticed the boy's look in the mirror, and he
took his time replacing his member in his pants before
taking a sink right next to Alex-Paul to wash his hands.

"Nice talking to you, mister. I gotta go! I'm late for
my meeting." Alex-Paul grabbed his clothes in one hand
and hurried out of the restroom into the hallway. He
stopped at the nearest bench and dropped his clothes on
it and started dressing. His flannel shirt was still wet and
felt cold against his body, but he shrugged off the incon-
venience. He had finished dressing when the restroom
door opened and the man came out into the hallway.

"Maybe later, young man?"

Alex-Paul didn't answer, hurrying away toward the
stairs. He could hear a soft chuckle behind him.

City hall was almost empty, for it was the week
between Christmas and New Year's and there was little
business being conducted. Alex-Paul didn't understand
why the probation department remained open during the
holiday week, but actually it was during the holidays
when the most people break probation. They take off
out of state to visit friends and relatives and then end up
not coming back.

Entering the office, Alex-Paul saw his probation officer standing next to a coffeepot with the man he had
seen in the restroom. He felt his face getting red.

The probation officer looked up and smiled. "Alex-
Paul Goldsmith. You're on time."

"Yes, sir."

"Good. I'll be with you in just a couple of minutes.
First, I've got to get Dr. Einstadt some records . . ." He
opened a nearby filing cabinet and started removing files
for the doctor.

Alex-Paul wondered how the man could have beat him
to the office and then realized that he had taken the
stairway at the far end of the hallway so that he wouldn't
have to pass the man by the restroom door. Alex-Paul

glanced up and saw the doctor staring at him. He blushed again.

"Dr. Einstadt, that's Alex-Paul, one of our youthful offenders." The probation officer spoke with his face in the filing cabinet. "Dr. Einstadt is one of our consultants—he was just hired to work with juveniles."

Dr. Einstadt's eyes narrowed and he smiled over at Alex-Paul.

"Dr. Einstadt is a licensed psychologist." The probation officer turned around and faced Alex-Paul. "You might want to talk to him."

"Is he married?"

"What kind of a question is that?"

"I don't mind answering him." Dr. Einstadt said, continuing to smile. It looked like something made out of plastic to Alex-Paul. "Yes, I'm married and I have three teenagers. Two boys and a girl. I actually have a son about your age. How old are you, Alex-Paul?"

"Seventeen."

"He just turned seventeen! His birthday is on Christmas Day." The probation officer smiled and winked at Alex-Paul.

"Don't we have a meeting, sir? I've got to get home as soon as we're done."

"Yes, you can wait in my office. I'll be with you in a minute."

"I'll be in the area for a little while, Alex-Paul. Could I give you a ride home?" Dr. Einstadt's smile hadn't left his face.

"Naw, I like to run."

"It's starting to sleet outside."

Alex-Paul shrugged. "I like to run in sleet."

The smile on the doctor's face shrank for a second and then expanded again. "Well, if you change your mind, Mr. Austin will know where to find me."

Alex-Paul went into the small office where his probation officer conducted his interviews and took a seat on a worn wooden straight-back chair.

The door opened a few minutes later, and Austin entered carrying Alex-Paul's file. "I think you've made a friend. Dr. Einstadt just asked me for your file to be assigned to him for evaluation. He can really help you, young man!"

Alex-Paul stared out the window. "Thanks, but I only have three more weeks left of probation."

"True, but his evaluation in your files could really help you in the future. It isn't often that a professional like Dr. Einstadt takes a personal interest in a juvenile offender. You should be happy."

"I don't have the ten dollars, Mr. Austin. I was mugged by some Pachucos on my way here . . ."

"Tsk, tsk—tsk." Austin made the sound using his tongue. "You know what we agreed upon."

"I know and I've paid you the ten dollars for the past five months—on time. I was mugged."

"Turn your head." The voice was a command. "What's that from? Were you fighting again?"

"That's where they punched me! I wasn't fighting. I was mugged—there is a difference, you know!"

"Don't get arrogant with me, young man!" Austin pushed his chair back away from the desk and looked out the window with a pencil pressed against his lips. "I'm sorry, young man, I can't allow for you to miss payments to the court. I told you the very first day that we met, I can allow for some minor infractions, but I cannot allow for missed payments!"

"But, sir!"

"Quiet! Wait here." Austin left the office and Alex-Paul heard the outer door slam.

He sat in the office, listening to the sleet hitting the window. He dreaded the run home in the icy rain. He would be soaked to the bone the first mile.

The office door opened and Austin appeared with a uniformed police officer. "Come!"

"Where are we going?"

"The judge wants to see you before he leaves for the day." Austin led the way out into the hallway with the police officer bringing up the rear.

The courtroom was empty and loud echoes amplified their footsteps as they walked to the front of the bench. Alex-Paul saw the plastic nametag in front of the judge: "JUDGE ROBERT E. WOLF."

"Well, young man, it seems as if you've broken your probation. Fighting?"

"No, sir, I was mugged."

The judge smiled and looked over at Austin, who smiled back. "Yes, Mr. Austin told me that was the excuse you used. Well, young man, you've got a thick file here for fighting. I see where you've even used a baseball bat to injure some kids who were waiting for their friends outside the school." The judge frowned down from his raised bench. "We cannot tolerate that kind of conduct. I'm going to have to agree with Mr. Austin. You violated your parole, so your jail sentence is activated—as of now." With that, the judge slammed down his gavel.

Alex-Paul felt the police officer's hand wrap around his upper arm and tug. "Let's go, fella."

Alex-Paul followed the cop to a side door that led directly into the city jail. He was in shock and had been completely intimidated by the courtroom surroundings. It still hadn't dawned on him what had happened.

The sound of the steel door slamming shut brought Lieutenant Goldsmith out of his thoughts. He realized that he had been breathing rapidly, and a cold sweat had broken out over his forehead in the air-conditioned room. He turned in his seat and saw that he was alone in the large operations room, but he could hear voices coming from the hallway where the area-studies teams planned their missions. The sound of a brewing coffeepot reached him from across the room. Goldsmith left his chair and walked along the raised platform in front of the wall map. The smell of the coffee was making him hungry. He looked at his watch and said to himself, "Shit! It's almost eight o'clock!" He had been staring at the map for over three hours!

Goldsmith poured black coffee in one of the paper cups provided for visitors and went back to his chair. Sitting down, he leaned against the padded back of the chair and crossed his legs in front of him. He liked how the valley coming out of Laos split when it entered South Vietnam. It looked like a snake's tongue. Also there were a number of prominent mountains that could be used to guide on, especially Hill 7195.

Slowly his thoughts slipped back to his confinement as a juvenile. All of a sudden the map in front of him seemed to show only the skull and crossbones that represented the POW camps, and there were hundreds of them on the huge battle map. His thoughts returned to the Saginaw County Jail.

"Strip down to your skin and stand over there by the scales." A sheriff's deputy pointed with his aluminum clipboard. The city police had taken Alex-Paul directly over to the county jail to serve his sentence. They wanted to keep their jail as empty as possible during the holiday week.

Alex-Paul obeyed the officer and stripped to his underwear. He folded his clothes neatly and placed each item in the cardboard box that had been provided.

"I said, down to your skin." The deputy glanced up from the papers attached to his clipboard. "It says here that your birthday is on Christmas—you just turned seventeen?"

"Yes . . . sir."

The deputy shook his head sympathetically. "If you had gotten in this fight before you turned seventeen, the worst they could have done is send you over to the juvenile hall for a couple of days."

Alex-Paul started opening his mouth to protest and then gave up. He remained standing against the dark green wall in front of his cardboard box.

"You're going to have to strip all the way down for a body-cavity search."

"What's a cavity search?"

The deputy gave Alex-Paul a sad look and shook his head. "What in the fuck are they doing back there, sending a good-looking kid like you in here?" The anger in the man's voice was directed to someone outside the small room.

The door opened and a man wearing a white doctor's smock entered the room, followed by another guard. "Well, let's get this over with, I've got other things to do! This is a holiday, you all should know!" The doctor nodded at Alex-Paul, but spoke to the deputy. "Why isn't he ready?"

"Take 'em off, kid." The guard glanced shyly up at the ceiling and noticed that the paint was peeling.

"Let's go!" The doctor motioned with his hand for the boy to hurry.

Alex-Paul noticed the rubber gloves on the doctor's hands and shook his head. "Fuck you!" He thought the doctor was going to shove his fingers in his mouth. That was a part of the inspection, but not the real reason why the doctor was wearing the rubber gloves.

"I told you that I'm in a hurry!" The doctor motioned for the guards to step forward.

The deputy laid the clipboard on a nearby shelf and grabbed Alex-Paul's left arm; the other guard took a hold of his right arm. The deputy said softly, "Look, kid, everybody who goes inside as a prisoner must have a complete body-cavity search to make sure they ain't smuggling in drugs or weapons. Cooperate and this will be over in a couple of minutes."

"You can see I don't have anything on me!" Alex-Paul tried stepping away from the approaching doctor.

The jail guard laughed under his breath. "You are a dumb little shit, aren't you?"

The doctor grabbed Alex-Paul by his lower jaw and ran two of his fingers under his tongue. "If you bite, I'll have these guards beat you senseless!"

The doctor grabbed his underwear on each side of his legs and pulled them down. Alex-Paul gasped when the man lifted his testicles with one hand and ran his other hand between his legs back to his anus. "What in the fuck do you think you're doing?"

"Turn him around and lean him over that table." The doctor sounded bored and angry.

Alex-Paul tried struggling, but the two men had been through this before and knew what to expect from a prisoner. The next thing Alex-Paul felt was a finger entering his rectum.

"He's clean. No drug packets and no weapons." The doctor stepped back and pulled off the rubber gloves with loud snaps. He threw the gloves into a nearby wastepaper basket. "Give me his papers and I'll sign them."

The two large men released Alex-Paul enough so that he could turn around. The deputy said, "Put your underwear back on. I'll issue you some prison clothes as soon as I take care of the doctor."

The doctor looked up from signing the paperwork and grinned over at the kid. "It wasn't that bad, was it?"

Alex-Paul tried taking a step forward, but the guard grabbed both of his arms and pulled them behind his back.

"You know, it's punks like you who give our fine city a bad name." The doctor took a couple of steps forward until he was standing a little to one side of the struggling teenager. "Having a rectal check by a doctor isn't anywhere as bad as what's going on in there." He jabbed his thumb over his shoulder at the steel door.

Feeling the pressure against his arms ease up a little, Alex-Paul twisted violently to one side and brought his right knee up as far as he could. As the guard's grip broke, Alex-Paul's knee connected with the doctor's jaw.

"Ugh!" the doctor grunted, dropping to his knees.

Alex-Paul tried kicking at the doctor's head, but the guard yanked him backward and shoved him into a corner.

Rushing over, the deputy saw blood pouring out of the doctor's mouth and down the front of his white smock.

"Mmmfff, ow!" The doctor tried talking, but the pain from his broken jaw prevented him from forming any words.

"You're in a lot of trouble, young man! A *lot* of trouble!" The deputy pushed a button on the wall, and a pair of burly guards rushed into the room.

"No one puts anything up my ass! Remember that, doctor!" Alex-Paul braced himself as the two guards approached him. He was expecting a beating, but the only thing the guards did was throw some prison clothes at him and roughly push him toward the steel door. Alex-Paul didn't resist. He had made his point, and he knew the word would spread through the whole jail.

The guards opened the door, and Alex-Paul stepped onto a raised steel platform and down some steps to the

main floor. He had a few seconds to glance down the
long aisle. It was over a hundred feet long. There was a
space left between the barred windows and the bars of
the bull pen, hundreds of cigarette butts lined the floor.

One of the guards led the way down the steps, holding
a ring of keys in his hand, and the other guard followed
behind Alex-Paul.

"Oh, look at this cute one!" someone said from the
back side of the bull pen.

Alex-Paul looked over his shoulder and noticed a large
rectangular barred area that occupied the center of the
floor had been divided right down the middle by a steel
wall that looked several inches thick. There were two
gates entering the large cage—one in each corner.

"You shut the fuck up, bitch!" The rear guard waved
his nightstick at the two men looking through the bars.

"Send him over here to us for the night, and we'll
make it worth your while—sweetie."

The cell door opened and the first guard stepped aside
so that Alex-Paul could enter the bull pen. He lost sight
of the pair of transvestites. The cell door clanged shut
behind him.

"We'll be coming back for you after we find out the
doctor's condition." The larger guard tapped his nightstick against the bars.

Alex-Paul looked at his surroundings. He was standing
at the end of a long walkway that had cells lining one
side of it. He started walking down the row of open cell
doors and saw that there were other prisoners occupying
the steel bunks. They stared back at him, but none of
them spoke. He found an empty cell and went inside. It
struck him as strange that an entire cell was empty and
the rest of the cells had three or four occupants, but he
figured that he had lucked out. Besides, he preferred the
privacy. He dropped his pillow and blanket onto a lower
bunk and went back out into the narrow run that continued on past his cell. Walking to the end, he found some
urinals and two commodes in what had been originally
the last cell, but had been converted into an open latrine.
A single shower stall had been built in a corner and was
surrounded on three sides by sheets of tin. The shower

curtain was a clear plastic so that the person taking a shower had no privacy.

Alex-Paul used the urinal and lit a cigarette while he waited. He stopped once on his way back to his cell to see if he could catch a glimpse of the world outside but saw only a six-square-inch picture of a portion of a large maple tree. When he entered his cell, he saw a man sitting on the bunk across from his.

"So, whatcha in here for?" The tall, skinny man's legs were bent in front of him with the heels of his jail-issued tennis shoes pressing against the edge of the bed.

"Breaking probation." Alex-Paul dropped onto his cot.

"You're lucky they put you in the juvenile section."

"Why?"

"You're cute."

Alex-Paul flashed the older guy a warning look that made him laugh.

"You don't have to worry about me." He jerked his thumb toward the steel wall. "It's them. Don't ask me why the sheriff has put sex offenders and juveniles on the same floor of this fucking jail, but he has."

"Sex offenders?"

"Yeah."

"Can they get over here?"

The man laughed and inhaled a long toke from his cigarette. "No, this steel wall runs the whole length of the bull pen, but if you volunteer to sweep up in the morning, you can earn yourself some money."

"Doing what?"

"When you sweep around to their side, you just pause for a while and put it through the bars."

"Fuck you! I don't get into that stuff."

The man flashed Alex-Paul a knowing look. "How long are you going to be here with us?"

"I think thirty days?"

"You don't know?"

"Something happened out there,"—Alex-Paul nodded toward the exit door—"so I might get some extra time."

The man nodded his head. "I'm Gary Fox."

"Didn't you play basketball for Saginaw High last year?"

"Yep."

"You were great! I thought you went on to college."

"I had a scholarship, but I got my girlfriend pregnant—and I got another girl pregnant also. I'm in here on charges of not paying child support."

"Fucking bummer."

"Yeah, a fucking bummer." Fox watched Alex-Paul closely every time the younger guy turned his head away. He was trying to size him up. "So what did you do in high school?"

"Not much—just try and survive." Alex-Paul looked up from the floor at the black guy sitting across from him. "I don't have your talent for basketball."

"You're also a short little fucker."

Alex-Paul shrugged. "What can I say?"

"So, are you going to stay in the cell?"

"Why not?"

"Some guy hung himself in here during Christmas Eve, and some of the other guys claim to have seen him sleeping in here at night when they went to the john." Fox grinned and nodded his head toward Alex-Paul. "In fact, you're sitting on the bunk."

"I don't believe in ghosts."

Fox twisted his lips and wiggled his eyebrows. "Lots of crazy things happen in this place. People go nuts on you."

Alex-Paul shrugged. He couldn't do anything about that. "I mind my own business."

"Well, I've got to get back to my buddies. But—if you get horny while you're here, all you have to do is go back by the wall in the john and knock on the steel wall. One of them will reach around and give you a hand job *and* give you five candy bars for doing it!"

"Thanks, but if the need arises, I can take care of myself while I'm in here." Alex-Paul winked over at Fox.

"That's unhealthy." Fox filled the open doorway to the cell. "So you're going to stay in here?"

"Yeah, for the next thirty days—or so." Alex-Paul stretched out on the mattress and finished his cigarette. He tried flicking the butt between the bars, but the still burning cigarette hit one of them and landed on the floor of his cell. He sat up and picked up the butt again. On his second try the butt landed in the narrow strip between the wall and the bull pen bars. He lit another cigarette and lay back on his bunk to think. He figured they would be coming back for him before long because of the doctor's broken jaw.

Occasionally one of the other prisoners would pass his cell on their way to the latrine, but they didn't look in. Alex-Paul realized that some kind of a game was being played with him, and he decided to let them make the next move. His earlier visit from Fox had also been a part of the game, but he couldn't piece it together.

A loud clanging of the main door to the floor brought a lot of activity in the bull pens. Alex-Paul could hear the sexual offenders on the other side of the wall moving around, and then he heard movement in his half. He got up off his bunk and stuck his head out of his cell. A cart had been placed at the end of the walkway, and the prisoners had lined up against the bars. The guards and the trustees from the floor below, where the adult offenders were housed, were handing out supper to the prisoners. Alex-Paul saw that each juvenile was given two sandwiches and an army canteen cup full of something hot. He looked around his cell for a cup but couldn't find any. He joined the end of the line and waited his turn.

"I need a cup," Alex Paul said to the guard when he reached the cart.

"You should have been issued one when you in-processed."

"I wasn't."

"Tough shit, kid."

Alex-Paul took the two bologna sandwiches the trustee handed him and was starting to turn away when he felt a warm canteen cup being pressed into his hand. He looked over and saw Fox grinning at him. He handed the cup out and watched as the man scooped it half full of a thin vegetable soup.

"I want that cup back before breakfast—washed out," Fox called out to Alex-Paul through the bars as he passed the tall black's cell. Alex-Paul paused and looked in at the four prisoners sitting on their bunks eating. He noticed that all of their sandwiches had thicker slices of bologna than his, and the cup of soup on the floor between the man's feet nearest him was almost full. It was obvious that there was some kind of pecking order within the jail.

"Thanks for the loan. I'll have your cup back soon." Alex-Paul left the group and returned to his cell. He drank the soup as fast as he could from the hot steel rim of the cup and went back to the latrine to wash the cup out. Then he noticed that the sandwich he had left on his mattress was gone. It had been a stupid thing to do, leaving it unguarded. He sat down and had a cigarette before getting up to return the cup to Fox.

"You're back quick."

"I don't like to borrow things for very long. Thanks for loaning it to me." Alex-Paul turned to leave.

"Wait, come on in and have a seat for a while. We's just talking shit." Fox beckoned him in and pointed to an empty spot on one of the bunks. There were almost a dozen prisoners sitting in the small cell. Fox didn't introduce any of the other men and continued talking to Alex-Paul. "We were just talking about Redman down in the last cell, near the john. He has fits at night and starts roaming around the place. Normally he don't bother no one, but if he's having a nightmare *and* a fit, he goes fucking crazy."

"He's as strong as ten fucking men when that happens!" The voice came from the bunk directly over Alex-Paul's head.

Fox continued, "But that rarely happens. Usually he just finds an empty bunk and goes back to sleep. If that happens to you—if he comes into your cell—just leave him alone."

"Fine." Alex-Paul lit up a cigarette and checked his pack. He had five left, so he didn't offer any to the other prisoners.

"If he does go crazy, just stay the fuck out of his way. I've been in here for eight months with him, and it's only happened once before." Fox rested his head against the wall of the cell.

"Who wants to play poker?"

"Yeah, let's get a game going!" A young-looking teenager dropped from the top bunk across from Alex-Paul and left the cell. "Let me get my loot."

The cell emptied for a couple of minutes before the men returned from their cells carrying packages of cigarettes and boxes of candy bars.

"You want to play?" Fox looked up from a makeshift poker table covered with an old army blanket.

"Sorry, I don't have any money."

"We use candy bars and cigarettes for money in here—or we bet meals."

"Sorry, I don't have anything to bet with."

"You can get yourself a box of candy bars in about five minutes," said one of the prisoners, who had a full box of Payday candy bars on the floor next to his feet.

"How?"

Everyone in the cell started laughing.

The Payday owner nodded toward the other half of the cell block. "Just volunteer to sweep up the cigarette butts in the morning. They'll probably pay you in advance—you're their type."

"Sorry, I don't eat candy," Alex-Paul said, taking the easy way out.

"Suit yourself." The prisoner shrugged and picked up the card that had been dealt to him.

Alex-Paul looked around the cell and noticed that all of the occupants, including Fox, had candy bars to bet with. He felt sick to his stomach and left the cell without saying anything.

Fox waited until Alex-Paul was gone and smiled. "Prime fucking meat!"

The rest of the occupants started chuckling but stopped when Fox signaled for them to be quiet. "Don't fuck this up! We're going to have some fun tonight!"

The main bank of lights were turned out on the floor at exactly ten o'clock. Four night lights were left on at each corner of the cell blocks, but they only sent shadows down the long bull pens. Alex-Paul's cell, near the center of the juvenile section, was almost totally dark inside. He could see the tip of his last cigarette glowing in the dark. The poker game was still going on under the light in the corner cell.

The loud clanging of the key in the lock of the exit

door echoed, and the deep voice of the guard followed. "Shut down that game! It's time for you little motherfuckers to get some sleep!" The guard walked around the outside of the cell blocks to make a security check and disappeared behind the steel divider.

"Send that new boy over here in the morning—please!" The voice that echoed back to the juvenile section was high-pitched. "He's so damn cute!"

"Shut the fuck up, bitch!" The guard hit the bars with his nightstick.

"Oh, I want to run my fingers through his curly hair and swallow—"

"If I have to come inside, bitch, I'll fuck you up!" The guard smashed his stick against the bars.

Alex-Paul swallowed and choked on the cigarette smoke he was exhaling. He knew they were talking about him, and if he could hear what the transvestite was saying, so could everyone else.

The voices dropped to whispers in the cells. No one wanted to be reported by the night guard. They waited until he left and locked the steel door again before talking in normal voices. The old-timers knew that they had two more hours before a guard would appear again.

Some time later, Alex-Paul woke up. He was still stretched out on his cot in the same position that he had dozed off, with his fingers laced behind his head. Then he heard someone snoring on the cot directly across from him. He used his Zippo lighter to see who had joined him in his cell and saw that his visitor was someone he hadn't seen before in Fox's cell. He closed the lid on his Zippo and got off his bunk. There was enough light coming from the security lights to see his way to the latrine.

Four prisoners were sitting in a corner of the latrine with a toilet paper lamp burning in the center of their circle. The lamp was made by wrapping toilet paper tightly around three of their fingers and then tucking both ends in to the center. When the top edge was lit, the tightly wound paper gave off a blue flame that burned for about a half hour and gave off enough light to see by.

"Who's in my cell?" Alex-Paul leaned against the cool steel wall of the divider between the cell blocks.

"Got me?" Fox looked up from staring at the blue flame coming from their lamp. "We're telling ghost stories. Ya wanta join us?"

"I'm tired." Alex-Paul left and went back to his cell. The other prisoner was still sleeping heavily on the other bunk. Alex-Paul dropped onto his mattress and wrapped the army blanket around his shoulders. He didn't believe in ghosts, but it was a little comforting having another person sleeping in the cell with him.

Alex-Paul dozed off and missed the midnight security check by the guard. He woke when he heard a gurgling sound coming from the cot across the cell. He sat up and saw a shadow sitting on the cot. The first thing he reached for was his Zippo, and the instant the wick caught on fire the face of the man appeared in the light. White foam dripped off his chin onto the floor. He groaned and more foam bubbled out of the man's mouth. He struggled to his feet and paused for only a second to look down at Alex-Paul before stumbling out of the cell. A few seconds later someone screamed and came running back his way.

"Redman's having a fucking fit!"

The whole cell block seemed to come alive with bodies flashing past Alex-Paul's cell. After what seemed like an hour, Fox's head appeared in the open doorway and he rasped out a warning: "Don't get trapped in your cell. Stay out here in the bull pen and avoid him!"

Alex-Paul took Fox's advice and left his cell. The run was filled with bodies trying to dodge the staggering Redman. Twice the madman turned and took a couple of steps in Alex-Paul's direction. Then he disappeared into a cell and a couple of prisoners came rushing out.

Alex-Paul moved back to the latrine, where there was more room to maneuver if Redman came back there. He noticed that three of the juvenile prisoners were hiding in the shower with the curtain drawn. He took up a position near the edge of the last cell wall, which was a solid sheet of steel, and waited. If Redman made it as far back as the latrine, he would be able to slip past him when he staggered by and run the full length of the bull pen to Fox's cell for safety. He figured that Fox would stand up for him in an emergency because they had attended the same high school together.

Less than a minute passed before Redman staggered past Alex-Paul and tore back the shower curtain. He growled and grabbed the nearest victim. The juve screamed and was tossed across the open floor before he scurried to hide behind a commode. Alex-Paul made his move while the crazy guy was mauling the shower crew and ran to Fox's cell.

"He's fucking crazy!" Alex-Paul started breathing heavily.

"I told you before that this could happen! Now remember! Whatever he does, *don't hit him!* If you do, he'll go nuts and kill you!"

"Don't fucking worry about that! He ain't going to catch me!" Alex-Paul glanced out the doorway and saw Redman heading down the hall toward him. "He's coming!"

"Oh, fuck me!" said one of the poker players, hiding under a mattress on a lower bunk.

Alex-Paul hopped onto the upper bunk opposite and crouched next to the bars. He figured he could leap down and be out of the cell if Redman stumbled inside.

A few seconds later, Redman filled the entrance to the cell and groaned.

Alex-Paul waited, remaining absolutely still so that his movement wouldn't catch the eye of the crazy guy.

Fox sat curled up in the far corner of the cell.

Redman stumbled over to the cot where the poker player was hiding under the mattress and fell onto it. Alex-Paul could hear a muffled scream, but Redman didn't seem to hear it. He laid down full length on the mattress and moaned again. From the security light, Alex-Paul saw the foam around Redman's mouth. The man's eyes were wide open.

Fox made a break for the door and ran down the hall. Redman tried raising himself up on one elbow and then fell back down on top of the man hiding under the mattress.

Seeing his opportunity, Alex-Paul dropped off the bunk and turned sharply to his right. It was a mistake.

The locked gate appeared instantly, and he realized that he had turned the wrong way in the bull pen.

He turned around. The space between him and safety was filled with the huge frame of Redman.

Alex-Paul kept backing up until he felt the bars pressing against his back. Redman spread his arms out and foamed at the mouth as he stumbled slowly forward.

"Help me!" Alex-Paul felt fear filling his stomach. He wanted to throw up. There was nowhere for him to escape. He tried ducking under Redman's arms, but the man moved too fast for him and blocked his escape.

Redman backed Alex-Paul into the corner, where the bars met the gate, and grabbed the bars on each side of Alex-Paul.

Up close, he saw the foaming mouth open and a hiss came from Redman's throat.

Alex-Paul brought his knee up, and air whooshed from Redman's lungs. The huge man had left his groin unguarded. He stumbled back a couple of steps, giving Alex-Paul room to use his arms. He started raining blows all over Redman as he struggled backward to escape.

Intense fear was giving Alex-Paul more power to his punches than he could ever muster on his own, and Redman's body shook each time one of the fists hit him.

"Stop! Damn it—stop!" The voice was close by, but Alex-Paul ignored it. He kept attacking the crazy man until he felt arms wrapping around him and through sheer weight of numbers he was wrestled to the floor.

Fox looked down at Alex-Paul. "You dumb fuck! It was just a fucking game!"

The steel door opened and four guards stormed in. They unlocked the bull pen and dragged Alex-Paul out. One of the guards had been present during his in-processing, and he used his nightstick under Alex-Paul's chin to restrain him. "You haven't been here a full day yet and you've attacked two people!" He released his hold on Alex-Paul and spoke to his comrades. "Put the little fucker in a solitary tank for the night. We'll let the sheriff decide what to do with his ass in the morning."

Alex-Paul heard Fox screaming as the door clanged shut, "It was just a fucking game!"

*   *   *

The loud clang of the steel vault door snapped Goldsmith from his thoughts.

"You still here, Lieutenant?" It was the operations sergeant returning. "You missed chow. Maybe you can pick something up over at the club."

Goldsmith looked around the windowless vault and immediately felt that the walls were somehow closing in on him. He jumped up from his seat and ran to the exit. He paused only long enough to flash his badge at the checkpoints and broke out into the fresh evening air. The sun had just set in the west, sending out a pale red glow in the sky. Goldsmith ran across the raked sand between the buildings, mindless of the fact it was off limits, and stopped running only when he reached his hootch near the beach. He didn't enter the small structure. He knew he couldn't tolerate the confined space, not after remembering the ten days that he had spent in solitary confinement as a teenager. They had even kept the lights turned off in his tiny cell as an extra punishment, and without light and being left alone, time blended together. The ten days might as well have been ten centuries. At seventeen years old, he had no defenses to protect him from such horrible mental torture.

"You okay, sir?" Tyriver asked, stepping out of the hootch.

"Yes . . ." Goldsmith thought for a second and then changed his mind. "No, I'm not. Can you run over to the club and buy me a fifth of bourbon?"

"Sure . . . no problem, Lieutenant." Tyriver started to leave and then stopped. "Why don't you walk over there with me? I could use the company."

Goldsmith nodded and joined his One-One. They walked over to the NCO club without saying another word. Tyriver entered the smoke-filled building alone.

Lieutenant Goldsmith waited outside in the fading light for his teammate to return.

CHAPTER EIGHT

✪✪✪✪✪✪✪✪✪✪✪✪✪✪✪✪✪

THE FIVE THOUSAND-YEAR-OLD WAR

Sergeant Tyriver ordered a fifth of Kessler's sipping whiskey and paid for it using two full books of bar chits. Goldsmith was waiting outside where he had left him. Tyriver knew better than to push his team leader, but it was obvious that something was bothering him, and it had to come out for the sake of the whole team. "Kessler's," he said as he handed the bottle to Goldsmith.

"Thanks," Goldsmith said, not looking away from the sky. It was the most open space he could find, and the effect was working on the attack of claustrophobia.

"I think we need to talk, Lieutenant. You looked like you saw a ghost back there." Tyriver squatted down Vietnamese style next to his lieutenant. "Maybe in the past no one needed to know, but . . ."

"You're right, Tyriver. You have a right to know. I suffer from a strange kind of claustrophobia. It only happens when I think about certain things *and* I'm in a really restricted place."

"It just happened in the TOC?" In Tyriver's medical training, a small portion had dealt with mental problems, but what was really helping him now was his session on a soothing bedside manner.

"Yeah." Goldsmith took a long pull from the bottle and sighed when he lowered it. "I should tell you the whole story so that you'll understand, but I'd appreciate it if you kept it to yourself."

"You have no problem here with loose lips, L.T."

Goldsmith proceeded to tell his One-One the whole story of his stay in the Saginaw County Jail and the term he had spent in solitary confinement.

Tyriver waited until the story had been told before asking the questions that had popped up in his mind. "If they were only playing a game with you, how did they get this guy Redman to foam at the mouth?"

"Colgate toothpaste."

"Shit, that's a slick trick. I bet he scared the shit out of you. I mean, there was no place for you to hide if everyone else was in on it."

"You got that right. When I went into a cell, the other guys pointed out where I was hiding to Redman."

"You kicked his ass?"

"Severely. I didn't realize how hard I was hitting him. The sheriff had to admit Redman to the county hospital, and he was still in there when I was released from jail two months later. The judge had doubled my sentence."

"Fuck! You were the victim!"

"Not after I cold-cocked the doctor."

"I forgot about that one." Tyriver took the bottle from Goldsmith. "You were a cocky little fucker back then."

"I tried surviving alone." Goldsmith's voice lowered. "I want you to do me a favor, David."

"Sure, anything. You know that."

"If something ever happens to me out in the field—like if I'm shot up really bad—I don't want to be left alive on the ground."

"Sir, I'm a medic!"

"You have to promise me, David. I couldn't stand being locked up in a fucking cage!"

There was a very long pause. The two recon men listened to the sound of the waves crashing on the beach. A storm was coming in off the South China Sea. Finally Tyriver looked up from staring at the sand. "Okay." His voice was husky with emotion. "Okay, I'll make sure that they never take you prisoner."

"Thanks, David. I'm going to hold you to that promise."

"What the fuck are you two doing out here in the dark?" The voice was brassy and struck Goldsmith as extremely irritating.

"Getting drunk, Captain," Tyriver answered the Hatchet Platoon commander.

"You too good to socialize with the rest of the recon men?" Captain Abou challenged.

"I thought you ran a platoon, Captain."

"Yeah, a recon platoon."

"We'd like to be left alone—if you and your friends don't mind." Goldsmith wasn't in the mood to take any of the captain's sarcasm.

"When does a fucking Jew second lieutenant tell a captain what to do?" Abou spat.

"What in the fuck are you talking about?" Goldsmith took another sip from the bottle, and replaced it in a hole Tyriver had made to keep the bottle from tipping over on the sand.

"Goldsmith, that's a fucking Jew name, isn't it?"

"Yeah, my grandfather was a Polish Jew, so what?"

"Abou is a Palestinian name! Now do you understand, Lieutenant?"

"Aw, fuck, you're not going to bring up the '67 War, are you?" Goldsmith didn't need to get involved in politics on the war that had been fought the year before in the Middle East. "Look, Captain, what went on over there is their business, not ours. We're Americans involved in our own fucking war."

"You fucking Jews have been fucking us Arabs for thousands of years!"

"Hold on, Captain," Tyriver said, trying to reason with the drunk Arab. "Didn't the Arabs attack Israel first?"

"Israel is Palestine! The fucking British took it from the Palestinians and gave it to the Jews!" The captain was slurring his words. He was very drunk.

Tyriver made the mistake of trying to reason with a drunk. "That war has been going on for five thousand fucking years. Can you name me one country in the Middle East—in fact, just one country on the face of this earth—that hasn't been formed because somebody conquered somebody else?"

"I'll tell you what, *Goldsmith*, if you tell me that all male Jews are cocksuckers and their women are whores, I'll forget all about our little differences." Captain Abou looked over his shoulder to see if his squad leaders caught his personal little joke.

"I don't think my dead grandfather would appreciate me saying something like that about my grandmother." Goldsmith started getting to his feet, sensing trouble even though he wanted to avoid getting into a fight with a captain. "Let's just drop this topic. All of us have been drinking—"

The punch came out of the shadows and hit Goldsmith so hard that he actually felt his feet leaving the ground and then his back impacted against the loose sand. He was back up on his feet almost instantly, but he was having a difficult time focusing.

Sergeant Tyriver caught a boot in his side before he could get to his feet, and then he felt the pressure of someone very heavy sitting on his chest. "Stay down! This fight is between our captain and your punk lieutenant."

Tyriver struggled to break free, but the squad leaders from Hatchet Platoon held him securely down on the sand. The only thing he could do was watch Abou beat the hell out of his lieutenant. It wasn't much of a fight. Goldsmith should have stayed down after the first punch.

Afterward, Tyriver struggled in the loose sand with Goldsmith. The lieutenant was dead weight and finally the small sergeant was forced to grab his One-Zero by his wrists and drag him over to their hootch. He pulled him into one of their sandbag beach chairs and made sure that Goldsmith's air passage was clear before he ran back to get what remained of their bottle.

It was an hour before Goldsmith could speak, and then his jaw hurt too much to say anything more than a couple of words. "Stupid!"

"He's an ass!"

"Stupid getting drunk!" Goldsmith cut his words short.

"He took a cheap shot at you!"

"Let it rest, David." Goldsmith ignored the pain from his bruised jaw.

"Hey, Lieutenant, are you really part Jew?"

"My grandfather was a Polish Jew—they murdered him."

"Sorry to hear that about your grandfather, but I think it's cool that you're part Hebrew." Tyriver stretched out on the homemade beach chair next to Goldsmith. He could feel the heat from the sand coming up through the legs of his trousers, and he used his heels to push away the top layer of sand so that his legs could rest against the cool layer underneath.

"They murdered three million Polish Jews during World War II." Goldsmith let the number sink in before continuing, "You know, when men die, we can blame them for being stupid and not paying attention to the politics that are being played out around them, but those bastards murdered pregnant women and children. I remember reading a passage in a book on the Holocaust where a Hebrew teacher was assigned to conduct classes in one of the concentration camps. In one day he watched SS guards round up over two *thousand* little boys between the ages of eight and twelve. The children were naked—it was late fall—and what stuck in my mind was how the teacher described the way the SS guards herded the terrified children to the gas chambers. They used sticks that reminded him of the goose girls back in his village guiding a flock of geese down a road. The teacher committed suicide the day after he witnessed the murders of the children."

"That's some heavy shit, sir." Tyriver noticed that Goldsmith's words were becoming clearer the more he spoke, and he encouraged him to continue talking. "Captain Abou is an ass!"

"No, he's probably from a family back in the States who still has relatives in Palestine. What none of them realize is that Israel is never going to give up an inch of land—never!"

Tyriver glanced over at his One-Zero. The last word had been said with a great deal of conviction. "Are you a practicing Jew?"

Goldsmith shook his head and then added, "No, I didn't even know that my grandfather was Jewish until a Jewish doctor spoke to me in Yiddish one day when I was getting a physical. He told me that my name was definitely Jewish. I went home and asked my grand-mother, and I found out that I had discovered a deep family secret. For a Polish girl to marry a Jew back in the old country caused both of them to be rejected by their families. And back in the old country, family was everything."

"We've got to do something about Abou," Tyriver said, already plotting revenge.

"Captain Abou isn't going to change. Racism and eth-nic hatred isn't going to go away. The most that we can hope for are laws that protect everyone." Goldsmith rubbed his sore jaw and stared up at the sky filled with stars. "It's a fucked-up world and it gets worse if you weaken."

Major Ricks paced in front of the assembled men in the area studies briefing room, as he had been doing for over five minutes without saying a word. Everyone knew that the major was extremely angry. Finally the executive officer stopped pacing and glared out at the recon men. "I've been informed that there was a fight outside of the NCO club last night. I've also been told that one member of a recon team, who is soon to be put in isolation for a *motherfucking mission!*"—Major Ricks' voice rose as spittle flew from his mouth—"I repeat, *a motherfucking mission*, was injured and his ability to perform his mis-sion is in question. Now, I would like to know the name of the sorry son of a bitch who would think so little of *me* that he would believe that he could beat the hell out of one of my men and me not do something about it!"

All of the assembled men avoided eye contact with the major. Goldsmith averted his head, pretending to stare at the gear displayed on the ready tables so that he could hide the large black-and-blue mark that went from his chin up to his eye.

"Now let me warn you, if I find out that a senior officer beat up a junior officer, I will personally write the court-marshal charges! I cannot believe that members of my recon unit would even think of fighting each other when we have a fucking jungle full of people who would love to fight us!"

Captain Abou flexed his jaws but remained sitting

silently in his chair. He knew that the major was talking to him directly, and it was becoming embarrassing in front of his squad leaders. He had gotten plastered at the club, and when he had seen Goldsmith sitting outside, it had been too much. His family back in Detroit had just written him about the suffering his relatives were going through living in refugee camps that were controlled by the Jews in Israel.

Major Ricks placed his hands on his hips. "Now, would one of you like to tell me what happened last night?"

Abou started to stand up, but Goldsmith beat him to the punch. "Sir, Sergeant Tyriver and I were up on the rappeling tower getting drunk, and we started grab-assing around and I fell off the tower. The side of my face hit one of the posts on my way down and sort of broke my fall. Because Captain Abou and I had a few words a couple of days ago, everybody thought that we had fought after seeing my face at breakfast this morning. That's how the rumor started, sir."

Major Ricks glared at the lieutenant standing at attention in front of him, and then he looked over at Captain Abou. "Is that how it happened, Captain?"

Abou shrugged. "If he says so, sir. I don't know anything about what happened to him. I was over at the club getting drunk with my teammates."

Major Ricks inhaled a huge lungful of air and held it in for a long time before exhaling. "All right, if that's the way it was, I apologize. Now let's get on with our mission briefing." Ricks flashed an angry look at Abou and then over at Goldsmith, but a tight smile crossed his face. He knew Goldsmith was lying. But a court-martial would really hurt the reputation of the SOG unit, and Abou was a valuable asset to the program. He was extremely aggressive in the field and volunteered his Hatchet Platoon for the most dangerous missions. Ricks paused to look at the huge bruise that covered Goldsmith's face on the left side and shuddered. He knew that Abou's eighteen-inch biceps packed one hell of a wallop. It was a wonder that Goldsmith's head hadn't been torn off.

"Listen up!" Ricks slipped into his briefing voice.

"This is the way we're going to handle this underwater-bridge mission. The insertion site is going to be fifteen clicks upriver. We're going to bring in fast-movers to bomb a portion of the river as if they were going after an underwater bridge, and then on both sides of the river we're going to bring in some large napalm runs to block your helicopters inserting your teams. We're going to use two shit-hooks—CH-47 Chinooks—for personnel, and you'll be covered by a platoon of Cobras that will be shooting up the jungle for a thousand meters.

"The effect of the massive air attack is going to look as if we are attacking the underwater bridge, and the NVA observers will figure that we screwed up and bombed the wrong site. It happens all of the time and they know it, so the attack will be an excellent cover for your insertion.

"Once you're on the ground—the napalm strike should give you enough cover to egress from the area—you'll head south and take up an ambush position at the real underwater bridge crossing. Then you'll wait there until a suitable target crosses the bridge. We are figuring that after the false air attack, the NVA will feel confident enough to maybe send something really important across the undamaged bridge."

"Like what, sir?" Abou interrupted.

"Tanks, special ammunition or personnel—stuff like that—but any suitable target will do. That will be your call, Captain Abou." Ricks pointed over at Goldsmith. "RT Massasauga will take the lead at the insertion site and move the Hatchet Platoon down to the actual bridge site. You've been there before. Goldsmith should recognize the area by sight. Once you're at the bridge site, Abou takes over command and conducts the primary mission."

At that moment Major Ricks paused and stared over the heads of the assembled recon men. Lieutenant Colonel MacCall had entered the room and taken a seat in the back. Ricks had argued violently with the CCN commander right before the meeting, and the colonel had finally given in and let him have his way. "Once the ambush has been executed, the Hatchet Platoon will move to their extraction site—either the primary or one of the alternates, depending on the situation—and RT Massasauga will move into hiding and act as a stay-behind unit." That was the part of the mission that had caused the argument the night before and was still very sensitive. MacCall crossed his arms, but he allowed Ricks to continue his briefing. "If for *any reason* you feel that a stay-behind mission would be in jeopardy, Lieutenant Goldsmith, you will cancel and move to one of your extraction sites. All of the FACs have been briefed and will be attending your final briefing in isolation."

"What's our mission, sir?" Tyriver asked, feeling the adrenaline starting to enter his bloodstream already.

"POW snatch. You'll cross over the river when the opportunity presents itself and move to one of three areas, depending on NVA resistance and activity. We have a lot of information that there are over a dozen small POW camps in that area operated by the Pathet Lao."

Major Ricks let the men whisper to one another for a half minute and then cut them off. "I want you to spend the rest of the day studying your mission areas and going over to the supply building to draw your special equipment. Captain Abou?"

"Yes, sir."

"Each one of your commandos will draw one LAW launcher. If the opportunity presents itself, we want to be able to destroy light tanks and trucks."

"Yes, sir."

"Now, get out of here and start your mission planning. And don't forget to take your special equipment over to the isolation building for my personal inspection at 0900 hours tomorrow!" Hopping down from the platform, Major Ricks walked to the back of the room and started talking in low tones to MacCall.

The team members were too excited talking about their mission to notice the head nodding going on between their leaders.

"Damn, sir! He took every one of your recommendations!" Tyriver patted Goldsmith on the back.

"It was logical."

"Right! Shit, is this going to be something to write home about—if we can pull it off!" Tyriver started walking toward the exit. "Let's get over to supply and draw our stuff."

Goldsmith looked up just as Captain Abou approached him. "Hey, Lieutenant, let's forget what happened last night. I was a little drunk and things got out of control."

Goldsmith waited for an apology, but when he saw that none was forthcoming, he smiled and slipped past the captain out into the main TOC area.

"Well, are we going to forget about it?" Abou's voice echoed across the area study tables.

Goldsmith stopped in the center of the room and turned back to face the captain. "Someday, *maybe*. Right now everything is going on hold until this mission is over with—Captain."

"Fuck you! Have it your way!" Abou flipped Goldsmith the finger and stalked toward his men, gathered around a map table.

Sergeant Tyriver held the door open for Lieutenant Goldsmith to enter the large barn-shaped tin building that housed the supplies for the Command and Control North recon teams. A captain met them as soon as they entered the building. He was leaning heavily on a bamboo cane.

"I saw you coming across the helipad." The captain waved for the members of RT Massasauga to follow him over to an enclosed area that housed specialty items.

"How's the leg healing, Captain?" Tyriver asked, taking up a position on the man's good side.

"Not very damn good! They told me over at the Navy hospital yesterday that they might be forced to ship me out to Japan for some special surgery"—Then the captain noticed the bruised side of Goldsmith's head. "You into some kind of kinky sex there, Lieutenant?"

"Right, Captain—whips and all that shit!" Goldsmith grinned, using one side of his mouth.

"Dangerous stuff!" He looked over at Tyriver. "You'd better steer him clear of that shit."

"You know how young officers are, sir." Tyriver shrugged his shoulders. "Hormones with feet!"

The captain proceeded to change the subject. He knew exactly what had happened between Goldsmith and

Abou the night before, but was trying to make light of the incident. "Now in here"—he rapped on a closed plywood door and a Vietnamese opened it—"are some very interesting items that I think you'll be happy with." The captain went over to a table where the Vietnamese worker was removing the protective coating from four brand-new Swedish-K submachine guns that had been supplied with blackened silencers. "You asked for these with ten extra magazines each."

"Great, Captain!" Tyriver hefted one of the folding-stock weapons.

"And"—the captain held up a common salt shaker for Goldsmith to see—"the powdered tear gas you asked for, complete with dispenser."

"A salt shaker?" Tyriver took the glass container from the captain's hand. "You've taped the top shut."

"It's easy to use. I guarantee that it will keep tracking dogs off your trail. Lieutenant Bourne developed this tactic and it works. Just sprinkle a little bit of the powered tear gas on a trail as you pass along it. Don't use too much or the NVA will get a whiff. Just enough to screw up the dogs."

Goldsmith nodded, wishing he had taken one of those salt shakers with him on his first mission.

"Strobe lights, cherry grenades, STABO rigs, indigenous rations, nylon space blankets, URC-10s, night goggles with spare batteries, mini-bolt cutters, and a special medical aid kit ordered specifically to Tyriver's orders." The captain tapped each item as he walked along the bench where they were displayed. "Anything we missed?"

"Excellent! As usual, you've done a great job in assembling this for us, Captain." Sergeant Tyriver knew that it had taken a lot of effort just to get the Swedish-Ks silenced.

"What else?" the captain asked Goldsmith, ignoring Tyriver's compliment. He had run recon until he had been shot. He had refused medical evacuation back to the States and had taken the S-4 job instead. He knew how important special equipment was to the success of a mission. "Oh, I almost forgot." He walked over to five sets of brand-new jungle boots lined up on a separate table.

"We don't need new boots, sir." Goldsmith didn't want to risk getting blisters breaking in a pair of new boots out in the jungle.

"You might want to try these." He lifted one of the boots so that Tyriver and Goldsmith could see the sole.

"Fuck me!" Tyriver took the boot from the captain and studied it. A human footprint was on the bottom of the boot instead of the normal tread. "It's even wide like a Montagnard's foot!"

"The idea is to leave a native footprint behind in soft soil, but still provide support and protection to your feet in the jungle. They're new and haven't been fully tested yet—do you want them?"

"Sure, let's try them out." Goldsmith nodded and smiled over at Tyriver. "Some good shit in here!"

"We do our best to please." The captain flinched and tried covering up the pain that flashed from his leg. "You won't be able to wear the boots inside the camp until you're in isolation. They're still secret equipment."

"Thanks, Captain." Goldsmith inspected the perfect rendition of a Montagnard footprint complete with broken-down arches and small scars.

"I'll have everything shipped over to the isolation building this afternoon. By the way, only RT Massasauga will be issued the new boots and silenced weapons for this mission. I really don't want a last-minute rush from the Hatchet Platoon for those items, if you know what I mean?"

"Yes, sir. We'll keep our mouths shut." Goldsmith nodded for Tyriver to depart the special-items area with him. "Thanks again, Captain."

The crippled captain just nodded his head as he watched the two young recon men leave his building. He was burning inside with jealousy, but he knew that he would never again be allowed to perform a recon mission. The AK-47 round through his kneecap had ended those glory days forever.

CHAPTER NINE

✪✪✪✪✪✪✪✪✪✪✪✪✪✪✪

OH! LORDY, LORDY!

RT Massasauga were the last ones to load up on the second Chinook. Abou's Hatchet Platoon, operating at full strength, numbered exactly sixty men, including the Americans. The normal load for the twin-rotor Chinooks was thirty-three men each, but SOG had the new C-models of the large helicopters and the average commando was only five-foot-three and weighed one hundred and forty pounds. The cargo capacity of the Chinooks was based on American soldiers.

Holding onto his Swedish-K with his right hand and his SOG short-brimmed camouflage cap with his left, Sergeant Tyriver lined up behind the Chinook's lowered rear ramp and leaned forward against the hot blast of air coming from the twin turbine engines located directly above the ramp. The helicopters had been idling the whole time the Hatchet Platoon had been loading up, and the PSP planking of the helipad was throwing off the heat of the engines.

Lieutenant Goldsmith, bringing up the rear of the five-man team, looked back over his shoulder and nodded at Major Ricks, who was standing off to one side with the SOG commander. They were watching the men load up for their insertion flight directly from the SOG headquarters pad instead of using one of the launch sites. The large Chinooks had a much longer range than the smaller attack helicopters that would join them when they flew over the 101st Airborne's base camp farther toward the Laotian border.

The blast from the turbine engines tugged at his navy watch cap, but Goldsmith didn't even try to push it down tighter on his head. He knew that the prop blast couldn't remove the cap.

Lieutenant Colonel MacCall shook his head and said to Ricks, "I have a bad feeling about this mission!"

"They've planned well!" Ricks yelled back as the turbine engines started to rev up for lift-off.

"Are you going to come with me to watch the insertion?" MacCall started walking toward the all black SOG helicopter on the far side of the pad. The helicopter had just finished refueling from his flight up from Saigon, and the door gunners were making a quick inspection of the chopper's airframe.

"No, I'll stay back here and work the special assets if things go wrong out there," Ricks said, barely keeping the contempt out of his voice. He knew that the SOG chopper had a brigadier general on board from the Saigon Support Command and at least three staff officers from the SOG staff riding as straphangers to watch the show from three thousand feet above the insertion site. MacCall always seemed to have a large entourage of staff officers from different Saigon headquarters flying with him during insertions. At first Ricks had only suspected what MacCall was up to, but now he was almost positive what was going on in the private office MacCall had established next to his commander's office. Ricks had assigned the SOG administrative officer, Rob Barr, to do a little snooping around.

"I'll probably go back to Saigon for the night and catch the fixed-wing flight back in the morning." MacCall started jogging toward the helicopter, which was starting up on the far side of the pad.

Tyriver had taken a place in the Chinook next to one of the side gunners, who was operating a .50-caliber heavy machine gun. The gunner smiled at the recon man and reached up to adjust his goggles. Tyriver squeezed between the barrel of the machine gun and the airframe in the open window and looked out at the jungle. The cool air coming in felt good.

An insertion was the worst part of a mission for Tyriver. He felt fear starting to develop in his stomach, knowing it would move to his lungs before long and he would start breathing heavily. He was concentrating on the jungle below them when he saw a flight of Huey Cobras catch up to them and start weaving over the tops of the jungle trees like wasps searching for spiders.

Goldsmith's gaze roved from man to man in the helicopter. He noticed both that the commandos were enjoying the ride and there was only a little tension surrounding the eyes of the platoon's American squad leaders. There was a big difference between a recon team and a Hatchet Platoon. Because of the small size of a recon team, an insertion could easily end up in all five team members being killed—in fact, that was a favorite tactic of the NVA. They would allow for insertion helicopters to drop off a five-man team, and they would wait until the choppers were gone before attacking and killing or capturing the members. A Hatchet Platoon was a different story. The thirty-five-man unit was designed to fight, and unless they landed in the center of an NVA battalion, they could kick a lot of ass. A normal NVA company only numbered sixty men, and they weren't as heavily armed as a Hatchet Platoon. Plus, one of the platoons was always brought up to full strength before an insertion, which was a key point. There were many United States Marine *companies* operating in the I Corps area that couldn't muster fifty men for the field—yet they were always referred to as companies on battle maps and maneuvered as such. A SOG Hatchet Platoon was a formidable force, and Goldsmith gave Captain Abou credit for having one of the best platoons in the SOG program. The whole purpose of the platoons was to exploit what the recon teams found, and they did their jobs extremely well.

The change of pitch in the rotor blades alerted Goldsmith and Tyriver that the Chinooks were heading down. Suddenly the jungle started getting closer. Tyriver left his position in the window when the gunner signaled that he needed to be able to maneuver the barrel of his weapon in the space. Tyriver caught a quick glimpse of a red ball of fire down on the jungle floor and a flash of blue. They were close to their insertion site. He hurried over to Goldsmith and took a seat on the floor. He tried keeping his eyes averted from the lieutenant's so that the fear he was feeling wouldn't show.

When they landed, the tailgate dropped open, and the crew chief signaled for the men to unload. Tyriver responded automatically and ran from the chopper, using Goldsmith as a guide. The other three men on RT Massasauga surrounded their two Americans as they moved into the high elephant grass. Goldsmith paused when they were far enough away from the Chinooks' rotor wash to gain his bearings and moved a little to his right to link up with Captain Abou's command element. The choppers had landed according to plan, facing south so that all of the men could move in a straight line for a hundred meters away from the choppers before forming a tight fighting perimeter. The tactic was designed not only to orient the ground commanders, but also, in the event that the chopper took a rocket, the men wouldn't be sprayed with debris. The door gunners sprayed the jungle with machine-gun fire, being careful to keep their ground fire to the sides of the choppers.

The huge double-rotor Chinooks lifted off the mat of pressed-down elephant grass and departed the area, staying as low to the ground as possible until they were a dozen miles away from the insertion site.

Locating Tyriver, Goldsmith dropped next to him so close that the sides of their legs touched. He felt Tyriver's muscles trembling, but ignored the sign of nervousness as coming from his own leg. Insertions were extremely dangerous and everyone was scared.

Tyriver pointed with his arm over to where Captain Abou had established his temporary command post. The sound of the choppers disappeared, replaced by the sound of the napalm fires and the loud popping sounds of the burning bamboo that lined the riverbanks on both sides.

Abou used hand and arm signals to organize his platoon, and in less than a minute he gave the hand signal for Goldsmith and RT Massasauga to take the point and move south. Tyriver didn't like the captain, but he respected the man's ability to perform in the field.

Y-Clack and Y-Brei took the point, followed by Gold-smith and Tyriver. Y-Bluc brought up the rear of the small team, carrying the radio in his rucksack. Abou and Goldsmith had decided on using the hand-held URC-10s as their primary means of communications. In addition, they had selected channel two, which was shared with their overhead FAC, who would remain above them con-stantly until the teams were extracted. The forward air controllers were a critical part of the SOG mission and had gained a reputation as being the best in their business.

A three-hundred-meter gap would separate the recon team and the Hatchet Platoon, a point that had been decided on after a great deal of arguing back in the brief-ing room. Abou wanted to travel much closer, but Gold-smith wanted the distance between them so that his team could listen to the surrounding jungle.

Tyriver felt much better now that the insertion was over with and they had not been attacked. As far as he was concerned, the hardest part of the mission was over. SOG recon teams had an over ninety-eight-percent con-tact rate with the NVA. *Knowing* that eventually he would end up in a firefight before the patrol was over made the idea much more acceptable. What had scared Tyriver was making contact initially, when they had very little control over their situation. Now that he had ori-ented himself on the ground and his team had formed up into a fighting unit, the fear left him. He was actually feeling a little cocky, knowing that a huge Hatchet Pla-toon was only a short distance away. This was the first time out on a recon mission that his RT had been so well protected.

The smell of burning flesh reached them from the napalm fires, and Goldsmith paused to sniff the air. It could be human or an animal that had gotten caught in the strike. There was no way of knowing, but he wasn't going to risk his team. He made a soft clicking noise to alert his point men to be more cautious.

Y-Bluc kept Goldsmith in sight as the team moved through the elephant grass. His main concern wasn't the lieutentant but the beautiful sword the American officer carried on his back. Y-Bluc's father was the sword maker for his village—and was renowned as one of the finest sword makers in the whole Montagnard nation—but he knew that his father could not make a sword as beautiful as the one the American carried. Y-Bluc had fallen in love with the smooth black blade, and all Goldsmith had to do was pull the short sword out of its leather sheath and Y-Bluc seemed to appear out of the air.

Montagnard forges were made using large bamboo sections for bellows and charcoal to heat the steel for shaping. Old car springs and scraps of metal were used to shape into swords and knives, but the fire never really got hot enough to smooth out the steel or produce carbon to harden the blades, and Montagnard swords always had the telltale bumps and ridges from a smith's hammer. The lieutenant's sword was smooth, and the double edges were sharper than anything he had ever touched before in his thirty-eight years of life. Y-Bluc knew that he would trade his eldest son into slavery to the American for the sword.

A large bird sounded an alarm and flew off in the direction of the river. Y-Bluc returned his attention to his job as rear guard for the recon team. He paused long enough to look back down the trail they were making through the tall grass. He knew the Hatchet Platoon would have no problem following them, but the danger lay in a small NVA unit getting between the platoon and the recon team. Y-Bluc had been working for the French and then the Americans since he was nine years old when his father sold him to a French colonel as a houseboy down in Ban Me Thout. The French bought slaves and worked them hard, but the Americans were a much different kind of white-skinned people. They did not buy people but paid them much more money, and every time the moon had a complete cycle, the Americans would give the Montagnards working for them some more money! The Americans were a foolish race of people, but Y-Bluc saw that they were very kind and always took time to help sick and injured Montagnards without demanding something in return.

Y-Bluc's gaze automatically moved to the hilt of the sword that stuck out between the lieutenant's shoulder blades and smiled. Maybe someday the American would sell him the sword. He would ask him and if the American said no, then he would go back to his original plan and kill him for the sword and disappear into the jungle. He knew he could live with his uncle's village, which was located high in the Laotian mountains, far away from the wars of the lowland people.

RT Massasauga moved quickly along the riverbank, pausing only long enough for Goldsmith to check their location on the map and that wasn't often. He knew that there was no way his Montagnard point men would miss the wide east–west trail, but he wanted to know his position in case they had an accidental encounter with an NVA force. The closer they got to the underwater bridge, the better the chances of their running into a large NVA force that was laagered and either waiting to cross the river or that had just finished crossing the river and were resting.

During the late afternoon, Y-Clack and Y-Brei started moving slower as the vegetation started changing from solid elephant grass to mixed patches of bamboo and secondary trees. They were picking up a lot of signs that the NVA were present in the area and in large numbers. Once they were forced to change direction and bypass a large, camouflaged bivouac site that was empty but not abandoned by the NVA.

Goldsmith marked the site on his map for a future target and checked his watch. They had been heading south for nine hours without taking a break. He signaled for his team to circle around and used the URC-10 to alert Captain Abou that they had stopped for a thirty-minute chow break.

Tyriver pulled a plastic tube of precooked indigenous rations from the side pocket of his rucksack and removed the rubber band over the end of another tube packed full of rice and shrimp. The commandos loved the rice and squid ration best, then the beef and rice, but the Americans favored the shrimp and rice ration. Tyriver always ate the indigenous rations in the field because not only were they nutritious and filled you up quickly, but they were easy to digest and bland enough not to give you an upset stomach. American rations were much too heavy to carry, and the variety that was designed not to bore the American combat soldier also caused indigestion—at least for him.

Almost as soon as the recon team stopped to eat, the jungle went back to normal around them. Monkeys started calling to one another in the tall trees, and insect life appeared from their hiding places on the leaves. Tyriver counted seventeen different species of bugs and spiders from his seat on his rucksack, and he didn't recognize a single one of them.

Goldsmith located their rest position and oriented himself before he ate. According to his map, they were very close to the underwater bridge site, and he started worrying they would be overtaken during the chow break. He hurried to finish eating and then signaled for his team to form up. The sound of running water had reached them as they sat silently, and Goldsmith wanted to make sure the sound they were hearing was the main waterway and not a stream feeding into it.

He took the lead and reached the riverbank after only a few minutes of weaving through the thick underbrush. He dropped down near a rocky outcrop and smiled. The narrow mountain river had widened, forming a pond that was over two hundred meters across at its widest point. Goldsmith recognized the site from aerial photographs and was pleased because it confirmed his prior guess of their location. They were only a few thousand meters from the underwater bridge site.

Tyriver nudged Goldsmith's side and pointed down into the clear water of the rock-lined mountain pond.

Goldsmith backed from the edge of the rocks automatically as soon as he noticed the huge reptiles in the water below them. One of the reptiles was almost twice the size of the other three and had a large bump on the end of its nose. It was difficult to judge the size of the creature without having something to gauge it against, but he estimated that it had to be close to twenty feet long and definitely big enough to eat a human.

Tyriver placed his hand over Goldsmith's ear and whispered, "Gavials—quite rare. They don't bother humans."

A shiver rippled down Goldsmith's spine all the same. A fucking crocodile was a crocodile as far as he was concerned, and he avoided all of them, even the little ones.

The URC-10 clicked, signaling Goldsmith that Abou wanted to talk to him. He removed the radio and, checking to make sure the volume on the radio was set low, answered.

"Massasauga One-Zero, this is Dragon One-Zero, over."

"Massasauga One-Zero, over."

"Are you ready to move out, over?"

"Roger, we are nearing our objective, over."

"Roger that. We will close the gap, over."

"Roger, we'll move out now, out."

Goldsmith signaled for his team to start moving again. Taking one last quick glance down at the male gavial and his harem, he followed Tyriver back to where they had taken their break. Then the team took up their positions again and headed south. As they did, Goldsmith started counting his paces as a means of judging distance in the thick jungle. He knew that they were approximately eighteen hundred meters above the site, and he would move his team another twelve hundred before stopping and letting the Hatchet Platoon catch up.

Out of nowhere, a flight of F4s passed overhead, flying so low that the sound of their engines startled Goldsmith so bad that he had to stop and move off a little ways into the brush to drop his pants. His nerves had been wound tightly as they closed the distance to the underwater bridge. Goldsmith cursed the pilots under his breath, not knowing that the flight of F4s had further relaxed the NVA detachment guarding the bridge. All of the activity upriver had convinced them that the Americans had selected the wrong site on the river to bomb and they were feeling very secure. A low-flying flight of fighters was nerve-racking to the recon team, but it was fairly common for the NVA who lived in the jungle.

Goldsmith moved his team as far south as he dared. When he stopped, he had them form up into a star laager position to wait for the Hatchet Platoon.

The sweat hadn't dried on his face before Captain Abou appeared. He joined Goldsmith and Tyriver and started pointing where he wanted his squad leaders to establish their defensive perimeter surrounding the recon team.

Abou waited until his perimeter was secured before speaking in a very low voice to Goldsmith. None of the animosity from the base camp was in his voice, but he hadn't been the one beaten up either. "Show me our location."

Goldsmith opened his small map and showed where they were in relation to the underwater bridge site. Abou nodded in agreement and smiled. "We've made damn good time! I think we should try and move into position around the site before nightfall. What do you think?"

Goldsmith looked over at Tyriver and nodded. "Sure—if we move *slow*."

"I agree. They should have a small unit guarding this side of the bridge and another unit on the opposite side."

"Let my recon team take out the guards. We have silenced weapons."

Abou frowned but then nodded in agreement. He didn't like sharing his mission with anyone, especially the glory. He had worked hard to establish a reputation as a tough fighter, and he didn't want a Jew to end up looking better than him. All the same, Goldsmith's reasoning was good: it would be smarter for a small, well-trained RT to take out the guards. "But don't fuck up this mission!"

Tyriver was about to retort and then thought better about it. He turned his back on the captain so that the look on his face couldn't be seen.

Goldsmith saw Tyriver's disgust and patted his One-One on his shoulder to calm him down. "We'll wait until dark and use night goggles."

"At first shadows! If there's a convoy waiting over there to cross the bridge, they'll start crossing as soon as it gets dark, and I want to have my men in position to use their LAWs!"

Goldsmith nodded and moved a few feet away so the man would stop talking. He signaled for his RT to circle around him and used Y-Bluc to interpret for him. Because they had only two pairs of night goggles, Goldsmith had decided that only Tyriver and he would go down to the crossing site, reconnoitering the area at the bridgehead if possible. The guard force would be small, maybe a half dozen men, and they would not be very alert, especially after the major air strike to the north. He told Y-Bluc that he was in charge of the rest of the team and Tyriver's and his rucksacks. Y-Bluc's eyes lit up. The beautiful sword would be in his care. He could hold it all night if he wished.

Goldsmith waited until an hour after the sun had slipped behind the western mountains to leave the laager site with Tyriver. He carried his silenced .22-caliber pistol and four hand grenades. Tyriver carried his silenced 9mm Swedish-K and a K-Bar fighting knife along with four hand grenades. He had copied Goldsmith's rigging on his STABO harness with three of the M-26 grenades rigged so that they could be removed for throwing and one of the grenades taped to his harness directly over his heart so that the pin could be pulled, but the grenade could not be removed. Tyriver had seen Goldsmith's rigged suicide grenade in the isolation ready room when Major Ricks was inspecting their gear. The major had taken his time inspecting Goldsmith's rigged grenade closely, but he didn't say a word. The lieutenant's message was very clear: he was not going to be taken prisoner.

The moon was so bright that it was almost unnecessary to use the night goggles, but Goldsmith decided to wear them anyway, just in case a cloud bank moved in and covered the moon. The additional light made the star-light-powered glasses work even better. It was like walking through the jungle during daylight.

Goldsmith took the lead. He had plotted a mental course from his map and hoped that he would not have to use his compass or map during the patrol. The two of them wouldn't have to travel more than six hundred meters—maybe less—before they reached the bridge. There was the ever present danger of running into a laager site, but the NVA were too shrewed to keep a large unit that close to the bridge. After all, the idea was to keep the crossing site as close to virgin jungle as possible so that it wouldn't draw attention.

Goldsmith remembered every step he took. He stopped often to listen to the jungle and search the surrounding vegetation for stationary guards. His sense of smell increased on demand, and he tilted his head back to sniff for smells of food or tobacco.

When the wind shifted, they both smelled the campfire at the same time. Tyriver's hand shot up and grabbed Goldsmith's arm. They froze and they turned their heads slowly, searching the jungle for the enemy. Goldsmith caught a glimpse of Tyriver, and the way he was standing and moving reminded him of a lizard who was hunting. Only his head was moving; his body was frozen in a half-step position.

Goldsmith kept looking back and forth until he located the direction the smell was coming from, and then he slowly started moving in that direction.

Tyriver moved his Swedish-K around from his back, where he had been carrying it to keep it from getting caught on vines and underbrush.

The NVA outpost had been built on a piece of high ground that looked down directly on the river crossing. Goldsmith counted five sleeping NVA soldiers. There was one NVA soldier sitting next to a large tree with an American landline telephone next to him. He had his hand resting on the handset so that he could feel the vibration if the telephone rang silently. The telephone watchman was also sleeping.

Nudging Goldsmith, Tyriver pointed to the three sleeping NVA on their side of the fire and then down at his Swedish-K. He was signaling that he would take out the three NVA closest to them and Goldsmith could have the other three.

Goldsmith tapped Tyriver's arm to gain his attention and then slowly shook his head. He raised a gloved finger to his lips. It was too early in the evening for the NVA to be sleeping—unless the guards knew they were going to be up later that night and they were trying to catch as much sleep as they could before the convoy arrived. Goldsmith could see that the fire they had smelled was only smoldering. The NVA were too well disciplined to burn fires at night and draw American reconnaissance aircraft to their location.

Goldsmith signaled for Tyriver to back off and follow him back to the laager site where Captain Abou was waiting. The trip back took a tenth of the time going to the bridge site.

Captain Abou looked angry when the two-man team passed through the platoon's perimeter. "What happened?"

"We found an observation post occupied by six NVA soldiers. They were all sleeping, but they had landline communications set up. It looked like a permanent site."

"So, did you kill them?"

"No."

"Why not?" Captain Abou's voice almost rose above a whisper.

"Because they were all sleeping and it's very early yet. I think they are trying to get some rest before a convoy arrives."

"So? That's all the more reason to kill them and get set up quicker!"

"I'd rather go back with your engineers and place the shape charges on the bridge and then kill the guards." Goldsmith opened his canteen and took a long drink as he waited for what he had said to sink into the rational part of Abou's brain.

The captain kept nodding his head and then he signaled for his NCO, who was acting as his executive officer, to crawl over. The bright moonlight filtering through the light overhead cover made it easy to see clearly as far as fifty feet away in the open areas. Abou whispered to his One-One, "Get the engineers together and get one of the squad leaders to carry the fuses."

Within a few minutes, two Special Forces-trained demolition men joined the officers, carrying their special back-packs that contained over forty pounds of plastic explosives each. The demo-men removed the electronic detonators and their zinc-chromium batteries from their packs. They then handed the detonators to Captain Abou and the batteries to their One-One. The man carrying the fuses sat twenty feet away; he would bring up the rear of the patrol when they moved out. As long as the plastic explosives were separate from the detonators, they were harmless. They wouldn't explode even if a bullet hit them.

"If you're not back by 0200 hours, we'll assume that

you've failed. I'll then take out the bridge guards and call in an air strike on the bridge." Captain Abou wasn't asking for the lieutenant's opinion. So far Goldsmith's recommendations had all been logical ones, and that bothered Abou.

"That should be plenty of time, sir," Goldsmith assured him, sensing that the captain was getting a little uptight over having to give in to him so much.

"I'll take the point, sir. You bring up the rear." Tyriver checked his gear quickly. He had stripped off everything but his fighting gear and left it with the Montagnards to carry in case they had to run. Y-Bluc snatched up Goldsmith's pack before anyone else could move.

"No, I'll take point, Tyriver. I have a good idea where the bridge is located under the water, and that will save time finding it. The engineers should follow behind me and then the detonator man. You bring up the rear guard and cover for us once we reach the bridge with your silenced weapon." Again, Goldsmith's logic was unquestionable. He was the most qualified to take the point, and a silenced weapon was the most practical to cover the engineers while they placed the charges. "We're going to go back down the same trail we took earlier, Tyriver, but I'm going to skirt around the NVA outpost. The bright moonlight is going to work for the NVA guards on the west side of the river when we try getting in the water to place the charges. We'll probably have to gather some kind of floating debris and make it look as if it had snagged on the bridge to hide our engineers. Be ready to do that." He was still speaking to Tyriver, but the engineers had been listening to the conversation.

"Let's cut it now and carry the vegetation with us." The recommendation was a good one, and Goldsmith nodded his approval. The engineers cut small bundles of vines and attached them to the backs of their packs.

Goldsmith checked his watch against Captain Abou's, and the small team slipped into the shadows. They had three hours to place the charges on the bridge and return to the laager site. It was plenty of time if they didn't run into any NVA soldiers.

It was harder locating the NVA outpost now that the fire had gone out completely, but Goldsmith located

them in enough time to make a wide detour to avoid
waking them up. The river's edge appeared suddenly at
his feet, and he rocked back to keep from falling into it
and making a splash. For a couple of seconds Goldsmith
thought that they had gone too far downriver and had
missed the bridge. Then he saw the ripple running across
the river where the current caught the edge of the steel
bridge. The trail on the west side ran directly to the
underwater structure, but on the east side the trail took
a sharp turn to the south for about a half mile before
turning back due east again. He could have missed the
bridge without crossing the trail until he was too far
downstream to realize it. The ripple in the water was a
welcome sight in the moonlight.

Goldsmith signaled with his hand and then pointed at
the ripple. The two engineers knew exactly what the officer was telling them and slipped into the river as quietly
as a pair of otters. They knew their profession extremely
well. The fuse man brought up the rear of the now three-
man team as Tyriver and Goldsmith covered them from
the east bank with their silenced weapons. Goldsmith's
.22-caliber pistol wouldn't be accurate enough to hit a
target on the opposite side of the river, but they could
throw their hand grenades to distract a small NVA force
if the engineers were spotted.

The night goggles revealed the engineers' heads in
detail even when surrounded by brush, but to the naked
eye in the moonlight, they looked as if clumps of the
riverbank had broken free and floated downstream.
Goldsmith also noticed a half-dozen clumps of sod floating on the other side of the river, which added to the
natural-looking camouflage the engineers were wearing.

Tyriver and Goldsmith watched as the engineers slowly
worked toward the center of the bridge. They had been
moving against the current, and it was only a matter of
time until anyone watching closely figured out that the
phenomenon was lasting too long to be a natural occur-
rence. Loose clods of riverbank did not move on their
own power.

The engineers placed charges all along the structure
out to the center of the bridge before turning back and
heading slowly toward Tyriver and Goldsmith. They

were within fifty feet of the riverbank when a dark spot in the vegetation broke free and started wading out onto the bridge.

Goldsmith quickly removed the small pieces of cloth tape he had covering his sights and lined up the two illuminus dots until he saw only one against the black head. Goldsmith had practiced shooting the silenced pistol with the goggles back in the base camp by shooting rats from the tops of the perimeter bunkers. The practice had paid off. The NVA bridge guard got almost within touching distance of the first engineer before he realized it wasn't just another clump of riverbank building up against the edge of the submerged bridge.

Goldsmith pulled the trigger and the soft *pop* barely reached his ears. The pistol didn't have a kick to it, and the only way he was sure the weapon had fired was when the NVA soldier's feet went out from under him and he fell backward into the current, which quickly swept him downstream.

The guard's partner called to him from where he had been watching on the riverbank. He flipped his AK-47 over his shoulder and started running along the riverbank to save his comrade, still thinking that he had slipped on the bridge.

This rescue attempt gave the engineers enough time to make it back to the riverbank and slip into the cover of the jungle. Tyriver, hearing the sloshing of the three men in their wet clothes, left his hiding place to guide them over to Goldsmith. The dead NVA's body had snagged downstream on a large tree that had fallen into the river, and his comrade was crawling out to rescue him. In only a few more seconds the guard would realize that his friend had been shot.

Goldsmith pushed the talk switch on his URC-10 and whispered, "Massasauga, detonate! I repeat, *detonate now!*"

There was a long pause, and then a dull thud sounded, followed by the sound of thousands of tons of water impacting again with the river. The demolition charges had been placed under the steel structure, and the bridge itself acted as a tamping device, sending the force of the explosion downward and digging a huge crater in the river bottom that would make the shallow ford unsuitable for another bridge.

The Hatchet Platoon's perimeter was alert and waiting for the return of the demolition team when Goldsmith nearly collided with Captain Abou.

"What happened?" Abou's voice nearly broke. He had been anxious that the URC-10 message had been some sort of mistake and that he had killed the engineers.

"We placed the charges, but before our men could get out of the water, they were discovered by a guard. We had to blow it right away." Goldsmith had dropped to his knees, exhausted from the emotion-wracked trip back to the platoon. He had expected to feel AK-47 rounds ripping through his back with every step he took.

"Good move!" Abou was relieved knowing that the underwater bridge had been destroyed and his mission was successful. Now he just had to get his Hatchet Platoon back to the SOG base camp, and he'd have another legendary mission under his belt.

The sound of whistles reached the laagered platoon and then gunshots. Goldsmith glanced over at Tyriver in the bright moonlight and saw the stress lines on the young sergeant's face. It was obvious that the NVA soldiers were sealing off the area.

"We're going to move back out of here the way that we came in. The NVA won't be expecting that maneuver, and they won't be expecting a fucking Hatchet Platoon!" Captain Abou told his squad leaders, who had joined him and the recon team.

Goldsmith wanted to tell the captain that going back down a trail they had already made seemed foolish, but decided against it at the last second. Abou was an experienced field soldier and knew the risk. Besides, now wasn't the time to question a commander's judgment. "We'll break away here and try crossing the river."

Goldsmith's comment shocked the American platoon members, and even Captain Abou stopped and stared at the lieutenant as if he had gone crazy. "This area will be fucking swarming with NVA within an hour! It's going to be tough going for a fucking platoon to fight our way out of here, let alone a five-man recon team! It's fucking suicidal!"

"Remember, Captain, whether my team stays behind or not is my decision." Goldsmith saw the fear on Tyriver's face. A stay-behind mission was always exciting to talk about inside a TOC surrounded by friendly faces, but it was a different ball game when you were surrounded by NVA soldiers blowing whistles and firing signal shots. Goldsmith added for Tyriver's benefit, "Besides, your platoon will act as the hare for the hound. The NVA will be tracking you, and our chances of crossing the river and continuing our mission are actually very good."

"It's your call, Lieutenant, but if we make contact, don't expect me to hold back air support because you might be out there somewheres!"

"I know the risk, sir"—Goldsmith moved closer to Tyriver so his One-One could see his face clearly in the moonlight—"but this POW mission means a lot to us."

That's all Tyriver needed to hear to get a hold of the fear running rampant through his veins. "Let's move it, sir!"

Goldsmith took his rucksack from Y-Bluc and threw it over his shoulders. He talked as he got ready to move out: "We're going to move north a few hundred meters along our old trail and then cut west to the river, sir."

"You'd better do it now. We're breaking camp and will be only a few minutes behind you—and, Lieutenant Goldsmith . . ."

"Yes, sir?"

"My men will have orders to fire at anything that fucking looks human!"

"I understand, sir—good hunting." Goldsmith didn't look back as he signaled Y-Clack and Y-Brei to head out on the matted-down trail.

RT Massasauga hurried along the trail at almost a run until they had cleared the platoon perimeter, and then Goldsmith slowed the team down a little until he felt that they were far enough away to veer off. He didn't want to get so far down the trail that he would risk running into an NVA force.

At his signal the Montagnard point stopped and backtracked to the two Americans. Y-Bluc joined them from the rear. Goldsmith signaled that they were going to leave the trail and then stepped into the underbrush, followed by Tyriver. The Montagnards lagged behind in order to weave the jungle growth back together so that not even the sharpest NVA tracker would detect their exit from the trail. Y-Bluc, the last one to exit the main trail, paused just long enough to sprinkle a light coating of powdered tear gas on the underbrush. He was very careful not to put down too much so that a human could detect it. The tear gas was for tracker dogs. They sniff the light coating of tear gas on the vegetation and move quickly past.

Tyriver took the point and moved serpentinely through the jungle to throw off an NVA patrol. The curving trail would be mistaken for a large animal moving through the jungle.

Tyriver stumbled on a large rock outcrop bordering the riverbank and followed the terrain around the northern edge of the rocks until he reached the water. Eons of flooding had worn away the northern side of the rock formation, carving a five-foot-high niche that ran all the way from the base of the formation to the river. It was an excellent place to take a break. It provided overhead protection in the jungle, which was rare, and protection from grazing fire in every direction except due south.

The recon team sat down with the granite wall against their backs, and all of them except Goldsmith reached into their rucksacks for something to eat.

Goldsmith pulled out his map and started plotting their location. He wanted to see how close they were to a ford. Their stay-behind mission was to head west into the Laotian mountains and reconnoiter two sites that had a high number of sightings of Caucasians and black Americans by wandering Montagnards.

All hell broke loose south of the RT's laager site. It started with a light exchange of small-arms fire and then quickly erupted into an all-out firefight. Listening, Tyriver identified the different weapons being fired, mixed in with an occasional LAW rocket and RPG launcher. Instead of the firefight dying down, it seemed to get more and more intense.

Goldsmith risked whispering to his One-One, "It looks like Abou found the fight he was looking for."

As Tyriver nodded back in answer, Goldsmith realized that he could see his face. Morning was breaking in the jungle as it usually did, quickly and without warning.

"We'll stay here until things die down a little. We're too close to the fight and might end up being an airstrike accident." Goldsmith was referring to Abou's comment when they had separated. He knew that right about now the captain was talking to their FAC and calling in all kinds of air support on the NVA positions in a 360-degree circle around his position. If the recon team wasn't out of the way, well, he had warned them.

The rock formation was a perfect place to wait out the air strikes. The men were safe from everything except a direct hit or napalm, and even then they could always slip into the river if the fires got too close.

Goldsmith pulled his camouflage parachute cloth around his shoulders, leaving only a tiny opening to see through, and listened to the battle taking place five hundred meters away.

CHAPTER TEN

✪✪✪✪✪✪✪✪✪✪✪✪✪✪✪

GUERRE ÀMORT!

The NVA company commander, thinking he was dealing with an American reconnaissance team, maneuvered his unit of one hundred and ten infantrymen aggressively. He had been assigned to guard duty along the Ho Chi Minh trail for over a year, and he knew how the Americans operated their small recon teams. The normal operating procedure for his company had been in platoon-size units, but he had been given orders only the week before to join the 10th Sapper Battalion just east of the underwater bridge.

The commander of the battalion sat in front of an area map and stared at the locations representing his troops. He felt his face giving off heat and his jaw muscles were causing his teeth to hurt, but he continued grinding his molars. Pain made the shame of being caught off guard by an American recon team less shameful. He commanded the best NVA sapper unit in the whole army! He knew the instant the bridge blew up what had happened. His 102nd Company had been late arriving, and the laager site bordering the river to the north had been empty for twelve hours. The Americans must have been lucky and slipped through the only hole in the bridge's defenses.

He tapped the map with a captured grease pen that had a retractable filler element. He knew he had the Americans trapped inside his defensive semicircle. The 102nd Company had moved into the empty laager site only a few hours earlier and had sealed the only possible escape route for the small American team. He had ordered the company commander to capture as many

Americans as they could so that he would have something to show for the destruction of the vital bridge.

Captain Abou signaled for his elite Chinese Nung recon squad to take the lead. He had decided that they would move aggressively back up the trail and occupy the NVA laager site, using the NVA bunkers and foxholes for protection, and then call in massive air strikes to destroy the NVA units he knew would consolidate around the bridgehead.

The Nung point element was well armed with two M-60 light machine guns and two M-79 grenade launchers. With these they could sustain a contact with an enemy element of any size until the rest of the platoon could maneuver. A Hatchet Platoon was designed to fight a violent, short battle and then withdraw so that the FAC could call in his air power to destroy the enemy. The tactic was normally very successful.

The two combat forces collided on the narrow trail with such force that the lead elements of the 102nd Company formed an accordion against their point squad and the Nung squad slaughtered the NVA caught along the first fifty meters of the trail.

Captain Abou maneuvered the rest of his platoon to get as many weapons firing as possible. Right away he realized that he had made contact with a large NVA force and called for air support.

"Bird Dog 5, this is Devil Cat 6, over."

"This is Bird Dog 5. Send your traffic, over." The response from the overhead aircraft was instantaneous. The FAC had been wearing a headset and monitoring the command frequencies of both the Hatchet Platoon and RT Massasauga. His sole purpose in being in a flight pattern above the inserted teams was to provide instant on-call air support.

"Devil Cat 6, I am in contact with a very large NVA force. I am popping smoke . . . now." Abou pulled the pin on a purple smoke grenade and threw it to the north side of his small command element.

"I identify purple smoke, over," the FAC said, dropping his call sign to save time in transmission.

"Roger, put some five-hundred pounders two hundred meters to my north from the river out three hundred meters. Also, plan some air cover to surround my position out one hundred and fifty meters of lighter stuff, over."

"Roger, Devil Cat, let me locate your perimeter first. I have two flights of A1Es on call."

"Hurry, or they'll get here too late."

Just then Abou saw an NVA soldier emerge from the elephant grass less than ten feet in front of him, and he fired a ten-round burst that threw the soldier back in the brush. He instantly became angry with himself for wasting so much ammo on one man, but the NVA had taken him by surprise. The appearance of the enemy soldier told him that his whole perimeter had been penetrated. His platoon was engaged in hand-to-hand fights with the NVA sapper company, which had recovered from the initial surprise encounter with a force that was much larger than they had been expecting.

The NVA company commander moved forward through the jungle surrounded by his bodyguards, and they stumbled onto the first dead Nung, whose body had fallen outside the tight fighting perimeter Abou had formed so that he could call in air strikes. The A1Es were much better for this type of fighting than F4s not only because the old World War II propeller aircraft could stay on station much longer than the jets, but they also laid down very accurate cannon fire.

The A1Es arrived just as the 102nd Company was starting their assault on the north side of Abou's perimeter. The grazing fire from the platoon's Nungs and the cannon fire from the aircraft cut down rows of elephant grass and vegetation, making fire lanes visible from the air so that the A1E pilots could lay down an even more accurate fire to protect the outnumbered platoon. The intense air support changed the tempo of the battle, and the Nungs on the ground started gaining the advantage as the NVA had to fire both on the ground and at the aircraft. The A1Es were taking numerous hits, but the old aircraft had been built to withstand small-caliber fire.

The attack from the south and east hit the Hatchet Platoon so hard that they had no time even to realize that they were fighting for their lives. The fighting became so intense, so fast, that Abou dropped the radio handset and started fighting hand-to-hand with the dozens of NVA soldiers overrunning his position. There were so many sappers inside the platoon's perimeter that the NVA were killing their own men with small-arms fire.

The whole 10th Sapper Battalion had been committed to the fight after the 102nd company commander had called in that he had engaged a large American unit.

A round hit Abou in his stomach, knocking the wind out of him. He gasped and then held his breath long enough to smash in the face of an NVA soldier with the steel butt plate of his CAR-15. A second round hit his shoulder right underneath his collarbone, and his hand released the weapon it was holding. The weapon hung from his shoulder by its carrying strap. Abou removed his fighting knife and tried crouching to brace himself for an NVA soldier approaching from his right side, but the stomach wound had taken the strength from his muscles and he collapsed onto his knees. Helplessly he watched the NVA running toward him with his bayonet aimed at his chest.

An M-79 grenade launcher went off only inches from his shoulder and sprayed the area in front of him with a hundred steel fleshettes. The NVA soldier's face reflected surprise before he sprawled to the ground.

"We're in deep shit, Captain." The platoon's NCO in charge dropped to one knee next to Abou and reloaded the M-79 with another one of the deadly antipersonnel rounds that could clear a ten-foot-wide path. "Can you move, Captain?"

"No, I'm gut shot."

"Try leaning against me and I'll drag you out of here. But I've got to keep my hands free—this fucking area is crawling with NVA. We must have gotten inside their defensive perimeter for the bridge somehow." The sergeant turned his back toward Abou and waited until he felt the captain's good arm wrap around his neck. He leaned forward, lifted the wounded officer off the ground, and started moving slowly toward the river. There was no doubt in his mind that the platoon was destroyed as a fighting unit. The only survivors from this fight were going to be the few men who could reach the river and float downstream to safety.

Two more Nungs joined the captain and the sergeant, and just before they reached the water, a third Nung appeared, carrying the platoon's PRC-25 radio on his back.

"Come here!" Taking the handset, Abou fell to the ground. The remaining members of his platoon made a fighting circle around him so that he could talk to the FAC. "Bird Dog, bad shit! We're finished. Too many NVA." Abou was having a very difficult time talking with his stomach wound, but he struggled desperately to talk. "Place fire on our position. I say again, fire on our position. NVA outnumbered us ten to one." He gasped and tasted blood. "Start laying it down to our east and work back to the river. That'll push the NVA into the water and make easy targets for the A1Es."

"What about the platoon?" the FAC pilot cried, unwilling to bring in an air strike on friendly forces. He had listened to a captain once before from the 101st who wanted napalm dropped on *his* location, and it had ended up on an airborne platoon that hadn't been wiped out but was trying to maneuver around the NVA. "Devil Cat 6, are you sure you want an air strike on your platoon's location?"

The NCO answered, "Bird Dog, that was an order!"

"Roger, Devil Dog, wilco!" The FAC still didn't like the idea. There could still be commandos down there fighting individual battles, but he was compelled to comply with a ground commander's request. He pushed his mike-control switch. "Blue Cloud Leader, this is Bird Dog 5, over."

A static-filled broadcast filled the FAC's headset: "This is Blue Cloud Leader. We monitored your last transmission, and I think it would be best to hit the edges of their perimeter and slowly work back toward the river. We can pretty much see where the battle lines are down there even though the NVA have broken through their perimeter in a couple of places. There's a rocky area along the riverbank a couple hundred meters away that would make a good place for them to defend—if they can make it there. We'll bring in some fast-movers with napalm to clear the far side of the river for them, over." The flight leader was calm. He had been in worse situations before when supporting Green Beret forces up in the A Shau Valley.

"Roger. Let's try that tactic." As the FAC pilot banked his light observation aircraft, a half-dozen AK-47 rounds shattered his side window. "Hot shit!" Overreacting, he turned the small airplane hard away from the ground fire and nearly crashed in the top of a giant mahogany tree.

The platoon had just gained two more Nung commandos, making the total of survivors seven, with the captain seriously wounded. The platoon NCO allowed for the Nungs to act as guards as he carried the captain back toward the river.

The firefight was just finishing its first hour. Casualties were very high on both sides, but the NVA sapper unit had suffered the most casualties because they had underestimated the size of the American force and had exposed themselves to grazing fire.

Goldsmith was sitting with his back pressed against the granite, listening to the occasional piece of bomb shrapnel that whistled over their heads. Some small-arms rounds had ricocheted off the rocks, but they were rare because of the dense jungle.

Goldsmith leaned over to speak in Tyriver's ear: "I think we should get out of here. The NVA will be swarming all over this place in a couple of hours. That's more than a squad the Hatchet Platoon has bitten into."

Tyriver shook his head. "A river crossing would be too dangerous during daylight."

"We can move along the riverbank until we've cleared this area. Any more NVA will be sticking to their trails to support whoever locked horns with Abou."

"Let's do it!" Tyriver was nervous even though they were well protected. He knew that the NVA would be sweeping the entire area around the battle site for at least a thousand meters searching for survivors, and they would be caught up in the sweep. The lieutenant was right: if they were going to be able to stay behind after what ever remained of the Hatchet Platoon was extracted, they had to be at least a thousand meters farther north.

Y-Clack took the point. No one had to tell the Montagnards that they were now moving through some very dangerous territory. They had heard the intensity of the firefight and knew there was a large NVA force roaming through the surrounding jungle.

The Hatchet Platoon's NCO took over completely from the captain, who was slipping in and out of consciousness. He decided on making a dangerous run for it along the riverbank. There were large portions of the river's edge that was made up of gravel deposits less than a foot underwater. He figured they could make faster time moving through the shallows, even though they would be exposed and easily spotted by any NVA observer who was watching from the other side of the river. He also figured that the NVA already knew they were there, and their only hope of making it out of the area alive depended on how fast they could get away from the battle site and call in for a STABO extraction. All of the commandos wore the STABO extraction gear as a part of their webgear. There wouldn't be enough time to blast a landing zone out of the jungle, and they were going to have to rely on ropes being dropped through the thick vegetation by hovering helicopters and being pulled up.

The NVA company commander saw a blood trail leading from the battle site toward the river. It was obvious from the matted-down area that a fairly numerous element had escaped in that direction. He formed up a hasty platoon and started after the Americans. The NVA captain had fifteen men with him when he broke out on the riverbank and took off at a lope over the rocks. He knew the escapees could be only a few hundred meters ahead of him and at least a couple of them were seriously wounded.

Water erupted a few scant feet ahead of him, and then the sharp crack of an AK-47 reached his ears. The NCO staggered and fell against the muddy riverbank, nearly dropping Captain Abou. The river turned a little to his right and gave the small group of Nungs a little cover. The NCO, seeing a deer trail leaving the riverbank a few meters ahead, decided on trying to make it to the trail and from there putting up a last-ditch fight. Two of the

Nungs hung back and acted as a rear guard until the NCO reached the trail, and then they ran as hard as they could to catch up.

The NVA captain had seen the seven-man party for only a couple of seconds on the river's edge ahead. One of his men had gotten off a shot before he could stop him. He had wanted to close the gap between them, hoping that the Americans would give up and surrender. Now that they had been alerted, he knew that they would fight. He slowed his patrol to a fast walk and moved forward with caution.

Goldsmith's team had heard the sound of people coming up the riverbank from the south and assumed that they were NVA. He signaled for his men to take cover. Goldsmith planned on letting the enemy unit pass by and remain hidden, but when he saw Captain Abou on the back of his NCO, Goldsmith nearly called out. If not for the bullet splashing out in the river, he would have given away his position. But as soon as he realized NVA force was following, he decided instantly that he would use his RT to ambush the NVA. It was obvious that Abou's survivors couldn't move much farther up the river and needed time to set up an extraction.

Goldsmith used hand signals to alert his team to spread out for an ambush. He removed his silenced pistol from its holster and held a spare clip in his free hand. The NVA would have to pass within twenty feet of their location, and that was prime range for his pistol. The prearranged signal to set off an ambush would be his first shot. Goldsmith held the center position and he would wait until enough of the NVA passed his location to supply targets for the two men to his right. He hadn't even settled into his ambush position when the first NVA appeared, hugging the undergrowth of the riverbank. There were only two men in the point element, which was a hopeful sign that the NVA unit was not very large.

Goldsmith waited until the first man appeared from what looked like the main body of the NVA unit before shooting. The soldier dropped dead in the shallow water without making a sound. Two more NVA appeared and stopped to help their comrade get back up on his feet.

Goldsmith killed both of them before a short burst of AK-47 fire raked the jungle above his head. The NVA were firing wildly, without a target to shoot at. There was another short burst and then everything became quiet again.

Goldsmith stepped out from his hiding place. It was creepy how quiet everything was as he looked down at the NVA bodies being swept downstream in the river current. The rest of his team joined him, and then it dawned on Goldsmith why it was so creepy. They had all used silenced weapons.

Tyriver moved back downstream for a couple of meters to make sure that there wasn't another NVA unit following the one they had eliminated so swiftly.

The NVA captain's body bounced over the rocks and was just about to be sucked into the main current when Goldsmith recognized the red collar tabs and grabbed the sleeve of the uniform. He went through the captain's pockets and removed everything, including his wallet and one of his collar tabs to confirm the identity of his rank, before giving the body a shove out into the current.

Tyriver, his Swedish-K pointing at the far river-back, nudged Goldsmith and nodded that it was time they took cover. The sound of the AK-47's short bursts might draw unwanted attention from the other side of the river. Tyriver patted the side of his silenced 9mm sub-machine gun; using silenced weapons had been a very good idea. Anyone who had been listening would have heard only NVA weapons firing and easily mistaken the sound as a jumpy patrol.

Abou groaned when he heard the sound of NVA automatic weapons so close behind them. He knew that it was only a matter of time before the NVA caught up to them. He moaned again at the pain coming from his shoulder. The bullet that had gone through his side wasn't causing much pain at all and that scared him. Pain meant that something was wrong with your body. No pain when you knew that you had been hit meant that something important wasn't working.

"Sergeant, put me down. I'll act as your rear guard, and maybe you and the rest of our men can break free," Abou said, releasing his hold around the sergeant's neck.

"Bullshit, Captain! I haven't left a teammate behind yet, and I'm not planning on starting now. Not alive!"

"That's an order, Sergeant!"

"Well, pardon me, Captain, but fuck you!" The sergeant signaled with both of his hands for the Nung commandos to form a loose skirmish line. He spoke loudly enough for all of the English-speaking Nungs to hear him. "Do not open fire until I do. If they pass us by, we might have a chance." The NCO grimaced and looked back down the trail they had just made. If the NVA came, he would fight to the death. It was a hell of a lot better than carrying the muscle-bound captain through the jungle on his back.

Abou rolled over onto his stomach and removed his fourteen-round Browning 9mm from his holster. He had lost his CAR-15 back at the firefight when he had taken the round through his shoulder and his sergeant tried putting a hasty bandage on his wound.

Tyriver and Y-Brei would have died if the platoon sergeant hadn't decided to hold his fire. Tyriver had taken the point for the recon team and followed the blood trail Captain Abou was leaving. The platoon sergeant left the trail at a backward angle so that any tracker would have to look back over his shoulder to see the exit.

Tyriver was too intent on following the blood trail to notice that the sergeant was watching him from less than ten feet away.

"Ty!"

The sound of the American voice saying his name froze Tyriver. He searched the jungle for the owner of the voice but couldn't locate him.

"Ty, over here!" The platoon sergeant pushed a large-leafed plant away from his face and beckoned for Tyriver to join him.

Tyriver in turn signaled back down the trail that he had found the platoon survivors, and Goldsmith moved forward.

Goldsmith didn't waste any time taking over the team. "There's a place on the map that shows a possible STABO extraction site only a few meters north of here. Let's go! Tyriver, help with Abou." Then he signaled for the Nungs to move out quickly. There was no contesting

Goldsmith's command and the men obeyed without question.

The SOG Command and Control North area-studies team had done their work extremely well. The detailed map of their area had been updated from aerial photographs and covered with symbols that gave a tremendous amount of information to the recon team leader on the ground. That was the primary reason why the maps were intentionally kept small, covering only a ten thousand-square-meter area, so that the map could be easily destroyed in the event the team leader felt it was necessary to do so.

Goldsmith's map was correct. Within twenty minutes he found the open area in the jungle. It wasn't more than a hundred feet across, having been formed from an old B-52 Arc Light's two thousand-pound bomb.

"Bird Dog 5, this is Massasauga One-One, over."

"Roger, Massasauga. Send your transmission, over."

"I'm at site twenty-three and I need a STABO extraction for seven, over."

"Roger, Massasauga. I have a STABO team standing by. They will reach your location in zero-five mikes, over." The FAC pilot had called ahead for a team capable of ground extractions, medevacs, or STABO extractions. The choppers had been rigged at the Quang Tri launch site and were manned by SOG men. "We also have two Brightlight teams standing by. Do you need assistance on the ground, over?" The FAC was referring to the special SOG teams designed to enter a very hot area to rescue a recon team too shot up to conduct their own extraction.

"Negative. I say again, negative with the Brightlight, over." Goldsmith looked over at Tyriver and said so that no one else could hear, "You can go out with Abou and his people if you like, David—no hard feelings. What I plan on doing is a little risky, and I can't order you to come along."

"Are you going to still stay behind?" Tyriver asked, surprised. He had assumed that RT Massasauga would be STABO-ing out along with the survivors of the platoon. They had performed better than any other recon team, and if they left now, no one would say that they had chickened out.

"It's personal, David. I just can't leave now without knowing for sure if those five POWs I saw last month are really dead."

"If it's personal for you, then it's personal for me too. I stay!"

The roar of the arriving extraction choppers cut the conversation short. Tyriver started helping the Nungs rig themselves for hanging from under the helicopters on long strands of nylon rope. The ropes were pre-cut to sixty-foot lengths and had sandbags attached to one end using D-rings so that the rope would hang straight down under the chopper. Two ropes were dropped out of each side of the choppers, and they could extract four fully loaded commandos at a time.

Goldsmith tore the tape away from the leg straps that had been folded and attached to Abou's pistol belt. He hooked the snaps together so that the harness would bear the captain's weight. Abou couldn't stand up for the extraction and was too weak from loss of blood to do much more than watch the lieutenant he hated save his life.

Goldsmith worked quickly, using both hands to hook as much of the captain's gear as possible to the extraction rigging. Looking up, he saw that the platoon sergeant had already popped yellow smoke and had two of his Nungs standing with their backs to each other about five feet apart. Goldsmith grabbed Abou by the back of his STABO harness and dragged him over to the spot that had been left for him. The chopper dropped out of the sky and ropes attached to sandbags flew out the open doors. Goldsmith grabbed one of the sandbags and unhooked it. In almost the same motion he attached one of the snap links to a D-ring on Abou's left shoulder and then quickly attached the second D-ring to the rope. He looked up: the helicopter's crew chief was watching from his position next to the door gunner.

By now four men were all rigged and standing with their legs spread apart to keep their balance in the prop wash. They had all linked arms, including Captain Abou, but they had their CAR-15s ready to fire when they were lifted up over the tops of the jungle canopy.

Goldsmith signaled for the chopper to lift off and his gaze locked for a couple of seconds with Abou's. He could see that the senior officer was saying, in his own way, that he was sorry.

Goldsmith smiled and winked at the wounded officer. They had made friends the hard way.

The second chopper, which had been hovering in the distance, darted over to pick up the remaining survivors from the Hatchet Platoon. Goldsmith glanced over at Tyriver. There was one string empty.

Tyriver shook his head violently and waved the chopper away. The three men hanging from the bottom of the chopper lifted off the ground for about five feet and then the chopper lost power. They came down hard on the ground, ramming their knees up against their chests before they could lock their leg muscles. The pilot gained control again and applied more power for the lift-off.

RT Massasauga watched the commandos disappear into the bright blue patch of sky. They would ride underneath the chopper for the whole forty-five-minute flight to the SOG launch site, located at Quang Tri. The instant the chopper was out of sight, the RT assembled and moved off toward the river. They all knew that the extraction would bring NVA soldiers to investigate, but at the same time the extraction gave the stay-behind team extra cover. The NVA wouldn't believe that an American recon team would have conducted a double stay-behind during one mission!

The forward air controller banked away from the site of the firefight. He was low on fuel, and with the extraction of what he thought was the stay-behind recon team, he had decided to leave the area, rearm his under-wing rockets, and get fuel at the SOG launch site.

Goldsmith didn't know that his air cover was leaving. He was concentrating on getting his team as far away from the area as possible before darkness fell.

The commander of the 10th Sapper Battalion sat at the edge of his bunker and listened to the sound of the battle. He loved the smell of cordite, and after fighting for over twenty-five years, he felt absolutely no fear. A runner approached him from the side and slowed to a tentative halt. The commander knew that the man was bringing him bad news. They always ran all the way up to him if the news was good.

"Well?" he asked gruffly.

"We have only three survivors from the 102nd Company. They took the brunt of the fighting and were struck twice with napalm." The soldier kept looking down at his feet as he talked. "The 409th Company did very well. They captured five Nung traitors and two American advisers!"

"Bring them to me!" Anger dripped from the NVA commander's words. He had taken over one hundred and ten dead sappers in the infantry assault, and his reports told him that he had at least the same number of wounded. He knew that it would be at least a month before replacements were shipped down from Hanoi. Sappers were highly trained saboteurs who had been handpicked from combat units in the south and shipped to Hanoi for over a year of specialized training. His battalion had been selected to work the whole I Corps area of South Vietnam, and his loss was much greater than just losing infantrymen.

Another messenger approached, holding his head down. He stopped five feet away from the commander and waited for permission to speak. A series of bombs going off in the distance kept the lieutenant colonel from speaking, and then he merely nodded his head.

"We found the body of the 102nd commander floating in the river, along with ten more of his company."

The commander waved for the man to leave him. It was good that the company commander had died after losing his whole command.

The noise from the trail leading toward the former fighting drew his attention in that direction. He saw his soldiers prodding prisoners along using their bayonets. The two Americans appeared and then five Nungs, who glared at him, knowing that their fate was already sealed. They knew from prior experience that any sign of fear would cause their immediate execution.

Taking his time, the battalion commander slipped off the roof of his bunker and adjusted his uniform before

strolling toward the waiting prisoners. The guards had
forced the seven men onto their knees by pushing down
on fresh-cut bamboo poles tied to their arms and running
behind their heads. All of their jungle boots had been
removed, and their uniforms had been stripped of every
item, including their belts.

The two Americans seemed to be in shock, still not
believing that they had actually been captured.

The NVA commander walked down the line, starting
with the Nungs. He paused in front of each one and
exchanged stares. The instant the Nungs had seen him
sitting on the bunker they knew that they were in serious
trouble. The NVA lieutenant colonel was also a Chinese
Nung.

When the commander approached the last commando,
the Nung whispered something. The NVA colonel stopped
and leaned forward so that the Nung could repeat what
he had said. A look of surprise crossed the commander's
face, and he barked out orders to have the man released.

One of the guards cut the Nung free from the bamboo
pole, and another ran forward and handed the Nung his
rucksack and weapon. The Nung nearest him kicked out
sideways and caught his ex-comrade in his side with his
callused foot. "Spy! Traitor!" he screamed. Everyone in
the clearing heard the man's ribs break.

The NVA commander removed his Russian-made pistol and shot the Nung in the head. Brains and blood
splattered against the side of the nearest American, who
looked on in shock. It would be a couple weeks later
before the Americans figured out what had happened.
The Nung who was released with all of his gear was an
NVA spy assigned to the SOG program. He would eventually find his way back to Da Nang and tell a story of
evading the NVA all the way back to the coast. He would
be believed. This had happened before, and the American sergeants would be left wondering how many other
commandos who had "miraculously" escaped were also
NVA spies.

The splattered American prisoner dropped his head.
He could not remove the Nung's blood from his face,
and none of the NVA guards would do it. Wishing he
was dead, he tried struggling to his feet and lunging at

the commander, but the guards were ready and pushed him back to the ground.

"So, Americans, what unit are you with?" The commander spoke English with a thick French accent.

"Fuck you!" the younger sergeant spat.

The commander arched an eyebrow and sneered at the young man. "Fucking is something you will never do again." The words carried so much finality that the sergeant also dropped his gaze and stared at the red laterite earth at his knees. It hit him totally: he was now a prisoner of war.

CHAPTER ELEVEN

✪✪✪✪✪✪✪✪✪✪✪✪✪✪✪✪✪✪✪

QUANG TRI
LAUNCH SITE

The side of the helipad was lined with area-studies team members who had planned the mission and had flown in from Da Nang as soon as they had heard about the disaster with Abou's Hatchet Platoon. It was common for a small recon team to get wiped out, but this was the first time that anyone could remember when a powerful Nung platoon had suffered so many casualties.

Major Ricks stood in the doorway of the command hootch, listening to the traffic on the radio. He heard the extraction pilots talking to each other, and he knew that so far there were only seven survivors of the forty men. The only factor making the huge loss even tolerable was the fact that the underwater bridge had been destroyed.

"They're five minutes out, sir. Do you want to meet the chopper?" a sandy-haired captain asked from inside the plywood hootch, which fulfilled the need for a control tower.

"No, there are enough people out there on the helipad now. I want all of the Americans who aren't wounded brought over her for a debriefing as soon as they touch down." Ricks shaded his eyes and looked west. He could just barely make out the tiny men hanging beneath the helicopters on invisible strings.

The captain left the hootch and started running toward the pad. Ricks called after him. "Captain Atkins! Bring them in here first!"

158

The captain kept running but waved his hand to confirm that he had heard the order. He knew what the major was up to. Lieutenant Colonel MacCall had arrived only a few minutes earlier with a chopper full of observers from Saigon, and Major Ricks wanted to make sure that the returning men were properly debriefed before stories became confused or were changed after the men had a few minutes to talk to one another.

The first chopper approaching the helipad was carrying Captain Abou. The medical team standing by didn't even waste the time trying to unhook his STABO rig. They cut the rope and slipped the wounded captain onto a stretcher for his ride over to the hospital substation, only a few hundred meters away. One of the SOG medics used a pair of tin snips to cut through the captain's web-gear, while another used scissors to cut the laces in the captain's boots, then along the seams of the captain's trousers and shirt so that his clothes could be pulled away from his body without disturbing him too much. The first medic identified the captain's wounds and used a jerry-rigged hose inside the Army ambulance to wash the mud and dirt from the captain's body. When they reached the nearby hospital, the only thing the Army medics and doctors would see was a naked, wounded soldier without any kind of identification. One of the SOG medics would stay with the captain to make sure that nothing was said while the officer was anesthetized. Furthermore, a SOG man would remain with the captain around the clock to make sure nothing was accidentally said when the officer was coming out from under his medication. As soon as Abou could be moved, he would be transferred to the commando hospital within the CCN compound and cared for by SOG doctors and medics until he was healed. The regular Army medical personnel hated the way that SOG people interfered with their hospital's operation, but the MACV commander himself had signed the orders as to what procedures would be followed with MAC-SOG patients.

Lieutenant Colonel MacCall and his friends from Saigon followed the stretcher carrying Captain Abou over to the ambulance. They tried talking to him while Captain Atkins hurried the platoon sergeant over to where Major Ricks was waiting.

Ricks handed the sergeant a cold beer. "Sounds like you guys found the tiger."

"Yes, sir." The sergeant drained the beer and closed his eyes for a couple of seconds. "We got the bridge, sir."

"I heard. What happened?"

"We must have slipped in between their defenses to reach the bridge because as soon as we blew that sucker, all hell broke loose!" The sergeant took another beer offered by one of the NCOs operating the bank of radios in the hootch. He nodded his thanks and continued talking to the major. "We wouldn't have gotten the bridge if it hadn't been for that lieutenant."

Major Ricks' eyebrows popped up and he suppressed a grin. "The lieutenant?"

"Yes, sir, he convinced my captain to set the charges instead of taking out a small NVA outpost. If we had waited, we would have made contact and not been able to reach the bridge."

"Where—where's RT Massasauga now?" Ricks asked, hesitating.

"The RT rigged us for extraction and stayed behind."

"What?" Captain Atkins asked from behind the major.

"His mission was to stay behind, and he took his option, sir." The sergeant finished his second beer and felt the relaxing effects of the booze already. "That L.T. has elephant balls!"

Ricks looked back at Atkins. "Does the FAC know there is still a functioning team on the ground?"

"I'll soon find out, sir." Atkins motioned with his hand, and one of the radio operators called the FAC control center.

"Before I forget, sir. We saw a number of orange panels when we were being lifted out."

Atkins had been a launch commander for over two years at Quang Tri and was one step ahead of the major. "I'll have Brightlight teams launched now, sir!"

The orange panels were issued to every man on a patrol and were to be used after a firefight to signal for extractions if they were separated from the main group.

Sometimes the NVA would use a captured commando as a decoy with his panel to draw in rescue helicopters and then shoot them down, so SOG Brightlight teams were used for all rescue missions and were backed up with a platoon of four Huey Cobra gunships. Over the years a system had been worked out so that a series of panel flashes were used to tell the rescue teams if it was safe to land for the pickup. One side of the panel was a bright orange and the backside a bright iridescent pink. The SOG communications people had worked out a Morse code using the orange side for dots and the pink side for dashes. Before a mission every man was taught the codes for that particular patrol. A single letter in the Morse code alphabet would be used to signal that it was safe to land and another letter meant that the NVA were nearby and the area should be attacked surrounding him. The wrong code or no code at all meant that an NVA soldier was wearing a commando uniform and trying to lure the choppers down. The system had been refined and was so effective that the NVA had given up trying to decoy American choppers, except at night when the commandos were instructed to use their strobe lights instead of the panels.

"It might not be as bad as it first looked." Ricks rubbed his chin. "How many panels did you see?"

"We left the area flying fast and low, sir, but I figure that I saw five or six."

"There should be more. Atkins, have all of their assembly points checked before dark."

"Yes, sir!" Atkins left the briefing and started to personally call his contacts with the 1st Cav and the 101st Airborne Division. They were going to need a large force to pull off the rescue attempt in such a short time, and he wanted pilots who had flown for them before so that SOG men didn't have to fly aboard each chopper. A lot of time would be saved, a prime consideration since it would be getting dark in a few hours.

Just then MacCall entered the hootch, followed by his entourage from Saigon. "Ricks, why didn't you tell me that you were conducting a briefing in here?"

"Sorry, sir, we've got a lot going on and I forgot you were here." Major Ricks went on quickly so that the colonel wouldn't have time to chew his ass: "We've spotted orange panels all around the battle site, and Captain Atkins is assembling as many Brightlight teams as possible before dark."

"Major, do you need the use of my chopper?" one of the Saigon colonels asked from the doorway.

"Yes, sir, that would save time and we could put one of my launch-site men on it," Atkins said from the bank of radios, where he was holding a handset.

"Good! It's refueled and ready to go. Would you mind if I rode along—as an observer only, of course. I don't mean to interfere with your operation." The colonel adjusted the belt with his .45-caliber pistol. Atkins saw at once that its black leather holster hadn't seen much wear.

"Sure, Colonel, but you'd better carry this." Atkins handed the colonel his CAR-15 and a belt of magazines.

"Do you really want to go out there yourself, sir?" MacCall saw from the looks of the other Saigon officers that they were none too anxious to fly out to the secret AO, especially when it was across the border in Laos. "Your chopper is our only ride back to Da Nang."

"You can wait here for me or catch another ride back. It seems that there is an emergency here, and they need the aircraft."

MacCall tried grinning, but his upper lip was trembling too much. "We are always having emergencies out here, sir."

The full colonel outranked MacCall, as well as everybody else who had come up from Saigon, and he snapped, "I'm going, MacCall. We'll be back right after dark."

Captain Atkins flashed Major Ricks a look and then smiled. They both knew what was going on, but it was a game that was not talked about in the SOG compound. "I'll ride with the colonel, sir. My XO can handle things back here."

"Fine. You're the launch-site commander," Ricks said, respecting Atkins' decision to go wherever he felt he should in his area of responsibility. Launch commanders had full authority to do whatever they felt was necessary when their teams were in danger or in contact with the enemy.

The Saigon colonel handed back Atkins' CAR-15, but the captain only grinned and removed a shotgun and a Claymore bag full of shotgun shells from the weapons rack near the exit door. "Let's go and eat up some glory, sir!"

The Saigon colonel paused in the doorway and looked back at the SOG commander. "You sure you don't want to come along, MacCall?"

"Thanks anyway, but you've already got enough straphangers with you." MacCall was referring to Atkins. Major Ricks knew why the captain had decided on going: not as one of the hated staff straphangers but as a bodyguard to the brave but naive Saigon colonel. The chances of the chopper being shot down were very high, and the colonel wouldn't have a chance of survival alone in the Laotian jungle. Little did he know that his capture would be a major victory for the NVA.

Ricks stood in the doorway until the helicopter had joined the flight of gunships and disappeared in the western sky. He turned around slowly and said to his boss, "Lieutenant Goldsmith set up the extraction for Captain Abou's people and then decided to stay behind."

MacCall's eyes widened in disbelief. He had assumed that RT Massasauga had stayed with the platoon and had been destroyed by the NVA. "What?"

"That was a part of his mission, if you recall, Jack." Ricks enjoyed calling his superior by his Christian name, especially in front of people MacCall was trying to impress. There was nothing MacCall could do to him. His career had already come to an end. Ricks would never get another promotion, and he was bright enough to know that once he had been put on the "do-not-promote" list, his name would never come off it. That was the reason he had joined the SOG program and stayed at the CCN site for over three years as the executive officer. The high command would always have a list of glory-seeking lieutenant colonels to command the operation, but every commander who had been appointed over him was smart enough to realize that Speedy Ricks was far more qualified to run the actual operations. MacCall had decided on working the public-relations end of the program. It was a sly move, for he had Ricks to blame for anything that went wrong in the program. And considering the extremely dangerous mission CCN had assigned to it, a lot of things could go wrong.

"He's actually going to try to locate those POW camps with all that NVA activity in the area?"

The platoon sergeant didn't bother to hide his look of contempt.

"Actually, Goldsmith is making a very smart move. All the activity is giving him a diversion. The NVA will not suspect that an American team had a special mission in addition to destroying the underwater bridge. He's got a better than fifty-fifty chance on making it to his new AO." Ricks went over to the launch-site map. "If he's just a little bit lucky, he can cross the river tonight and be inside of his AO before nightfall tomorrow." Ricks looked back at the platoon sergeant. "Were any of RT Massasauga wounded?"

"No, sir, not that I could see."

"Good! Very, very good!" Ricks eyed the target AO for Goldsmith's team and grinned. The kid had elephant nuts to try to pull this off, but he was also a hell of a lot smarter than he projected. Ricks would have to remember that when Goldsmith's team returned.

One of the VRC-47 radios started crackling and a loud voice came over the speaker. Two of the pilots were talking to each other, and Captain Atkins' voice broke through the chatter to provide information to the nervous crews on the choppers. No one wanted to land in the Laotian countryside for a lone commando, and Atkins was trying to give the pilots confidence.

"See it?"

"Where?"

"To our left front about ten o'clock. It's an orange panel."

"Roger, ten o'clock!" The pilot banked his helicopter for another look. "What was that code again?"

Atkins' voice came on over the air: "The letter R."

"What in the fuck is that?"

"You'll see him flash orange, then pink, then orange

again, in that order. He'll pause and repeat the code again. Orange, pink, orange—"

"I see it!" one of the door gunners cut in on the open channel. "Orange . . . pink and orange! He's one of ours!"

"Let's go get him!" The open-doored chopper banked hard and almost went into a nose dive before leveling off and dropping so that the lone commando could climb in. The crew chief had to help him up over the side of the floorboard. The commando was favoring his side, suffering from a few broken ribs.

"Look, three o'clock! Another panel!" The weapons man in a Huey Cobra above the chopper picking up the commando spotted a new panel. "It's not the same code, though: pink, orange, pink, orange."

Captain Atkins' voice cut into the communications: "They're in danger! Where are they?"

"Can you see us circling?" the Cobra pilot said, scanning the sky for Atkins' chopper.

"Roger!" Atkins was leaning way out of the chopper door on his safety strap. "Listen, circle the area with fire! He's signaling that he's surrounded and can't move!"

"Roger!" The Cobra pilot lined up for a pass and opened up with his mini-gun.

"There are five of them!"

Two more Huey Cobras joined the first and made team passes over five men who were lying down in elephant grass with their feet spread apart, touching each other. They formed an almost perfect star. The pilots saw that the men were firing at something and continued making their gun runs, clearing the area for a hundred meters around the group.

"We need a slick to pick them up."

"We're the closest." It was Captain Atkins' voice again, and the men listening in the launch-site hootch all smiled. Their commander sounded like John Wayne. "Are you for it, sir?"

"The Saigon colonel's voice came over the air. "Absolutely!"

MacCall felt his face getting warm as he listened to the

166 DONALD E. ZLOTNIK

staff officer's voice. He knew that he should have been
in that chopper instead.

The action quickly became so intense that Atkins forgot to turn off his headset, and he yelled over the air
without knowing that his words were being broadcast.
"Just *pull* him in the chopper, Colonel! We can be fucking gentle later! Move your asses! *Move it! Move it!* In
here!" There was a slight pause. "Get the fuck gone!"

The slick pilot's voice came on the air: "Did we get
them all?"

"Roger, let's get home! Low-level this crate until we
get far enough away!"

"Roger that, Wild Bill!" the pilot cried, referring to
Atkins by his old nickname.

"Fuck you! You owe me a beer!"

"For what?" The pilot's voice reflected the relief that
they were flying away from the area.

"For scaring the shit out of me with that fucking nose-
dive! This ain't a fucking jet!"

The launch-site team were all smiling as they listened
to the small talk over the radio.

"It might not be as bad as we thought," Ricks said to
MacCall. "It we can find a few more of the platoon."

MacCall nodded in agreement. For some reason he
was terrified, and he hadn't even been in the chopper.

A thin line of black smoke trailed the helicopter carrying Atkins and the platoon survivors. The chopper
landed hard on the PSP pad, behind a helicopter that
had landed only a few seconds earlier to deliver the single
injured commando they had rescued. Medics from the
launch site were removing the Nung's shirt when the five
survivors rescued by Atkins and the Saigon colonel stumbled past.

One of the rescued Americans broke away from the
group. He recognized the scar on the Nung's chin.
"Aren't you in O'Mallory's squad!"

The Nung shook his head violently.

"Yes, you are! I remember seeing you out on the rifle
range with O'Mallory!"

"Come on, Sarge, let's get over to the hootch and
debrief the major," Atkins said, grabbing the sergeant's
arm and directing him away from the wounded Nung.

He waited until they were almost to the hootch before speaking again. "What does his being in O'Mallory's squad have to do with anything?"

The sergeant's voice filled with emotion: "Ruiz and I were trying to slip behind the NVA after we had gotten separated from the platoon. We saw an NVA team tying O'Mallory and McDonald to bamboo poles. They had been captured." The sergeant looked Atkins square in the eye and added, "There were too many NVA around the area for us to rescue them."

Atkins nodded in agreement. It was always easier to be judgmental when you were safe inside of a large base camp. "What happened with the Nung?"

"He was being tied up with them! *He had been captured!*" The sergeant looked back over his shoulder at the Nung, now being carried away on the stretcher.

"Are you sure?" Atkins' eyes narrowed to slits.

"Positive! That scar on his chin—I remember it because it's so large. You would think whatever had caused it would have taken the bottom half of his head with it." The sergeant was taking a step toward the wounded Nung when Atkins stopped him.

"Let me take care of this, Sergeant."

"He told me that he wasn't in O'Mallory's squad, which is a fucking lie! Why would he lie about something like that?"

"Maybe he was surprised that you survived the fight and recognized him. Do you think he knows that you saw him with O'Mallory and McDonald being tied up?"

"Hell, no!"

"Good, then let me follow up on this. We might have something very nasty going on." With that, Atkins hurried away to find Major Ricks and brief him on what the sergeant had told him.

Five days had passed since Abou's Hatchet Platoon had made contact with the NVA. Listening posts in Laos had intercepted NVA radio messages that had the losses for the 10th Sapper Battalion, and the numbers were impressive considering that the elite NVA unit had run into a platoon. The encounter was one of the few fights during the war when the NVA had controlled the area and had numerical superiority at the same time. The official NVA reports listed 133 NVA soldiers KIA and 171 WIA, due mostly to the air strikes. They listed over two hundred Americans killed in action and two Americans captured.

Major Ricks held the translated NVA report in his hand. After reading it, he had rolled it up and tapped his desktop thoughtfully. Captain Abou sat across from him, waiting patiently for the CCN executive officer to speak. He was having a difficult time reading the senior officer.

Ricks looked up at Abou as if he had just realized the captain was there. "So—Abou. What do you think?"

"About what, sir?"

"These figures the NVA have reported to their HQ."

Abou twisted his lips and seemed to give the matter a lot of thought before speaking. "I think my platoon kicked a lot of ass!"

Ricks nodded. "With the support of the United States Air Force, we should add."

Abou nodded in agreement. The Air Force's support had been superb.

"We still have seventeen Nungs unaccounted for and two Americans—sergeants O'Mallory and McDonald, our Irish twosome," Ricks said, referring to the nickname the two had been known by in the camp. They were always seen together and had taken a large amount of teasing from the other recon men because of it.

"I thought we listed them as POWs, sir."

"Yes, they were seen alive and captured by the NVA by members of the platoon—which brings up the matter of the Nung."

"Do *you* think he's a traitor, sir?"

"It's not a matter of what I think, it's what the facts point to."

"He's got a fantastic war record, with over fifteen confirmed kills. If he is an enemy agent, he's been killing his own people."

"He told Sergeant Riggs that he wasn't a member of O'Mallory's squad and he is."

"Maybe he was confused, sir. Riggs asked him in

English right after he had been rescued. The commando could have been confused."

Ricks nodded his head. "I'll give him the benefit of the doubt, but I think we should pay this Nung a visit. He doesn't know that Sergeant Riggs saw him tied to a bamboo pole along with O'Mallory and McDonald. Let's see what our commando has to say about being captured and then escaping. We've given him five days to relax and get his story straight."

"I agree, sir. We've got to clear the matter up. I'm thinking of promoting him to Nung platoon leader."

"Really?"

"Like I said, sir, he's a fighter and well respected by the rest of the Nungs." Abou winced from the pain in his shoulder as he tried getting to his feet. The stomach wound had been minor compared to this other wound. He wore his arm in a shoulder harness to prevent unwanted movement.

"You don't have to come with me if you're in pain," Ricks said, nodding at the captain's shoulder.

"Naw, keeping busy keeps my mind off it. Let's go. He's over at the platoon barracks. He suffered three broken ribs, but he's healing fast."

Ricks and Abou walked over to the platoon's longhouse without talking. Both men were gathering their thoughts for the interview, knowing that the Nung was not expecting it. Abou waved one of his platoon's interpreters over to the back door of the hootch and told him to bring the Nung outside with the Nung company commander.

Ricks lit a thin cigar and offered Abou one from his leather case. The smoke burned his nose, but he liked the strong smell of the tobacco. "I'll do all of the talking. You can support my line of questioning if you like, but let me lead." Ricks held the match out for Abou's cigar.

The Nung appeared at the door, and Ricks smiled. "Hello. I am here to talk about the big fight."

The Nung smiled back and nodded as the interpreter spoke.

"I would like to know about what happened to you in the fight. How did you hurt your side?"

The Nung, knowing that all SOG missions were debriefed in detail, wasn't suspicious about the major and captain coming to ask him questions. He dropped to a squat on the shady side of the longhouse and started telling his story. He paused often for the interpreter to translate for him. "I was with the point element when we made contact with a very big NVA force. We killed many of them, but there were many more following them on the trail. I lost sight of Sergeant O'Mallory and linked up with Sergeant McDonald. We fought hard and killed many NVA, and then the NVA surrounded us and we fought with our knives. I was fighting with one NVA soldier when another one hit me in the side with his rifle butt. That is how my ribs were broken. I escaped by fighting very hard and got separated from my squad. I fought my way through the NVA until I was alone in the elephant grass, and then I used my orange panel to signal for help. That is my story."

The Nung company commander had been listening to his soldier speaking in Chinese to the interpreter and had been drawing Chinese letters in the sand. He looked up when the major spoke. He spoke English well, but he waited for the Chinese translation just to be sure that he had heard correctly.

"Sergeant Riggs said that he saw you captured along with Sergeant O'Mallory, Sergeant McDonald, and a couple other Nungs."

A flash of panic passed over the Nung's face. "Oh, that's right—I forgot that part!"

"You were captured?" Ricks glanced over at the Nung commander and saw the anger in his eyes.

"Yes, but for only a short while. I escaped when they ignored me."

The Nung commander swiftly removed his .45-caliber pistol and shot the Nung traitor above his left ear. The right half of the man's head disappeared.

"Damn! I wish you hadn't done that!" Major Ricks shouted, taking a step back.

The Nung commander was yelling so loud and so fast that the interpreter gave up trying to translate. He waited until the commander slowed down to catch his breath and said, "My captain is very angry. He is a traitor to the Nung people!"

"I wonder how many more of our men are working for the other side," Ricks said in a low voice to Abou. "This could be a real problem for us." Suspiciously he eyed the Nung commander kicking the body of the dead traitor. The man's anger seemed genuine, but it was still possible that the Nung leader had killed the commando to keep him from talking. Ricks felt himself becoming a little paranoid, but paranoia if kept under control kept you alive in combat. "Let's run a check on how many of our commandos mysteriously reappeared after a firefight in the jungle."

"That happens all of the time, sir! It wouldn't be fair to question every commando who's survived a firefight!"

"True, but we've grown a little lax with our Chinese Nungs. Because they originally hated the Vietnamese, we've assumed that they are loyal to us." Ricks spoke in a low voice so that neither the Nung commander nor the interpreter could hear him.

"Well, if they get wind that we don't trust them, I think we'll lose the whole lot of them. They'll desert as a unit!" Abou was sticking up for his Nungs, but deep inside he was starting to wonder himself. He had been about to make that Nung traitor his platoon leader.

"Let's move slow. We might have to bring in some polygraph experts and test the whole fucking camp." Ricks spoke as if he was only thinking about the idea, but he had actually made up his mind to do just that. Double agents would have layers of covers to protect them. He was beginning to get angry at himself for falling for the Nung myth of loyalty to their paymasters. "Stay here, Captain, and make sure that body is taken care of. Say that he died in a training accident and have our medics sterilize the body. We don't want rumors starting that we assassinate double agents and spies—do we?"

Abou shook his head and stared down at the Nung with half of his head missing.

He walked through the double doors and nodded over at the two military policemen who stood behind the shellacked wooden desk. For a second he paused to look back at the sign over the doors: "STUDIES AND OBSERVATION AUGMENTATION."

The military policemen came to attention, and the gray-haired colonel smiled. "I'll be down the hall if I'm needed."

"Yes, sir!" The senior MP quickly scribbled down the location of the SOG commander in case he was called at the desk.

Colonel Shunball took his time walking down the long hallway, carrying a large manila envelope at his side. He was in his element: he knew how the game was played in the large headquarters building. Where your office was located could carry more weight than the rank on your collar, and the SOG offices that he commanded occupied the end of the long hallway, at the opposite end from the MACV commander. If you couldn't have the office next to the four-star general, then having the offices at the opposite end was next best because every time the commander of all of the American forces in Vietnam left his office, he saw your unit's logo.

Shunball stopped halfway down the hall and entered a set of offices composed of two rooms: one for three sergeants and two junior officers and a section in the corner that had been subdivided by Plexiglas to give the colonel privacy. The walls were lined with charts that were covered with figures and highlighted with subtotals and estimates. The office controlled the budget for the entire Vietnam War.

Colonel Shunball leaned against the door frame and waited until a young bespectacled major finished briefing his colonel on the fuel figures for the IV Corps area. Finally he held up the manila envelope. "I heard that you found the time to visit our Quang Tri launch site up north."

"Yes, I did, Shunball, and I must say that I was very impressed with the courage of your people—especially a young captain named Atkins."

"MacCall told me that you not only loaned us your helicopter but even rode along during an actual rescue mission. I'm impressed, and I guess so was Captain Atkins and Lieutenant Colonel MacCall." Shunball took his time placing the sealed envelope on the colonel's desk.

"What's in there? Another one of your requests for

special funds?" The staff colonel immediately put on his financial expert's hat. He knew that the SOG commander had invited him out to a SOG field location to butter him up, trying to keep the blank-check door open for the program. There were only four special programs in South Vietnam that had blank-check privileges, and the SOG programs spent more money than the other three combined. He had been trying to turn off the money flow to the program since he had arrived in Saigon.

"Open it and see. It arrived just this morning from Da Nang." Shunball crossed his arms over his chest, just below the seven rows of ribbons he wore on the left side and the display of badges that covered the right pocket. Wearing a field uniform or khakis was optional on the staff, and Shunball always chose to wear his khakis so that he could show off his ribbons. He enjoyed watching the eyes of fellow staff officers when they talked to him. Eventually the other man's gaze would float down to his ribbons and he would see their envy.

Shunball had served in the army with special units since World War II, but if someone had checked his personnel files—kept in a special file because of his assignment to SOG—they would have seen that all of his valor awards had been issued in Vietnam.

The colonel tore open one end of the large envelope and dumped two blue leather boxes on top of his desk. He reached in the open end of the envelope and removed a quarter-inch-thick package of paperwork and military orders. "What's all this?"

"Read it. Like I said, it just came in with our special courier this morning." Shunball knew exactly what was inside the envelope. He had talked about it with MacCall only five days earlier and was impressed with the efficiency of the CCN commander's operation.

The colonel turned the blue boxes over to read what was stamped on the front, and Shunball heard the air catch in his throat. He was forced to suppress a smile as the colonel opened the first box slowly and then quickly opened the second box. He sat staring in at their contents and then looked away from the boxes and up at Shunball. "I ca—can't accept these awards!"

"Like I said, you must have impressed my people out at the launch site."

"But . . . a Silver Star!" The colonel reached over and picked up the open second blue leather box. "And a Purple Heart!" He quickly looked back at Shunball. "For what?"

"Obviously, the Purple Heart is for that cut you received while you were out on that recovery mission."

"But I cut my hand on something inside the helicopter!"

"Read your regulations!" Shunball allowed his voice to raise as if he was angry. "I hope that you aren't implying that we recommended you for awards that weren't justified. If you are—"

"No, no! I don't mean to offend your people. It's just that . . ."

Shunball smiled as he watched the staff officer staring at the two awards on his desk. "You might not think that you deserve those awards, but believe me, friend, my people would not have recommended a staff officer for a Silver Star if they didn't think you really deserved it. They hate staff officers!"

"I've got to send a message to Captain Atkins and thank him—"

"There's no need to do that. You'd just embarrass him. I'll tell Atkins the next time I see him. Shunball grinned and left the staff colonel alone to goggle over his awards. He smiled all the way back to his office. He was quite sure that he would have no problems in the future getting special funding.

CHAPTER TWELVE

✪✪✪✪✪✪✪✪✪✪✪✪✪✪✪✪✪✪✪✪✪

Y-BLUC'S VILLAGE

RT Massasauga had tried crossing the river three times during the past five days, but each time they had been stopped by NVA sightings during their observation of the selected fords.

Tyriver nudged Goldsmith with the toe of his boot. He had been watching the opposite side of the river, letting the Montagnards and the lieutenant sleep. What had caught his attention was the dark clouds forming upstream from the ford that Y-Bluc had found for them the night before. The middle-aged Yard had lived in that part of Laos as a young boy, and many of the landmarks were familiar to him.

Goldsmith pressed his mouth against Tyriver's ear to whisper, "Monsoon coming." The lieutenant's breath tickled the sergeant's ear and he shivered.

"The river will be rising soon. We're going to have to risk a crossing as soon as it gets dark or find someplace else."

It was Goldsmith's turn to feel the chill down his spine from the whisper placed directly in his ear.

Tyriver smiled and faked a kiss when Goldsmith looked his way. If a woman had done it to him, he would have considered it sexual foreplay, but in the hostile jungle it was a survival tactic. Goldsmith grinned back at Tyriver's attempt at humor and winked.

The exchange between the two momentarily eased the tremendous tension they had been under since they had inserted with the platoon.

"We cross here. Before the river rises up too high for our commandos to wade across."

Nodding, Tyriver slipped back from the edge of the river. He checked his Swedish-K to make sure that it was clean and the bolt operated smoothly, and then he removed a magazine from its carrying pouch and checked to make sure the 9mm rounds were lined up properly and wouldn't jam in the chamber of the submachine gun. He was keeping himself busy so that he wouldn't think about the huge gavials they had seen downstream in the river. He knew his fears were unfounded. Gavials were fish eaters and very shy creatures. He hadn't been too worried about a late-night river crossing when the water was only knee deep because he figured he could see the gavials coming, but if a monsoon upstream made the river rise to their chests, it would be a much different story. It was the way gavials looked. They looked just like crocodiles!

Goldsmith took Tyriver's spot on the riverbank and scanned in both directions. He saw the ripples where the rocky ford angled across the water, and then he looked along the opposite riverbank for any sign of NVA activity. The ford should have been watched by NVA trail watchers, but Y-Bluc said that his people kept this crossing site a secret for their own private use just in case they had to make a hurried retreat out of Laos or South Vietnam to avoid a major battle. The Montagnards lived a dangerous existence in the jungle trying to live between the NVA and the American forces. The South Vietnamese government tried keeping them in resettlement village, but the program only added to the problem, since the Montagnards seemed to wilt like a picked wildflower. Jungle villages were kept clean and so were their longhouses, but the Montagnards forced to live in settlements exchanged their beautiful jungle jackets and loincloths for discarded Vietnamese clothes that didn't fit them. What's more, they ended up picking through Vietnamese and American garbage dumps for their food. They were a wild people that were at home only in the highland jungles.

In thinking about the Montagnard tribes, Goldsmith hadn't been paying much attention to what was going on in front of him. When he finally realized that there were people crossing the river, they were already halfway across.

"Look! Get Y-Bluc!" Goldsmith's voice carried farther than he wanted it to and reached the spot where Y-Bluc had been curled up under a wide-leafed jungle plant trying to sleep. The Yard lifted his head and looked over at the lieutenant. Goldsmith beckoned for him to come to the riverbank.

Y-Bluc took only a glance at the river and then stood up. He waved and the Montagnard family smiled and waved back. The members of the recon team met the man and his wife, who was carrying a newborn baby in a sling around her neck, when they reached their side of the river.

Y-Bluc and the other two Montagnard commandos talked for a long time with the young man before Y-Brei turned toward Goldsmith and smiled. "This man is from Y-Bluc's old village. He is telling us that the village chief decided to move to this old camp before the monsoons came. The man tells us that there are no lowland soldiers near here." He pointed up and down the river before speaking again. "Many NVA where we come from, and there are many to the mountains. We can cross the river now if you like, Lieutenant. It is safe."

Goldsmith didn't like the idea of crossing a river in broad daylight, but the Montagnards knew what was going on around them in their jungle.

Y-Brei understood his lieutenant's concern and added as a convincing argument: "Y-Bluc's father is in this village and Y-Bluc is very happy!"

"Come on, Tyriver. Let's get our asses across the river." It felt strange talking in a normal tone of voice.

"Oh, thank the Lord! I wasn't looking forward to a night crossing with those damn gavials swimming around out there!"

Y-Bluc shook the young Montagnard's hand in both of his and then reached into his rucksack and gave the man a small half-pound cotton sack full of table salt. The gift brought a tremendous response from the man and his young wife. Salt was worth more than gold to the Montagnards living in the highland jungles. The gift would insure that if the young Yard ran into any NVA soldiers on his trip to visit his relatives to the east, he would keep his mouth shut about seeing any Americans.

Just as the Montagnard family was starting to leave, Goldsmith got an idea. Writing a quick note, he handed it to Y-Bluc. "Tell him to give this note to any Americans that he sees on his trip." Goldsmith looked over at Tyriver. "Just letting the folks back home know that we're all right. They should be getting a little worried that we haven't been making any BTBs." He was referring to the blind-transmission broadcasts they were supposed to be sending up to the FAC aircraft flying above the clouds. Goldsmith didn't want to risk any radio communications after having seen so many NVA in the area. A radio broadcast could be picked up through triangulation by the enemy.

"What did you say?" Tyriver felt uncomfortable talking in a normal voice so close to the river, where sound carried a long distance.

"Massasauga—SAFE—Will call later."

"Don't you think we should risk making a broadcast now that we know that the NVA aren't nearby?" Anxious over the long delay in communications, Tyriver was afraid that the launch site would chalk them off as missing and remove their FAC coverage.

"What do you think, David? You've been with the program a lot longer than I have. Personally, I think that we have the advantage over the NVA as long as they don't know we have been inserted, and I think that Major Ricks is smart enough not to try and insert another team in our AO until he's sure that we are dead."

Tyriver thought for a long time before answering his lieutenant. "You've got a point there, sir. No news could be good news."

"Let's take advantage of this opportunity that has been given to us. Maybe the Yards will know of POWs that are being held in the area, especially if they're from Y-Bluc's tribe. We should be able to get the truth out of them."

"We'd better cross over now, sir, before the situation changes." Tyriver flipped his rucksack over his shoulders and then checked his weapon one more time before following Y-Clack out into the open river. After spending almost a week hiding in dense jungle, he felt naked out in the river. It was as if he was suffering an extreme fear of open places. He felt his heart starting to beat faster and his mouth dried up. Tyriver hurried toward the opposite bank and even passed Y-Clack on his way. The Montagnard was taking his time crossing the river, enjoying the cool water against his legs.

A Montagnard boy who had been assigned to watch that side of the river ford stepped out from the undergrowth when Tyriver drew near. He had never seen an American before, even though he had heard many stories about the tall race of people. Tyriver didn't look that much different to him because he had dark hair and brown eyes, but the American crossing the river behind him was much different! He had eyes the color of the sky, and they changed colors when you stared at him! The boy drew back away from Goldsmith, thinking he was a sky god. Goldsmith's eyebrows gave the young Montagnard a hint that the American's hair was also a different color than what was normal for a human being. Most Montagnards had black hair, but a few had hair that drifted toward brown or a reddish brown. But there had never been a Montagnard born with white hair! There had been stories told in the villages about a Montagnard girl who had been born years ago with white skin and red eyes that could not hold the light of the sun. She had lived her whole life in a cave and came out only when the moon was full. The young boy had no way of knowing that the girl would be classified as an albino by modern medicine.

Goldsmith wore his favorite Navy SEALs watch cap pulled down low around his ears, and he wore his camouflage cape over his head like an Arabian sheik. In the jungle the outfit very effectively kept the bugs off him, and what worked for him he turned into a habit. Tyriver had brought along a large piece of parachute cloth to use in the same manner when the mosquitos got too bad at night, but during the day he liked wearing his short-brimmed SOG hat that matched his tiger suit. All of the recon men developed superstitions after they had pulled a few missions, and items that they had worn during successful missions seemed to appear more often during subsequent missions, but an idea that was really good, like Goldsmith's parachute cloth, was adapted almost instantly by all of the recon men. The cloth could be used for a wide variety of chores in the field. It was lightweight, strong, and made out of a camouflage pattern. The cloth could be used to drag wounded men through the jungle, or to use as a stretcher if there was enough time. It could be used at night as a bug shield, and because it was so light it didn't retain heat.

The Montagnard teenager stared openly as Goldsmith passed his position on the hidden trail. Y-Bluc spoke a couple of sharp words and the boy went back to watching the river crossing. Y-Bluc spoke to Y-Brei, who translated for the elder Yard: "Y-Bluc says that his people asked why we stayed so long hiding over on the riverbank. They saw us when we came yesterday and thought that we were resting before signaling that we would cross over!" Y-Brei make a clicking sound by pressing and releasing his tongue against his palate in self-reproachment. He had also failed to pick up the signals that the river ford was watched by his own people. Y-Brei brushed off the error as having been caused from living for too long with the lowlanders, but Y-Bluc was upset with himself for missing so many obvious clues and wasting a whole day next to the river.

The Montagnards walked close together, talking all the way down the guarded trail to the hidden village. Chickens wandered in a small clearing between some longhouses, running to beat their neighbors to the insects that made the mistake of jumping off the surrounding jungle growth into the clearing.

Y-Brei guided the two Americans over to the guest section of the longhouse reserved for unmarried young men who were of age. Meanwhile Y-Bluc hurried over to his family's longhouse. He had not seen his parents in almost two years, and the reunion would be private. They had left the resettlement village without having the opportunity to say good-bye to him and his wife, who had given their eldest son to his parents to keep the boy away from the vices that had filled the Vietnamese-controlled settlement. Y-Bluc had approved of her decision but had missed the boy.

The Montagnard commando found his father working a piece of metal in his outdoor forge. Y-Bluc's son was operating the bellows and smiled when he saw his father approaching, but he could not stop heating the coals his grandfather was holding the piece of steel in.

Y-Bluc greeted his father and then reached over and gently touched his son's bare shoulder. The greeting carried with it the tenderness of the pain of the long separation.

"You have stayed away a long time, Y-Bluc." The old man started beating out a rhythm with his hammer against the steel after glancing to see if the guard posted up in a tree nearby approved of his making the noise. Any sign of NVA or Pathet Lao activity and the forge would be shut down.

"The Americans have paid me well and we have worked very hard."

"Do you still hunt the northern lowlanders?"

Y-Bluc grunted an affirmative.

"They are always making our people dig holes in the jungle for them, and they steal our young men. We must hide them now from the lowlanders, who make them carry heavy loads far to the south in the land of the Kampuchea people."

"It is good, Father, that you have found a place for our people to still live well."

"Ugh." The old man worked the metal with his hammer.

"I have seen a beautiful sword, Father. Tonight I will ask my American officer to show it to you. It is truly beautiful!"

Y-Brei and Y-Clack led the way over to the village bachelor longhouse and showed Goldsmith and Tyriver where they could put their gear for the night. As curious as the villagers were about the Americans, they would be left in total privacy inside the longhouse, and their rucksacks would be safer than inside a Swiss bank vault. The Montagnards were a nation that did not possess locks, so a person's personal space was respected.

"There is a place to wash nearby." Y-Brei knew from living in the American camp that Americans were like the Montagnard people: they enjoyed being clean.

"Do you think we should risk it?" Tyriver's skin started itching with just the suggestion of getting clean.

"If Y-Brei thinks it's safe here, I don't want to insult the villagers." Goldsmith dropped his rucksack on the woven bamboo mat in the longhouse.

"It much safe in this village." Y-Brei started toward the door at the end of the building, which had been constructed on a raised platform three feet off the ground.

"Let's take our weapons." Goldsmith trusted the Yards, but he wasn't going to be foolish. "Did you bring any soap?"

Tyriver shook his head. "I'm a medic, remember? Of course I brought some soap!"

"I swear, Tyriver, just how do you get all of that stuff inside one rucksack?"

"It takes a little planning, sir." Tyriver removed a bar of surgical soap from the side pocket of his rucksack and held it up for Goldsmith to see. "The secret of packing a rucksack is to bring exactly the amount you need." He turned the bar of soap so that Goldsmith could see it had been cut in half—lengthwise.

Y-Brei led the way down a narrow path away from the village. They entered a patch of thick triple-canopy jungle, and then they broke out individually into a small clearing that was nothing more than a shallow, clear jungle pond that had been created by a six-foot waterfall.

"Damn!" Tyriver's voice reflected the awe over the beautiful setting. The vegetation surrounding the waterfalls was a bright green, and the rocks were being constantly washed from the spray and mist of the cool mountain falls. "I was expecting a stream, not a shower!"

A small group of children who had been playing in the pond started giggling and slipped off into the cover of the jungle to watch the strangers. Montagnards were extremely shy people, and even though their normal clothing was only a loincloth and short vest-type jacket for the men and a wraparound skirt for the women, the Yards were very modest concerning complete nakedness in adults.

Y-Brei removed his tiger camouflage uniform and folded it neatly on a rock before stepping under the refreshing waterfall. He was careful to keep his back to the Americans, and even then he kept one of his hands covering his genitals as he used his free hand to rub the dirt off the rest of his body. This was a common Montagnard courtesy when bathing in a communal group.

Goldsmith took his time undressing in the jungle. He was not comfortable with the idea of standing unarmed and naked under a noisy waterfall, but Tyriver had accepted the Montagnards' hidden security measures and was wading across the pond before Goldsmith had even unlaced his boots.

"Ahhh! It's great!" Tyriver called back after he had completely soaked himself under the water. "It's *cold* but good!"

Goldsmith kept scanning the surrounding jungle as he undressed, and he picked out a couple of shiny faces staring at them through the wide-leafed plants. Finally the children stopped watching them, and slowly they started coming back to the pond.

"Are you coming in?" Tyriver rubbed the bar of soap in his hair and tried making suds from the surgical cleaner in the cold water.

"Yeah!" Goldsmith unsnapped the safety on his holster, slipped his pistol under his folded jacket to keep the mist off it, and then started wading into the knee-deep water. The chance to clean up was just too tantalizing to pass up. Besides, if the villagers were going to turn them over to the NVA, they could do it at any time now that they had found them. Just as Goldsmith reached the waterfall, he noticed movement on the trail leading to the pond and took a step back toward his weapons. But it was only the Montagnard boy on guard duty at the ford coming down to bathe. Goldsmith took a deep breath and ducked down to get his matted-down hair wet. The shock of the cold water felt good after spending so much time sweating in the muggy jungle.

The Montagnard boy undressed quickly and started walking across the pond toward Y-Brei, but the Yard commando waved his hand and spoke harshly to the youth. Tyriver saw that the boy was embarrassed as he started leaving to return to his clothes. "Y-Brei! It's all right if he wants to use the waterfall when we're here. There's plenty of room for a dozen guys under here!"

Tyriver motioned with his hand for the youth to come and stand under the water on his side of the falls. The boy glanced shyly over at Y-Brei, who gave him a dirty look but did not interfere.

Goldsmith used up half the bar of soap just cleaning his hair. The watch cap had plastered his hair against his skull. As he rinsed it, he failed to notice that the Montagnard boy was staring at him.

He had been separated from his family when he was eight, and the tribe had taken him in and taken care of him as they would for any orphaned Montagnard child. He hadn't been assigned to any longhouse, and he slept with whichever family he ended up with at the end of the day. The same principle held for meals until he had reached puberty, and then he had been assigned to live in the bachelors' longhouse. Because he was orphaned and didn't have a family to protect him, he had become the village's *common one*. If there was a homosexual boy in a village, then he would become the common one, but if there were none, then one of the orphans was designated as the common one and sent to live in the bachelors' longhouse. It was unacceptable for single males to have sex with unmarried girls of the tribe, and the common one was provided by the tribe to take care of the young males until they selected a wife and married. The practice was accepted as a normal part of life by the jungle villagers, but in the settlements and lowland camps, there were many Vietnamese whores to service the young men, and the old practice was not enforced.

Tyriver washed under the waterfalls, not realizing that by signaling for the boy to join him under the water that he was also saying that he was interested in him as a common one. Y-Brei was married, and that was why he had scolded and sent the boy away when he had tried joining him. Y-Brei knew that the young American sergeant wasn't married, and according to his age-old customs, he accepted Tyriver's decision to bathe with the common one as normal. He, of course, assumed that the sergeant knew the custom.

Goldsmith left the waterfall and wandered across the pond back to where he had left his clothes. The children started giggling when he passed by them. He was not holding one hand over his genitals in the common practice, and the little ones thought that was funny.

Tyriver left the waterfall, followed by the Montagnard boy. "Damn, that felt good!"

"It looks like you've found yourself a little friend." Goldsmith stood on a rock and kicked his legs individually, and then shook his arms to remove the excess water from his body. They didn't have anything to dry them except the warm sunshine coming through the hole in the trees directly above the pond.

The Montagnard boy stared so hard at Goldsmith's private parts that the lieutenant became very uncomfortable and decided that he would slip his trousers back on even though he was still a little wet.

What the boy was staring at was Goldsmith's blond pubic hair. It was something he had never seen before, and he was intrigued by the sun-colored, curly hair that was all over the American's body. The boy was sure that he was the son of the sun.

Tyriver had noticed the boy staring as well. "I think he's curious about the color of your hair, sir. I'd bet that he hasn't seen a Frenchman or an American in his life."

"How old do you think he is, Tyriver?"

"Thirteen, maybe fourteen." Tyriver saw that Y-Brei had finished washing and called over to where the Montagnard was dressing. "Y-Brei! How old is this kid?"

Y-Brei spoke sharply to the boy and then shook his head. "He doesn't know. Maybe twelve or thirteen year."

"Has he ever been down in one of those resettlement villages?"

Y-Brei grimaced, not liking to talk to the boy, but he would translate if that was what the Americans wanted. "He say no. He live in jungle with no family. He is the village common one."

Both Tyriver and Goldsmith took the term of common one as meaning that the boy was an orphan.

"It's too bad that we couldn't take him back to Marble Mountain with us." Tyriver was trying to say something nice. "He could be the camp mascot."

"You want *him*?" Y-Brei couldn't understand why the Americans would want a common one back in Da Nang, where there were plenty of women who met the commandos and Americans down on the beach and had sex with them.

"Why not? The kid needs a decent home."

Y-Brei shook his head and translated what the American had said to the Montagnard boy. The boy's eyes lit up and he smiled for the first time in many months.

"Let's get back to the village." Goldsmith felt much better after the refreshing mountain stream shower. "Did you see those kids, Ty?"

"Yes, I was thinking of conducting a MEDCAP, but my medical supplies are very limited. I brought mostly stuff for combat wounds and not much medicine. I noticed that a couple of those kids back there are suffering from worms and infections."

"Do what you can. We might win some hearts and minds on this mission just by doing some small things for them."

"Will do, L.T.!" Tyriver loved being a recon man, but his heart was that of a medic. He enjoyed helping people, especially when only a little modern medicine could cure a very painful disease. He spoke to Y-Brei about a medical sick call in the village, and the Yard agreed that it would be a very good idea. "I set it up for this afternoon."

The whole village assembled around the clearing where the Americans were and watched as the dark-haired American performed his magic on the sick members of their group. He took his time feeling different places on their bodies and even looked in the mouths of those who complained of pain inside their bodies, as if he were looking down their throats to see the demon that was causing it. The Americans were great entertainment for the villagers and filled the late afternoon with many opportunities to laugh. Meanwhile the elders prepared and roasted the pig the village chief had selected for the feast that would take place in honor of Y-Bluc's return.

"Look at that little one over there." Tyriver pointed at a little girl sitting on her mother's lap. The child's eyes did not focus, and she acted as if she was blind. "Do you know what her problem is, Lieutenant?"

Goldsmith shrugged his shoulders.

"It's nothing that a dime's worth of vitamin A can't cure, but if she goes another month like that, she'll be blinded for life." Tyriver searched through the pockets of his aid kit and found the small plastic container that held twenty large 50,000 USP capsules of the vitamin. "I brought only adult doses, but maybe I can save her eyesight. Would you take this capsule and break it open in her mouth, L.T.?"

"Sure. What should I do?" Goldsmith took the soft capsule in his fingers.

"First have the mother open the child's mouth. Then bite off a corner of the capsule and squirt the vitamin A directly in the child's mouth. Use about half of it and you can use the rest on any of the other kids. They're all suffering from some level of vitamin A deficiency." Tyriver looked up and saw a pregnant girl sitting off to one side of the clearing under a shaded porch. "Give the rest to that woman over there. She's going to need all the vitamins she can get."

Tyriver spent most of the afternoon treating over half of the village for different ailments. All of the elderly people were suffering from some kind of upper-respiratory disease, and the children all had the extremely protruding stomachs that signaled malnutrition. There was an extremely small age band among the Montagnards that looked physically healthy, approximately the mid-teens to the mid-thirties.

The Montagnard boy waited by himself in the shade of the undergrowth until everyone else had finished seeing the American witch doctor. He hoped that the miracle man still had enough of his magical jars left to treat his pain.

Seeing the boy walking toward Tyriver, Y-Brei guessed that he was going to ask for some kind of treatment. The older Yard hissed something between his teeth, and the youth took a step backward. It was the tone of Y-Brei's voice that caused Tyriver to look up and see the boy leaving. "Y-Brei! Stop him!" Anger filled the medic's voice. "Why are you being so mean to that kid?"

"Him a common one. Don't waste good medicine on him!"

Tyriver again assumed Y-Brei's anger was because the boy was an orphan. "Bring him here and I will treat him, just as I treated the rest of the people in this village. I don't care if he is a common one." Tyriver's voice dropped and he allowed his anger to show through. "I am a *bac se*! A doctor! I treat all of the people!" Tyriver had seen the same kind of discrimination among the South Vietnamese when it came to treatment for the different levels of their society. The extremely poor were left to die, especially the half-breed children the French had left behind after their war in Vietnam. He was not going to tolerate the same kind of racism and social hatred from his own men.

"Fine, treat him if you like, but go in hut!" Y-Brei pointed to a nearby storage hut.

Tyriver was a little confused why of all of the people he had treated during the afternoon, only one required the privacy of a hut, but he decided on compromising with his interpreter and motioned for the boy to go inside the hut. The boy acted very shy when Tyriver dropped his aid kit down on a basket containing some kind of root.

"What is wrong with him, Y-Brei?"

The Yard spoke sharply to the boy and then shook his head before translating. "His bottom end is in pain."

It took Tyriver a couple of seconds to understand what Y-Brei was referring to, and then he felt his face getting warm when he realized what part of the body the Yard was talking about. Gaining control of himself, he motioned for Y-Brei to leave them in privacy. Tyriver waited until the older Yard left to stand outside of the doorway before motioning for the boy to remove his loin-cloth and turn around. The youth obeyed and bent over.

Goldsmith heard Tyriver's gasp all the way on the other side of the clearing. He got up and walked over to the hut. "Is everything all right in there?"

"Shit! This kid has a severely infected anal passage and he's got a dozen fissures *in ano*. The poor kid must be passing bricks instead of stool!"

"Do you need some help?"

"No, he's already embarrassed just by me looking at it. I think I can maybe stop the infection with some penicillin. I wish I had some stool softeners with me, but a low-residue diet should help if I can get Y-Brei to translate correctly for me." A sigh came from behind the closed door of the hut. "Now comes the hard part of being a medic."

"What's happening?" Goldsmith glanced around the clearing and noticed that it was totally empty. Automatically he reached for his pistol and searched the area for his commandos.

"I've got to put some salve on this kid's butt hole! Ugh!"

Goldsmith smiled despite his concern of the disappearance of the villagers and answered, "It can't be as bad as a finger wag during a physical."

"If you saw the condition of this kid's rear end, you'd retract that statement."

"You'd better hurry up in there. I don't like what's going on out here."

The door to the hut opened, and Tyriver stepped out holding his open aid kit at his side and his silenced Swedish-K at the ready. "What's wrong?" He had made the transition instantly from medic to warrior.

"The villagers are all gone."

Y-Brei appeared from the back side of the hut. "They go to feast. We go now too!"

Goldsmith looked over at Tyriver wryly. He had overreacted. In that moment he remembered that the Montagnards were hiding from the North Vietnamese as well as the Laotians and American bombers. Their survival in the dense jungle was based on not being discovered by anyone, and if Y-Bluc hadn't been with the recon team, the Montagnards would never have taken them to their village.

"Hey, Lieutenant, it's better to be a little over cautious out here." It was as if Tyriver was reading Goldsmith's thoughts. "I've even relaxed too much in this village. It's hard to believe that we're sitting in Laos a few thousand meters away from the bad guys."

Goldsmith nodded in agreement. "Let's go eat."

"Here." Tyriver held out his hand.

"What are these?" Goldsmith looked down at the half-dozen different-colored pills.

"To kill the bugs before they can make you sick. Yards have a habit of not cooking their food enough, and we're having pig meat for dinner."

"Thanks." Goldsmith saw the Montagnard boy watching them from the shadows. "I feel sorry for that kid. I was pretty much an orphan growing up."

"Really?" Tyriver walked on Goldsmith's right side so that his Swedish-K wasn't trapped between their bodies.

"Yeah, I was raised by my grandmother after my mother died and my father dumped us."

"Us?"

"My brother and I."

"Where's your brother?"

"He was with the 101st but got out and got himself married. He's got two kids and wants two more." Goldsmith realized that he had talked about a lot of things with Tyriver, but they had never talked much about their personal lives. He recalled Tyriver bringing up the topic several times back in the base camp, but he had avoided talking about his family. "What about you?"

"Me? My father is a famous surgeon who flies all over the world performing operations. We have a huge house—some people call it a mansion—and my mother is what you might call the perfect mother. Our house was where all of the kids would end up during the day when we were little, and when I was in high school, our house was where everyone met to just come and talk. Now that I look back on it, my mother should have been a child psychologist. She sure helped a lot of rich kids get through puberty in our town."

"So what are you doing here? You should be in Harvard Medical School."

Tyriver's head snapped around as if Goldsmith had struck a sensitive nerve ending. "In fact, L.T., I just might be doing that when we leave the jungle and my tour of duty is over with. My father has arranged for that, but it will be the University of Michigan's medical school—it's better than Harvard's."

"And full of fucking left-wing hippies!"

Tyriver shrugged. "Won't they be surprised when I get there!"

"Hey, dinner is served!" Goldsmith followed Y-Brei

over to where Y-Bluc and his family was sitting in front of a fire pit and a roasted pig. The pig had been provided by Y-Bluc's father, and the whole village had contributed food and come and listen to the group of gong musicians.

Y-Bluc smiled when he saw that the lieutenant was wearing his STABO harness and the sword. Goldsmith had rigged the leather sheath on his two shoulder straps so that he could reach back with his right hand and grab the handle of the sword.

"Let's eat just enough to be polite and fill up when we get back to our longhouse on what's in our packs," Goldsmith whispered to Tyriver as they were taking their seats. "This pig isn't going to feed all of these people."

"They must be having a difficult time finding a rice source. I don't see any *nump-hai* jugs."

"Well, we lucked out." Goldsmith smiled over at Y-Bluc and his family. "We don't need a rice-wine hangover out here in the fucking Laotian jungle."

The gongs started filling the surrounding area with their mystic sounds, and some of the women began chanting softly to the beat. The villagers ate talking and laughing politely and constantly sneaking glances over at the Americans, especially the young man whose curly hair seemed to reflect the light of the sun in the firelight.

Y-Bluc cut huge pieces of pork from the belly of the pig and piled fist-sized globs of fat on the large leaves that were being used as plates. The grease dripped off the leaves as they were passed over to Goldsmith and Tyriver. Y-Bluc had sprinkled liberal portions of the precious salt over the meat to show the villagers his wealth and his gift to them. Four of the half-pound cloth bags were lined up in front of Y-Bluc's father. Even though the salt was his gift to his father, the villagers knew that the life-supporting white grains would be shared with all of them.

"My God! Do these people love fat!" Goldsmith held the leaf out away from his body so that the dripping grease wouldn't get on his trousers as he sat cross-legged on a bamboo mat.

"Fat is rare in their diets, and when they do find an animal like a pig, they make sure all of the fat is eaten. It's an honor to be given so much fat." Tyriver picked through the lean meat on the leaf, looking for a piece that was well done. Most of the meat was still red. "We're going to catch trichinosis for sure!" Tyriver closed his eyes as he bit down on the pork and felt the fat and blood fill his mouth.

The absence of the rice wine the Montagnards called *nump-pai* made the evening more somber, and the ceremony seemed to go by slower. Tyriver saw the Montagnard boy he had treated for anal infections sitting back away from the rest of the villagers in the shadows of a longhouse. He felt sorry for the orphan and figured that he would get little of the pig after all of the families had taken their shares. He reached over and took three pieces of fat still piled up on Goldsmith's leaf and added it to the fat and pieces of red pork still on his leaf plate.

"You aren't going to eat all of that, are you?" Goldsmith was relieved to have the fat gone from his leaf, but he didn't want Tyriver to feel that he had to eat it for him.

"No, I've got to go relieve my kidneys. Hold my place at the table, L.T." Tyriver got up and stretched his legs before wandering off in the direction of the longhouse and the boy. He dropped the greasy leaf plate on the boy's lap as he passed him and continued walking toward the open area the village had designated as a latrine.

Glancing at the boy on his return trip, Tyriver saw the white teeth smiling at him in the reflected firelight.

Goldsmith figured that they had waited long enough since their arrival to start asking some polite questions. He had learned in his Special Forces training that it was rude to start asking questions as soon as you arrived in a Montagnard village. Plus, it was very important whom you asked the questions from. "Y-Brei."

The Montagnard interpreter turned in Goldsmith's direction, still holding a piece of the pig's brain in his hand.

"Y-Brei, ask the chief if he or any of his villagers have seen any more people like us that are being kept by the lowland people or the Pathet Lao."

Y-Brei nodded and leaned over to get the chief's attention. When he asked the questions, the villagers sitting nearby stopped talking and listened to their chief's answer. Y-Brei shook his head. "No, they see no Americans, except you and the sergeant in over one full year."

"Ask him about POW camps."

When Y-Brei translated, it seemed to Goldsmith that he was asking a lot more than a single question. What's more, the answer was a lot longer than he thought it should be.

"He say that the NVA stay near their road on the other side of the mountains. No NVA are near. One-day walk to NVA."

"I think we're being bullshitted, sir," Tyriver said, leaning over so that only Goldsmith could hear. "They know that if they tell us the truth, we'll stir up the NVA and then the NVA will search for us and find their village."

"We can't really blame them, can we?" Goldsmith smiled over at the chief. "We'll leave in the morning and see what we can find on our own."

Y-Bluc left his place next to his father's side and walked bent over the short distance to his lieutenant. "Lieu-ten-et. You honor my family and show Father your long knife?"

"People are very interested in your sword," Y-Brei added. He had already talked to Y-Bluc about it and had agreed to support him when he asked the lieutenant to show it.

"Sure." As Goldsmith pulled the sword from its sheath, every eye in the village was on the black blade. He heard gasps of admiration from the village craftsmen. They knew a work of art when they saw one. Goldsmith stood up and handed the sword, hilt first, to the old man. Y-Bluc's eyes shone with pride in the firelight from just knowing someone who owned such a fine weapon. The Montagnards had lived in the jungle for years with only short spears, knives, and small crossbows to protect themselves. Rifles and modern weapons of war were new items and didn't receive the same respect as the old weapons.

Y-Bluc's father spent a long time touching the smooth blade and inspecting the sword. He was visibly impressed by the sword's balance. He nodded in respect at Gold-

smith and passed the sword over to the village chief so
that he could inspect it.

"I think your blade is drawing too much attention,
sir." Tyriver was trying to wipe the grease off his chin
using his sleeve, and his words came out muffled.

"What do you mean?"

"You might have to end up giving it away."

"Whoa! I had that sword made special! It's an exact
copy of a Roman short sword. Damn, it cost me over a
thousand bucks!"

"I'm just saying, sir, that the Yards have a thing about
gifts. We might get some information that wasn't available earlier."

"Like what?"

"I don't know, but giving that sword to Y-Bluc's father
might jar some memories around here and save our lives.
I don't think they've told us everything."

"Damn, Tyriver, you're making sense, but I really
don't want to part with my blade."

Tyriver shrugged. "I thought my sick call in the village
would get them to open up, but I guess it hasn't."

"Oh, fuck it!" Goldsmith unbuckled his webgear and
slipped his arms out of the harness. He hurried to remove
the sheath before he changed his mind.

Y-Bluc watched as his lieutenant walked over to where
the sword was being passed among the villagers and
took the blade back, placing it slowly into the leather
sheath. The Montagnard interpreter felt his envy turn to
a copper taste in his mouth.

Goldsmith stepped in front of the village chief, holding
the Roman short sword and sheath down in front of him
parallel to the ground. "Y-Brei, translate for me."

The Yard stepped out from among the guests and
stood next to Goldsmith in the flickering firelight.

"Chief, your village has been good to me, and my
men and I would like to honor your great hospitality by
presenting this sword to your village sword maker."
While Y-Brei translated, Goldsmith went over and handed
the prized blade to Y-Bluc's father. A collective gasp
came from the assembled villagers as the old man took
the weapon.

Y-Bluc felt his hands shaking. In his wildest dreams

he had not thought that the lieutenant would part with that sword willingly. In fact, he had secretly made plans with several Montagnards in the village to kill the Americans while they were sleeping and keep the sword. Without knowing it, Goldsmith had saved his and Tyriver's lives.

The chief started speaking rapidly to the other elders, and one of the younger men disappeared into the chief's longhouse. The Montagnard leader spoke again, this time sharply and with some contempt. Another one of the younger men left the campfire to go back to the village.

When Goldsmith rejoined Tyriver on the bamboo mat they had been sharing for the feast, Tyriver shook his head. "Well, by giving that sword away, you've got them excited."

"I hated doing that."

"Yeah, I know, L.T., but let's see if it jogs their memories."

Exiting the longhouse, the young Yard returned carrying a red silk bag about the size of a milk carton. He gave the bag to the chief.

Y-Brei listened to the chief for a couple of minutes and then turned to translate for Goldsmith. "Chief say that your gift is too great for his poor village to accept without giving something in return." With both hands Y-Brei took the red silk bag from the chief and handed it to Goldsmith. "Chief say that the lowlanders like this kind of stone, and he would like for you to have this."

Taking the heavy bag in one hand, Goldsmith was surprised by its weight. He nearly dropped it on the mat in front of him.

"What's in it, sir?" Tyriver leaned forward to watch as Goldsmith opened the thin silk drawstrings and poured a portion of the contents out onto the mat. "Fuck me! Is that gold?"

"It looks like gold nuggets to me!" Goldsmith held up one of the marble-sized nuggets in the firelight, and the firelight made the untarnished metal sparkle. He hefted the bag a couple of times. "Feels like it weighs ten pounds!"

"Well, you can buy yourself another sword with that stuff," Tyriver said, grinning.

"*Ten* swords!" Goldsmith smiled over at the village chief and said to Y-Brei, "Tell the chief that I am very honored with his gift."

Y-Brei translated and then added, "Chief say that village find the small sun stones in river and stream to trade with the lowlanders, but the NVA torture village men who bring them the stones, trying to get them to tell where they find, so chief stop trading stones for rice with the NVA because stones are found too close to village. NVA come and take women and young men!"

Goldsmith nodded in understanding and smiled again at the chief. As far as cost went, he had come out ahead in the trade.

"Chief also gives you Y-Roc."

"Who?"

"Y-Roc, common one of village. Chief see that Tyriver like Y-Roc and he give Y-Roc to you." Y-Brei wasn't happy over translating that part of the gift giving, but it was his job. The whole village knew not only that the American *bac si* Tyriver had spent time in the storage hut with the common one, but also that Tyriver had given him the choice portions of both his and Goldsmith's food. No one in the village was passing judgment on the two Americans. Y-Brei had told them that neither of them had selected a wife yet, even though they both looked old enough to be married. Secretly, many of the fathers in the village liked the idea because the Americans wouldn't ask to sleep with their daughters during the night.

"What do you think, Ty? Do we take the kid out with us when we leave? We still have a mission."

"He's an orphan. His life would be a hell of a lot better back at CCN than living here."

"Do you think it would be wise taking him with us on the mission? He's just a kid."

"That kid knows his way around this fucking jungle better than either of us! He could carry the radio for us, and besides, L.T., I don't think these villagers would be too happy if we turned down a gift. Anyway, I think we can get him better treatment for his bowel problems back in Da Nang. I'm no expert at internal problems, and I'd like one of the doctors to look him over."

"Okay, we'll take him along. But I'm going to feel really bad if we get the kid killed."

Goldsmith nodded to indicate that he would accept responsibility for the boy.

"Chief says that one of his warriors just remember that he see NVA with two American warriors on poles."

Goldsmith dropped the bag of gold down on the mat. "Where?" His interest brought a smile to the chief's face. He had finally found a gift that was equal to the sword.

"Chief say that American warriors are being kept in cage on Bla-Krong."

"What is that?" Goldsmith asked excitedly.

"A mountain—over there." Y-Brei pointed and talked to the chief at the same time and then answered Goldsmith. "One part of a day's walk from village."

"Shit! They must be keeping the Americans on the back side of those mountains!" Excited as well, Tyriver was now getting to his knees. "Fuck, L.T.! We might be able to go home with some American POWs after all."

"Finding them and getting them out are two different things, Tyriver."

Y-Brei interrupted the conversation: "Chief say that he will have his warrior take you to NVA camp when the sun come back."

In the midst of the excitement over the gifts of gold and the POW information, Y-Roc arrived at Goldsmith's mat. The boy dropped behind the Americans and sat with his head lowered both in humility and to hide the excitement of belonging to the yellow-haired American.

Most of the villagers left the dying campfire, but the warriors stayed to talk with their chief and the Americans about the best way to approach the NVA campsite the next morning. The group talked until the wee hours of the morning, and a cold fog started creeping through the village.

"I'm totally beat. Tell the chief that we thank him, but we must get some rest now for tomorrow." Goldsmith stood up on blood-starved legs and walked around a bit to get his circulation going again.

The chief said a few sharp words, and his warriors

slipped away from the camp fire to return to the longhouses.

"Well, sir, we might be back home by tomorrow night if everything goes all right. The way I figure it, there aren't more than a dozen NVA in the POW camp at any given time. Also, it seems like they don't put more than three or four Americans in a single camp at a time. Apparently there are dozens of these camps spread out along the Ho Chi Minh trail."

"We've gotten more information tonight about how the NVA run their field POW sites than CCN has gathered in five years!" Goldsmith stretched and yawned. "If we leave right now, this is a successful mission."

"All for the price of one sword. I'd call that very good horse trading, sir. Your Jewish relatives will be proud of your ability to bargain."

"Dumb luck, friend. Just a case of dumb luck." Goldsmith led the way over to the bachelors' longhouse. "I'm so fucking tired that I think if I closed my eyes for a second, I wouldn't be able to open them again."

Unnoticed, Y-Roc followed quietly behind the two Americans. He waited until they were inside the dark longhouse before joining them.

Fumbling around in the dark, Goldsmith pulled his nylon poncho liner out of his rucksack and wrapped it around him before dropping onto a woven bamboo mat on the floor that served as a bed. Tyriver placed his submachine gun down next to him and lay down a few feet away from Goldsmith in the dark. "Fuck, am I beat!"

Goldsmith struggled to listen to the night jungle before drifting into a deep sleep. His last conscious thought was having one of his team pull guard before he realized that the villagers were watching their own village.

Y-Roc listened to the two Americans breathing deeply. His eyes adjusted to the faint moonlight, and he saw the yellow-haired American sleeping on the floor. He took a position between the two of them and waited.

Sensing someone lying down on the mat, Tyriver lifted his head off his rucksack, which he was using for a pillow. "Y-Roc?"

The boy grunted softly when he heard his name, even though it had been horribly pronounced.

Tyriver dropped his head back onto his rucksack and reached over to touch his submachine gun in the dark. He could feel the mat shaking from the boy's body, and as he drifted off in a much needed sleep his medic's mind realized that the boy was cold and he threw a part of his poncho liner over Y-Roc.

The boy didn't move, but the strange material soon made his whole body warm. He was used to nearly freezing at night in the longhouse, especially after the bachelors had finished with him. It was a new experience being warm at night. He stopped shivering and slowly eased himself over until he was touching the American.

Tyriver moaned in his sleep, ignoring Y-Roc's advances. The boy lay awake for hours, waiting for Tyriver to use him, before finally he fell asleep under the luxurious warmth of the American's cloth. He smiled in his sleep as he dreamed of a happy life living with the Americans.

CHAPTER THIRTEEN

✪✪✪✪✪✪✪✪✪✪✪✪✪✪✪✪✪✪✪✪✪✪

BAMBOO CAGES

The sound of a domesticated jungle rooster woke Tyriver up. He opened his eyes without moving his head and felt a warm body pressing up against him that he couldn't identify. Backing away a little, Tyriver rose on one elbow and then realized that the person sleeping with him was Y-Roc. He felt his face getting warm and looked over to see if Goldsmith was still sleeping. The sectioned-off portion of the bachelor's longhouse was empty.

Tyriver hurried out of the longhouse and stopped to search for Goldsmith on the small raised back porch. He saw the lieutenant and the rest of RT Massasauga squatting around a small pot of boiling water. It had been placed in the center of the village's night fire, which supplied hot coals to light the breakfast fires in all of the longhouses.

"Ready for some breakfast?" Goldsmith smiled back over his shoulder at Tyriver. "I threw in a packet of rice and shrimp for you."

"Yeah, sure." Tyriver glanced over his shoulder nervously.

"It looks like Y-Roc has taken a real liking to you." Goldsmith fished a reheated packet of indigenous rations out of the boiling water and held it up between two fingers for the hot water to drain off before handing it over to Tyriver.

"Too much!" Tyriver felt his face getting red again. "He must have slipped under my poncho liner when I was sleeping like a dead man last night."

"It's no big deal, Tyriver, especially to the Yards. That's how they sleep at night in family groups. The parents together to keep warm and all the siblings together. Blankets out here are rare and are usually given to the old people. Look around." Goldsmith motioned toward an old man sitting near one of the morning fires with an Army blanket wrapped around his shoulders. Nearby a young Montagnard mother bare from the waist up squatted across from the old man.

"I'm not used to stuff like that." Tyriver was still blushing.

"It doesn't bother me. I slept in the same bed with my brother when we were little." Goldsmith shrugged and opened the plastic packet of rice.

"Well, it bothers me. The only person who's ever been in a bed with me is the woman I was fucking."

Goldsmith frowned and changed the subject: "Eat up. We move out in an hour. The village chief has given us a guide—I think more to make sure that we get away from his village than because he gives a hoot about us once we leave here."

"I'm ready." Tyriver glanced back at the longhouse. "All I need to do is get my rucksack."

"I don't know about you, but I really needed that rest last night. I slept like a fucking baby—once I got used to the idea the Montagnards weren't going to run off and get the NVA while we slept."

Tyriver was going to say that he had slept well too but caught himself in time. "When did you get up?"

"Y-Bluc woke me before dawn."

"Why didn't you wake me?"

"There was no sense in both of us getting up. If you feel bad about me letting you sleep a little longer, you can take an extra watch tonight when we're in the jungle." Goldsmith shoved a plastic spoon of over-cooked rice into his mouth and talked around it. "Damn, David, stop being so fucking sensitive."

Tyriver grinned, using only one side of his mouth. "Yeah, I'm overreacting, aren't I?"

"Just a touch. Remember, he's just a kid and an orphan to boot. He's probably scared and grateful that we've shown him a little kindness. After all, not everyone would rub your butt for you."

Tyriver flashed a hostile look over at his lieutenant's stab at humor. "I'm a fucking *medic*, sir!"

"I'm just teasing, Tyriver. It's just a joke."

"I don't think that was a bit funny, *sir*!" Tyriver left the fire and stormed back to the longhouse to pack his rucksack.

To his relief, the longhouse was empty. Tyriver folded his poncho liner and shoved it back into his rucksack before slipping the pack on. He looked down the narrow hallway running through the longhouse but still didn't see the boy. He was about to exit, but changed his mind and walked the full length of the longhouse and exited at the opposite end. A small group of bachelors were sitting around a small fire, waiting for a pot of rice to boil. Tyriver saw Y-Roc sitting away from the group with his arms wrapped around himself.

"Y-Roc!" Tyriver beckoned for the boy to join him, but he didn't wait for him to catch up as he hurried around the building toward RT Massasauga's fire.

Goldsmith removed the last packet of rice from the boiling water and handed it to Y-Roc without saying a word or making eye contact with Tyriver. He knew that he had gone out of bounds by joking about Tyriver's medical duties. Tyriver was an excellent medic and would do whatever he had to do to cure a person.

Taking the packet in his hand, Y-Roc felt the heat of the rice, but he didn't drop it. He kept looking at the ground, as was proper for one who was inferior. The three Montagnards meanwhile had seen their lieutenant give the common one food right out where everyone could see it, and Y-Brei figured that this was just too much. He had to warn his lieutenant or they all would be shamed. "Lieutenant, Y-Roc is a common one. He get food by himself. Not good you give him food in front of village."

Goldsmith looked up in puzzlement. Something just wasn't right with the way the villagers treated Y-Roc. They weren't mean or cruel to him, but he sensed that there was something about the boy that required ignoring him in public. When Y-Brei had entered their longhouse to wake him, he hadn't said anything about Y-Roc sleeping so close to Tyriver, but giving the kid some food brought disapproval. Goldsmith decided not to press the issue. "Let's move out."

Nodding, Y-Brei spoke sharply to the Montagnard guide. Everything was packed, and they only had to pick which direction they wished to leave the village from. The guide carried a Montagnard sword in the waistband of his loincloth and a crossbow quiver with a dozen arrows. The crossbow he carried was meant for monkeys, but it would inflict a painful wound in a human.

Watching the guide take the lead, Goldsmith thought about how those small men spent days foraging alone, in a jungle filled with tigers and dangerous snakes, and had only those simple weapons to defend themselves with. It was a wonder they had survived as a people.

The village chief and Y-Bluc's family were waiting for them when they reached the edge of the village. Y-Bluc's father was wearing the sword across his back just as Goldsmith had. Goldsmith felt a twinge of regret when he saw the sword, but he knew that the trade had been well worth it. The chief wouldn't have told them about the POWs if not for the sword. What bothered him the most was that his weapons were reduced to his small-caliber pistol and a couple of hand grenades.

The recon team moved slowly through the jungle, and Y-Brei had to tell the guide over a dozen times to slow down. When they reached a small cut in the mountains to the west of the village, though, the guide's attitude changed completely. He started creeping down the well-hidden trail as if stalking game. It was obvious even to the Americans that they had just entered dangerous territory.

Only when Tyriver pushed the jungle growth away from his body and looked down did he see that they were walking on a well-used trail that was no more than a foot wide. The thick jungle growth clung to him as he walked along the path and blocked his view of the trail, but as they walked, he started seeing little nicks in the bark of trees and small sticks placed in tree forks to show the way. Like anything else in life, he thought, once you break the code, everything becomes very clear.

The trail came to an abrupt halt when the recon team reached a fast-running jungle stream. The team gathered around the tiny rock clearing barely large enough for the seven of them pressed tightly together. The Montagnard guide pointed downstream, gave a curt nod of his head, and disappeared back in the direction they had just come from without saying a word. He had done his job and wanted to get far away from the lowlanders' camps before they found the Americans.

Goldsmith signaled for a break and removed his map and compass from his side pocket. Being guided down the trail had completely confused him in the dense jungle growth, and he figured that he needed to find a landmark to orient himself on. The nearby stream was a year-round source of water and should appear on the map. He laid it on a flat rock and then, checking to see if the rock contained any metal, he placed his compass down and oriented the map toward due north. He had spent a lot of time locating the Montagnard village on the map the night before, and he knew the general direction they had taken from the village. It had been difficult both counting paces on the trail and paying attention to the jungle, but he had gotten a decent estimate as to the distance they had traveled and he found the stream on the map. It was only a matter of figuring out the lay of the land and selecting the narrow gorge they had traveled through.

Goldsmith tapped the map with his finger and looked over at Tyriver, who had been watching for confirmation of their location. Tyriver nodded in agreement.

A flock of parrots flew over the recon team, making a racket. Both Tyriver and Goldsmith automatically ducked closer to the ground and reached for their weapons.

Y-Roc squatted next to the stream and watched the two Americans. He saw that they were very worried about something, but the jungle wasn't giving any sign that there was danger nearby.

The map shook in Goldsmith's hand as he studied the narrow valley that the stream ran into to join up with a small river. He recalled the area west of his small recon map from the main battle map back in the TOC. This stream originated another few thousand meters up in the mountains, and he guessed that they were about three thousand meters away from the closest suspected site for a POW camp. The more he studied the map, the more he realized that the best location for a POW camp would be along this very stream.

It dropped in elevation rapidly and that meant a constant supply of fresh water for the camp and for a water latrine, which was important not only for hygiene but to decrease the smell of an open-pit latrine. The sides of the gorge were extremely steep and turned into vine-covered cliffs periodically.

Goldsmith could feel the excitement growing in his stomach. There was an excellent chance that the villagers were telling the truth and that there were two American POWs being kept in a small camp nearby.

The roar of a small-engine aircraft reached them. Tyriver looked directly up through the trees, but knew that he wouldn't catch a glimpse of the small plane. The sound told him that it was flying at some three thousand feet. He glanced at Goldsmith and raised his eyebrows. The lieutenant was thinking the same thing, and Tyriver made the sign of holding a telephone up to his ear. Goldsmith shook his head. He would have liked to make contact with a FAC, but they were too close now to finding POWs to risk giving away their location. All he could do was hope that the note he had given to the Montagnard at the ford would reach an American unit that had the sense to research his recon team's code name. Then too, Major Ricks would keep a FAC circling their area of operations until he was sure the team was killed.

Tyriver leaned back against his rucksack and rested while Goldsmith studied his map and tried figuring out which was the best way to proceed down the stream.

Leaning forward, Y-Roc touched Tyriver's sleeve and tugged gently to make him move a little forward, away from the bamboo bordering the streambank.

Tyriver frowned at the boy. He was still upset about the kid sneaking under his poncho liner the night before and had been ignoring him all morning.

The boy tugged again, this time a little harder, and pointed behind Tyriver with his free hand.

He moved toward the stream and turned to see where the Montagnard youth was pointing. He saw only a thick wall of young bamboo. Realizing that the American didn't see the danger, Y-Roc picked up a bamboo stick about four feet long and pointed directly at a spot in the bamboo.

It still took Tyriver several moments to detect the snake coiled around a half-dozen of the bamboo stalks, because the bright green back side of the snake matched the green leaves and its underside was the cream-colored yellow of the stalks.

Once Tyriver saw the bamboo viper, including the two-inch fangs, he nearly scurried into the stream. The reptile had been less than a foot away from the back of his neck when Y-Roc warned him. Y-Roc knew the snake wouldn't have attacked unless provoked, but he didn't know if the American was going to lean back harder on his pack and thus hit the snake with his head.

A light sweat broke out over Tyriver's forehead as he thought about what could have happened. He had studied the bite of the bamboo viper during his Special Forces medical training. The venom was very toxic, but what made the bite so bad was that the viper almost always struck its victim on the hands or head because it hunted up in the young bamboo at about that height for a human.

The kid had saved him from a very nasty snake bite that could have cost him his life and at the very least ended the mission, since they would have had to call for an extraction.

Goldsmith looked up from his map just in time to see Y-Roc point out the viper to Tyriver. He reached for his silenced pistol and took his time lining up the sights on the large triangular head before firing. A bright red spot appeared just behind the snake's eyes, and it twisted violently in its death throes. Y-Roc waited until the snake's activity had died down a little, and then he reached out with lightning speed and grabbed the viper behind its head. To the astonishment of the watching Americans, he placed the snake in his mouth and bit the head off in one quick bite. Y-Roc was careful not to step on the snake's head when it dropped to the ground, for the severed head was still capable of delivering a deadly bite.

Tyriver's nose wrinkled in disgust as he watched the

boy skinning the snake using his teeth. The teenager was going to eat the snake's flesh raw.

The three Montagnards on the team glanced over to see what was occupying their lieutenant's attention, but turned away when they saw that it was only the boy preparing the snake to eat. Raw meat eaten in the jungle was as common a sight to them as a child eating candy back in the States. Flesh spoiled quickly in the jungle heat, so small animals were eaten on the spot by the Yards.

Seeing the boy struggling with the snake skin, Tyriver reached to his belt and removed his K-Bar knife, sharpened to a razor's edge. He handed the boy the knife and received a warm smile for a thank-you. The spaces between the youth's teeth were filled with red blood.

Goldsmith snapped his fingers to gain Tyriver's attention and signaled with his hand for him to join him. Tyriver, only too glad to get his mind off the snake, hurried to Goldsmith's side. "You know where we're at, L.T.?"

"Here." He tapped the map with his index finger. "And from what I can tell"—Goldsmith looked downstream—"the POW camp should be down that way." His voice was barely above a whisper. "We move until we find some sign of habitation, and then we stop and leave our Yards in a larger site so that you and I can recon the area."

Tyriver nodded his head. He wasn't sure how the kid would react if they stumbled on the NVA, and the more he thought about it, the more he wished that they had left the kid back in the village.

Goldsmith slipped over to Y-Brei, resting in the shade of a plant, and whispered in his ear, "Tell Y-Roc to stay close to Sergeant Tyriver and to hide if we run into any NVA."

Y-Brei nodded and left to pass on the information to the boy.

Tyriver approached Y-Roc first, and the boy handed the knife back to him. He had cleaned off the blade in the stream and the leather handle was wet. Tyriver thought for a couple of seconds and then undid the harness of his STABO rig to remove the leather sheath from his pistol belt. It would be cruel to bring the kid along with them and not give him some kind of weapon to defend himself.

Y-Roc understood instantly that Tyriver was giving the knife to him and started nodding his head in gratitude, but Tyriver didn't want him to make too much out of the gift and turned abruptly to join Goldsmith again. As he did, he struggled to clear his mind of the snake incident and concentrate on the dangerous task at hand, of locating the NVA.

Y-Bluc took the point, but for the first time since they had been on patrol, he looked very worried. He stealthily left the small clearing as if breaking a single twig would give the team's location away.

There was no visible reason why the Montagnards would suddenly start acting so cautious, but Goldsmith respected their instincts in the highland jungle. In fact, what had alerted Y-Bluc was a rock formation that appeared off to their left above the secondary jungle growth. He had been told that it was near that formation the lowlanders were camped with the two American slaves.

It took the recon team an hour to move three hundred meters in the virgin jungle bordering the stream. The ravine widened considerably as the team moved toward its mouth, and a cool breeze came out of nowhere with the setting of the warm sun. The sweat that had saturated the uniforms of the recon team acted to make the breeze even cooler, and Goldsmith shivered as he crouched down. All along, the team had maintained visual contact with each other, but now they moved closer together than normal because of the pending fear of making contact with the enemy.

Goldsmith emitted a soft click that carried only a few meters in the thick jungle. This alerted his team and then he signaled for the recon team to assemble around him. It took a couple of minutes for Y-Clack, who was working the point, to return to the rest of the team, but Goldsmith waited patiently. When Y-Clack joined the tight circle, Goldsmith held out his hand with his fingers splayed apart and then made a fist. This meant they would laager at that location for the night.

The Montagnards had rehearsed a recon team's laager site a hundred times with the Americans, and they all knew that they would spend the night in a star formation on the ground, with each one responsible for one fifth of the very tight perimeter. Goldsmith put Y-Roc in the center of the formation and dropped his rucksack where he wanted the boy to stay and guard it. Tyriver removed his rucksack and medical-aid kit and placed it next to the lieutenant's.

Y-Brei bent over to listen as the lieutenant whispered to him, "Tyriver and I are going alone to recon downstream before dark, and we might stay longer." Goldsmith pulled his night goggles out of his rucksack and held them up for the Montagnard interpreter to see. The Yard had tried the magic glasses several times, and he knew that they turned night into a green-colored daylight. "*Rally*"—Goldsmith said the word as a command and pointed back at the large rock formation on the side of the ravine—"use *panel*, make *R*." Goldsmith emphasized the key words for Y-Brei, and when he said the letter R, he held his hand palm up and turned it over and then back up again. The Yards had been trained that an open palm was a dot in Morse code and the back of the hand was a dash. Closing the hand in either position meant that the dot or dash was repeated.

Y-Brei nodded to show he understood the lieutenant's orders.

"Y-Roc will carry our rucksacks if you must go to the rally site." Goldsmith pointed over at the boy.

Y-Brei gave a curt nod.

Tyriver had removed his set of night goggles and a couple of amphetamine tablets to keep him awake and alert. Normally adrenaline kept him awake in the field, but his body had been running on adrenaline since their insertion, and it was only a matter of time before his body would need help staying awake. He took a few extra tablets for the lieutenant and handed his rucksack to Y-Roc. He hoped that the team wasn't discovered while he was gone because the boy didn't look big enough to carry two rucksacks through the jungle.

Goldsmith and Tyriver stopped at the stream just long

enough to take the amphetamine tablets with a double handful of cold water before disappearing in the jungle.

Goldsmith took the lead, carrying his silenced .22-caliber pistol in his hand. Tyriver followed close behind with his silenced Swedish-K, ready to back up the lieutenant if they ran into trouble. The silenced submachine gun would make quick work of any NVA trail watchers, but if they ran into a tiger on the trail, the small-caliber weapon would only piss it off unless they were very lucky and hit a vital spot. Tyriver quickly got his mind off stray tigers and listened to the sounds of the jungle.

The sound of the jungle stream made Goldsmith nervous because it covered the more subdued sounds, but at the same time the gurgling stream covered any rustles they made.

As the sun dropped behind the ridge, the light faded from gray to near darkness. Goldsmith was about to stop Tyriver and wait until they could use their night goggles when the distinct scrape of metal against metal reached them.

Tyriver's hand shot forward and grabbed Goldsmith's arm. The warning was unnecessary. Goldsmith was already dropping in a low crouch, trying to locate the exact direction of the sound.

Tyriver released his grip and pointed downstream. Goldsmith nodded his head in agreement and wished that fading daylight would hold for just another hour.

The two recon men inched forward next to the stream. A South American sloth could have moved faster, but both of them knew that movement was usually what gave you away in the jungle, and they were very well camouflaged.

The metal against metal sound reached them again, only this time it was only a few feet away. A voice close by caught them completely off guard, and the voice that answered the first one made Goldsmith lean backward. The second voice had come from only a few meters away.

It took Goldsmith a few minutes before he mustered the courage to part the jungle growth in front of him with his gloved hand. The two men were less than fifteen feet away. They were both squatting next to the stream, washing a small stack of metal bowls. Goldsmith quickly scanned the small open area and saw two bamboo cages that contained shadowy figures curled up on the floor of the small enclosures. Off to the right of the stream was a well-camouflaged bamboo hootch that would be impossible to detect from the air. The entire encampment had been constructed so that none of the secondary trees had been removed.

A voice from the hootch called down to the two men cleaning the metal bowls. Goldsmith didn't recognize the language at first. He had been expecting an Oriental language and was shocked when he realized that he was listening to an Arabic dialect.

Tyriver had reacted in the same manner as Goldsmith, but neither could risk a glance at each other. The whole idea of an Arab living in the Laotian jungle was absurd, and then it dawned on Goldsmith both why Arabs were there and where they were from. He kept the brush parted and continued watching the two men kneeling by the stream. One of them turned toward the man near the hootch and said something that seemed to end in a question. There was a pause before the other man answered.

Goldsmith was losing sight of the men in the fading light and risked letting the thick vegetation close in front of him. Turning slowly to look over at Tyriver, he noticed that even his face had lost its detail in the rapidly encroaching darkness. He removed his night goggles and slipped them on. At the same time he adjusted his navy watch cap to pad his head against the elastic strap of the goggles. Goldsmith turned on the battery, and everything around him sprang into detail again.

He parted the vegetation and got a very clear look at the two men. One of them was wearing a checkered headpiece in an Arab fashion. He knew from the brief glimpse he had earlier that the checkered cloth was white and red. Goldsmith knew that he had seen the same pattern before: these were the scarves the Pathet Lao wore. In the next moment the whole picture came together. The man wearing the Arab headdress was from the PLO!

The idea was startling. The high command in Saigon knew that there were a number of communist advisers—

Chinese, Russian, and Cuban—working the main POW compounds in North Vietnam, but no one had ever reported seeing members of the Palestinian Liberation Organization working with the North Vietnamese before. The PLO wasn't working with the NVA, but were advisers to the Pathet Lao! That would explain the ruthlessness of the Laotian communists and the reason they wore red and white scarves as a symbol of their organization. Everyone had thought that the colors had something to do with ancient Khmer societies, but actually it was in honor of their PLO advisers.

Goldsmith blinked his eyes slowly to clear the thoughts racing through his mind, and he returned his attention to the small clearing. He scanned the area slowly and noticed that there were two hootches with thatched bamboo roofs. These could hold five or six men each. There was a smaller hootch that looked like a storage shed, and then straddling the stream were the two small bamboo cages with one human form in each. The one closest to Goldsmith was curled up with his back to him, and Goldsmith couldn't tell if the person was an American or not, but he saw that he was naked. A small tin bowl and a bamboo sleeping mat were the only two items in the cage.

The person in the second cage was blocked from view by the bamboo bars of both cages, but Goldsmith saw that he was sitting upright and facing the two men down by the stream.

Goldsmith was starting to scan back to the hootches when he heard a voice speaking perfect English. He felt Tyriver's hand grab his shoulder, and he jerked as if the words had been bullets.

"Would you at least give him a blanket for the night?"

Goldsmith recognized the voice. It was Sergeant O'Mallory speaking. "He's sick."

The man wearing the Arab headdress and khaki fatigues stood up and took a step toward the cages. "We do not care if he is sick. We do not care if he dies! We do not care if you die!"

"I thought you Muslims are supposed to show compassion to your enemies."

"You! You do not tell me about my religion!" The

man raised his arm as if he was going to strike Sergeant O'Mallory through the bamboo bars.

"Give him some clothes to wear, then."

"We have no more uniforms for prisoners!"

"Then give him mine!"

"Ha!" The man still washing the dinner bowls looked up. "We might just take your clothes too, and then you can show your private parts to everyone!"

"He's just a kid. Show a little pity, will ya?" O'Mallory pleaded with the PLO representative.

"Pity? Do you Jew supporters show pity on my people? Do you care if my people starve to death or that their homeland has been taken from them?"

"I don't know anything about what's going on in the Mideast," O'Mallory said, playing dumb.

"Well then, maybe tonight we will bring you into the office for a long discussion on the matter."

Hearing the threat in the man's voice, Goldsmith guessed that the reference to the office meant an interrogation room.

The two men left the stream laughing over a private joke. Tyriver moved closer to Goldsmith and pressed his leg against the lieutenant's side. He wanted to speak, but then changed his mind because of the risk involved. Goldsmith understood what Tyriver wanted to say and reached over and patted his One-One's leg.

A series of loud coughs filled the clearing. Tyriver could tell from the sound that the infection was deep in the man's lungs and that the coughs were causing him a great deal of pain. The man in the cage wheezed and choked as he struggled to catch his breath.

"Hang in there, Mac." It was O'Mallory's voice again, but much softer. "Don't leave me, kid, not alone with those monsters!"

"I don't think I can make it much longer, O'Mallory. I'm freezing . . ." The voice trailed off in a whisper.

Goldsmith started shaking from his tremendous desire to charge and murder these vermin. His worst nightmare was being acted out only a few meters away, and the victims were two men he had known as fellow soldiers.

Fear jumped to the forefront of his thoughts, and Goldsmith felt his mind beginning to turn itself off as a protective measure. Then he felt Tyriver's reassuring hand touch his shoulder. He turned his head and his night goggles allowed him to see Tyriver grinning tightly. Goldsmith was glad that his teammate could not see the fear in his eyes.

Tyriver nudged him and pointed over to the nearest hootch. Someone had lit a gasoline lantern, and the light glowed through the partially open window. Tyriver sniffed the air once and then again to make sure before risking a whisper in Goldsmith's ear. "Monsoon coming."

Goldsmith nodded in agreement and took in a deep breath. A cool breeze was racing up the narrow ravine. The storm was coming in from the east, which was unusual but the high ravine walls could be throwing off the direction the storm was coming from. In any case, he knew that a heavy downpour was approaching rapidly. He had to make a snap decision. His original intention had been just to reconnoiter the area and then return to the rest of the team, but the approaching monsoon would provide the perfect cover for a raid on the small camp. What bothered Goldsmith was the lack of posted guards. He figured that there were at least six enemy in the camp, but they should be easy to take out. He had the element of complete surprise on his side, and the storm would be an additional bonus because when it hit, the enemy soldiers would be hesitant to come out of their hootches.

Goldsmith turned his head and peered at the small gates to the bamboo cages. Steel chains were wrapped around the bamboo, and he assumed that they were secured with some kind of padlock. They had left their bolt cutters back in their rucksacks and would have to return to get them, unless Tyriver and he could kill all of the enemy and use their keys to open the cages.

The first huge raindrops hit the nearby leaves, and Goldsmith knew that within a couple of minutes the jungle would be saturated in a torrent of water that would block out all sound. They could actually run back to the laager site without being heard and get the rest of the team.

Goldsmith's thoughts were disturbed by the sight of

someone leaving the PLO hootch and running over to the cage that contained McDonald.

"Why don't you take me tonight and give the kid a fucking break?" O'Mallory screamed from his cage at the PLO adviser.

"You shut your mouth or I'll come back for you later!"

Goldsmith and Tyriver watched as the adviser unlocked McDonald's cage and reached in to pull the young soldier out for another night of entertainment.

Goldsmith quickly memorized the PLO adviser's face. He was the one who had the keys to the cages.

The rain arrived in a solid wall of water before the PLO adviser had half carried, half dragged the skinny Special Forces soldier to the hootch. The PLO adviser cursed and tried kneeing McDonald for being so slow. Tyriver was watching every step the pair took and caught himself grinding his teeth.

Suddenly Goldsmith's fear evaporated, replaced by a familiar feeling he had developed over the years living as a white kid in a black ghetto. It was up to him to act. No help was forthcoming from the outside, and he could expect no mercy if he failed.

The rain was coming down so hard that he knew he could speak in a normal voice. It wouldn't carry more than a foot in the jungle. Goldsmith turned toward Tyriver and said, "We'll take them now."

"Let's do it!" Tyriver started to move forward, but Goldsmith caught his shoulder to slow him down.

"We take the other hootch first and then the one they took Mac into."

"Roger!"

Five NVA soldiers were sleeping in hammocks inside the first hootch. Three of the NVA were awake, talking to one another, and the other two were sleeping.

Tyriver filled the doorway under the extended roof and pulled the trigger on his Swedish-K. The only way he knew it was firing was from the gentle vibration in his hands and the NVA bodies sprouting red marks on their bare skin and uniforms. He killed all five of them with the first magazine from his submachine gun.

Goldsmith pushed past him through the doorway and ran over to make sure each of the NVA were dead. He administered a coup de grace on two of the bodies and turned toward Tyriver. They were still wearing their night goggles and looked like space warriors in the dim light of the single lantern.

"Let's get our guys!" Tyriver, more than ready for more bloodletting, led the way toward the second hootch. He moved alongside the building, checking for guards. That the NVA didn't have guards posted at least to watch the two Americans in the cages, was almost unbelievable but the NVA obviously felt very secure.

From inside the hootch came a shriek that rose above the sound of the rain. Goldsmith pulled his night goggles down around his neck and reached over to do the same for Tyriver. They were entering a well-lit space, and Goldsmith wanted to ensure that McDonald wasn't hit by mistake. It had been all right using the goggles for the first hootch because anything inside it had been fair game.

They took up positions on either side of the split bamboo door, taking several seconds to let their eyes get used to the bright light coming from inside.

McDonald shrieked again, a sound that sent a chill down Goldsmith's spine. He nodded over at Tyriver in the half-light and reached over to push the door open.

The two PLO advisers were working on McDonald, who sat naked on a bamboo bench. One NVA officer sat in a hammock in a corner of the room, and watching from the far side of the room, another NVA officer sat behind a bamboo desk next to a Latino soldier sitting cross-legged. It was a regular international communist terrorist classroom.

The only one who saw the two Americans enter was the NVA officer in the hammock. He received a .22-caliber round in his forehead for his interest.

Tyriver took out the Cuban and the NVA officer behind the desk in a silent burst from the Swedish-K.

Surprisingly, the two PLO advisers had their backs to the door, concentrating on McDonald, and didn't realize that their comrades were dead.

"So, big American soldier! Would you like to talk to us for the colonel?"

Goldsmith shot the man in the back of the head. His

friend turned around to see what was happening and died before he could even open his mouth in surprise.

Tyriver dropped his Swedish-K down on its carrying strap and rushed over to Sergeant McDonald. "Mac! We're here!"

McDonald looked up and struggled to open his eyes. He recognized Tyriver and smiled. "What took you so fucking long to get here?" His voice was filled with emotion.

"We had a problem with the transfer tickets on our bus and besides, we didn't know that you were having so much fun."

"Oh, fuck me," McDonald groaned.

"Let's get O'Mallory and get out of here!" Tyriver was helping McDonald up but was stopped by his lieutenant's voice.

"Let's not rush. This camp is ours, Tyriver. Let's take home some souvenirs." Goldsmith used the barrel of his pistol to point with. "That Cuban's uniform should fit Mac," he said, noting that the Cuban's uniform was dark green and would blend in better out in the jungle. "Here." He handed Tyriver the keys to the cages. "Go get O'Mallory."

A new life force seemed to enter Sergeant McDonald. He had been a POW less than two weeks, but the Cuban and PLO advisers had taken a special interest in him for some reason and had directed most of their torture against him. The first day that he had entered the small camp, they had stripped both him and Sergeant O'Mallory of their tiger-stripe camouflage uniforms, but they had issued only O'Mallory a POW uniform, keeping him naked for some reason. The PLO advisers would start out their torture by whipping him, but they always got around to doing something to his anus or his genitalia and the pain had been intolerable. At first he had tried holding back the screams, but that had lasted less than a day. Soon he learned that the longer he held out, the more pain was inflicted on him.

"Hurry, Mac," Goldsmith said as he riffled through the paperwork on the NVA colonel's desk. He saw several steel 12.7mm ammunition boxes stacked behind the dead colonel and placed one of them on the desk before opening it. Three passports were right on top of the can full of documents. Goldsmith stuffed as much from the desk as he could in the box and resealed it. He opened the second box: it contained the personal effects of what looked like American and South Vietnamese POWs. Not wanting to carry both boxes, he glanced over at McDonald. "Do you feel strong enough to carry one of these until we get back to the rest of the team?"

McDonald nodded his head. He was still very ill, but hope was giving him strength. "I'll take that AK-47 along too."

"Good, but don't fire it unless it is absolutely necessary. I want to use silenced weapons as long as we can to keep the NVA off our asses."

Goldsmith was nudging the sergeant toward the door when he saw a map on the wall. The mountain masses were extremely familiar, and he paused to take a better look. He identified all of the major landmarks from the main battle map at the TOC, but what caught his eye were the grease-pencil markings that represented a whole miniature city of two- and three-man POW camps spread out over a ten thousand-meter area. Goldsmith realized instantly why there had been no guards. First, they had bypassed all of the NVA bunker lines by going through the Montagnard village, and second, the Montagnard guide had taken them along trails that the NVA considered impassable mountainside jungle. RT Massasagua had actually entered the whole NVA compound from the rear. Even better, the POW camp they had stumbled on first was the colonel's headquarters camp that he had personally located at the highest point along the stream so that they would have fresh water.

O'Mallory saw the dark shape heading toward him when the door to the hootch opened. He felt his stomach tighten because the man was alone, which meant that he was coming for him. The PLO adviser was keeping his word: they were going to use both of them for their entertainment. He had seen a couple of what he had thought were NVA soldiers enter the main hootch earlier and took an educated guess that a class was being conducted by the advisers on how to properly break an

American prisoner. The worst torture wasn't committed by the NVA, but by the advisers.

As the dark shape paused at his cage door, O'Mallory pressed against the far side of his bamboo prison. "Are you ready to go home, O'Mallory?"

He was shocked. Not only was the voice American, but he recognized whose it was. Wondering if his mind had snapped in the cold monsoon rain, he reached out to see if he could feel the vision. He wrapped his hand around Tyriver's wrist and squeezed hard when he felt flesh. "Oh, my God!"

"Let go so I can find the right key for this fucking lock!" Tyriver struggled with the key chain in the downpour.

"Is it really you, Tyriver?"

"You can bet your sweet ass it's me! What did you think? That no one would come for you?"

"Thank you—thank you—thank you!"

"Calm down, O'Mallory. We've still got to get back to an extraction site."

"I don't give a fuck if I never leave this fucking jungle. Just give me a fucking weapon so that I can fight back again!"

Tyriver opened the bamboo gate to the cage and helped O'Mallory out. He stumbled for a half-dozen steps as he worked the blood back into his cramped legs in his rush to reach the hootch.

Seeing McDonald lacing the larger PLO adviser's boots on, O'Mallory flashed a tight grin from the doorway. The color had come back in the junior sergeant's face. They were free again, and that was the medicine the young warrior needed to fight the virus that had attacked his lungs. McDonald was still very ill, but the fire in his eyes told the older sergeant that he would make it.

O'Mallory searched the room until he found the folding-stock AK-50 and the canvas chest pack that held a dozen full magazines for the weapon. He picked up the semi-automatic rifle and pulled the bolt back to check if there was a round in the chamber. Walking over to the now naked Cuban adviser, O'Mallory kicked him as hard as he could and then spat in the dead man's face. "I wish I was the one that had killed you!"

Tyriver helped McDonald up on his feet. He was very worried because he knew that the POW was running on the excitement of being rescued. It wouldn't be long before his energy gave out.

"Here, Mac, put this map in your shirt." Goldsmith had torn the NVA map off the wall. The information it contained could be used for additional Brightlight and Project Cherry rescues if they moved quickly back in Saigon. It was obvious to Goldsmith that all of the POW camps were temporary and they moved them often. "Sergeant O'Mallory, enough of that shit!"

O'Mallory was still kicking the dead Cuban's body, trying to get revenge for the hours the adviser had spent torturing him and especially McDonald. Goldsmith's sharp command finally brought him back to the situation at hand.

"Tear out those telephone lines. They'll assume the storm is the cause, and it'll give us a few more hours' head start."

O'Mallory became the recon man again.

Gauging McDonald's condition, Goldsmith decided that they could move faster if they carried him. "Tyriver, you bring up the rear with your submachine gun. Next will be O'Mallory, but I don't want you firing that AK unless it is absolutely necessary. Mac, I'm going to carry you out of here—"

"Sir, I can walk!"

Goldsmith ignored McDonald's plea. "O'Mallory, shoulder that weapon and carry these ammo cans—they're full of good information. Tyriver, we'll take the stream back to the laager. In this fucking monsoon it will be impossible to find our way through the jungle."

Tyriver agreed and nodded his head.

"Let's move it!" Holstering his pistol, Goldsmith removed the AK-47 from McDonald's shoulder and threw it back to its NVA owner. "Sorry, Mac, but we've got to make things as light as possible." Goldsmith turned around, bent his legs, and waited for the sergeant to hop onto his back. He waited a couple of seconds and barked an order. "Let's go, Mac!" Goldsmith had braced

himself for a much heavier load and was surprised at how
light the sergeant was. "Try locking your legs around my
waist and your arms around my neck so that I can free
my hands."

McDonald obeyed the lieutenant, making some adjust-
ment to avoid the gear Goldsmith was carrying.

"Ready, Ty?"

"Let's do it, sir, this fucking place is making me nervous!" Tyriver waited until everyone else had left the
hootch before smashing the gasoline lantern against the
homemade desk. The fire spread rapidly inside the building, but the monsoon rain would extinguish it once it
broke through the roof.

The rain saturated them the instant they left the
hootch. Goldsmith licked the water from around his
mouth and realized that he was very thirsty. He continued licking the water from his face as he hurried toward
the stream. He adjusted McDonald on his back before
taking a cautious step in the fast-moving, rain-swollen
stream and rebalanced himself against the current before
heading upstream. The water came only midway up his
calf, but it was moving with a great deal of force. At
least, Goldsmith thought thankfully, we're high up in the
mountains.

The small recon party moved quickly up the stream,
stepping gingerly on the slippery rocks. They were moving much faster in the water than they could in the jungle, and Goldsmith knew that the stream passed the
laager site. He guessed that the rest of his team was less
than a thousand meters away, and he started counting
his paces the instant he entered the stream in order to
judge the distance they traveled.

Y-Clack was on guard duty when the rescue team came
splashing up the stream. He nudged Y-Brei, who had
been dozing off in the downpour, wrapped in his nylon
poncho liner to retain his body heat. Y-Brei listened to
the noise of someone, or something, splashing in the
water. He let the first struggling black mass pass their
position and in the very poor light saw two more figures
coming behind the first one. Y-Brei assumed that the
men were NVA and was going to let them pass until the

last black figure slipped and fell to his knees. "Shit!" he cried softly.

Y-Brei rose to his feet and called out, "Ty-river?"

Tyriver hurried forward to catch up to Goldsmith and stop him. "We just passed the team."

Goldsmith sighed in relief. He had counted over fifteen hundred paces and was beginning to worry that they had somehow passed the Yards in the rain.

Once the team was reunited, they all felt better. Tyriver opened his rucksack and handed O'Mallory and McDonald the last two pre-cooked packets of his rice. He figured that they could use the food more than him. He fumbled around in the dark trying to find his aid kit and finally put on his night goggles. Now that they were stationary, he could hold his head down so that the rain wouldn't cover the lenses in a moving sheet of water. He saw Y-Roc curled up in a tight ball next to the rucksacks. The boy was nearly frozen lying there in the cold rain, and Tyriver felt himself getting angry. There was a warm poncho liner in his pack, yet the kid had chosen to lie there freezing rather than take one of his personal possessions without asking first. Tyriver pulled his liner out of his rucksack and wrapped it around the kid's shoulders. Tyriver saw in the green light the goggles gave off that the kid had stopped shaking, and he smiled to himself. He had made too much out of what had happened in the village. Goldsmith was right about accepting the customs of the natives when you were in their environment.

McDonald's cough brought him back to what he had been looking for in his aid kit. Tyriver opened a box of five morphine Syrettes, removed one of the collapsible tubes, and unscrewed the plastic cap that protected the needle before tapping McDonald's arm. "I'm going to give you some morphine, Mac, to control your cough until we get out of here."

"You're not going to put me out, are you, Doc?"

"If we have to. Your cough could cause us some problems."

"I understand." McDonald didn't want to be unconscious in the jungle, but he understood the danger of his coughing once the monsoon rain had stopped.

Tyriver had no way of knowing the effect of the morphine on McDonald's weakened condition, but he was
hoping that the drug would numb McDonald's nervous
system just enough to reduce his need to cough, but not
so much that he would choke on his own sputum. Tyriver
pushed the short needle deep in McDonald's muscle and
squeezed the aluminum tube. He withdrew the needle
and shoved it deep into the dirt at his feet. "Here, take
a couple of these—penicillin."

Goldsmith removed the top half of the PRC-25 radio
from his rucksack and released the antenna. He said a
short but emotion-filled prayer before turning the set on
and placing the wet handset up against his ear. He looked
down at the dimly lit frequency band and turned the
knob until he reached the FAC's air-emergency frequency. Every aircraft flying over Southeast Asia monitored that particular band. He had decided that he would
make only one short broadcast, and if the FAC had been
called back to the launch site, he would accept help from
anyone.

Goldsmith sighed, closed his eyes, and pressed the
transmit button. "Bird Dog 6, this is Massasauga 10,
over." He released the switch and listened to the static.

The forward air controller had been flying in the rear
seat of the L-19 above the monsoon storm. The pilot was
near exhaustion from fighting the controls of the small
fixed-wing aircraft in the severe air currents the storm
had created.

The launch-site FAC had been puking on and off for
over an hour since the storm hit their area, and they had
to increase their altitude to remain above the recon
team's AO. He had been tempted a hundred times to
tell the pilot to return to the launch site and wait out the
storm, but something inside of him told him that even
though it had been days since they had heard from the
team, he could not leave the area uncovered.

Goldsmith's broadcast was heard by the FAC, but at
that moment he had to push the microphone away from
his mouth so that he could puke. The aircraft jerked
violently in an updraft, and his helmet struck the side
window. He tried wiping the vomit off his mouth, but the

aircraft jerked again and he ended up punching himself, drawing blood from his lips.

Goldsmith didn't realize the FAC was struggling to communicate with him. He pushed the talk switch again and sent out an emergency call. "Any aircraft, any aircraft, this is RT Massasauga. Emergency, emergency. Mayday, Mayday, over."

The response was instant. "RT Massasauga, this is Hexagon 34. Identify yourself, over."

The sound of an American voice gave Goldsmith tremendous confidence. "Hexagon 34, this is Recon Team Massasauga. We're in deep shit and need help, over."

"Roger, Massasauga, what can we do for you? We're high flyers on a bomb run to Hanoi, over."

Goldsmith realized that he had made contact with a flight of B-52 bombers. "Relay a message to my higher headquarters. Their call sign was Eagle Feather 6 when we started this mission, and you can reach them on 73.9, over."

"Roger, Massasauga, what do you want us to tell them, over."

"*Break, break.* This is Bird Dog 6, over." The FAC had finally broken into the transmission. He had to swallow the vomit trying to come up his throat, but he finished the transmission.

"Massasauga, I think you've found your people, over."

"Roger, Hexagon 34. Thanks for your help."

"I'll still pass on your call to your higher, out." The unknown B52 bomber pilot, continuing on his mission to Hanoi, looked over at his co-pilot and shook his head. "And we thought we had it bad."

"Bird Dog 54, Massasauga, over."

"Send your traffic, Massasauga, over."

"We need extraction for eight—I say again—eight, over."

"Roger, what number, over . . ." The FAC had barely gotten the words out when the L-19 dropped over a hundred feet into an air pocket over the storm clouds. The vomit tried creeping up his throat again, but he continued to swallow it back down. The FAC felt his throat burning from his own stomach acids.

The pilot came on over the intercom: "Do you want me to take over?"

"Negative, they're my people."

The pilot was impressed with the Army FAC's guts. He knew how miserable it was to be extremely airsick and have to continue a mission.

Goldsmith used a known extraction site as a base guidepost and walked the FAC to a spot where he thought they could be pulled out on their STABO rigs. "From site nine, go west one point five and south point seven. We'll be in that area, over."

The FAC repeated Goldsmith's message and then added, "We'll pull you out as soon as the storm passes, over."

"Roger, Bird Dog. Be advised that three—I say again—three McGuire rigs are needed, over."

"Roger, Massasauga. Three McGuire rigs and five STABO extractions coming up! Out."

Goldsmith replaced the handset in his rucksack and looked up at the three Americans grouped around him, listening to the broadcast. "We're going home as soon as the monsoon passes."

"Thank God!" McDonald lowered his head and laced his fingers together. He didn't care if the whole world was watching as he prayed.

CHAPTER FOURTEEN

✪✪✪✪✪✪✪✪✪✪✪✪✪✪✪✪✪✪✪✪✪✪

STABOS AND MCGUIRE RIGS

The B-52 flight leader immediately called the CCN tactical operations center, using the frequency Goldsmith had provided, and left the short message with a shocked duty officer. The CCN headquarters had already written RT Massasauga off as missing in action and had changed the identification pin on the operations map from green, which meant the team was active, to yellow, signifying MIA status.

Captain Atkins had kept the L-19 flying over RT Massasauga's area of operations on his own accord and against the direct orders of Lieutenant Colonel MacCall, who wanted the aircraft used for air-reconnaissance missions until another team was inserted. Atkins had covered his forward air controller by assigning him reconnaissance missions that were all in RT Massasauga's area.

The duty officer used the direct telephone lines from the TOC to the CCN commander's and Major Ricks' quarters to alert them that RT Massasauga had called in for a STABO extraction for eight people.

Ricks met MacCall in the hallway of the officers' hootch. He couldn't help smiling. "It looks like Goldsmith has pulled off his stay-behind mission."

"Let's see what he's bringing out first before we jump to conclusions." Instinctively MacCall pushed his black SOG hat down on his head to cover up his uncombed hair. The hat was something else that bothered the recon men in the camp. The lieutenant colonel had never been out on a mission and yet he wore the coveted hat. It was a converted version of the issued jungle hat, but the SOG team members had the wide rims cut back to two inches and then the hats were dyed black and the SOG patch was sewn on the front. Most of the recon men had two of the hats made up, one for the field and one for the rear areas, showing them off at the bars that supported the large nurse populations in Da Nang. These hats for profiling had the SOG patch in living color and displayed a white skull wearing a green beret with blood dripping out of the corner of its mouth, all surrounded by a lightning bolt pattern. The patch was one of the best unauthorized patches in Vietnam and was highly respected by all of the units.

Ricks brushed his hair back with his fingers and followed MacCall out of the hootch. "Why do you have a hard-on for Goldsmith?"

MacCall stopped and whirled around to face his executive officer in the light coming from the perimeter floodlights. "I just don't like him, and I don't need a damn reason!"

Ricks held his ground, but he was surprised all the same that MacCall even had the guts to stand up to him. "He's pulled more than his share of the load since he's been here, and his first mission gets a gold star. Just not liking him isn't enough—Colonel."

"You don't know the whole story about him, Ricks. Trust me on this one!" MacCall turned away and stormed toward the TOC.

Ricks followed the senior officer into the cement bunker, having no intention of trusting him. He liked the cocky lieutenant who was upsetting the whole operation at CCN by doing what even his fellow recon men thought was impossible. Ricks remembered the last recon man who had pulled missions like that off, and he wondered idly if the tremendous courage both of those men showed had anything to do with their hootch on the beach. Lieutenant Bourne had led RT Viper out of the same hootch that Lieutenant Goldsmith was now living in. Ricks shook his head to rid his thoughts of ghosts. He didn't want to bring bad luck on Goldsmith's team.

The duty officer had alerted the area-studies team that was assigned to RT Massasauga's AO, and the men hurried into the bunker in different stages of dress.

MacCall stood in front of the main battle map with his hands resting on his hips. From the rear, he looked like George Patton. "Damn it! Change that damn map pin!" Seeing the yellow pin reminded him of the shortsighted decision he had made earlier to withdraw support from RT Massasauga—and the big argument he had had over it with Ricks.

Ricks glanced over at MacCall and saw that he was waiting for him to join him at the map and make suggestions on what they should do. Ricks went over to the large coffeepot and filled his cup. He took his time stirring the coffee, even though he drank it black. The physical chore seemed to help him think.

"Ricks, get your ass over here! We have work to do. You can drink coffee later!"

Ricks paused at the duty officer's station and spoke to him softly. "Have you made contact with the Quang Tri launch site?"

"Yes, sir. Captain Atkins has a FAC over the team. They have requested extraction, sir."

"What kind?"

"STABO for five, sir, and three McGuire rigs."

Ricks placed his left index finger against his mouth and bit gently down, as he usually did when he was deep in thought. The STABO system for extraction had been designed by five Special Forces men. In fact, the first letter from each of their last names made up the name for the extraction gear. It was designed basically like a parachute harness, except that the leg straps were folded and taped on the wearer's pistol belt and the shoulder straps had a D-ring attached and taped on each side. The rig was designed to haul a recon man out of the jungle without having to land a chopper to get him.

The McGuire rig had also been designed by a Special Forces man—and named after him—but it could extract anyone from the jungle. It looked like a large horse collar with a small wrist strap attached to one side up at the top. When dropped from a hovering chopper, the person on the ground could strap himself into the horse collar even in a sitting position and be lifted out. In an emergency the evacuated man could slip his wrist into the wrist loop and be hauled out of the jungle hanging by one arm.

The duty officer broke into Major Riggs' thoughts. "We think he might have found three POWs, sir."

"Possible, very possible." Ricks had been running the SOG program for too many years to make assumptions so early. Goldsmith could have NVA prisoners or villagers that he wanted to bring out.

Seeing Ricks talking softly to the duty officer, MacCall was forced to leave the map and join his executive officer to hear what was going on. Having to walk over to the duty officer's desk made him furious, and he arrived in a state of near hysteria.

Ricks ignored his leader and continued talking to the duty officer: "Get me Captain Atkins on the secure voice radio, but don't pull him away from what he's doing. Tell him to call me as soon as he gets a break."

"Yes, sir."

"Is what I hear true, Major?" Captain Martin asked, joining the two senior officers.

"As far as we can make out, RT Massasauga is alive and well out there in their AO. They've requested an extraction for eight."

"Hot shit! I knew they were safe! I damn sure knew it!" Martin didn't see that his words were offending Mac-Call until the commander roared:

"If you had done your job, Goldsmith wouldn't have been left out there without an air cap!" MacCall's words sounded like gunshots in the bunker.

Ricks intervened. "He did his job, Jack. There's been an air cap over RT Massasauga constantly since they were inserted."

"I thought . . ." MacCall snapped his head around to face his executive officer. The unspoken word *traitor* was written on his face.

"The aircraft were conducting reconnaissance missions with a secondary mission to monitor RT Massasauga's frequencies. That was Captain Martin's idea, and I approved of it." Ricks knew that the request had been

Captain Atkins's, but he lied to get Martin out of trouble with MacCall.

"Why wasn't I informed?"

"I thought you assigned me to operate the TOC. Do you want to be briefed on every little order I give?"

MacCall shook his head.

"Well then, it worked out all right and that's what counts—right?"

MacCall nodded in agreement. He didn't trust himself to speak. He knew Ricks was making an ass out of him in front of the area-studies officer, but he controlled himself because he knew that he had only thirty-six days left of his command. After that he would be transferred back to the States to the Pentagon assignment he had already been given. His career was nearly guaranteed up to two stars, and all he had to do was leave Vietnam now without a major disaster. He knew that once he got back to the Pentagon, he could eliminate every damn one of the CNN officers and NCOs who had laughed at him behind his back. MacCall knew that there would be a major reduction in force after the war and the officer corps would muster out half of their numbers. He would make sure that people like Captain Martin and Major Ricks were on that list, along with those arrogant bastards operating the launch sites like Atkins.

Realizing what he would do, MacCall actually smiled. "Continue, Major. You're doing a great job. I'm going over to the mess hall for an early breakfast."

Martin waited until MacCall left the TOC and the steel door clanged shut behind him before speaking. "What a flaming asshole, sir!"

"Careful, Captain. He's our commander." Ricks cut the captain short. "Let's see what we can do to help Atkins with that extraction. Check and see what kind of air assets are on call. And while you're at it"—Ricks tapped the desk in front of the duty officer to gain his attention—"put two Brightlight teams on call."

The duty officer was on the secure voice radio talking to someone and only nodded to acknowledge that he had heard the order.

"I think MacCall is going to screw me on my efficiency report, sir," Martin said to Ricks.

"I'm the one who's rating you, Martin, and he's endorsing you. After I'm done, he'd be a fool to try to make you look bad. Just do your job, Martin, and I'll do mine."

"Thanks, sir."

"Check the extraction sites in RT Massasauga's AO." Ricks became the TOC director again. "Site six is on the board. Work it!" He was referring to the large operations board where all of the data was posted for the recon team's extraction. This way any visiting officers wouldn't interrupt those who were working to gather information.

"Yes, sir!" Martin hurried over to join the rest of his team. He felt much better after receiving the major's support. Many careers had been ruined in Vietnam through bunker politics.

"Sir, Captain Atkins is on secure voice." The duty officer held the handset up for Major Ricks.

"Atkins?"

"Yes, sir."

"I'm not disturbing you, am I?"

"No, sir, my team is preparing the helicopters for the extraction. We've got a FAC over the area, and the monsoon is moving away from the area. We should have clear skies when our team arrives."

"I'm concerned about the McGuire-rig extractions. We don't know what condition Goldsmith's people are in, and I would like to move two Brightlight teams into an old fire-support base on our side of the border. Let's have the choppers land there so that the team and their guests can get inside the choppers and receive medical support on the ride back if they need it." Ricks tapped the bottom of his coffee cup against the desk and added, "What do you think?"

"I agree." The ride back from RT Massasauga's area of operations to the Quang Tri launch site was forty-three minutes in good weather, and that was an awfully long time to be hanging underneath a chopper from a nylon climbing rope, especially if you were wounded or wet.

"I'll set that part of the extraction up from here to let you concentrate on the actual pickup."

"Thanks, sir."

"Is there anything else I can help you with?" Ricks said, honoring the SOG directive that the launch-site commander made all the decisions during the extraction or the insertion of a team. The directive had been designed to keep the layers of command from interfering with the critical process at hand.

"None, sir, but if you can think of anything else, let us know. I think Goldsmith has pulled off another legendary mission." There was a twinge of honest jealousy in the captain's voice.

"Have you heard who the extra three rigs are for yet?"

"We just received a call from the FAC. He's bringing out two POWs and a Yard kid."

"Names?"

"O'Mallory and McDonald." Atkins knew the effect his broadcast was making in the command TOC. "I was going to save that bit of info for you until they returned home."

"We've got to get them out of there first before we celebrate." Ricks knew that if the men assigned to the Brightlight teams knew they were going to be rescuing two of their own recon men held prisoner by the NVA, they would fight to the death to save them. "You're doing a good job, Atkins."

"Thanks, sir."

"Ricks, out." The major handed the handset back to the duty officer. He didn't need to say anything to the staff inside the TOC: he saw the looks on their faces. All of them had been eavesdropping on his conversation. Ricks strode over to the main map and selected an old fire-support base the 1st Air Cavalry Division had occupied only a month earlier during one of their sweeps of the border. Captain Martin stood at his side. "Get the Brightlight teams there as soon as possible! Have our doctor fly out with them and a couple of our medics. Tell the Brightlights who we're picking up. And tell them to go armed for bear!"

Martin nodded and waved for a couple of his NCOs to join him at the map.

Ricks leaned back against a desktop and smiled into his coffee cup as he watched his team operate with the efficiency of a Russian ballet.

*   *   *

The moonsoon rain stopped.

Water flowed over the ground in a solid sheet, making walking difficult in the jungle. Everything was soaked through, and the vegetation was still dripping water as if it was still raining.

RT Massasauga had used the heavy rains as a cover to move out of their night laager site toward the spot that Goldsmith had selected for their extraction. The rain would make tracking the team very difficult and the vegetation wouldn't give away their passage to an observer. Tyriver had taken the extra precaution of sprinkling the area with a light coating of powdered tear gas as he brought up the rear guard.

Goldsmith had taken the point with Y-Bluc after O'Mallory had insisted on carrying McDonald on his back so that the lieutenant would be free to fight if he had to. Where O'Mallory was getting the strength to carry his teammate was a mystery, but Goldsmith had given in, figuring he would be taking only a short break before O'Mallory fell exhausted with his load. The old sergeant was surprising everyone and hadn't once slipped with MacDonald on his back.

Y-Bluc spotted a wide animal track and decided to risk using it, since the lieutenant had told him to hurry. At first it looked as if the trail had been made by humans, but it was littered with huge piles of scat that varied in age. Y-Bluc turned toward Goldsmith and whispered the Montagnard word for the animals, but Goldsmith frowned, not recognizing the word. Y-bluc knew that the animal was much larger than the similar American beast but said it anyway: "Cow."

Even more confused, Goldsmith nodded for Y-Bluc to move out along the wide trail. They were still heading up the ravine, which was narrowing rapidly as they headed toward the source of the stream. After a hundred meters of fairly easy walking on the trail, the path disappeared as it made a sharp turn to the left toward the wall of the ravine. Goldsmith thought that they had reached the end of the trail, but Y-Bluc knew better. Animals always followed the natural lay of the land that took the

least amount of energy to negotiate. The trail wove its
way up a crack in the ravine wall to the top.

O'Mallory struggled with McDonald on his back, but
Y-Roc helped both of them up the steep incline by pushing on McDonald's back. The young sergeant was passing
in and out of consciousness, but the morphine had
worked and he wasn't coughing anymore.

At the top of the ravine, Goldsmith regained his bearings and located their position on his map. They were
less than five hundred meters from their extraction site.

The NVA executive officer had his telephone operator
try again to make contact with the commander's camp in
the ravine. He knew that the telephone was located in
the commander's office, which doubled as his personal
quarters, and someone was always in the hootch. After
the first attempt he had assumed the telephone line had
been damaged by the storm and had sent a runner to
deliver his status report, but he still had his operator try
every fifteen minutes to make contact. He had never
been late making a report, and he wasn't going to let a
monsoon break his perfect record.

The operator felt the handset vibrating in his hand just
as he was getting ready to ring the commander's camp
again. He pushed the talk switch and answered cautiously. "Hello?"

The voice coming over the line was heard by the NVA
officer standing ten feet away. He couldn't make out the
man's words, but he could tell that the caller was
extremely excited. As his operator listened, his eyes widened more and more. He finally cut the caller off and
turned toward the executive officer. "The commander is
dead! The advisers are all dead along with the camp
guards! The Americans have escaped from the camp!"

The NVA officer couldn't believe that two Americans
had overpowered so many guards and escaped. He didn't
even consider that an American recon team had penetrated so deeply through the NVA defenses. One of their
special teams had always made contact with the Americans within hours of their insertion, and besides, there
hadn't been any American helicopters within twenty
thousand meters of the colonel's camp in weeks. "Alert

the special teams! Find those two Americans, and I want them back here alive!"

The staff officer gave a curt nod and started working the radios. They had established an elaborate network throughout the area of squad-size units designed to patrol a thousand-square-meter zone. Any contact with an American unit, from escaped POWs to an American battalion, could easily be engaged and held in place until the squads could mass into as large a unit as necessary to destroy the airborne invaders. The system had always worked and it had prevented American recon teams from reaching the vital areas inside the NVA-held areas of Laos. There had been a few exceptions when Americans had stumbled on vital storage sites or had been dropped right on top of senior headquarters, but those instances had been rare.

The staff officer alerted the headquarters of the checkerboard defense system, and within an hour all of the NVA squads surrounding the POW complex were alerted. It would be impossible for two lone Americans to make it through their lines, especially if they went east toward South Vietnam.

The NVA squad occupying the top of the ridge line overlooking the colonel's POW camp received their alert within minutes. The squad was led by a sergeant who had fought against the French and had over thirty years of combat experience. He was old but very tough, and even though they were in one of the most secure areas of the war zone, he had made his men practice their tactics everyday, and he had spent hours planning how he would react to a POW escape. The thousand-square-meter area he controlled included the entire ravine. He had used two-man teams to patrol the entire area every single day since it had been assigned to him.

The squad leader barked orders for the squad to start searching along the edge of the ravine for any sign of the POWs breaking a new trail. If they had gone up the ravine instead of trying to break through the main POW complex, they would be in his AO. Chances were, that was exactly what the POWs would do.

He snapped his fingers and pointed at the two bamboo

shelters they had made for their tracking dogs. "We use the dogs today!"

Goldsmith followed the wide animal trail until its direction changed again, veering away from the direction of the assigned extraction site. He knew he was getting very close to the overgrown clearing that years before had been a Meo or Montagnard farm site. Secondary trees had reached fifteen feet, but none of the huge jungle giants had had enough time to take over the area and a chopper could hover fifty feet above and drop their ropes.

Tyriver paused where the team left the animal trail and dusted the ground with powdered tear gas. The exit was well marked with broken vegetation because the team moved without caring if they disturbed the jungle or not. It was only a matter of time before the NVA camp was discovered and the whole area alerted.

Everyone on the team sensed that they had to reach the extraction site quickly so that the FAC could use air power to saturate the surrounding area if needed in order to get them out. Once they were on site, they could just sit there while the FAC destroyed anything within a hundred meters of them.

Forcing his way through the jungle, Goldsmith almost fell out of a solid wall of young bamboo and vines into a relatively open area. He would have passed through the overgrown clearing if not for Y-Clack, who pointed out an old Montagnard sleeping platform that had been built between several trees. The grass roof had collapsed, but the bamboo floor was still recognizable.

The recon team formed a loose circle with Y-Roc and McDonald in the center next to Goldsmith, who set up the radio. "Bird Dog, Massasauga, over."

The FAC answered almost before Goldsmith had finished. "Roger, Massasauga."

"We're here. Popping smoke, over."

"I see yellow smoke, over." The FAC pilot banked his L-19 in a tight circle over the smoke. It was up to the pilot to determine whether the smoke was friendly or an NVA deception. If they were monitoring American radio broadcasts, they could confuse an extraction. They had been known to pull tricks like that in the past during major battles.

"Roger, yellow smoke, over."

"I have a surprise for you, Massasauga. We've got a Spooky on station." The forward air controller smiled into the mouth mike attached to his headset. The AC-47 fixed-wing airplane had been converted into a gunship with mini-guns that could fire thousands of rounds a minute and saturate an area the size of a football field with rounds six inches apart. The main advantage of the old aircraft was its stay time over a target. Jets could barely remain long enough to drop their bombs and then had to return to their bases to refuel, but the propeller-driven AC-47s could stay over a target area for hours.

"Bird Dog, use only small arms and cannon fire to support us. This area is saturated with small POW camps. Do you read me, over."

"Roger, Massasauga. I'm glad you mentioned that. I've got fast-movers coming in carrying five hundred pounders, over."

"If they have to drop them, put the bombs in the ravine to my northeast, over."

The FAC pilot banked his small aircraft so the SOG observer riding the backseat could observe the narrow ravine Goldsmith was talking about. Then the FAC saw a flight of helicopters coming in the distance. They looked like a swarm of hornets. "Massasauga, prepare yourselves for extraction, over."

Goldsmith signaled his team and they helped each other rig their STABO equipment. O'Mallory sat next to McDonald, supporting the younger sergeant wearing the Cuban officer's uniform. Y-Roc sat with Tyriver's rucksack on one side of him and the lieutenant's rucksack on the other. He was so small that he blended in with the baggage and was forgotten in the excitement.

Goldsmith broke his group into two extraction parties: O'Mallory, McDonald, and Y-Bluc would go out on the first lift with Tyriver, and he would supervise the second lift, which would take out the rest of the team and the Montagnard boy.

*   *   *

The NVA squad leader dropped to one knee and looked at where the new trail broke away from the animal trail. He was sure that he had found where the Americans had panicked and left the easy trail. He was still under the assumption that he was tracking two American POWs, who at the most had taken a couple of AK-47s from their guards during their escape.

The loud snort brought the squad leader's attention back to the animal trail. A full-grown bull gaur stood less than twenty feet away. The dogs had tried warning their masters by whining, but their warnings had been mistaken for excitement. The huge bull stood at least seven feet at his shoulder and totally filled up the wide trail.

He snorted again and tossed his respectable rack of horns. The NVA soldiers, hearing a number of gaur from the herd answering the bull, started to panic. Even a tiger did not mess with an adult gaur.

The squad leader pushed the safety off his AK-47 and fired a short burst in the air. The bull jerked his head sideways and left the trail, using his two thousand pounds to break through the jungle. The herd panicked and followed him. The sound of crashing gaurs filled the jungle for hundreds of meters. One female moved slower through the jungle so that she wouldn't lose her month-old calf in the underbrush. Several older cows stayed close to her, and they moved through the jungle in the protective pattern the herd took when spooked by a tiger. The calves were in the center, surrounded by their mothers, and the younger bulls acted as guards. The herd was headed directly toward RT Massasauga's extraction site.

Goldsmith heard the AK-47 fire at the same time the NVA squad leader looked up and saw the circling L-19. He knew exactly what was happening. The airplane was familiar to all NVA soldiers in the field. It always symbolized the prelude to a bomb strike or an American recon team. He didn't know how his two POWs had contacted the aircraft, but it was now up to him to kill the team before they could be rescued and then to hold the small aircraft on the site until reinforcements came.

He had only eight men in his squad and two dogs, but the men were all combat-tested veterans.

The first extraction helicopter appeared over the clearing and dropped their ropes. Two large McGuire rigs hung from the ropes, and a STABO rig had been attached to each so that the lighter rigs would reach the ground in the wash of the chopper.

Goldsmith gave a sigh of relief that his request for McGuire rigs hadn't been screwed up. The aircraft had been rigged as he had requested, with two McGuires with the first aircraft and one with the second. He knew that Captain Atkins would obey his request without question, but sometimes even the best requests were second-guessed and things got screwed up.

Tyriver hurried to help O'Mallory get McDonald in the rig and strap him in, and then he helped O'Mallory before hooking his own STABO rig to the D-rings.

An NVA soldier appeared out of the thick grass, holding his AK-47 out in front of him with the round bayonet pointed directly at Tyriver's back. The sound of the hovering helicopter had covered the NVA squad's approach.

O'Mallory had been facing the spot where the NVA had appeared. His eyes widened and he pointed behind Tyriver, but neither of them had time to react.

Goldsmith was looking up at the hovering chopper, and Y-Brei and Y-Clack were watching the jungle in the direction they had come to cover their back trail.

The NVA soldier cocked his arms to thrust his bayonet in Tyriver's back, but the expression on his face changed from hate to shocked disbelief as a K-Bar knife was buried deep in his throat where his collarbones met. The weight of Y-Roc on his back pulled the NVA soldier away from Tyriver, and the sharp point of his bayonet caught Tyriver across the back of his neck and then caught on the extraction rope and was deflected. It left a two-inch gash that caused Tyriver to turn around to see what had caused the pain.

Y-Roc still had his legs wrapped around the dead NVA's waist and was clinging to the man's back. He withdrew the knife and shoved the blade back in again before pushing the NVA away and struggling to his feet. Blood covered the front of Y-Roc's chest and arms.

The boy looked over to see if Tyriver was all right and smiled. His American was safe. Y-Roc jerked, tried recovering his balance, and jerked again as a second AK-47 round tore through his body, and then fell backward to the ground.

Tyriver screamed and tried unhooking himself from his extraction rig, but the crew chief had seen everything from his position hanging out of the aircraft and had signaled for the chopper to depart. The pitch changed with a roar, and the helicopter jerked the four men off the ground and flew straight up until the men dangling under its belly had cleared the trees before changing direction and within a couple of seconds had left the area.

Goldsmith saw the NVA soldier who had shot Y-Roc and fired twice with his pistol, but it was the burst from Y-Clack's submachine gun that killed the soldier.

Y-Brei was sweeping the jungle in a steady stream of 9mm rounds and was using magazines as fast as he could put them in his weapon. He killed three more NVA before they could engage in the small clearing.

The FAC saw the NVA closing in around the remainder of RT Massasauga. The sight down on the ground was very confusing, but the trails the NVA had made in the tall grass and young bamboo gave away their positions, and the FAC ordered the gunships to make a couple of runs so that the second helicopter could slip in and pick them up.

The Huey Cobras appeared out of the sky and hovered above the extraction site. Short bursts came from their mini-guns. The gunners knew that their marksmanship was critical because of the close-in fighting below.

The NVA squad leader blew his whistle, and the two survivors from his squad pulled back into the gaur-infested jungle. The herd was confused and angry. They had taken the dogs as their main threat to their calves and had attacked them. The human smell was irritating, but in the past the humans had always left them alone. The sounds coming from the sky confused the herd even more, and the animals had darted and spread out in small bands to hide from the loud sounds.

Goldsmith watched the second rescue chopper coming

in with both door gunners firing solid bursts from their
M-60 machine guns. He knew he would only have a few
seconds to rig up before the chopper pulled away. The
crew chief was hanging out of the open side door of the
aircraft, waving his arms frantically for Goldsmith to
hurry. The sergeant was secured by a safety strap, but it
still took elephant balls to expose himself like that to
ground fire. Goldsmith knew the crew chief would be
giving the helicopter pilot the signal to lift off.

Y-Brei and Y-Clack had already hooked up to their
ropes and were standing with their feet spread apart,
their submachine guns at the ready. Goldsmith ran over
to the two rucksacks containing the documents they had
confiscated from the POW camp. The information was
too valuable to leave behind. He used the waist strap on
the empty McGuire rig meant for Y-Roc to secure the
packs and was starting to grab the attached STABO rig
when he saw the boy's body lying on the ground. Goldsmith knew that he couldn't leave the kid's body there
for jungle animals to devour. Grabbing Y-Roc's arm, he
slipped the boy's wrist into the McGuire rig's wrist loop
and left the boy hanging there while he rigged up.

The crew chief gave the hand signal and yelled over
his intercom at the same time. The chopper rocketed
skyward for a hundred meters and halted before changing
directions and heading due east for the South Vietnam
border.

Perched in a tree, the NVA squad leader had been
waiting for the second extraction helicopter to lift off.
From much prior experience, he knew that the chopper
would stop for several seconds in midair to change direction. He fired an entire magazine at the men hanging
from the bottom of the chopper and had enough time to
put another magazine at the copper as it flew away.

Goldsmith felt himself spinning at the end of the rope
and tried stabilizing himself, to no avail. Feeling that he
was going to puke, he spread his arms out to attain a
free-fall position and regain control of his body. It helped
a little and his eyes focused on the spinning mass that
was the rucksacks and Y-Roc's body. He reached out
and his fingers caught one of the shoulder straps of a
rucksack. The spinning stopped and he stabilized himself

as well, facing the direction the helicopter was flying in. After a couple of minutes the urge to vomit stopped. Nearby Y-Clack was hanging in his harness and Y-Brei was stabilizing himself by holding onto Y-Clack's STABO harness, a method they had been taught to prevent spinning at the end of the ropes.

Goldsmith felt a sharp pain in his leg, but he was more concerned with the pain of the STABO harness between his legs. All of his body weight was focused on the leg straps, and it was worse than hanging from the suspended harnesses during training in jump school. Realizing that he was still holding his pistol in his right hand, he shoved it into his pistol belt. Instantly he started shaking at the end of his rope, and he quickly moved his arm back to stabilize himself. He had had enough spinning to last him a lifetime.

The forward air controller called in the Spooky AC-47 to sweep the immediate area around the extraction site, and the NVA squad leader died instantly as a dozen bullets tore through his body.

The herd bull had led his herd far enough away from the noisy place, and all of them escaped death from above. One of the larger cows suffered a deep gash in a foreleg from one of the dogs as she was trampling it, but she would heal.

Goldsmith took a deep breath, trying to ignore the pain coming from his crotch. He dreaded the long ride back to the launch site, but at least he was alive.

The helicopter slowed and changed direction. Goldsmith spotted an open patch of red laterite and two helicopters that were parked there. A great sense of relief filled him as he realized that his chopper was going to land there and allow for them to change choppers and fly the rest of the way back to the launch site inside the aircraft.

The pain from the straps in his crotch stopped the instant his feet touched the ground, but then the other pain overwhelmed him. He staggered and his right leg buckled under him. Before he hit the ground, arms grabbed him and carried him to the open door of the waiting chopper. A medic helped him down onto a stretcher. Goldsmith didn't realize how weak he had become until he tried sitting up. The medics laid Y-Roc's body on a stretcher next to him, and he turned his head to watch what they were doing to the dead boy. Goldsmith ignored the medics who were working on the gunshot wound in his own leg.

The helicopter lifted off as the two medics conducting CPR on the boy. Goldsmith wondered why they were wasting their time until he saw the boy's chest jerk and Y-Roc's eyelids flutter.

The Montagnard boy was still alive!

CHAPTER FIFTEEN

✪✪✪✪✪✪✪✪✪✪✪✪✪✪✪✪✪✪✪✪✪✪✪✪

CAMP ROTARY, B.S.A.

He had the driver of the black SOG jeep drop him off in front of the NCO club with his gear. The right leg of his camouflage trousers had been cut off at the knee by the doctors at the Da Nang Naval Hospital, and a clean bandage contrasted with the rest of him, which was still very dirty from the mission. It was bad manners to enter the social club after you had returned from a mission without first having cleaned up and changed uniforms, but Goldsmith hadn't spent enough time in the SOG compound to learn all of the little social rules of the elite reconnaissance unit.

Entering the smoky haze of the bar, he dropped his rucksack near the entrance and quickly made his way through the crowded room to the end of the bar. He signaled with his hand for the SOG sergeant who was taking his turn acting as the bartender to wait on him. Goldsmith reached in his pocket for his chit book and realized that he was still wearing his sterile mission uniform. All of his military-payment certificates and his club chit books were locked up in the safe in the TOC's mission-prep room.

"How about giving me a fifth of Kessler's on credit? I'll have the chits here tomorrow."

The acting bartender pressed his lips together and gave a curt nod. "It's a done deal." Reaching behind the bar, he pulled a bottle of the popular sipping whiskey out of a cardboard box behind the bar and set it on the worn plywood bar top. "That was a good stay-behind mission RT Massasauga just pulled, *sir*." The last word was heavily accented. SOG NCOs rarely addressed lieutenants as sir. They used L.T., lieutenant, or if they commanded a recon team, they would call them One-Zero.

"Thanks." Goldsmith grabbed the bottle around its neck and dropped it down at his side.

"How's Ty doing?"

"He took a round through his mouth." Goldsmith shifted the bottle to his left hand and used his right to show the sergeant the trajectory the AK-47 round had taken, through Tyriver's open mouth and exiting through his left cheek. "But the bullet didn't hit his jawbone. A clean hole through flesh. He lucked out."

The recon bartender nodded at the bottle of Kessler's. "This one is on me."

"Thanks." Goldsmith turned and left the bar without realizing that all conversation had stopped and everyone had been listening to his conversation with the bartender. The club remained silent until the door closed behind him.

"He's already a fucking legend with only two fucking missions!" The voice came from behind a cloud of cigar smoke at one of the felt-covered poker tables in the corner.

"Fuck that shit. Two fucking missions don't make a legend. You've got to have seniority!" The recon man who spoke had over fifty missions under his belt and had been with the SOG program for over three years. He commanded the coveted All-Asian Team, who were known to carry NVA weapons and act like the enemy on occasions in the AO.

The bartender, an old-timer in the program himself, looked over at the Asian team leader and winked at him. "Over fifty missions and not one of them comes even close to either of the missions Goldsmith has pulled off."

The team leader stood up and his chair fell backward on the plywood floor. "Are you trying to say something?"

"Nope, I said it already." The bartender started busying himself with some dirty glasses on the bar. He was neither afraid of the recon leader, nor was he giving in to the man's envy. He had said his piece, and everyone else in the bar knew that he was right. There were certain topics the recon team members did not talk about, and one was what went on out in the field with certain teams. There were rumors that some teams would insert and then hide for a couple of days before faking contact with the enemy and requesting extraction. Some of the rumors had even gone so far as saying that they put a couple of rounds through their extraction helicopters to make it look even better. But of course, there had never been any proof that teams did stuff like that—but in elite units, rumors were powerful.

Goldsmith struggled as he walked in the loose sand, favoring his right leg. The bullet had cut across the front of his shinbone and had caused a lot more pain than actual damage to his leg. As he moved through the hot sand, each step he took was directed in a half-upward motion.

He felt his breath quickening when he reached the door of his hootch, and he leaned over to feel along the raised beams of the floorboards until his fingers touched a key hanging on a nail. His hands shook as he unlocked the padlocked door and then dropped his rucksack and webgear in a pile on the floor, covered with a thin layer of sand that had blown in through the cracks of the hootch. He tore his clothes off in a near frenzy and threw them on the growing pile of field gear. Slipping on a pair of cutoff camouflage leopard trousers he used for lounging around, he started to open the bottle of Kessler's and changed his mind. The hootch was too confining. Goldsmith looked over at Tyriver's empty cot and noticed that a layer of sand had covered the white mattress cover. He jumped up and grabbed his poncho liner off his bed, sending a shower of fine granules through the air that caught the light of the late afternoon sun. He stepped out of his hootch carrying his poncho liner in one hand and the bottle of Kessler's in the other.

The path he took headed directly toward the rappeling tower, but he hadn't yet realized where he was going. He changed his course only to negotiate around buildings and parked vehicles in his way. He acted as if he was walking through a sea of quicksand, and the tower was the only safe refuge left for him. The tower offered him

the solitude he required to work out his problems. SOG
debriefers had swarmed around the survivors from his
team as soon as their extraction helicopters had touched
down at the Quang Tri launch site, and they had been
besieged with hundreds of questions that he knew could
come back to haunt him if he answered them the wrong
way. He had struggled all afternoon to keep the images
of Y-Clack and Y-Brei out of his mind, but he knew he
was losing that battle. He would have to face it, and he
wanted to be alone when it happened.

His hand reached out and touched the bottom rung of
the ladder of the rappeling tower. His sigh of relief came
out of his lungs with enough force to blow the accumu-
lated sand off the wooden rung at head level. He threw
his poncho liner around his neck and sucked in his stomach so that he would have room to shove the quart bottle
down the front of his cutoffs. Then he climbed the ladder
so fast that when he reached the top, he fell forward on
the deck when his hands ran out of places to grab. The
whiskey bottle was jammed against his scrotum, and a
sharp pain warned him to be more careful in the future.

He felt as if a huge weight had been lifted off his back.
He stood with the front third of his jungle boots stuck
out over the edge of the tower and rocked back and forth
just enough to make the act dangerous. It was a danger
that he could control and it felt good. Goldsmith stared
out over the camp and at the South China Sea to the
east. The water was so calm that only a slight strip of
white showed where it met the beach. There was absolutely no wind: it was as if nature was holding her breath
in anticipation of what Goldsmith was going to do. Smiling, he stepped away from the edge and kicked off his
unlaced jungle boots. One of them slid to the edge of the
platform and stopped just short of going over. Goldsmith
frowned. He did not remember putting the boots back
on when he had changed into his cutoffs, and that tiny
fact bothered him. He closed his eyes and inhaled a deep
breath as he told himself it did not matter that he
couldn't remember putting his boots back on. It was a
routine task that he had done automatically.

He forced his thoughts off his boots and spread his
poncho liner out on the deck close enough to the edge

so that he could lean forward and look down at the bottom of the tower. He dropped into an Indian lotus position with his bottle of whiskey in his hand and looked out over the tops of the buildings.

The complete memory of flying underneath the extraction helicopter flooded back. He had stablized himself by grabbing onto Y-Roc's McGuire rig and had taken up a free-fall position for the flight back. Y-Roc's rig had been attached to the opposite side of the aircraft, and the spinning had stopped as soon as he had grabbed a hold of the Montagnard boy.

Y-Brei and Y-Clack were spinning at the ends of their ropes. For a moment Goldsmith wondered why only a minute earlier they had grabbed each other's rigging and stabilized themselves. Then Y-Clack turned with the wind and Goldsmith saw that the whole front of his head was missing. An AK-47 round had hit him at the base of his chin and blown his face off. Goldsmith looked away immediately, but the sight kept reappearing in his mind. And when the body shifted in the wind, blood and tissue from Y-Clack's exposed head sprayed on Goldsmith's face and body and then moved on.

Goldsmith had been sitting on the tower for over an hour when he saw a thin black line appear on the horizon. It explained why the sea had been so calm. A major storm was moving in from the east.

He took another sip of his whiskey. He had thrown the bottle cap over the edge of the tower when he had opened the bottle. Goldsmith wasn't intending on getting shit-faced, but using the liquor as a conduit back to the mission. He was reliving every step of the long patrol and analyzing what he had done wrong and what he could do in the future to make sure that the same mistakes wouldn't happen again. The alcohol dulled the agony of the awful parts.

The wind increased, sending clouds of sand billowing up behind the tower. A large raindrop splattered next to him and was instantly absorbed by the extremely dry wood. He watched as the tempo of the falling raindrops increased and spotted the tower deck. At first his eyes focused on the wet spots, and as the rain started falling harder, he sought out the rare dry spots on the deck.

The main storm hit with the force of a gale, and the tower was covered with a sheet of moving water. Goldsmith was forced to lean forward as the wind attempted to push him off the platform. Adjusting to the force of the wind, he stood up. Instantly his poncho liner was sucked off the tower deck and went sailing through the air like a camouflaged flying carpet.

Leaning into the wind, Goldsmith moved closer to the eastern edge of the platform. Any sudden shift in the velocity of the gale and he would have fallen forward before he could compensate for the change. He wouldn't land on soft, dry sand but on brick-hard wet sand fifty feet below.

Goldsmith lifted his arms from his sides and held them out at a forty-five-degree angle. The power of the sudden storm and standing almost naked in it transported him back to the happiest time of his adolescence. Goldsmith's brain was kicking in its survival-defense system, forcing him to avoid the thoughts of death.

Major Ricks and the SOG supply officer watched Goldsmith standing on the edge of the rappeling tower with his arms held away from his sides and his head lifted toward the black sky. It looked as if the lieutenant was taunting Mother Nature. Gales were notorious for quickly changing the direction of their winds.

Since the storm was coming directly from the east, the supply officer had opened the huge barn doors of the prefab steel warehouse on its western side to equalize the pressure inside the building and keep the wind from tearing holes in the tin roof. Ricks and the captain were standing in the open entrance and watching Goldsmith as the force of the storm drove the rain almost parallel to the ground.

"We're losing him, sir," the supply officer said, keeping his eyes on the lieutenant. "Do you think I should climb up there and get him down?"

Ricks continued staring at Goldsmith and lit a custom-made cigar.

The captain, assuming that Ricks's silence meant that he should go, took a step forward. The major's hand shot out like a cobra striking and grabbed the captain by his elbow. "No, leave him alone. He's okay."

"Looks like he's losing it to me, sir."

Ricks smiled and twisted his lips around his cigar. "Haven't you ever just stood out under the rain on a summer's day, Captain?"

"Fuck, no! Why in the hell would a person do something like that when they can stay dry?" The captain was a practical man.

The smile on Ricks's face widened as he watched the lieutenant lean more into the wind. He was actually leaning out over the edge of the tower so far that if the wind suddenly stopped, Goldsmith would drop like a stone. "Well, if you haven't done it, Captain, you couldn't possibly understand the joy it brings." Ricks was recalling a similar experience he had had as a boy growing up in rural Virginia.

"Joy? In doing that? He's going to fucking kill himself, Major, and then you've got yourself a pile of paperwork!" The captain shook his head and left the major. "I've got to inspect a new shipment of weapons."

Ricks leaned against the side of the door frame and watched Goldsmith conduct his cleansing ceremony.

Goldsmith's thoughts left the rappeling tower and returned to an incident that had occurred when he was seventeen years old.

Alex-Paul sat in a captain's chair that had been placed in the waiting room of the office. The coffee table was covered with old issues of *Boy's Life* and *Popular Mechanics*. The double doors opened under a handmade sign that had the words Valley Trails Council etched in burned letters to make them look like rope. A smiling middle-aged man stepped out, wearing an adult version of the Boy Scout uniform.

"Alex-Paul Goldsmith?"

He was the only one in the waiting room, but he smiled and nodded his head.

"I'm Max Sheall. I'll be the camp director this summer." He motioned toward the open double doors. "Let's go back to my office and talk a little so that we can get to know each other a little bit."

Alex-Paul followed the scout leader into the office and took the offered seat in front of a wide desk. The decor of the office was pure scouting. Nature projects covered the tables along the walls, and stuffed animals were displayed in glass cases along with a display of coiled poisonous snakes.

Sheall saw where the teenager was looking and smiled. "Most scouts get a kick out of that display. I have it moved to Camp Rotary during the summer and keep it in the main office."

Alex-Paul turned to face the scouting official. He wanted to get on with the reason he had been asked to come to the scouting headquarters.

"I see you're wearing a jacket from the 101st Airborne Division. Do you have a relative with the division?"

"My brother's a paratrooper." Alex-Paul kept his answer short.

Sheall nodded and laced his fingers in front of him. The process of interviewing the boy was going to be more difficult than he had figured. "So, you want to be a camp counselor this summer."

Alex-Paul shrugged. He was intrigued by the idea, but he was realistic enough to know that poor kids from the east side of Saginaw didn't get jobs counseling the sons of the wealthy people who lived on the west side. He figured that the reason he had been asked to interview for the job was to meet some kind of quota.

"You don't seem very excited about working for us. Don't you want the job?"

"Sure, I want the job, but why are you interested in me?" Alex-Paul stared directly at the older man, forcing him to look away out the window. "I just got out of jail, and I don't think that is the kind of a person a Boy Scout camp would be looking for."

"Normally we don't hire juvenile delinquents to work for us, but you have some special talents that we are interested in—"

"Like what?" Alex-Paul had taken the initiative and wasn't letting the scout leader off the hook. "I've never been a Boy Scout. Hell, I don't even know your pledge!"

Sheall raised his hand. "Now, we don't curse around here."

Alex-Paul grimaced and started to get up to leave. It was obvious to him that the interview was over.

"Sit back down!" Sheall shouted, sounding like an irritated father. "I can see this isn't going the way I had planned. I might as well tell you the truth. I was shocked when Bob Gilbert called me and asked for a favor."

"Bob Gilbert—from the Big Brothers?"

"Do you know him?"

"Yeah, I was a little brother for a while in that program." Alex-Paul recalled the half-dozen big brothers who had been assigned to him. He wouldn't talk to the men assigned to him, and all of the relationships had folded after only a few weeks.

"Well, you've got a friend in Gilbert. He called us and asked if we would hire you for the summer. I must admit that I wasn't too pleased with the idea . . ."

"What changed your mind?"

Sheall flashed Alex-Paul a look that told him he was entering dangerous ground. "Actually, it was my son. He's going to be a counselor at the camp this summer too."

"You mean that everybody is going to know that I served time in jail?" Alex-Paul shifted to the edge of the chair, ready to walk out.

"Relax! The only people who will know about your background are the adult staff at the camp and my son. Everyone else will think that you're a scout who's been hired like they have."

"You're talking like I've already been hired."

"You have. My son Ted will pick you up in the morning if you want the job."

"What's the job?" Alex-Paul was still waiting for the real reason why they wanted to hire him. He was expecting something like they needed a dishwasher or janitor.

"Counselor. We haven't decided exactly what you're best suited for, but during the two-week orientation period, we'll figure out something that you can do." Sheall saw the blank look on Alex-Paul's face and added, "We have a two-week period at the beginning of the summer when the senior staff open the camp. My son and you will be the only teenagers up there, but I think that you'll enjoy the extra time to get adjusted to the woods before the scouting staff arrives."

"Will I get paid?"

Sheall smiled. "Sure, you'll be paid."

"I'll take the job." Alex-Paul shrugged, trying to act as though he wasn't excited. He would have taken a dishwasher's position to escape from the ghetto during the summer.

The next morning, Alex-Paul sat on the front steps of his small white house with dark green trim. He had been waiting for over two hours for Ted Sheall to pick him up, but he neither wanted to risk going back inside and leaving his suitcase out on the porch, nor did he want to take his suitcase back inside and have Sheall come and his grandmother invite him inside their house. It was only him and her now that his grandfather had died and his older brother had joined the paratroopers. They lived off her Social Security check and whatever money he could make doing odd jobs, but even then they were extremely poor. The inside of the house reflected their poverty. His grandmother made sure that the house was always painted and in good repair, and he took care of the yard. They had one of the neatest houses on the block from the outside, but everything on the inside was threadbare and he was ashamed of their poverty. The last thing Alex-Paul wanted was for some rich kid from the west side to see how they lived and then spread it all over the camp.

Three black teenagers walked slowly past the front of the house, acting like they were casing it out for a future robbery. Alex-Paul stared back with the same intensity of hatred they were giving him. He knew that the slightest sign of fear would bring the blacks on him. It was a game that they played with each other also. You had to be strong in the ghetto, and you had to protect what you owned with a fierceness that Alex-Paul often thought belonged back in the days of the cavemen.

The blacks passed slowly, and Alex-Paul turned toward Janes Street, which would be the most likely way the kid from the west side would come. Lapeer Street came through the heart of the First Ward and was the worst street in the city for crime and violence. Suddenly he saw a new car turn slowly off Janes onto 16th Street. He knew instantly that it was Sheall's son because his neighbors owned only junkers and the car was driving way too slow, as if the driver was afraid.

Alex-Paul called a good-bye over his shoulder to his grandmother and grabbed the handle on his small suitcase. He had already made arrangements to pay one of the black kids on his street to watch out for his grandmother while he was gone, and he had made sure that a line of credit had been set up at the corner grocery store so that the kid could draw groceries for her. She was too old to shop for herself anymore, and Alex-Paul felt a little guilty leaving her alone.

The car pulled up to the curb, and a teenager looked out of the rolled-up window at him. Alex-Paul hurried around to the passenger's side and waited for the kid to reach over and unlock the door. He threw his suitcase in the only open space on the backseat and slipped into the car. Ted Sheall's eyes widened as Alex-Paul rolled down the window. "It's hot in here."

Sweat dripped off the driver's chin. "I got lost. I've been driving around for the past half hour. Sorry I'm late."

"No problem, I just came outside. Good timing!" Alex-Paul continued eyeing the driver. "Are we ready to go?"

"Yeah—yeah. How do we get out of here?" Ted's voice broke a little.

"Go straight and turn left on Lapeer Street." Alex-Paul could see that the driver was scared shitless just driving through the black ghetto.

They drove in a silence broken only when Alex-Paul gave Ted directions. Every time they had to stop for a red light, the teenager constantly swiveled his head around to see if anyone was sneaking up from behind or from the sides of the car. When they reached downtown, Sheall relaxed a little, and once they had turned onto Washington Boulevard and the faces started turning white, he sighed with relief.

"You can roll your window down now." Alex-Paul smiled over at the teenager, who looked like he had just turned sixteen.

"Shit!" Ted caught himself and glanced over at Alex-

Paul, feeling his face getting red. "You actually live in there?"

"You get used to it." Alex-Paul shrugged.

"I've really made an ass out of myself, haven't I?"

"Yep." Alex-Paul continued looking out the window.

"Sorry, that was the first time that I've driven—or even gone—into the ghetto. I heard about it, but I never thought it was like that."

Alex-Paul pressed his lips together and remained silent. He knew that Ted's adventure into the ghetto would be a hot topic of conversation at the scout camp, and there was nothing he could do to stop it.

Several times Ted tried making small talk as they drove along the highway, but every time Alex-Paul brushed him off. Finally Ted turned his head when they reached a straight stretch of highway and said rapidly, "Look, if you don't tell the guys about how scared I was back there, I'd appreciate it a lot!"

Alex-Paul kept a poker face and nodded. "No problem, I can keep a secret. Let's just drop the whole thing. If you don't say anything about me, I can keep quiet."

"Deal!"

"I mean nothing!" Alex-Paul acted as if he was referring to the jail sentence he had served, but actually he didn't want Ted telling the others how poor he was.

"Sure, nothing. I don't even know you. Never seen you before in my life!" Ted started chuckling, relieved that Alex-Paul had agreed not to tell on him. "You're a ghost!" He knew from previous years as a camper how cruel the kids were if they found anything to tease a person about. He had been worrying ever since he had picked up Alex-Paul that he would tell everyone how scared he had been. It hadn't dawned on Ted that Alex-Paul had been just as worried.

The first week flashed by, and the rest of the summer staff would be arriving during the next couple of days to put the finishing touches on the camp before the campers started arriving on Saturday. Alex-Paul had fallen in love with the large scout camp the first day he arrived. He had never been in the woods before—he had rarely left his neighborhood except to go to school and when he had gone to jail. He had been more than a little apprehensive about living in the woods, and it had been a case of wasted worrying over nothing. Max Sheall had agreed to let him use the woodland cabin by himself during the first two weeks of camp. He had been surprised when Alex-Paul had asked to sleep in the cabin that was off by itself in the woods. The camp director had known a number of adult counselors who had passed up the opportunity to stay in the cabin alone during previous years, and because of the isolation of the cabin, campers had worked up a number of ghost stories about the place. The cabin, built to hold two counselors and six campers, had been situated away from the main campsite so that campers could study animal lore close up and not have to walk long distances. Over the years the cabin had been converted into a staff cabin because the smaller campers had become afraid of the place, and during the winter Explorer Scouts used the cabin for overnights.

Alex-Paul followed the narrow trail bordering the lake until he reached the docks at the main camp. Max Sheall and the graduate student in medicine who was going to run the swimming program that summer were standing waist deep in the water, trying to bolt a lifeguard's chair to the dock. Sheall waved for Alex-Paul to join them. "Alex-Paul, we've decided on letting you operate the rifle range. Do you think you can handle that?"

Alex-Paul was shocked. Normally that position was given to one of the adults because of the danger in using live ammunition. He had hinted that he would like to be the range officer's assistant, but he hadn't dreamed of being the range officer. "Sure, I can handle that!"

"Go draw the .22s from Al, and make sure they are cleaned and in good working order. You might want to take one of them down to the range and try firing a couple of rounds."

"Yes, sir!" Alex-Paul cut across the parade grounds over to the main office, where the rifles were kept in a large locked box.

The couple of rounds the camp director had recommended turned into a whole case. Alex-Paul spent every possible daylight hour he could on the rifle range, firing and sighting in the .22-caliber rifles. Al Fenner, the assistant camp director, had spent a half day showing him how to operate the range safely, and then he gave Alex-Paul a crash course in marksmanship. By the end of the week Alex-Paul was lighting wooden matches from fifty feet away.

The counselors, who were made up from the Explorer and scouting troops, arrived the Friday before the campers were due to arrive. There was little for them to do besides taking care of their personal belongings and set up the final camping areas. Cabin assignments were made by the camp director, and Alex-Paul noticed that no one had been assigned to his cabin. He waited until supper to corner Ted in the dining room.

"Ted!" Alex-Paul caught him just as he was heading toward a table filled with counselors from the previous year. It was like a homecoming. Ted glanced over at Alex-Paul with an expression that said he hoped that he wasn't going to ask to sit with them. Alex-Paul read the expression and waved Ted away. He figured that he would find out on his own why no one had been assigned to his cabin.

"Alex-Paul." Al had seen what had occurred between the two teenagers and quickly figured out that Ted wasn't too happy about introducing Alex-Paul to the old scout clique, which had been together since they had been campers at Rotary. "Over here! I need to talk to you." Al waved Alex-Paul over to the senior staff table.

Alex-Paul set his tray on the picnic table so that his back would be to the dining room.

"You've done a great job setting up the rifle range."

"Thanks."

"I'll sort of appear during your first class to make sure that everything is set up all right and you've got a grasp on the safety procedures, and then you'll be all on your own." Al looked at Alex-Paul and added, "You don't seem very happy."

Alex-Paul got to the point quickly: "I checked the cabin assignments, and I've noticed that I'm the only one in my cabin. Is there a reason for that?"

"Do you think there might be a reason?"

"Yes, I do!" Alex-Paul was thinking about his time in jail.

"You're wrong—about your reason." Al understood

Alex-Paul's concern. "The counselors are mailed an application, and on it they are asked where they want to work for the summer. We try to accommodate everyone. If they ask to be assigned to the swimming area, they live in the cabins down by the dock; arts and crafts, they live in the cabins near the center. The cabin you've decided to live in has always been left vacant, except on special occasions. No one has intentionally kept people away from your cabin, Alex-Paul."

He felt his face getting red and looked down at his tray of food. "Thanks for explaining that to me, Mr. Fenner."

"No problem, Alex-Paul. But in the future, give us a break. We are your *friends*. And I promise that the rest of the counselors will not know about your past back in Saginaw."

"Thanks." Too embarrassed to stay at the table, Alex-Paul got up to leave. "I've got to go."

"You haven't finished eating."

"I'm not hungry." Alex-Paul carried his tray over to the garbage cans, and just before he threw his food away, he caught himself and made a huge meatloaf sandwich. He left the mess hall carrying a carton of milk and the sandwich. He picked up the trail to the cabin and hurried until he was out of sight of the main complex before slowing down enough to eat. He had gone off half-cocked over the cabin assignments and was glad that he hadn't asked Ted about them. He had an hour before the counselors were going to assemble down at the lake campfire site for their first staff meeting.

As soon as Alex-Paul opened the door of the cabin, he noticed a suitcase and athletic bag on the bunk bed opposite his. The cabin assignments must have been incomplete. Alex-Paul went over and checked for a nametag on the baggage but couldn't find one. He figured he'd wait and see who the brave counselor was, to volunteer living in a haunted cabin.

The counselors left the dining hall and wandered over to the meeting site in small groups to wait for Max Sheall and the adult staff. Alex-Paul arrived just as the camp director was leaving the dining hall with Al Fenner at his side. There wasn't enough time to find out who his roommate was before the meeting. He took a seat on the stone retainer wall a little away from the rows of logs that functioned as seats in the small beachfront amphitheater.

One by one the adult staff briefed the teenage counselors on their respective duties and on the new changes in the camping rules for the summer. As each additional rule was read to the group, a collective groan went up from the counselors.

"Now, before we take questions from the audience, I would like to settle one final detail—the camp-fire skit for tomorrow night. Which cabin would like to volunteer for the first skit?" Max Sheall looked slowly around the camp fire. The first skit of the season was always the most difficult because the cabin had only a day to prepare for it. What was worse, a bad skit could give a counselor's cabin a bad reputation for the rest of the summer. Because of this, the counselors avoided the first-night skit like the plague. "How about the Waterfront Cabin? You guys have been together for three years now and should be able to put something together for tomorrow night."

The senior counselor for the lifesaving and swimming group was quick with his answer. "Sorry, we've got to get our lanes in the water tomorrow, Mr. Sheall. But we'd be glad to take the second week's skit."

Sheall nodded and marked the Waterfront Cabin down for the second week. Hands shot up as cabin leaders picked weeks for their skits throughout the summer. When they had finished, the first skit was still open. "I need a cabin to volunteer!"

Alex-Paul raised his hand.

"Yes, the Woodland Cabin will do tomorrow night's skit! Great! That's solved, then!" Sheall slapped his clipboard against his leg as all of the counselors turned around to see who was dumb enough to volunteer.

Alex-Paul slipped off his rock wall and disappeared into the shadows. He heard the camp director's voice behind him: "You can take tomorrow off to prepare for the skit."

Hearing someone running up the path behind him, Alex-Paul stopped and turned around. In the light reflecting off the lake, he saw a slight figure.

"Are you living in the Woodland Cabin?"

"Yes."

"Hi, I'm you're cabin mate! My name is Dave Spaulding."

Alex-Paul took the hand that was held out to him. "Alex-Paul Goldsmith."

"Great! I'm glad that someone else picked the Woodland Cabin to live in this year. I love that place!"

Alex-Paul couldn't help but smiling over the smaller counselor's enthusiasm.

"You volunteered us for tomorrow night's skit. So what do you have planned for us to do?" David kept turning sideways as he walked in front of Alex-Paul up the path to the cabin.

"I don't know yet. Do you have any ideas?"

"Well, it's going to be difficult with only two of us— so it'll have to be something simple."

"Have you done this before?"

"Sure. I've been a camper here since I was ten years old."

"How old are you now?"

"Fourteen."

Alex-Paul realized that he had gotten himself a little brother instead of a cabin mate. Nonetheless, he was starting to like the kid. "Well then, tell me how these skits operate."

David sat on one of the large, flat rocks outside the cabin and started briefing Alex-Paul on how the skits operated. Halfway through, he stopped. "Have you ever been a camper before? You ask a lot of questions."

"My first year."

"How old are you?"

"Seventeen."

"Man! And they hired you?"

Alex-Paul felt his stomach tighten. "Yes—and gave me the rifle range."

"Range officer?"

"Yes."

"Whew, you must be a good shot!'

"So, besides coming up with a good skit for the campers, our reputation is going to be on the line—is that right?" Alex-Paul said, getting back to the subject at hand.

"Absolutely. Guys have been shunned for the whole summer for putting on a bad camp-fire skit." David looked back down the trail, and his voice changed to a more melodramatic tone. "This could ruin me as a counselor—and it's my first year too!"

"Don't hang up your jockstrap yet. I've got a couple of ideas that might work."

David frowned. "There's only two of us. Most of the cabins have five or six counselors in them."

"Can you tell a good ghost story?"

"Can I tell a ghost story? I was born telling ghost stories to campers!" David leaned forward on his seat. "Are you going to do a ghost-story skit?"

"Not exactly . . ."

When Alex-Paul finished telling David what he had in mind, the younger counselor started hopping around in uncontrolled excitement. "It's great, Alex-Paul! Absolutely the greatest idea for a skit that has ever been conceived at Camp Rotary."

"I don't know if it's *that* good. We've still got to do a lot of work. In fact, I think we better start now."

"Tonight?"

"It's going to take that long for parts of it to dry."

"What about the Cracker Barrel tonight in the dining hall?" David asked, referring to the social hour where all of the staff gathered to have a late-night snack before lights out.

"I'd rather work on our skit."

"So would I!" David started running down the path and then stopped to return to the cabin to get a couple of items.

"I'll meet you by the dining hall right before lights out, and we can walk back to the cabin together," Alex-Paul said, starting ahead of the smaller counselor on the trail.

"Sure, if you're scared of the dark, I'll walk back with you," David said seriously.

"I'm the one who's been living out here alone for the past couple of weeks. It was you that I was thinking about."

"Don't worry about me. I love the dark. The woods don't bother me at all."

"Let's still meet at the dining hall and make sure

everything is done. I'll be over at the arts and crafts building most of the night, but make sure you get me that old wet suit and flippers you said Waterfront Cabin has in its rafters."

"It might take awhile if they stay in their cabin, but I know that stuff is up there because I put it there myself last summer."

"Good, then let's get to work." Alex-Paul jogged down the dark trail toward the large arts and crafts building, feeling excitement flowing through his body.

David Spaulding sat in front of the dying camp fire with his back to the lake. He had been telling ghost stories for over an hour, and some of them had been quite good. Picking up a small drum, he began tapping out a soft rhythm and his young voice lowered. A light mist started rolling in off the lake, adding to the spooky drumbeat, and a couple of the younger campers moved a little closer to each other. The ghost stories had reached the under-twelve campers, but the older boys were amused but nowhere near scared.

David caught the look on the faces of the counselors, and he saw that none of them were amused. The ghost stories were entertaining, but did not fulfill the requirements for a skit.

Just at that moment Max Sheall turned his head to see where Alex-Paul was sitting in the group of gathered campers and couldn't locate him anywhere. He couldn't believe that he had left a fourteen-year-old to handle the whole skit by himself.

David slowed the beat of the drum and his voice rose. "And now I will tell you the story of Ke-Che-Wan-ka, the water demon of the Chippewas. He is an ancient demon who lives in all of the lakes in Michigan. Many, many moons ago the demon dug inner-connecting tunnels between all of the lakes, and he travels at will between them." David lowered his head and looked out at the group of scouts through lowered eyebrows. "Ke-Che-Wan-ka is a very evil demon who lives to suck the marrow out of young bones!"

A couple of the older scouts started chuckling, and the senior staff had to calm them down.

David continued talking to the beat of the drum. "Blood—human blood—is what keeps Ke-Che-Wan-ka immortal, and he always moves through his tunnels under the lakes to hunt in lakes that are used by unsuspecting humans. Like Lake Rotary—that hasn't been used for half a year." David leered and slowly nodded his head. He was a very good actor. "But there's no reason to fear him here. He hasn't been seen in over a hundred years. He must be very hungry—hssss."

Several campers chuckled.

"Now, here is the story how Ke-Che-Wan-ka was created . . ." David spent ten minutes telling the story, and when he reached the end, he stood up. "And so that is the story of Ke-Che-Wan-ka—good night, campers!"

Max Sheall started a polite round of applause for the effort that David Spaulding had put into the story telling, but he figured that he would wait until the next morning to tell the first-year counselor that his stories did not qualify as a skit.

The older counselors had already chalked off the Woodland Cabin's skit as a total flop and were talking among themselves when they heard a high-pitched scream.

At first the object that appeared in the mist covering the water didn't have a distinct shape, but as it drew closer to the camp fire in the amphitheater, the campers saw scales covering the creature's black skin and water weeds hanging from its body. A couple of the older counselors tried laughing, but the sounds came out as nervous titters. The younger campers, who had been seated the closest to the water's edge, got a good look at the lake monster and didn't stick around to see if it was real or not. They took off running and disappeared over the parade grounds.

Dave Spaulding stood with his back to the water. "What's going on?"

"Run!" one of the eleven-year-olds screamed as he dashed after the rest of his troop.

"Why?" David performed his part in the skit perfectly, standing with his hands held out as the lake monster approached him from behind.

Some of the older campers stopped running when they reached the stone wall surrounding the amphitheater.

They watched as the lake monster wrapped his arms around Spaulding and pulled his long claws across the teenager's chest. Blood gushed from underneath his shirt and ran down his legs to his knee socks.

David screamed and started pleading for someone to help him as the lake monster began dragging him backward into the water.

An Explorer scout from Waterfront Cabin hopped up on the stone wall and gathered his courage to yell at Spaulding, who was starting to disappear in the mist. "All right, stop the crap! You're starting to scare the little kids!"

A high-pitched scream answered the scout: "Help me! Oh, please help me!" The scream ended with the gurgle of someone being pulled under the water.

The staff counselor in charge of the waterfront stepped out onto the wooden dock and cupped his hands around his mouth. "Okay, it was impressive, now come on back to shore! You're scaring the little kids!"

A loon answered from the other side of the lake.

The older campers were the first ones to return to the campfire, but they moved cautiously, ready to run back to the stone wall at the first sign of anything coming up out of the water. They weren't ready to believe a monster had actually appeared out of the lake and grabbed Spaulding—but they weren't totally convinced that it hadn't happened either. The lake monster had looked too real.

"Look at this!" One of the older campers was kneeling down at the spot where the monster had grabbed Spaulding. "This is real blood!"

"Awe shit!" A nearby camper started running for the stone wall, and that was all it took to panic all of them.

The camp-fire amphitheater emptied. Even the counselors left the area, using the excuse that they were trying to calm down the campers, but the real reason was that what had happened was making them very nervous. They hadn't fallen for the monster theme yet, but something was strange and they figured that it was smarter to proceed with caution. David Spaulding's ghost stories had worked their magic.

Alex-Paul had to hold his hand over Spaulding's mouth

to prevent his giggling from reaching the shore. They were standing in chest-deep water under the dock, watching the scouts panicking.

"That was a good touch, having the scout find the blood," Alex-Paul whispered in David's ear. "Let's go, before they come back with flashlights and find us here." Taking a deep breath, Alex-Paul leaned down into the water to secure the papier-mâché monster's head to the sandy bottom of the swimming area, next to one of the dock's support posts. He had shoved Spaulding's clothes inside the full-sized mask along with his monster gloves. Spaulding had been wearing a swimming suit under his scout uniform.

"I love it!" David's voice was a little above a whisper as he started breast stroking over the dark surface of the lake.

"Shhh. Voices carry far over water. We don't want to get caught now and ruin everything!" Alex-Paul said, swimming next to David in the dark. The mist over the water made visibility less than a yard, but he knew exactly where he was going. At the same time he felt the current underwater from David's kicking and heard his breathing. He was keeping track of the young counselor as well.

Alex-Paul found the canoe they had hidden a hundred meters down the shoreline and held it steady so that David could get in it. They paddled quietly across the lake to the campsite they had set up for the night.

Max Sheall sent a couple of counselors to get Alex-Paul and David for the Cracker Barrel, but when the counselors returned, they told him that they weren't in their cabin. He waited until after the Cracker Barrel to pick a dozen of the older counselors to form search parties. He was beginning to worry that the pair might have drowned in the lake after pulling off their skit. The junior counselors were forced to sleep with the younger campers in their tents to calm them down. The ghost stories and the open-ended skit had worked on their young imaginations.

The search parties stayed up all night, checking the shoreline until the first rays of the sun broke over the east. Sheall had decided that he would have to call the sheriff's office, but he figured that he would wait until after breakfast.

The campers fell out of their tents and formed up in the main parade area for reveille. The area surrounding the campfire didn't look as sinister as it had during the night, but the campers were still nervous and rumors had spread quickly that the two counselors had drowned in the lake.

The first campers to enter the dining hall were shocked to see Alex-Paul and David sitting at the staff table behind plates piled high with pancakes and sausages. David struggled not to laugh and was forced to jam his mouth full of pancakes.

Sheall shoved his way past the open-mouthed scouts and reached the table with his hands already placed on his hips. "Explain yourselves! And it had better be good!"

Alex-Paul stood up slowly and addressed the crowd filling the dining room. "The Woodland Cabin's skit is now officially over." He took his seat again, wearing a broad smile.

"Wh—at did you just say?" Sheall was about ready to burst from anger. "Do you know that I had search parties up all night looking for the two of you?"

"Yes, sir, we could hear you calling to each other from our campsite on the opposite side of the lake." David struggled to swallow his food and talk at the same time.

"Then why in the—why didn't you answer us?" Sheall caught himself just in time before he swore in front of the whole camp.

"It was a part of our skit. Group participation in the legend of Ke-Che-Wan-ka." Alex-Paul wiggled his eyebrows, trying to add a little humor to what was quickly becoming a crisis situation. "You didn't give us a time limit for the skit and no one told us that we couldn't use group participation, so we decided we would bring the whole camp into the skit. After all, Mr. Sheall, there were only two of us in our cabin."

The silence in the dining hall was complete. Sheall looked over at Al Fenner, who shrugged his shoulders. The Woodland Cabin skit had broken no rules, and the intent of the skit was to scare the campers *and* staff—

they had accomplished both of their goals. Sheall's anger left him and he struggled to suppress the smile forming on his face. He knew that he had to maintain discipline in the camp, but Alex-Paul and David had created the near-perfect skit. He nodded his head and smiled. "Well done . . . very well done!"

The campers burst out in a roar of approval, and the Woodland Cabin's skit became a classic at Camp Rotary.

Goldsmith felt the cold and his body began shivering uncontrollably in an effort to generate heat. He leaned back from the edge of the tower deck and then took a step backward. He was still holding the bottle of Kessler's in his hand. He had lost all track of time. An hour or a dozen hours could have passed. The storm was still raging and didn't look as though it was going to let up. Goldsmith looked for his poncho liner, but it was gone. One of his jungle boots was still lying on its side in the center of the rappeling platform, but the second boot had been blown over the edge of the tower.

Goldsmith took his time climbing down off the tower and paused only long enough to glance over at the open barn doors of the supply building before heading back to his hootch. He thought he saw a shadow leaning against the frame of the door, but he wasn't sure.

The hootch was still empty when Goldsmith returned. The force of the gale had caused the roof to leak in a couple of places, and the gear and clothes he had left on the floor were all soaked. His cot was dry, though, along with everything else that was up off the floor. He used one of his olive drab towels to dry off and slipped into a pair of tiger cammies. The inside of the hootch was warm compared to standing nearly naked in the storm. His body regained its normal temperature, and a tremendous hunger engulfed him. He checked his watch to see if he had missed dinner at the mess hall. They were still serving, but still he didn't want to see anyone. Even hunger couldn't get him to join his peers, where there would be hundreds of well-intentioned questions that he did not want to answer. Goldsmith opened a wooden ammo box they kept in the hootch and sorted through the cans of C-rations they kept for midnight snacks. He selected four

cans of the high-calorie main meals and sat on his cot to
devour them. His thoughts bounced back and forth
between his summer at Camp Rotary and the storm raging outside his hootch.

What had made the two and a half months at the Boy
Scout camp so special for him was that it was the first
time in his life that he had realized that he was something
more than poor white trash. He had spent most of his
teen years living in the black ghetto without any close
friends. White kids who lived outside the ghetto shunned
him, and the few white kids who lived in the neighborhood were in the same position as he was and they tried
not being noticed by the blacks. As far as the blacks
went, they would let him hang around them, but only if
he accepted the lowest position in their social order. He
really didn't need that kind of ego busting, so he had
choosen to be a loner.

Goldsmith caught himself grinding his teeth as he
thought about his screwed-up childhood. Not until his
summer at Camp Rotary, where he had been surrounded
by white kids his own age, had he realized that he was
intelligent. Answering questions in class always caused
trouble after class. After years of trying to act dumb, he
has assumed that he was dumb.

Camp Rotary opened his eyes and showed him that he
was much more than he had given himself credit for
being. The Woodland Cabin's skit was only the first coup
he pulled off that summer.

Goldsmith set the empty C-ration can on the wet floor
of his hootch and picked up his half-full bottle of Kessler's. He took a long drink of the smooth whiskey and
crossed his legs on his cot. The Army blanket curtain
that covered the Plexiglas window overlooking the sea
had been drawn back, and he stared out at the raging
storm. He was beginning to feel very good. He was
warm, safe, and fed, and the whiskey was starting to
work its mellow charm on the jagged edges of his
emotions.

Al Fenner called Alex-Paul and David into his office
after the evening chores had been finished and the campers were all back at their campsites. "Well, it looks as if

the two of you have become very popular. I've received nine requests from the other counselors to transfer to your cabin."

David glanced quickly over at Alex-Paul, who caught the look on his cabin mate's face. "I don't know if we want to share our cabin with anyone else. I've sort of gotten used to Spaulding's snoring, and I don't know if anyone else can put up with it."

David grinned. He didn't snore, but it was about as good excuse as any to keep the mystique of the cabin from being shared with the rest of the counselors. Scouts had been coming up to him all day congratulating him on the skit, and it was unusual for a first-year counselor to receive so much attention. "I agree, sir. We're happy the way things are and we shouldn't disturb the status quo."

Fenner nodded his head and suppressed a grin. "I figured the two of you were happy the way things are. So, I'll just tear up these requests to transfer to your cabin—for now." He knew that it was wise to keep the door open. Everyone in camp knew that the two Woodland cabin mates were going to bear watching for the whole summer. Sheall had called both of them into his office and had given them firm warnings about getting carried away again, but Fenner had been around long enough in scouting to know that a legend was being created. The Woodland Cabin was being talked about all over camp.

During the staff's Cracker Barrel meeting that night, the Waterfront Cabin counselors sat together around the table. Sheall had made his debriefing of the day's events short and the meeting was breaking up early. The skit that Alex-Paul and David had pulled off had placed them in a tough position. They were going to have to perform the next skit in front of the same group of campers. Normally, the second week's skit was easy because the first week's skit usually bombed. Not only had Woodland Cabin put together a legendary skit, but they had violated the sanctuary of the lake, which had always been Waterfront Cabin's private area.

The head counselor for Waterfront Cabin left the table and went over to Alex-Paul and David. "Hey, that was a great skit!"

"Thanks." Alex-Paul sized up the older counselor, waiting for a smart remark to follow. The elite waterfront clique had ignored him since the camp had opened, and the sudden friendliness was something he was taking with caution.

"Look, why don't you and Shorty there stop by down at the docks after we're finished here?"

"Why?" Alex-Paul's eyes glowed with their own light as he stared at the pre-med student.

"Well, we just want to be friendly, that's all."

"We're busy," Alex-Paul said, turning away.

The rebuff hadn't been expected. The other counselors were usually thrilled to be asked down to the docks by the waterfront clique. "Hey! We're trying to be friendly. Now, if you want to spend the rest of the summer at each other's throats, we can do that too!"

Alex-Paul glanced over at the senior staff's table and saw that both Fenner and Sheall were watching them. "Fine, we'll stop by for a couple of minutes."

"Good!" The pre-med student slapped Alex-Paul on his shoulder and left to join his clique.

David waited until the waterfront counselor had gotten out of hearing range before he spoke. "I don't know if this is such a good idea, Alex-Paul. Those guys can be real pricks when they feel that their status is threatened. I should know. I apprenticed with them last summer and they made my life pure hell."

"How? Tricks?" Alex-Paul finished his cup of cocoa. He was listening to David, but his eyes were on the waterfront crew, who started laughing over some private joke as soon as their leader returned. Alex-Paul knew something was up.

"Uh, yeah, stuff like that. I was only thirteen last year and I, uh, didn't have very much *stuff* down there"—David nodded his head down toward his crotch—"and they teased me a lot!"

"Real mature guys."

"Assholes is more like it!"

"Well, let's see what they have planned for us." Alex-Paul left the table and carried his cup over to the kitchen, where he rinsed it out before putting it in the dish rack.

David followed closely behind Alex-Paul as he led the

way down the dark path. The waterfront was illuminated at night by four large floodlights as a safety precaution. The whole group of counselors from Waterfront Cabin were sitting out at the far end of the docks, where the two safety canoes were tied up.

"Hey, Alex-Paul, David! Come on and have a seat!" The pre-med student patted a spot next to him that had been left open.

Alex-Paul quickly scanned the faces that were staring at him in the floodlights. He could see that they were too interested in his arrival. He took a seat next to the pre-med student, but instead of letting his legs hang over the edge of the dock as the other counselors were doing, he crossed them Indian-style on the dock. David followed suit next to him.

Noticing Alex-Paul's precaution, the pre-med student smiled to ease the tension. "Thanks for coming down to smoke the peace pipe with us. We don't want any hard feelings to develop between our two cabins." The counselor reached over the edge of the dock as he talked and pulled up on a rope tied to four cans of Coke left from a six-pack. He pulled two cans free from the container and handed them to Alex-Paul and David. "Peace?"

"Peace." Alex-Paul took the Coke but kept his feet away from the edge of the dock. He was expecting some kind of a surprise initiation.

"That was a great stunt you pulled off at the camp fire last night."

"Thanks."

"Even though you used all the stuff we had stashed up in our roof for your skit."

"Come on! You guys didn't even remember that that stuff was up there!" David shook his head. He knew that the waterfront guys were trying to find some excuse to take a cheap shot at them because of the smashing success with their skit. "I put it up there on my own after being told to throw the wet suit and flippers away."

The pre-med student flashed an angry look at the first-year counselor but remained calm. "Maybe so, but you guys have sure put the pressure on our cabin for next week. You're going to be hard to beat."

David shrugged. "Isn't that what the skit competition is all about?"

The angry look was repeated, but this time the pre-med student made sure that David saw it. "Probably."

The warning had been received, and David shut his mouth.

"Hey, do you think old Scarback is still in the lake?" one of the lifeguards asked from the shadows.

"Probably. He's been living in this lake for a long time. They say snapping turtles can live to be over a hundred years old and weigh two hundred pounds!"

"He's probably out there right now in the dark swimming around looking for something to grab hold of. Maybe a finger or a toe hanging over the edge of the dock!"

All of the waterfront crew pulled their legs up out of the dark water.

"Naw, he wouldn't be this far away from his favorite haunts back by the dam lagoon."

Alex-Paul followed the conversation. The lake was kidney-shaped, but there was a small narrows near the dam on the far side of the lake, which fed into a waist-deep lagoon filled with turtles and water lilies.

"There was a scout a couple of years ago who went fishing back there and lost two toes to snapping turtles. He had his feet hanging over the edge of the boat."

"Oh man, that's sick!" One of the waterfront staff pretended to gag.

"Can you imagine what a snapping turtle would do to a guy who was skinny-dipping!" The gathered waterfront crew joined the speaker in groaning and holding their crotches in mock pain.

"I'll race you guys to the dock!" the pre-med student cried, slipping out of his scout shorts. He was wearing a nylon racing suit underneath, which was normal for those who worked all day on the docks. "Come on! I'll race anyone out to the floating dock and back!"

"That's over fifty meters in the dark!" the apprentice counselor for the waterfront said too loudly, letting everyone know that his line had been rehearsed.

Alex-Paul realized that David and he were being set up for a test of courage.

"Not me! I'm not swimming in the water. You can't see anything and the weeds wrap around your legs!" a second voice piped in with the same rehearsed tone.

The pre-med student turned slowly around and looked directly at Alex-Paul under the spotlight. "How about you? Want to give it a try?"

"I'm not a very fast swimmer." Alex-Paul saw smiles break out on the faces of the waterfront crew. They wanted him to back down from a challenge to regain their status as the lords of the camp. He knew that the rumor that would be spread around the camp wasn't that he backed down from a race, but that he chickened out because he was afraid of the dark water. It wouldn't make any difference that he had stood chest-deep in the same lake the night before for over an hour and had swam a much farther distance to his hidden canoe. David had been with him, and they would say that made the difference.

"I'll give you a head start. I'll let you reach the dock before I even start!" The pre-med student was very confident of his swimming ability. He had been a member of the Arthur Hill varsity swim team and had been on the University of Michigan's team since he was a freshman in college.

"Sure, why not." Alex-Paul leaned over and whispered something in David's ear before slipping out of his clothes. David's eyes popped open and he started to protest, but Alex-Paul shook his head and added, "Just do it!"

"But—"

"Do it!" Alex-Paul balanced himself on the edge of the dock, curling his toes around the last two-by-six plank. Then he pushed off in a passable racing dive and bent at the waist to form an air pocket to protect his groin. He had stripped all the way down and entered the water naked.

The pre-med student smiled and winked over at his co-conspirators. He was impressed that Alex-Paul had the guts to race naked after the stories about the large snapping turtles, and he slipped out of his nylon trucks to make the race equal in the courage department. He had little doubt that he could beat Alex-Paul even with a fifty-meter head start.

David slipped away from the group, watching Alex-Paul swimming in the floodlights toward the dock, and untied one of the canoes tied to the end. Life vests and rescue hooks had already been placed inside the canoes, since they were rescue craft. He was not happy about what Alex-Paul had told him, but he would do his part. He didn't like even being out on the lake at night alone, let alone being responsible for Alex-Paul's safety.

David moved the canoe next to the dock until he reached the spot where Alex-Paul had left his clothes, and he leaned over and pulled the clothes into the canoe with him. Everyone was watching Alex-Paul swimming and cheering their representative on even before he entered the water.

"What's he doing?" The pre-med student had started dropping into position to dive as Alex-Paul neared the dock, but he stopped when he saw that Alex-Paul was swimming past the floating dock out into deep water. "Damn, he's missed the dock! He must be swimming with his eyes closed!" The comment brought loud laughter from the crew.

David had to shout to be heard. "He's swimming back to the dam!"

"What did you say?" The pre-med student turned, and the waterfront crew noticed David in the canoe for the first time.

"I said, he's swimming back to the dam. If you would like to witness it, you'd better get in the other canoe." David shoved away from the dock using his paddle so that no one else could join him. He wanted to keep enough room for Alex-Paul to ride back with him.

"Hot damn!" The apprentice counselor was the first one to respond to what had been said. All of the older guys were in a state of mild shock. No one had ever swam all of the way across the lake through the lagoon to the dam! Scouts had swam across the lake proper to the opposite shore, but the thick weed beds and lily pads in the lagoon made swimming difficult even in the daytime. Alex-Paul wasn't only swimming the distance at night, but he was doing it naked! Every boy standing on the dock unconsciously placed a hand over his crotch.

The pre-med student started reaching for his shorts but

stopped halfway down to the deck. He realized that if Alex-Paul pulled that stunt off alone, the waterfront crew would forever lose their status in the camp. It was too late to stop the crazy kid, but he could at least make the score even. He sprang from the dock and hit the water with hardly a splash. He swam underwater for at least twenty-five meters until the filtered light from the spotlights stopped and he broke the surface. He made up the distance between him and Alex-Paul quickly and started breast stroking alongside him. "You're fucking crazy, you know that?"

"Thanks for joining me. It's a little scary out here." Alex-Paul's white teeth reflected in the distant floodlights.

"Where are you going?"

"I thought I would swim back to the dam and check it out."

"Have you ever been back there?"

"Once in the daylight."

"That place is filled with snapping turtles, and the water is very shallow."

"I know. Are you coming?"

The pre-med student shook his head in the dark and took up a position next to Alex-Paul. "I guess I'll have to. Someone has to keep you from drowning when old Scarback decides to bite your cock off!"

Alex-Paul chuckled and started stroking harder. The two of them swam without talking, followed by a small flotilla of canoes that the waterfront crew had unlocked from the shore racks. No one wanted to be left behind during the historic night swim.

The water changed temperature quickly and Alex-Paul realized that it was becoming shallower. He changed direction slightly to line up with the narrows leading to the lagoon and took a deep breath when a cold patch of weeds rubbed against his chest and down his body to his feet. The feeling sent a chill down his spine.

"Are you sure that you want to enter the lagoon?" the pre-med student asked, feeling his scrotum tighten against his body.

"Yep." Alex-Paul conserved his breath. He wasn't a swimmer and the long swim had tired him. He tried leveling off more over the water to keep his feet from kicking too deep and touching the water plants, but that only made him splash the surface. He resigned himself to touching the underwater plants and started swimming as fast as he could through the lily pads. All he could think of was a snapping turtle coming up off the bottom and biting off his penis.

The pre-med student reached the dam fifty feet ahead of Alex-Paul and struggled to his feet before wading through the shallows and the mud. He ran ten feet up on shore before turning around and hollering at the top of his lungs. "Yeah!"

Alex-Paul didn't waste any time following the waterfront leader up on the bank. He reached down and touched his penis. "Whew, it's still there!"

The two swimmers started laughing. A friendship had been formed.

David beached his canoe and called over to Alex-Paul, "You're crazy!"

"I know it!" Alex-Paul called back to his cabin mate. "Did you bring my clothes?"

"Yes, here!" David threw the bundle of clothes on shore. He had wrapped the bundle in Alex-Paul's belt to hold it together.

Alex-Paul slipped on his underwear and handed the pre-med student his scout shorts. "Here, wear these back."

"Thanks." The older scout took the shorts and slipped them on over his wet hips. He felt the same way that Alex-Paul did in his underwear, as if he had slipped on a steel jock.

The gale's force rattled the Plexiglas window of the hootch, bringing Goldsmith's thoughts back to the present. He caught himself smiling and he laughed. The summer he had spent at Camp Rotary was the best summer of his life. He had learned how to fire a rifle, lead people and most of all, he had learned the meaning of courage and had conquered his fears.

Goldsmith lifted the bottle of Kessler's to his mouth and wondered what had become of David Spaulding.

CHAPTER SIXTEEN

✪✪✪✪✪✪✪✪✪✪✪✪✪✪✪✪✪✪✪✪

MARBLE MOUNTAIN

The rain stopped beating against the window, and the light from a full moon reflected off the wet sand in the SOG compound. Goldsmith opened the door of his hootch and looked out. A strong breeze was still blowing in off the South China Sea, but the dark storm clouds were gone. He took a few steps outside and stretched. Surprisingly, he wasn't drunk. Half the bottle was gone, but the smooth sipping whiskey had only relaxed Goldsmith, allowing him to make the transition from the battlefield to the base camp.

The sound of crashing waves drew him to the huge sand berm surrounding the camp, which was in constant need of repair because of the blowing winds. Goldsmith found himself a comfortable spot between two large fighting bunkers and dropped down to watch the giant waves created by the storm crash on the beach. Goldsmith looked over at the bunkers on the perimeter and saw that the guards had taken up positions on the roofs. Seeing the glow of their cigarettes in the distance, he knew they were awake. Storms always made the guards nervous because NVA sappers loved to sneak up on a permanent installation and blow up a couple of bunkers or ammunition piles just to let the Americans know that they were around. After a storm all of the guards relaxed and checked the area around their bunkers for hidden shape charges.

The nearby waves masked the sound of the approaching

jeep, and Goldsmith didn't hear until it was almost on top of him. He turned around on the sand and saw Major Ricks exit from the vehicle. He was alone.

"Evening, sir." Goldsmith turned back around to face the sea as Ricks took a seat on the sand next to him.

"I'm out checking the camp. That storm did a lot of minor damage. It damn near blew the rappeling tower over!" Ricks grinned and saw a smile creeping over Goldsmith's face.

"It's a good place to go sometimes to get your head screwed on right." Goldsmith figured out that Ricks had seen him up on the tower.

"O'Mallory and McDonald are going to make it."

"That's great." Goldsmith handed the open bottle over to the major, and he took a long pull before handing it back.

"They told me to thank you, especially McDonald. They've diagnosed him as having double pneumonia. He would have been dead in a week."

"So the mission was worthwhile." Goldsmith sipped from the bottle and swished the booze around inside his mouth before swallowing it.

"Yeah, it was worthwhile." Ricks sensed that something was troubling Goldsmith and waited for the lieutenant to speak.

"I lost Y-Brei and Y-Clack."

"War has a habit of doing that to soldiers."

"Have you seen Sergeant Tyriver?"

"He insisted on staying with the kid you brought out with you. He's worried that they will ship him to a South Vietnamese hospital, and you know how they treat Yards . . ."

Goldsmith nodded. "Y-Roc saved Tyriver's life during the extraction. The kid hopped on the back of an NVA who was about to bayonet Tyriver, and then he cut the sucker's throat." Goldsmith kept his eyes on the surf.

"That explains it, then."

"Explains what?" Goldsmith didn't like the tone in the major's voice.

"The doctors told us that the kid had a lot of anal damage."

"So?"

"Well, the Montagnards sometimes select a kid—orphaned, usually—to service the bachelors."

"A queer?"

"Well, it doesn't mean the kid is homosexual, but yeah, he's used that way."

"And you thought that because Tyriver was looking after the kid that Tyriver was—"

"Don't jump to conclusions, Lieutenant!" Ricks was forced to reach over and pull Goldsmith back down on the sand. "There were a couple of rumors."

"I recommend that you or someone stops those kinds of rumors quickly—before Ty gets back in camp—or he's going to waste some people! That's a crock of shit!"

"Nothing has gotten out of the TOC. I'm glad, though, that you mentioned the incident during the extraction. It explains a lot."

Goldsmith flashed the major a hostile look in reply.

Ricks stood and brushed the wet sand off the seat of his pants. "Thanks for the drink. There is going to be a full debriefing in the morning at the TOC. I would like you there. Captain Abou and his people will also be there, and we'll go over the whole patrol from insertion to extractions." Ricks paused with one leg inside the jeep. "You've done a damn fine job, Goldsmith."

"Thanks, sir."

The jeep engine revved and the gears ground as the major tried finding first gear. Goldsmith struggled to control his anger. He knew what the major had been hinting at, and the more he thought about it, the angrier he became. He filled his mouth with whiskey and swallowed it in small doses, enjoying the burning sensation the alcohol was producing inside his mouth.

"Nice night."

"Fuck! Can't a person have a little fucking privacy around here?" Goldsmith lashed out at the newcomer.

"Sorry, I saw you sitting up here talking to the major, and I thought I'd stop and say congratulations on your mission." Captain Barr started stepping backward down the berm.

Now Goldsmith felt guilty. Barr had treated him like a friend since he had arrived at Command and Control North, and he didn't deserve being snapped at. "Sir, I'm

sorry. Come on back and have a drink." He held the
bottle out for the captain.

"Thanks." Barr took the peace offering and drank a
healthy amount before handing it back to Goldsmith,
who shoved the bottle down into the sand between his
feet.

"This war is some sorry shit."

"Was it tough out there?" Barr thought he meant the
mission, but Goldsmith had been referring to his conversation with the major.

"It wasn't as tough out there as it is back here. Fucking
politics!"

The lieutenant was now talking about something that
Barr was the expert at. He had been the SOG-CCN personnel officer for almost a year, and he had seen just
about every political trick that could be pulled, especially
in the awards and decorations department. "Thinking
about politics has reminded me that there are a lot of
award recommendations coming from your mission. Captain Abou has already submitted his for his platoon, and
you should get yours in before things cool off."

Goldsmith looked down at the bottle between his feet
and thought for a long time before he answered. "I'll
write up a recommendation for Tyriver—make it a Silver
Star—and I want to get Y-Roc a Bronze Star with a *V*
for valor."

"Sure, we can do that. I'm assuming that Y-Roc is a
Montagnard?"

"Yeah."

"We are authorized to go as high as a Silver Star for
Yards."

Goldsmith thought for a couple of seconds. "No, a
Bronze Star will do. He's only a kid. A damn brave kid,
but just a kid. We don't want to get the commandos
jealous or they'll take it out on him."

"I'll stop by the hospital tomorrow and get Tyriver's
recommendations," Barr noted, not expecting Goldsmith
to react.

"Why would you do that?"

"Well, you know, to complete all of the recommendations."

"I just gave you mine and they're complete."

"How about you?" Barr's voice lowered. "Someone has to recommend you, and it has to be an American."

Goldsmith shook his head. He was remembering how Lieutenant Colonel MacCall had reacted to the award recommendation for his first mission, downgrading the award to a Bronze Star. "I don't need anymore bullshit with the C.O. Just leave me off the list. If he sees a recommendation for me signed off by Tyriver and my recommendation for a Silver Star for Ty"—Goldsmith made eye contact with Barr for the first time since the captain had joined him on the berm—"I don't need that kind of shit spreading around."

"You're pretty fucking naive, aren't you?"

The hostility of the normally mellow captain startled Goldsmith. "Naive about what?"

"That's how things are done around here! Shit, having Tyriver submit you for an award is the honest method. Most of the time the One-Zeros use their own after-action reports as evidence for their own award recommendations! When you have only two Americans on a team, that's the way it's done. Friend submitting a friend for an award. And that goes all the way up to the big one."

Goldsmith shook his head. "It doesn't mean that much to me."

"You are fucking amazing! You stand back and let MacCall fuck you out of DSC, and now you could actually make a legitimate Medal of Honor and you say that it isn't a big deal."

"It isn't—not to me." Goldsmith stared directly into Rob Barr's eyes, and the captain realized that the lieutenant wasn't playing any game with him.

"You're serious, aren't you?"

"Yeah, serious." Goldsmith looked back out over the beach.

"What do you think you deserve for this mission?"

Goldsmith thought about what the CCN commander had done to his award recommendation for his first mission. "A Bronze Star would do just fine."

"A Bronze Star?"

"Yeah, for achievement." Goldsmith was deadly serious. "I didn't do much out there on the mission, but I think if I deserve anything, it should be for the planning part. I did a good job." He glanced back over at Barr to emphasize his statement and to check to make sure the captain wasn't laughing at him.

"A Bronze Star for achievement for the best mission to come out of CCN since it has been established?" Barr couldn't believe what he was hearing. "Do you have any idea what kind of an operation our commander is running out of that little cubbyhole attached to his office?"

Goldsmith looked puzzled. "No."

"He's running a—" Barr caught himself just in time. "It's no big thing . . ." He waved his hand at Goldsmith. "It's just that you deserve more, much more . . ."

"A Bronze Star would be fine, really." Goldsmith took another sip from the bottle and handed it over to Barr.

"God, yes!" He held the bottle up and drained it before handing back the empty to Goldsmith.

"Another dead soldier." Goldsmith took the empty fifth bottle and stood up to throw it as far as he could out into the surf.

"You are one fucking amazing recon man—do you know that, Lieutenant Goldsmith?"

Goldsmith shrugged. "I've lived through worse times."

"Worse?"

"Try living as the only white boy in a black ghetto sometime." Goldsmith struggled to his feet. The whiskey was finally finding its way to his head. "Not only a white boy, but a blond-haired, blue-eyed white boy. Now that's survival, Captain."

Barr stayed on the berm and watched Goldsmith struggle through the wet sand over to his hootch. He was already making plans on how he was going to help the lieutenant.

There were too many men attending the briefing for everyone to fit into one of the small recon-team debriefing rooms, so Major Ricks decided to use the main work area to conduct the meeting. There were eleven teams still in the Prairie Fire area of operations and five teams in the dangerous Nickel Steel AO, but the area-studies teams were constantly monitoring them and Ricks had prearranged with Captain Martin that the TOC would be cleared quickly if one of the inserted teams got into deep trouble.

Captain Abou sat in the front row, surrounded by the survivors of his Hatchet Platoon plus the new men who had filled the empty slots on the team. Recon teams and Hatchet Platoons were put back into operation as soon as possible after a disaster to maintain the morale of the program. Men had a tendency to sulk when they were reminded too often that a team had been wiped out.

Goldsmith sat in the back of the room, keeping the seat next to him open for Sergeant Tyriver, who hadn't shown up yet.

"We'll start the debriefing with Captain Abou and work our way through the events in chronological order." Ricks pointed at the staff member operating the built-in tape-recording system in the TOC and nodded his head. "I don't need to remind you that your debriefings are being taped, so think before you speak and try to be as thorough as possible—yet keep it brief so that our clerks won't be working for weeks to type the transcript for Saigon." Ricks nodded for Abou to take the platform and took a seat next to the CCN commander.

Tyriver entered the TOC and tiptoed over to the seat next to Goldsmith and sat down. He smiled, using the good side of his mouth.

Seeing the stitches in Tyriver's cheek, Goldsmith shook his head. The doctor had put some kind of antibiotic ointment over the gunshot wound but left it unbandaged so that it could heal faster. Goldsmith smiled at his One-One and leaned over to whisper, "How's Y-Roc?"

"They stabilized his condition at the naval hospital and were going to ship him over to the Ninth ARVN Hospital, but I smuggled him to our commando clinic. That's what took so long."

Goldsmith nodded and then returned his attention to Captain Abou on the platform. The captain was just about ready to make a sarcastic remark directed at Goldsmith and Tyriver when the lieutenant redirected his attention to him.

Abou's debriefing centered on the successful destruction of the underwater bridge and the large number of casualties his platoon had inflicted on the NVA. He avoided talking about leaving the area with two live Americans still on the ground and a large number of his commandos.

"Lieutenant Goldsmith, would you please brief us on your stay-behind mission?" Ricks turned in his chair so that his voice carried to the back of the room.

Goldsmith left his seat and walked down the center aisle to where all of the captured NVA equipment was displayed, including the documents. He glanced over at MacCall and saw that the commander was struggling to keep a poker face. Goldsmith had heard that MacCall and his ex-battalion commander from the 5th Division had been classmates. What's more, he had been warned about the popular Stateside trick of writing a bad efficiency report on an officer; then, in the spirit of making things fair, the senior officer would transfer the delinquent officer out of his unit. What actually happened was that the senior officer had the man transferred to one of his buddies' units. A back-channel message would insure that the junior officer received another bad OER, which would result in his discharge from the service for having two bad officer-efficiency reports back-to-back. Once the career-ending game had been completed, especially in combat, it was virtually impossible to appeal the reports.

Goldsmith was positive that MacCall had downgraded his award from his first SOG mission because it would look bad if he won a high valor award and received a low rating on his OER.

Ricks cleared his voice and Goldsmith realized where he was. Everyone was watching him, even the straphangers who were pretending that they had something to do in the large room so that they could eavesdrop on the debriefing. "Excuse me, sir," he said, addressing MacCall, and then moved down to the end of the table and picked up the first item. He gave a short explanation of how it had been captured and what was different about the piece of NVA military equipment. The experts from SOG headquarters in Saigon were still going over the documents, which were providing a wealth of information. Goldsmith had been right in guessing that the whole area in Laos was saturated with small two- and three-man POW compounds. The NVA had established a POW compound near every one of their major troop laager sites so that their new recruits could see that the Americans were not giants or super humans, but weak and scared in their cages.

Ricks noticed that Goldsmith's hand skipped over the stack of passports on the table as the lieutenant briefed the items his recon team had captured in their raid on the POW camp.

It took Goldsmith nearly an hour to complete the item briefing, and he went over to the map and showed the route they had taken to the POW site and the Montagnard village. Goldsmith tapped the map and looked over at Ricks. "Has Saigon decided on our request yet?"

"They agree with you. There will be an eight-sortie bomb strike in the area to cover for the LOWLEX drop of ten tons of vitamin-fortified rice near the village. Saigon has also taken your advice of attaching a small piece of Y-Bluc's loincloth and jacket to each of the rice bags so the villagers will know that the rice came from Y-Bluc and us." Ricks rolled the cigar he was holding in his fingertips. "That was a good idea, Goldsmith."

"Thank you, sir, but the credit should go to Sergeant Tyriver." Goldsmith nodded to his One-One as he walked back to the table. He removed the passports and tapped them against his fist as he walked over to Abou in the front row. "Have you noticed these, *sir*?"

"Passports," Abou said cautiously, not sure what Goldsmith was up to.

Goldsmith opened the top passport and pointed to the country of record. "Jordan."

"So?" Abou leaned back on his seat.

"O'Mallory and McDonald have both testified that the two Arab advisers who tortured them the most were members of the PLO."

"That makes sense. The communists all stick together, and the PLO has received money from the commies. So what's new about that?"

"What's new, sir, is that the Pathet Lao are being advised by the PLO. *Arabs.* So in the future, Captain, you can lay off all of that Jewish-baiting crap with me!"

"That is enough!" MacCall growled. "Lieutenant, I will not tolerate that kind of disrespectful talk!"

Ricks bit down on his cigar to keep from smiling. He knew the whole story about Abou's assault on Goldsmith, and Goldsmith obviously wasn't passing up the opportunity to get even.

"Yes, sir!" Goldsmith turned away from Abou and replaced the passports on the table. "In closing, sir, I would like to state that all of the men that went in with RT Massasagua came out—plus two POWs left behind from Captain Abou's platoon."

"Damn it, Goldsmith! I said, enough of that kind of inflammatory talk!" MacCall left his seat. "O'Mallory and McDonald were not left behind!"

Goldsmith, though, was watching Captain Abou, who was sitting speechlessly in his chair. The whole camp knew that what Goldsmith had said was true. Abou had panicked and left people behind on the ground. That was as bad as a SOG leader could get. Nor could he say anything to defend himself after the two Irish sergeants had made their damning statements.

The SOG commander replaced Goldsmith on the platform, cutting the lieutenant's briefing short.

Goldsmith saw a red silk pouch at the end of the table and went over and removed it. "I believe this is mine, sir."

"Put that gold back, Lieutenant!" MacCall's face started turning red. "That is government property!"

"Sir?" Ricks stood up, taking his time walking to the front of the room. "We just received a message from Colonel Shunball that authorizes Lieutenant Goldsmith to keep the gold. Saigon agrees that he traded the gold for a personal weapon. Also, the trade was the key element in the Montagnards releasing the information about the POW camps."

MacCall was trapped in front of the recon men. Goldsmith, with Ricks' help, was making an ass out of him. He looked over to Abou for help, but saw none forthcoming. He glanced to the back of the room, where all of the staff officers were standing. Captain Martin held up a yellow piece of teletype paper. "Sir, that information just came over the wire. We didn't have time to brief you on it before this meeting."

Seeing his opening, MacCall took it, small as it was. "Okay, fine. Keep the gold." He waved Goldsmith away with the back of his hand. "I don't think that it looks right for an officer to make such a huge profit off the ignorance of the Montagnards, but I will obey higher headquarters."

Goldsmith took his pouch of gold and returned to his seat. Tyriver was sitting with his head down to hide the smile on his face from the colonel, who watched every step Goldsmith took toward the back of the room.

"Lieutenant Goldsmith, see me in my office after this meeting, please." Ricks sat down sideways in his chair and turned his attention back to the CCN commander, who was recapping the mission for the assembled officers and NCOs. There wasn't much MacCall could say except that the mission was receiving a great deal of attention in Saigon from the MACV staff. The commanding general himself had requested a complete briefing on the POW camps.

Afterward, Goldsmith paused outside the major's office and turned to face Tyriver. "I'll meet you over at the hootch later."

"If I'm not there, I'll be with Y-Roc at the commando clinic. He's doing pretty good, but seeing a familiar face helps him. He's never been out of the jungle before! Can you believe that? I mean, he's never been in a city. The only vehicles he's seen are trucks on the roads and aircraft in the sky! He was shocked the first time he was served ice cream in the hospital. It's like bringing a person out of the Stone Age!"

"Let me take care of business and I'll join you over there later." Goldsmith knocked on the door and entered when Ricks called for him to enter.

"Come in, take a seat." Ricks sat behind his desk with his feet crossed over one corner. "I'm sorry about what happened in the TOC. It seems that everyone is trying to cut a piece out of that particular pie. You pulled off a great mission, but I'm afraid that Captain Abou is going to be the one named as the commander and receive the credit."

"He was the senior officer on the ground—for part of the time, sir."

Ricks grinned and lifted his eyebrows. "You're right about that, but our leader has ordered that Captain Abou receive all of the credit."

Goldsmith shrugged. "I don't know anyone in Saigon, so it doesn't matter to me. My friends here at CCN know the truth and that's all that counts."

"And so do the people at Saigon and the other SOG units. The truth has a way of getting around. You've received the true credit for the mission, but Abou will receive the official credit and the Distinguished Service Cross." Ricks waited for a reaction from Goldsmith and saw none. "Captain Barr tells me that you mentioned something about a Bronze Star for achievement?"

"We talked about awards for my men, sir."

Ricks nodded his head. "That's all you want for this?"

"Sir, are the officers so underemployed back here that they've got to play politics with everything?"

Ricks didn't answer, instead changing the subject. "So, Lieutenant, what are you going to do with your gold now that Saigon said you could keep it? Are you interested in investing it?"

"In what, sir?"

The major lifted a small stone statue off his desk and handed it to Goldsmith. "That's a Cham Dynasty piece worth maybe ten thousand dollars back in the States."

Goldsmith held the small statue and looked around the office. There were at least fifteen more statues and carvings. When Goldsmith had finished scanning the room, his gaze returned to the major, who was smiling. "You must have a small fortune sitting right out in the open."

"Two hundred thousand dollars. Some of the pieces are quite valuable."

"So how do you acquire this stuff?" Goldsmith handed the statue back to the major, who placed it on a stack of paperwork.

"The Cham were probably the first human beings to inhabit what is now Vietnam. They are considered the forebearers of the current people occupying the coastal area. The original Cham settlements are on the coast between Saigon and Nha Trang, so you can see that the diggings aren't very close to Da Nang, but that works in my favor. No one realizes that the stone carvings I'm shipping back to San Francisco are genuine items of Vietnamese antiquity. I've built up a reputation for buying carvings from the stonecutters at Marble Mountain, and I bring the carvings back here and smash them into powder and replace the Marble Mountain carving with a Cham carving for shipment back to the States. The customs inspectors see the familiar Marble Mountain shipping boxes and pass the items right through." Ricks smiled and laced his fingers together behind his neck. "I have a friend in San Francisco who sells the pieces to museums—he takes a hefty twenty percent cut—and ships me back money so that I can buy more pieces."

"It sounds like you've got it all set up—so why me?"

"Your gold. I can get a better rate bartering for the statues with pure gold than even American hundred-dollar bills." Ricks leaned forward in his chair and stretched his hands out on the top of the desk. "I can get you a three thousand percent profit on your gold—in just one deal."

"It sounds like a good deal, but is it illegal?"

"Since the war started, no one has been watching the old Cham temples, and we've been having diggers working the sites since 1965."

"We?"

"I have a Vietnamese partner. He's the stonecutter at Marble Mountain."

"You haven't answered me, sir. Is it illegal?"

"It's illegal to *ship* Cham antiquities to the States, but once they are there, it's legal to own them. It's legal for you to own gold in Vietnam, but once you ship it to the United States, it's illegal." Ricks shrugged his shoulders. "So you decide what in the fuck is legal or not!"

"I don't know, sir. Gold is thirty-five dollars an ounce and it might go up a couple of bucks. It might be illegal for us to own gold, but it doesn't feel illegal. I think I'll just take the risk trying to get it back to the States. Besides, there's an emotional part to all this. I traded my custom-made Roman short sword for this gold." Goldsmith hefted the red silk bag in his hands.

Ricks wasn't about to give up so easily. "Look, I'll square with you. The stone carver has a particularly good piece on the market right now, and I've got all of my available cash tied up in these pieces." Ricks waved his hand around at the statues in the office. "It wouldn't be so bad, except there are others who are buying from him. A couple of black marketers from the quartermaster depot have already looked at the piece, but they're not smart enough to realize just how valuable it is. Plus, they can only offer him military-payment certificates, which he doesn't like to take."

Goldsmith didn't say no and the major misinterpreted his neutrality as a sign that he was weakening. Actually, though, Goldsmith didn't want to offend the major, especially now that MacCall was pissed at him.

"Look, come with me over to the stonecutter's. He's got a shop right outside the gate at the base of Marble Mountain. You can look at the piece and judge for yourself. I'm telling you, Goldsmith, you can make enough profit off that one piece to buy yourself a fucking house back in the States—and I mean a decent house!"

"I don't like breaking the law."

"Whose fucking laws? You know, I served in Korea and I watched people get fucking rich off that war selling black-market shit. I was like you were—honest until it hurt! Where did it get me? I damn near starved when I returned to the States and no one was hiring vets. I was forced to rejoin the Army, and I swore that if there ever was another war that I would leave it rich. I don't black-market or sell weapons to the enemy, like some of these guys are doing. I just buy and sell stone carvings." Ricks nodded in the direction of Colonel MacCall's office. "We all have our little hang-ups from Korea. MacCall feels that he got cheated out of a chestful of medals during that war, and he's making up for it here and so are his old buddies. I'm after money, MacCall's after glory—and what are you after, Lieutenant?"

Goldsmith refrained from saying out loud what he was thinking. He merely smiled. "Let's go see what the stone carver has that's got your motor going, sir."

"Now, that's the way I like to hear my people talk!"

Ricks stood up and grabbed his hat off a small shelf next to the office door.

"Aren't you going to lock your door?" Goldsmith looked back at the statues placed haphazardly around the office.

"Hell, no! There's nothing in there worth stealing." Ricks grinned. "And besides, I know exactly what's in there."

The major drove the black SOG jeep through the compound gate. U.S. Army vehicles were all painted an olive-drab color, but in order to add a little mystique to the already off-limits top-secret base, the commander had authorized all CCN-SOG vehicles to be repainted with a little black mixed into the olive paint and the CCN-SOG emblem of a skull wearing a green beret with blood dripping from its mouth painted in the center of the window frame where the hood met the front fold-down windows. The commander's jeep and the executive officer's jeep had camouflage parachute seat covers and two VRC-47 radios permanently mounted in the back so that they could maintain contact at all times with the TOC.

"You didn't need to bring all that with you," Ricks said, glancing at the CAR-15 submachine gun Goldsmith had lying across his lap. "We're just going over to the mountain. The Marines have the area very well secured." Ricks pointed up to the top of the mountain. "They've established an outpost up there, and on the south side they have a base camp. We own the land to the north of the mountain and the sea front is a wall of barbed wire."

"Is the marble quarry open to the Vietnamese?"

"Sure. And so is the Buddhist temple built inside the mountain. That temple was carved out of solid marble and is over a thousand years old." Ricks smiled at the young lieutenant. "You're a little paranoid, but I can understand why."

"Wasn't that Marine driver from the Third Marine Division kidnapped near here?"

"Garwood?"

"Yes, sir."

"He's on our capture list. There are a lot of unanswered questions about that young man. We've received reports that he's turned coat and is working for the NVA." Ricks stopped on Highway 1 to make a left-hand turn, and immediately traffic started building up behind the jeep. Highway 1 was the main north–south artery along the coast and was pretty much left alone by the Vietcong and NVA because they used it almost as much for their supplies as the South Vietnamese and Americans.

One of the drivers from the oncoming convoy stopped and blocked traffic so that Ricks could make his left-hand turn into the small parking area the stonecutter had made for his American customers. He had a profitable little business going selling marble desk nameplates to the staffs stationed at Da Nang, and he gave free ornately carved nameplates to all of the new commanders.

Ricks got out of the jeep and spoke in fluent Vietnamese to one of the stonecutter's apprentices before turning to face Goldsmith. "He's doing some repairs on the dragon pillars that guard the entrance to the temple. Come on, you'll enjoy seeing this."

Goldsmith paused long enough to look over the apprentice's shoulder. The teenager was carving the name of the new 24th Corps commanding general in the marble. The youth stopped working and smiled up at Goldsmith.

"Are you coming?" Ricks asked, waiting at the entrance of a small path that led around the side of the mountain.

"Do they carve nameplates for everyone in Da Nang?"

"I guess. He does a lot of business." Ricks started walking ahead of Goldsmith on the path.

"It sure makes it easy, then, for the Vietcong to know the names of the new commanders—before they arrive."

Ricks stopped and turned around to face Goldsmith. "What are you talking about?"

"Back there"—Goldsmith jabbed his thumb back over his shoulder—"that kid was working on a marble nameplate for the new 24th Corps commander, and I didn't even know that there was going to be a change of command."

Ricks frowned. "There isn't going to be a change of command. The commanding general just got here a few months ago."

"Well then, someone gave that stone carver back there the wrong name to carve on that nameplate, or there's going to be *two* lieutenant generals in 24th Corps. You know, sir, someone over at the corps might know about the change of command, come over here to get the new commanding general a nameplate for his desk, and make a few brownie points when the old boy reports in."

"Damn you, Goldsmith! You're making sense."

"I'm not saying that the Vietcong would have one of their men working here at Marble Mountain, but it would sure be nice to know about changes of command among your enemies, wouldn't it?"

Ricks stored the information for another time. He planned on having his counterpart in the secret police check out the workers at the quarry. Ricks thought about the traditional gifts the stone carver gave to every one of the staff at the CCN compound. Every staff officer received a free nameplate. Rob Barr submitted the name of the new staff officer to the stone carver along with the man's rank. Ricks was going to tell Barr to stop the practice of nameplates entirely. There was too much potential for the information to fall into the wrong hands. Major troop changes would reflect in CCN's ability to field teams in the AO, and the NVA would know that there would be large holes in the recon-teams sectors in Laos.

"Damn it!" Ricks shook his head as he walked along the marble path to the temple.

"What's wrong, sir?"

"You've got me thinking."

"That can't be all that bad, sir."

"Watch your mouth, Lieutenant!" Ricks looked back over his shoulder and smiled.

"It's nice to know that staff officers think every once in a while."

The smile on Ricks' face turned to a frown. "Careful, now . . ."

The stone carver appeared at the entrance of the temple, looking surprised. He quickly flashed a warm smile, but it was too late. Goldsmith had seen both the look on the man's face and that a silk curtain behind the stonecutter was being drawn shut by another person. Or had it been the wind? Goldsmith checked the curtain, hanging on the opposite side of the marble Buddha, and noticed that it hung absolutely still in the still air of the temple. The incense sticks burning in front of the Buddha sent their smoke curling straight up in the air and confirmed Goldsmith's suspicion.

"Are you still interested in the Cham carving, Major?" The stonecutter kept glancing from Ricks over to Goldsmith. He saw the interest the young lieutenant had in the drawn silk curtain, and it was making him visibly nervous. "Come, and I will show it to you again. We might be able to come to an agreement on the price this time," the stone carver said, anxious to get the two Americans out of the temple.

Ricks' attention was on the Cham carving, and he failed to pick up on the queerness of that curtain.

Goldsmith walked around to the side of the large Buddha and looked behind the statues. There was a space about four feet wide behind the back of the Buddha and the ornately carved wall. Goldsmith scanned the narrow space, and just as he was about to return to the major, he saw a spot of blood on the floor in the shadows. He took one step toward the blood, but then quickly stepped away, acting as if he had lost interest in the temple altogether. "Are you ready to leave, sir?"

"Yes, let's go over to his shop and look at the piece I told you about. He said that it's already crated for shipment to the States and that he's going to sell it today— either to us or the American black marketeers. It's getting too dangerous for him to keep such a large antiquity in his shop."

"Sure, let's go." Goldsmith shoved the major's shoulder to get him to move, and Ricks flashed the junior officer a dirty look.

The stonecutter kept a poker face when they stepped out into the sunshine, but inside, he felt a rush of relief and became almost giddy over having escaped the close call inside the temple. Ricks followed the middle-aged man to the small shop that functioned as the stonecutter's office and show room, and he was led over to a crate set on two low sawhorses. He spoke without checking on the whereabouts of his lieutenant. "You're going to love this piece, Goldsmith. It's a true piece of art."

"He isn't here." Just then the stonecutter saw the lieutenant standing outside by the jeep with a radio handset
up to his mouth. "He seems very nervous for a person
so young."

Ricks' face became red with anger. He had about
enough of Goldsmith's nonchalance. "Goldsmith! Come
here!"

Goldsmith joined the major and leaned over the open
shipping crate. He could see the front of a well-carved
statue of a young male and a female surrounded by jungle beasts. "Nice work."

"Why were you on the radio?" Ricks asked, still
angry.

Goldsmith glanced over at the stonecutter and saw that
he too was interested in the major's question. He smiled.
"I forgot to tell the TOC where we were going. You
know the rules, Major."

"Fine!" Ricks said, satisfied with Goldsmith's answer.
They were supposed to let the duty officer at the TOC
know their whereabouts at all times in case of an emergency. "How much pure gold do you want for the
piece?"

"Gold?" The stonecutter's interest in the statue
became keener, and he stopped glancing over at the path
leading to the temple. "The statue is very old and depicts
the female fertility goddess and her consort. It is very
rare."

"How much gold?"

"I cannot ask less than . . . one hundred and sixty
ounces."

"That's robbery!" Ricks began the opening volley of
the bargaining.

The stonecutter shrugged. "It is the best piece I have
seen in over twenty years of dealing in Cham Dynasty
carvings."

Ricks and the stonecutter haggled back and forth while
Goldsmith wandered around the small shop, looking at
the pieces of marblework on display. He made sure his
back was to the stonecutter each time he checked
outside.

All the same, the stonecutter caught Goldsmith glancing out of the window and stopped bargaining long

enough to blurt out. "Your jeep is safe parked there. My apprentices will watch so that no one steals from it."

Goldsmith answered the stonecutter with a broad grin and took a couple of steps toward the door. Sergeant Tyriver entered the bamboo-and-thatch structure holding a 12-gauge shotgun at the ready. He was followed by a half-dozen recon men and Nung commandos from the CCN compound.

"What in the hell is going on here?" Ricks cried, angry over so many CCN personnel seeing him at the stone carver's office.

The stone carver answered the major's question for him. He realized that somehow his real operation had been uncovered, and he tried making his escape through a hidden side entrance to the hootch. He ran into the rifle barrel of a Nung's M-16. He turned around to face the occupants of his office wearing so much hate on his face that he looked like a different human being.

"Take a team and check out the temple. Be careful. There's a secret entrance that leads somewhere behind the statue of the main Buddha." Goldsmith pointed the direction to the path, using the barrel of his CAR-15.

"What in the hell is going on here?" Ricks was still puzzled.

"Let's step outside, sir." Goldsmith led the way out of the office. There were commandos everywhere, rounding up the stonecutters and apprentices who had tried escaping from the quarry.

"What in the fuck?" Ricks was beginning to worry that his real reason for coming to the quarry would be uncovered. He thought it was a raid on the Cham antiquities smuggling and wasn't focusing on the real operation that had been going on right under his nose.

"He's VC and so are his men." Goldsmith pointed at the stonecutter, who was being guarded closely by two Nung commandos.

"You're kidding me, Goldsmith! I've known him for two years! He's been cleared by the Da Nang secret police!" Ricks looked over at the stonecutter, hoping to see confirmation in his eyes. He saw instead the hate the man had for him.

"You are a fucking fool, Major!" The stonecutter realized that his cover was blown, and he knew that he would not survive the South Vietnamese's secret police interrogation. He knew too much to live, and he was seeking a fast death. "How do you think I got all those carvings you wanted? Who do you think smuggled them up here to Da Nang?" The smile that crossed the stonecutter's face told Ricks everything he needed to know.

"You're a Vietcong?"

The stonecutter spat at the major and received a butt stroke from one of the Nungs that knocked him to his knees. "North Vietnamese! A colonel, in fact—you fool!"

Ricks stared at the humble stonecutter in shock. He had been totally suckered in by the man. Nevertheless, he knew that he hadn't provided the NVA colonel with any information about the CCN operation. His only dealings with the man had been over the Cham antiquities.

An M-16 opened fire, but it sounded muffled. It was answered by the muffled reply from an AK-47. There was a pause and then all hell broke loose around the base of the mountain. Trucks passing by on the highway pulled off to the side of the road, and the machine gunners on the trucks tried locating targets among the mass of civilians.

Ricks reached for his pistol and then realized he hadn't brought a weapon from the nearby SOG compound. He had made the trip so often to the mountain that he felt secure—or he had felt secure. Now he felt very vulnerable.

"Here, sir." Goldsmith handed the major his silenced .22-caliber pistol. "It's not much, but it's better than nothing until you can find something with more firepower."

Ricks took the offered weapon and turned around just in time to see the NVA colonel struggling with the remaining Nung guard. He had dropped the first guard with a side kick that had silently broken the Nung's neck. Ricks took aim and fired the pistol without thinking. The bullet entered the NVA colonel's head in the back, and he dropped down dead. Running over, Ricks stripped the dead Nung of his ammunition belt and took the M-16 out of his still quivering hands.

By this time Goldsmith had already left the stonecut-

ter's office and was making his way slowly down the path,
which was now littered with wounded commandos. The
NVA had cut firing ports into the side of the mountain
and were placing extremely effective fire on the exposed
troops.

Seeing Goldsmith leave, Ricks beckoned to the remaining Nung to help him carry the shipping crate over
to his jeep.

A light machine gun opened fire only a few meters in
front of Tyriver, and he pressed his back against the temple wall. He could feel the coolness of the marble seep
through his damp jacket. Only the barrel of the weapon
stuck through the small opening in the wall. There wasn't
enough room for even a hand grenade to be pushed
through. Tyriver waited until the NVA machine gunner
was forced to change ammunition drums before he used
the barrel of his shotgun to push the barrel of the
machine gun out of the opening. Then he started firing
rounds of fleshettes through the hole. This was an incredibly risky stunt, but the trick worked. He killed all of the
NVA on the other side of the wall. Now it was possible
for some commandos to get from the entrance of the
temple back to the area behind the Buddha. They needed
only a few minutes to figure out how to open the secret
panel that led into the interior of the mountain.

Tyriver followed the first of the commandos into a
well-lit tunnel. Electric bulbs were spaced out along the
side of the marble corridor, but the long passageway was
empty. Tyriver passed rooms that had been set up as
operating rooms and storage areas for medical supplies.
The NVA had been using Marble Mountain as a major
hospital, complete with the most modern operating
equipment available to Americans. Clearly, Tyriver realized, the equipment had come off the docks in Da Nang.

Outside the mountain, Marine amphibious vehicles
that had been conducting their normal patrol on the
beach were taken by surprise when a rock wall on the
mountain opened up and a horde of NVA soldiers
poured out. The firefight lasted only a couple of minutes
before the NVA surrendered. They were hopelessly out-
gunned on the open sand, and most of them were medical personal and not infantry. Their main concern was

the safety of the wounded soldiers they had been trying to evacuate from the mountain hospital.

The Marine lieutenant in charge of the patrol approached the open beach entrance to the hospital with caution and shook his head in wonder as he noticed that the doors to the cave entrance were made out of molded plastic that blended in perfectly with the rest of the mountainside. He had passed that entrance a hundred times while on patrol, and he hadn't even suspected that it was there. Worse, the outpost on top of the mountain had never caught anyone slipping up on the mountain at night. The reason was because the NVA had brought their wounded in during the day, using the stonecutter's operation as a cover and the temple as the main entrance to the hospital. NVA soldiers and medical personnel entered and exited the hospital dressed as Buddhist monks in their long yellow and orange robes.

The fighting lasted less than an hour, and the POWs taken numbered five NVA surgeons who had received their training in France and the United States, along with eight NVA doctors and fifteen nurses. The losses in medical personnel to the NVA was disastrous. The mountain hospital had been one of the best facilities of its kind in South Vietnam and was considered so secure that it was used to treat seriously wounded officers.

The South Vietnamese police found that they had captured two NVA generals and one Vietcong main force general along with a dozen minor colonels and junior officers who were recovering from their wounds in the cool air of the mountain passageways.

The underground hospital revealed over a half mile of corridors and thirty well-stocked rooms carved by the stonecutters from the original caves and passageways within the mountain. Portions of the hospital dated back to the days when the Viet Minh had been fighting against the French! The hospital had been operating continuously for over forty years.

Ricks was standing by his jeep when Goldsmith and Tyriver joined him. The major had been guarding the contents in the shipping crate from harm.

"It was a bit more than I had expected, sir." Goldsmith placed his foot up against the seat well of the jeep and leaned forward to speak in a lower voice. "I hope that *our* purchase wasn't damaged during the fight."

Ricks looked shocked and then he smiled. "It's safe."

"Half?"

Ricks gave the lieutenant a curt nod and changed the subject. The Cham statue was worth over a half-million dollars, and half of that amount was still a lot of money. "How in the hell did you know this was a VC operation?"

Goldsmith shrugged his shoulders. "First I saw a spot of blood behind the Bhudda. But there was another spot that was smeared in an arc that stopped at the base of the wall behind the statue. It had to have been done by a hidden door closing, so I assumed that there was some kind of a hiding place built behind the Buddha. Judging by the stonecutter's nervousness, it was being used to hide VC."

Ricks shook his head. "A lot more than a couple of VC were back there!"

"Luck, I guess." Goldsmith glanced over at Tyriver, who was watching him with cat's eyes. "Thanks for reacting so fast."

"Lucky timing. One of the Nung companies was getting ready to go to the rifle range and were already on the trucks when you called the TOC."

"See, sir? Luck." Goldsmith crawled over the front seat of the major's jeep and patted the crate with his palm. "We should get this shipped out today, sir, before something happens to it."

Tyriver stared at the markings on the side of the crate and looked back and forth between the major and the lieutenant.

"Are you coming back to the camp with us, Tyriver?" Ricks asked, slipping behind the wheel.

"Sure, sir." Tyriver took the shotgun seat up front.

Ricks threw his arm over the back of his seat and looked at Goldsmith. "Remind me *not* to take you with me again when I go outside the compound!"

CHAPTER SEVENTEEN

✪✪✪✪✪✪✪✪✪✪✪✪✪✪✪✪✪✪✪✪✪✪✪✪

HIGH GOSSIP

The strong wind coming in off the South China Sea whistled in the open microphone that had been set up on the portable raised platform in front of the Command and Control North headquarters building. The director from the 24th Corps band kept glancing over at the open mike, hoping that someone would put a cover over it, because the magnified sound of the wind was interfering with the music.

Normally, award ceremonies were held out on the CCN helipad, but the huge PSP pad was packed with helicopters from the visiting dignitaries. It seemed like every general officer stationed in Vietnam had visited the NVA hospital in Marble Mountain. A special detachment of Navy SPs had been assigned to guard the captured prize, and within a day they had been turned into tour guides and a Marine company replaced them as guards. The NVA hospital was the hottest tour ticket in Vietnam, drawing visitors from as far away as the Pentagon. No one believed that the NVA had the balls to establish a major facility right in the heart of the American complex in Da Nang, and the fact that they had done it scared the hell out of the high command.

The formation in front of the headquarters building had been standing there for over an hour. Major Ricks had given the men permission to smoke and stand at ease until the MACV commanding general's party arrived at the main gate. Lieutenant Colonel MacCall was acting as the guide for the motorcade that would have at least a half-dozen junior general officers tagging along.

Ricks stood facing the formation and checked the men

to make sure that all ranks were uniform. The front center rank was composed of five men: Captain Abou, who was going to receive the Distinguished Service Cross for commanding the highly successful underwater bridge mission, and four NCOs who were receiving Silver Stars. Tyriver was one of them, and Ricks noticed the sergeant was constantly looking back in the rank of soldiers behind him, where Goldsmith stood. Much longer, the back rank was made up of the men receiving minor awards, mostly for achievement and service during their tours in Vietnam. The first eight were receiving Purple Hearts for wounds received in combat. Goldsmith was the first man in the back rank because he was receiving a Bronze Star medal with a *V* device attached for valor and several Purple Hearts.

Captain Barr stood inside the headquarters building, watching the entrance road for the four-star general's convoy. He checked the stack of general orders in front of him for at least the hundredth time, to make sure they were in the same order as the men standing out in the formation. He had underlined the name of each man on the GOs, and he had underlined the body of their award citation that he would be reading over the inside microphone as the commanding general and his party pinned the awards on the left jacket pockets of the recipients. He had been up since four in the morning setting the awards ceremony up, and originally he had placed his microphone and podium outside, but the strong wind made it nearly impossible to control the stack of papers on the podium, and he had received permission from Ricks to move his operation inside out of the wind. Barr knew that the CCN commander would chew his ass for moving his adjutant's station indoors, but it would be worth it. MacCall had been acting like a paranoid old spinster with a gentleman caller over the general's visit, and had personally supervised every detail of the ceremony.

Ricks saw an MP jeep turn off the main highway and called the formation to attention. The back four ranks of the award formation was made up of two commando companies. Each of the Nung and Cambodian commandos had been issued a new tiger suit for the ceremony, and they looked very impressive with their weapons slung over their shoulders. MacCall had insisted that every commandos be inspected to make sure that none of them carried a full magazine of ammunition on them. It had been a good idea, just in case one of the commandos was a Vietcong willing to give his life to execute a half-dozen American and South Vietnamese generals.

The convoy of jeeps stopped on the perimeter road and unloaded their cargo of stars. It looked like every general in South Vietnam had accompanied the four-star general, along with a couple of civilians. Ricks felt a growing nervousness in his stomach and wanted to light up a cigar. Then he recognized one of the civilians and found himself smiling. Seeing the friendly face of a man he had gotten drunk with on a number of occasions eased his fear, and he barked out the order for the ceremony to begin.

As the band played martial music, the four-star general took up his position in front of the open microphone. The generals accompanying him then took their positions in front of the row of chairs behind him. There were more generals than chairs, and all but one of the brigadier generals were forced to stand behind the platform. And the lone general, seeing his peers leaving the platform, decided it would be politically wiser to join them and leave the seat vacant.

Goldsmith, seeing the brigadier general leave the seat on the platform, wondered if there were *any* generals in Vietnam who were fighting the war, not just on paper but with every fiber in their bodies—like infantry privates were.

The martial music stopped and the sound of the sea wind coming over the loudspeakers filled the CCN compound for what seemed like minutes as the four-star general scanned the assembled troops. The gray-haired soldier reached inside his shirt pocket and removed a three-by-five card. He took his time buttoning the pocket again before he looked out at the formation. He commanded everything he could see in Vietnam, and after doing that for a year, he knew he set the pace.

A flight of helicopters circling the Marine outpost on top of Marble Mountain caught the general's attention for a second, and Goldsmith almost turned his head to

see what he was looking at. Then the familiar deep voice
came over the loudspeakers:

"I am honored to be here today among such an elite
gathering of paratroopers." He paused to allow the statement to sink in. He was well known for his love of airborne soldiers, and he made that point known every time
he spoke to them. "I had my adjutant back in Saigon do
a little homework for me, and I must admit that I am
very surprised over the results." The general held the
card out, giving away the fact that he was farsighted by
holding the card out nearly at arm's length. He hated
wearing his glasses in front of the troops. "Three Medal
of Honors; eleven Distinguished Service Crosses; one
hundred and thirty-two Silver Stars; and two hundred
and fifty-eight Purple Hearts for wounds suffered in combat—that, Gentlemen, is what I call a very well-
decorated unit, especially when it's smaller than a
battalion!"

Barr stopped shuffling through his general orders, and
his head snapped up to look out at the general. The
numbers he had just rattled off were wrong. Command
and Control North personnel had received three Medal
of Honors and another one was currently pending, but
the unit had received only five Distinguished Service
Crosses and sixty-three Silver Stars. Barr was positive
that his figures were correct because the A&D files were
one of his pet projects. There was so much pressure put
on him to upgrade awards that he had read every citation
awarded to CCN so that he could be objective when he
compared feats of valor for current award recommendations. Because he had never served in the field with a
recon team, he was very sensitive over the whole awards
process. He wanted to make sure that he was treating
the recon men fairly.

Barr glanced over at the two clerks who worked
directly for Lieutenant Colonel MacCall. They were the
only two personnel men who did not work for him, and
that had bothered him when he took over the section.
The few times he had visited them in the office MacCall
had set up for them next to his own office had been
very short. He had always felt uncomfortable in the small
office, and when he entered, the clerks stopped working

and covered the papers on their desks. That practice made him uneasy: why didn't they trust him? MacCall had explained to him that the clerks were working on a top-secret project for Saigon headquarters, and there was a strict need-to-know before anyone could read the documents the office generated. Barr had fallen for that line only because there were a dozen of those kinds of projects going on in the TOC all the time.

One of the clerks turned his head away so that his eyes wouldn't meet Barr's, but the second clerk glared back at him as if he wanted to shout something in his face. Instead the clerk only mumbled something that didn't make sense. "I was promised an appointment to Officers' Candidate School—"

"Shut the fuck up! It wasn't his fault that you had a prison record back in the States!" the other clerk cried, cutting the angry clerk off in mid-sentence.

"He promised me that nothing would prevent my appointment!"

The band music drew Captain Barr's attention away from the bickering clerks. The general, accompanied by MacCall and two staff NCOs from CCN carrying green velvet pillows with the medals that the general was going to present, started walking across the sand to the first rank of awardees.

Barr, making one last check to see that Captain Abou was still the first man in the rank, held up his citation so that he could read the paragraph explaining what the captain had done to earn the second highest valor award in the United States Army. The paragraph was very short and when Barr had finished reading it over the loudspeaker, the general was still trying to clip the medal on Abou's jacket.

Barr looked up and smiled as the general moved on and presented the next soldier with a Silver Star. Sergeant Tyriver blushed when the powerful general attached the award to his jacket and he heard the citation being read over the loudspeaker. It was twice as long as Abou's had been.

Then the general passed behind the first rank and started walking to the end of the second rank, where Goldsmith was standing at attention.

Barr felt a cold sweat break out on his upper lip, and for a second he almost backed out on what he had planned. He closed his eyelids tight together and took a deep breath that could be heard over the loudspeakers. Then he picked up the thick packet of general orders and removed the large note card he had hidden between the papers.

"Lieutenant Alex-Paul Goldsmith . . ." Barr felt his vocal cords tightening. He was rapidly losing his courage. One of the generals standing behind the raised platform casually glanced over at Barr standing behind the Plexiglas window. A pause of only a few seconds during a well-executed ceremony always seemed like minutes. Barr ground his teeth and spoke in a loud, commanding voice: ". . . is awarded the Bronze Star medal with *fourteen* oak leaf clusters. He is awarded thirteen Bronze Stars for valor and one for achievement for planning the highly successful underwater bridge mission."

MacCall's head seemed to snap around on its own accord as he sought out the source of the voice. He searched the area but failed to see Barr inside the headquarters. Anger seethed out of the commander in the form of a hiss. He couldn't leave his position next to the general, but was forced to stand there and listen. He tried locking gazes with Goldsmith's, but the lieutenant was staring directly ahead, at strict attention, as the four-star general reached over to remove the Bronze Star from the pillow.

Barr continued reading off the note card he had prepared especially for the occasion. At first the assembled officers thought the reading over the loudspeakers was a part of the planned ceremony, but as Barr continued, it started to become clear that the young lieutenant standing in front of the four-star general was quite a unique soldier.

Goldsmith stood ramrod-stiff, trying not to focus his eyes on anything with the powerful general standing directly in front of him, holding his Bronze Star in both hands. Then Goldsmith's eyes focused for a second, and he saw the general looking down. The award had two silver oak-leaf clusters and three bronze oak-leaf clusters attached to the cloth above a bronze *V*.

Goldsmith felt his cheeks getting warm as the general remained standing in front of him for what seemed like hours. He hoped the officer would just pin the award on his pocket and leave. Meanwhile, snatches of Barr's voice penetrated his defenses:

"He spent eleven days alone in the jungle after losing his team in a North Vietnamese ambush . . ."

Goldsmith thought about Sergeant Archer.

"It was Lieutenant Goldsmith's accurate location of the underwater bridge that allowed for its destruction . . ."

Goldsmith thought about the American POWs he had seen passing his position from the 101st Airborne Division.

"He killed two NVA soldiers and prevented them from alerting their comrades . . ."

Goldsmith thought about the looks on the dead NVA soldiers' faces.

"The pipeline coming from North Vietnam severed in numerous places . . ."

Goldsmith felt the fear returning again when he was placing the charges on the steel pipe. He had expected bullets to tear through his body.

". . . and he was directly responsible for the rescue of two fellow Americans from a North Vietnamese POW camp . . ."

Goldsmith envisioned the look on McDonald's face when he had stepped into the NVA hootch, and he smiled. The general, who had been staring at the young lieutenant, saw the smile and smiled back, but Goldsmith was in another world and didn't see it.

Barr's voice droned on as he flipped through the individual general orders that awarded Goldsmith his thirteen valor awards. He paused often, and there was a whole series of orders about which the only thing he could say was that the citation was classified.

The Command and Control North personnel, who had been standing off to the sides of the ceremony as observers, started talking to each other, and a buzz replaced the sound of the wind.

MacCall was turning to break formation to stop Barr when he saw that the general smiling at Lieutenant Goldsmith. He realized that it was now too late—the damage had already been done.

"The Purple Heart with three oak-leaf clusters is awarded to Lieutenant Alex-Paul Goldsmith for wounds received while in combat with an enemy of the United States . . ." Barr's voice increased in volume, as if he was struggling to finish a difficult task.

The general attached the Purple Heart next to the Bronze Star on Goldsmith's pocket. Because the lieutenant was so short, he was forced to lean over to take a hold of the young officer's hand, pressed against the seam in his trousers. The general took the hand in both of his and shook it with a firm grip.

The movement of his arm brought Goldsmith's mind back to the present, and his eyes focused again on the general's tanned face.

The four-star general saw a sparkle enter the lieutenant's eyes, and he smiled. "I'm very impressed, Alex-Paul—*very* impressed, young man." The general looked over his shoulder at an immaculately dressed colonel who had been standing in the background. The colonel removed a leather notepad and wrote something down in it.

Seeing the unspoken message pass between the four star general and his aide-de-camp, MacCall realized that he could never write a bad officer-efficiency report now to support his classmate's request from the 5th Division. In any case, he knew his old classmate would understand once he had explained the reason why—four-star generals were wild cards in the political game within the military, and they could foul up the best-laid plans.

Seeing movement out of the corner of his eye, the general turned his head to catch the sergeant just awarded the Silver Star looking back over his shoulder at the lieutenant. The general rarely missed anything involving his soldiers, and he realized that the two were war buddies. He smiled and winked at the sergeant, who quickly returned to the position of attention and then back to parade rest with the rest of the men in his rank. The look of absolute pride on the sergeant's face remained in the general's mind as he finished passing out the awards on the pillow that kept appearing next to his right hand. The general was very good at doing one thing and thinking about something else, and his thoughts were

back with the handsome lieutenant who had received
such an extraordinary number of Bronze Stars for Valor.

Barr saw MacCall turn around the instant the last of
the four-star general's convoy had left the main gate of
the compound. The lieutenant colonel's boots sent showers of dry sand behind him as he strutted toward the
headquarters building. There was little doubt in the captain's mind whom MacCall was coming to see.

"Aw, fuck." The expression slipped out of Barr's
mouth.

"Forget something, Captain?"

"Sorry, sir." Barr turned to face Major Ricks and saw
that the Command and Control North executive officer
was standing almost on top of him with a civilian and
another major. They had approached while he was
watching MacCall cross the empty parade grounds. All
of the award recipients and CCN personnel had already
left for the mess hall, where a large party was being held
for them.

"I'd like for you to meet an old friend of mine—
LeBlonde. He's the station chief here for the CIA."

"That's supposed to be a secret, Ricks!" The white-
haired man wearing civilian clothes and mirrored sun-
glasses shook hands with Barr and chuckled to show that
he was only teasing his old friend. "That was some reading you did for that lieutenant. It sounded more like he
should have been awarded a couple higher awards than
fourteen Bronze Stars." LeBlonde had seen through
Barr's thinly veiled plan, along with the rest of the award-
ceremony's observers. There was little doubt which award
the lieutenant should have won.

"Thank you, sir," Barr said returning his attention to
his approaching doom, which had just reached the front
door of the headquarters. He had completely passed over
the major who was with Ricks and the fact that both of
MacCall's private clerks were standing against the hall in
the background.

MacCall entered the building in a rage. He turned
toward Barr's office and bellowed, "Barr, get your fucking ass out here!"

"Yes, sir?" Barr's voice answered the commander

from the opposite direction in the hall, which threw the senior officer off balance, but only for a second.

MacCall whirled around and choked on his first word before he could speak clearly. "You're relieved! Get the fuck off my compound! *Now!*"

Barr started turning around but was stopped by Ricks' hand on his elbow. "You're not going anywhere, just yet."

"Damn you, Ricks!" MacCall threw out his arm and pointed directly at the captain. "He's fired! He's a goddamn traitor! He made a fool out of me and my command in front of—of all goddamn people! The commanding general of all the goddamn forces in Vietnam!" MacCall's voice broke and he came close to tears.

"I don't think that is your biggest problem right now, boss." Ricks pointed over at the major standing quietly by himself in the background. "This is Major Archon, from MACV headquarters in Saigon. He's been sent here by the MACV commanding general to investigate some charges."

"What damn charges?"

"It seems that one of your private clerks has contacted the Criminal Investigations Division and reported an illegal operation."

For the first time MacCall noticed his two clerks standing in the background. One of them was looking down at his boots, but the other clerk was glaring at him. It was the one whose OCS application had been rejected. MacCall had promised to make him a sergeant first class before he left CCN, but his Stateside criminal record had prevented it. Yes, there was a traitor at CCN, but it wasn't Captain Barr. MacCall realized that he was in very deep trouble. He knew that he should have caught it when the general mentioned the number of DSCs and Silver Stars awarded out of CCN.

Major Archon nodded at Ricks. "Thanks, I think I can handle it from here." He looked over at MacCall. "I'm not from the CID's office. The general has appointed me to handle this personally for him. It seems that the names on your personal awards list are too sensitive to be revealed all together. That's what is going to save your

ass from Fort Leavenworth's stockade—much to the cha-
grin of the commanding general."

"Can we talk in private?" MacCall said, seeing his
opening.

"Sure, but be advised, there isn't going to be any bargaining. You'll sign your retirement papers and will be
discharged from Vietnam."

"What?" MacCall started stuttering, "I—I was third in
my class from West Point! I have ten more years of service left!"

The major shook his head. "I was first in my class—
and you are a disgrace to the Academy. I'm embarrassed
we both graduated from the same school."

"Listen here, Major!"

The special-operations major shook his head and
glanced over at Ricks and the CIA station chief. "Some
people have a difficult time understanding English, don't
they?"

Ricks shrugged. "Come on, LeBlonde, let's go over to
the mess hall and have a couple of well-deserved drinks."

"That sounds like a good idea. I'd like to meet this
lieutenant who won fourteen Bronze Stars."

"He is a character—you'll like him." Ricks paused in the
doorway and looked back at Barr. "Are you coming?"

Barr glanced over at MacCall and then back at Ricks.
"I've been relieved."

"Not by me, and I've been commanding CCN since
one minute after midnight—according to these orders
that have been signed by the MACV commander himself." Ricks held up the folded set of orders and then
slipped them back into his shirt pocket.

"I'll need a copy of those for your records, sir." Barr
hurried to catch up to Ricks. He paused long enough to
look back at MacCall. He felt sorry for the man, but the
pity lasted only until he remembered what the lieutenant
colonel had wanted to do to him.

Barr caught up to Ricks and LeBlonde on the sandy
road leading back to the mess hall. "What were they
actually doing in that office next to MacCall's?"

"He was running a phony awards program out of
there. It was the perfect cover for that kind of operation.
Command and Control North was a top-secret operation.

Very few people had the authority to check even our
paperwork, and those who did really didn't have any reason to question the large number of high decorations
coming out of here. They all knew that we were running
missions into Laos and North Vietnam."

"But the awards were being given to senior officers."

"True, but we use senior officers for a number of sensitive programs." Ricks flashed Barr a look that filled in
the missing top-secret words for the projects he was
referring to, ones that couldn't even be spoken outside
the TOC.

Barr nodded in agreement. "But why? What kind of
a general or full colonel would want to wear a phony
award?"

Ricks glanced over at LeBlonde and grinned.

"Maybe I can answer that for you, Captain."
LeBlonde moved a little closer to Barr as they walked
down the road toward the sea. "You see, all of these
generals and colonels serving in Vietnam were lieutenants and captains in Korea. Valor awards in Korea were
very hard to come by, especially during the time periods
when we were getting our asses kicked by the Chinese
and we were retreating south. Quite a few young lieutenants during that war actually performed great feats of
courage and didn't receive a damn thing for their valor.
You see, it seems like the policy at the time was that if
we were retreating, our soldiers couldn't be fighting with
valor, and they turned down many of the recommendations for valor." LeBlonde stopped and pointed at Barr's
chest. "You administration officers have a tough job during a war keeping things honest. Probably one of the
toughest jobs during a war. Oh, Korea produced its share
of questionable awards—hell, even the Medal of Honor
can be questioned in some cases. S.L.A. 'Slam' Marshall
claims to have been the main cause for getting a captain
the MOH for a bayonet charge by writing about him in
one of his books."

"What LeBlonde is saying, Barr, is that there is always
a group of people during a war who feel that they have
been screwed out of winning a medal—and there's always
truth in their claims—and there's that group who use
high valor awards as career moves. Vietnam is producing

more than their share of that kind of officer." Ricks shook his head. "MacCall falls into both categories, and when he was given the opportunity to do something about it, he did. He contacted his old combat buddies from Korea when they came over here, reminded them of the awards they didn't get over there, and he offered to give it to them here. Most of them fell for the trick and accepted Distinguished Service Crosses and Silver Stars for minor actions here in Vietnam. But in their minds it was for actions in Korea. That's why the commanding general isn't going to revoke their awards. It's cutting things pretty fine, I agree, but there are just too many fine officers whose careers will be ruined that the Army needs right now to serve during this war. Besides, if this kind of a scandal got to the press back in the States, it would cause way too much trouble with the doves. They're looking for any excuse to give the military a black eye."

"I agree, but it really sucks when you look at what guys like Goldsmith have done and the awards they've ended up with." Barr looked down at the sand as they walked. "We should do something to correct the wrong MacCall did to him. Maybe upgrade a couple of his Bronze Stars—"

"Sorry, we can't do that. Goldsmith is going to end up being a victim of the system. What you did for him out there today was really gutsy." Ricks reached over and laid his hand on Barr's shoulder. "Now that MacCall is gone, we might be able to work something out for the future."

"Goldsmith is due to rotate back to the states soon . . ."

Ricks sighed. "Well, at least MacCall was stopped."

"That's not enough, sir." Barr was getting angry over what the lieutenant colonel had gotten away with. Being forced to retire but still being allowed to keep all of the phony medals he had submitted for himself and his buddies just wasn't enough punishment to the young officer's way of thinking.

"Trust us, Barr. We've been around awhile and MacCall is only the tip of the iceberg on the awards system. Good, brave men are looked over for valor awards because they don't have friends in the right positions. I would like to know the percentage of valor awards that were handed out in all of our wars between friends—"

"What do you mean, friends?"

"That's when a senior officer or NCO makes sure that a junior soldier he likes receives an award." Ricks patted Barr's shoulder as they neared the mess hall. "If someone hates someone serving underneath them, do you think they'll recommend them for an award? MacCall and Goldsmith are the perfect example. I think we all agree that if MacCall had liked Lieutenant Goldsmith, he would have recommended him for the Medal of Honor—but he didn't like him."

"True, but Goldsmith got fourteen Bronze Stars!" Barr smiled over at Ricks and the CIA station chief as they entered the mess hall.

There were a few recon men standing around Captain Abou, congratulating him for winning the Distinguished Service Cross, but the majority were gathered around Goldsmith and Tyriver. The crowd made way for Major Ricks and opened a path between him and his guest.

Ricks saw the lieutenant reach into his pocket and slip something in his right hand before he shook hands with him. He could feel a piece of paper against his palm, and he curled his fingers around it as their hands separated. "Lieutenant Goldsmith, I'd like for you to meet a very good friend of mine—LeBlonde."

As the old CIA station chief shook hands with Goldsmith, Ricks used the time to open the small piece of paper the lieutenant had slipped him. The name of a bank and an account number had been printed neatly on the paper. He looked up and saw Goldsmith smiling at him. A grin formed at the corner of the major's mouth, and he couldn't stop the smile from spreading out.

EPILOGUE

❋❋❋❋❋❋❋❋❋❋

THE SALMON
RIVER
MOUNTAINS

He held an open blue leather box in both of his hands and looked down at the red ribbon that had a narrow blue stripe bordered in white in its center. The bronze *V* had tarnished over the years along with the silver and bronze oak-leaf clusters, but the medal still brought back a flood of memories.

The cough filtered into the bank vault, and he looked up at his reflection in the mirror attached to a corner of the ceiling. He wore a full beard that was cut short. He had been surprised when the beard had grown in with a red-blond tinge, but after a while he had gotten used to it. His electric blue eyes flashed back at him in the mirror.

The bank guard coughed again.

Closing the case, Alex-Paul replaced the award in his safety deposit box and hurried to finish what he had come to do in the first place. He removed a heavy cardboard box from his hunting jacket and opened it. There were four plastic tubes inside that contained ten one-ounce gold Krugerrands each. He placed the plastic tubes next to the stack inside his safety deposit box. He had been forced over the years to go from a small box to a medium and then a large. Next year he would have to rent another box to hold his growing horde of gold.

The bank guard stuck his head in the vault entrance. "Mr. Goldsmith, we're closing in five minutes."

"I'll be right there. I've just got to lock up." Alex-Paul reached back in the box, hefted the red silk bag of Montagnard gold, and smiled. The gold had been his security blanket for years. He had come close to spending it a number of times, but just when he was about to cash it in, something always happened and he returned it to the safety deposit box.

He shoved the box back into its slot and removed the key. The weight of the gold made the bottom of the steel container squeak, and the guard stuck his head in to see what was going on.

"I'm coming out." Alex-Paul turned his key, locking the box in place, and removed it.

The timber shepherd lifted its head off the cool marble floor and whined. Alex-Paul smiled over at the dog and the twins, who had been sitting against the wall of the bank, waiting patiently for him. He stared at the boys as he approached them and felt a rush of emotions. When he returned from memories of Vietnam, it was his family that made everything worthwhile.

"Mom is going to have a cow, Dad. We're late."

"She's with Nicole shopping, Paul," the other twin said. "We'll be the ones who will end up waiting for them." The second twin struggled up on his feet and stretched.

"I agree with Alex. We'll be waiting on those two women until dark!" Alex-Paul felt the timber shepherd's nose against his palm. He reached over and petted the huge dog to reassure him that everything was okay. The dog hated the city and the smells coming from so many strange things.

"So what do you keep hidden in that vault, Pops?" Alex asked, nudging his father with his elbow. The twin fourteen-year-olds were at the age where they were constantly testing their strength against their father's.

Alex-Paul's hand shot out and caught Alex around his neck. He pulled the struggling boy up against his chest and gave him a quick butch rub and then released him. "A box of gold. Tons of it!"

"Right, Dad. If you had that much gold, we'd be living in the city, like Uncle David."

"There's Mom and Nicole!" Paul pointed down the street to the pair of moving packages.

She smiled from two blocks away when she saw the three men in her life walking toward her. The twins were identical, but what had made it even stranger was that they were clones of their father. The boys possessed his curly blond hair and had inherited the same electric fire in his blue eyes. They were identical miniatures of their father. They even walked with his cocky stride.

"Darn it, Mom! There they are!" Nicole's voice reflected her disappointment in the ending of their shopping spree.

"Now, Nicole, you'll have plenty of time to shop in Los Angeles, believe me."

The teenage girl's eyes lit up with the mention of the huge city. "Really, Mom?"

"Really." She tried waving to her men, but gave up trying with her arms filled with packages. She just waited until they were close enough to smile a greeting. "Well! Help me with some of these packages!"

The twins rushed to their mother's rescue and removed the packages from her arms so that she could hug Alex-Paul. "So, have you finished doing whatever you do in that bank vault?"

"Yep. Let's go home." He wrapped his arm around his wife's waist and led the procession down to their Jeep. Dixie, Idaho, was the only town the children really knew, and as far as they were concerned, it was a big city. "Ty and his family should be arriving pretty soon back at the camp."

"Well, if we're a little late, they can make themselves at home. I just couldn't let Nicole leave without some new clothes to take with her."

The twins shoved most of the packages into the carryall attached to the top of the Jeep Cherokee, which was normally used to haul the fishing camp's clients' gear in.

"You drive." Alex-Paul handed his wife the keys and took a seat on the passenger's side.

She flashed him a quick look of concern as she started the Jeep. She knew that he always got melancholy when he thought about the war. The best cure was to leave him alone.

Soon the Jeep turned off the asphalt highway onto the old timber trail that led back to the thousand acres surrounding the fishing and hunting camp. Alex-Paul pointed at the sign and said over his shoulder, "The letters are coming loose. You boys come back here with the Wrangler and fix it, okay?"

"Sure, Pops," Alex answered for both of them. He had seen the letters of their last name starting to come away from the back board when they had left the camp and had already made a mental note to come back and fix them.

At the sound of a helicopter passing overhead, Alex-Paul leaned forward and pressed his head against the windshield so that he could look up. He caught a quick glimpse of the chopper through the trees. "They've arrived."

"No problem, Alex-Paul. The place isn't locked and they know their way around," she said, keeping her eyes on the trail.

The excitement started showing in the kids as they neared the large camp. It was always exciting when their dad's war buddy and his family visited them for two weeks in the fall at the end of the season. They all called the famous surgeon from Los Angeles Uncle David and his wife Aunt Margie, but the kids knew that their fathers were much closer than brothers—if that was possible. The war had done something between the two men that had bonded them.

"I'm so excited!" Nicole was the one who broke the silence from the backseat. "I'm going to live in Los Angeles for a whole year!"

Alex-Paul smiled over at his wife. He wasn't happy with the idea of switching kids for a year, but Nicole was almost seventeen and she had never been away from the mountains. It was time she had a chance to see a little bit of the real world, and he had reluctantly agreed to allow her to complete her senior year of high school living with Tyriver and his family in Beverly Hills. Ty's eldest son was going to spend the same amount of time living with them at the campsite. The boy was having some problems with drugs, and Tyriver thought that the mountains would be a perfect place for the boy to get his head screwed on right. He was the same age as the twins, and the three of them had always gotten along great.

Tyriver was stacking logs in the fire pit outside the main house when the Jeep pulled into the yard. Alex-Paul hopped out while the vehicle was still moving and ran toward his best friend. The two men hugged each other in front of their smiling families, and then everyone started talking at once. There were no walls between the Goldsmiths and the Tyrivers.

The sun had set and a chill covered the mountains. The hardwood trees had already lost their leaves, but the evergreens filled the woods with their greenery and sweet smell of freshness. The women had gone inside the large main house, which also served as a lodge during the hunting and fishing season, and the men and boys had taken up seats around the camp fire for the traditional telling of tales. Over the years it had become a tradition between the two families to sit around the camp fire and share the highlights of the past year. When the children had been smaller, they just listened to the adults talk, but now they freely participated. All of the family talk was over, and the women had gotten bored listening to the tales of machismo that were beginning to dominate the conversation. The males outnumbered the females in the two families, but the girls held their own. Nicole was the one who hinted that the women should withdraw to the lodge. She wanted to talk about Los Angeles.

Alex-Paul waited until the women were out of sight before fetching the quart of Kessler's sipping whiskey he had hidden. He removed the cap and threw it into the fire before handing the bottle over to Tyriver.

The boys smiled at each other in the flickering firelight. They all knew that now the really good stories would start. As long as they had been sitting around the camp fire, the stories had never been the same, and they kept the boys wide awake until the wee hours of the morning.

"So how's Y-Roc doing?" Alex-Paul took the bottle

back from Tyriver and sat down on a section of log used for a seat.

"I bought him a liquor store and he's got his whole family working in it. I think they'll do just fine once they get used to L.A."

"Whatever happened to MacCall?"

"I hear he inherited a fortune and built himself a house overlooking the ocean at Carmel by the Sea." Tyriver reached over for the bottle. "He tried calling me once at my office, but I never returned his call."

"He wrote me a letter . . ." Alex-Paul said, handing the bottle to his war buddy, "but I never wrote back."

Alex leaned against his father's back and hooked his chin over his shoulder. Then the boy wrapped his arms over his father's shoulders and stared into the fire. Tyriver's youngest son followed suit with his father.

Paul dropped in front of his dad and sat cross-legged between Alex-Paul's feet. The Tyriver boy having problems with drugs hesitated and then moved closer to his father, acting as if he was drawing closer to the warmth of the fire pit.

It was the traditional gathering of the clan, and there was a lot more warmth around the campfire than the flames were producing.

Tyriver looked over at Alex-Paul, and the two middle-aged men smiled at each other. They had survived the war, and it didn't get much better than what they were experiencing now. Feeling his son leaning against his leg, Tyriver reached down and touched the teenager's head. His hand slipped down to the troubled boy's shoulder and gently patted the side of the boy's neck.

Tyriver felt a cool hand touch his, and for the first time in months, he knew that there was hope for the kid's recovery.

A pine knot popped in the fire, sending up a spray of red flowers. A great gray owl called from the deep forest, and a buck stomped his hoof to alert his harem.

Alex-Paul smiled. Life was good.